Praise for the novels of Robyn Carr

"Carr has hit her stride with this captivating series."
—*Library Journal* on the Virgin River series

"This book is an utter delight."
—*RT Book Reviews* on *Moonlight Road*

"Strong conflict, humor and well-written characters are Carr's calling cards, and they're all present here…. You won't want to put this one down."
—*RT Book Reviews* on *Angel's Peak*

"This story has everything: a courageous, outspoken heroine, a to-die-for hero and a plot that will touch readers' hearts on several different levels. Truly excellent."
—*RT Book Reviews* on *Forbidden Falls*

"An intensely satisfying read. By turns humorous and gut-wrenchingly emotional, it won't soon be forgotten."
—*RT Book Reviews* on *Paradise Valley*

"The Virgin River books are so compelling—I connected instantly with the characters and just wanted more and more and more."
—#1 *New York Times* bestselling author Debbie Macomber

Also by Robyn Carr

Sullivan's Crossing

THE COUNTRY GUESTHOUSE
THE BEST OF US
THE FAMILY GATHERING
ANY DAY NOW
WHAT WE FIND

Thunder Point

WILDEST DREAMS
A NEW HOPE
ONE WISH
THE HOMECOMING
THE PROMISE
THE CHANCE
THE HERO
THE NEWCOMER
THE WANDERER

Virgin River

MY KIND OF CHRISTMAS
SUNRISE POINT
REDWOOD BEND
HIDDEN SUMMIT
BRING ME HOME FOR CHRISTMAS
HARVEST MOON
WILD MAN CREEK
PROMISE CANYON
MOONLIGHT ROAD
ANGEL'S PEAK
FORBIDDEN FALLS
PARADISE VALLEY
TEMPTATION RIDGE
SECOND CHANCE PASS
A VIRGIN RIVER CHRISTMAS
WHISPERING ROCK
SHELTER MOUNTAIN
VIRGIN RIVER

Grace Valley

DEEP IN THE VALLEY
JUST OVER THE MOUNTAIN
DOWN BY THE RIVER

Novels

SUNRISE ON HALF MOON BAY
THE VIEW FROM ALAMEDA ISLAND
THE SUMMER THAT MADE US
THE LIFE SHE WANTS
FOUR FRIENDS
A SUMMER IN SONOMA
NEVER TOO LATE
SWEPT AWAY (formerly titled
   RUNAWAY MISTRESS)
BLUE SKIES
THE WEDDING PARTY
THE HOUSE ON OLIVE STREET

Look for Robyn Carr's next novel
RETURN TO VIRGIN RIVER,
available soon from MIRA.

ROBYN CARR

WHISPERING ROCK

mira

ISBN-13: 978-0-7783-8620-9

Whispering Rock

First published in 2007. This edition published in 2021.

This edition published by arrangement with Harlequin Books S.A.

For questions and comments about the quality of this book, please contact us at CustomerService@Harlequin.com.

Mira
22 Adelaide St. West, 40th Floor
Toronto, Ontario M5H 4E3, Canada
BookClubbish.com

Printed in U.S.A.

Michelle Mazzanti and Kristy Price, an author's best friends.

VIRGIN RIVER

WHISPERING ROCK

1

Mike Valenzuela was up and had his Jeep SUV packed long before sunrise. He had a long drive to Los Angeles and meant to get an early start. Depending on traffic around the Bay Area, the drive would be eight to ten hours from Virgin River. He locked up his RV, which was his home. It sat on the property at Jack's bar and grill; Jack and Preacher would keep an eye on it for him, not that Mike expected any kind of trouble. That was one of several reasons he'd chosen to live here—it was quiet. Small, peaceful, beautiful and nothing to disturb one's peace of mind. Mike had had enough of that in his former life.

Before coming to Virgin River permanently, Mike had made many trips to this Humboldt County mountain town for hunting and fishing, for gathering with an old Marine squad that was still close. His full-time job had been with LAPD, a sergeant in the gangs division. That had all ended when he was shot on the job—he'd taken three bullets and had a lot of hard work getting his body back. He'd needed Preacher's robust food and Jack's wife Mel's assistance with physical therapy on his shoulder. After six months, Mike was as close to completely recovered as he'd get.

Since moving to Virgin River he'd been home only once to visit his parents, siblings and their families. He planned to take a week—one day driving each way and five days with that crowd of laughing, dancing Mexicans. Knowing the traditions of his family, it would be a nonstop celebration. His mother and sisters would cook from morning to night, his brothers would stock the refrigerator with cerveza, family friends and cop buddies from the department would drop by the house. It would be a good time—a great homecoming after his long recovery.

He was three hours into his drive when his cell phone rang. The noise startled him. There was no cell phone reception in Virgin River so the last thing he expected was a phone call.

"Hello?" he answered.

"I need a favor," Jack said without preamble. His voice sounded gravelly, as though he was barely awake. He must not have remembered Mike was heading south.

Mike looked at the dash clock. It wasn't yet 7:00 a.m. He laughed. "Well, sure, but I'm nearly in Santa Rosa, so it might be inconvenient to run over to Garberville and get you ice for the bar, but hey—"

"Mike, it's Brie," Jack said. Brie was Jack's youngest sister, his pet, his favorite. And she was really special to Mike. "She's in the hospital."

Mike actually swerved on the highway. "Hold on," he said.

"Stay there." He pulled off the road onto a safe-looking shoulder. Then he took a deep breath. "Go ahead," he said.

"She was assaulted sometime last night," Jack said. "Beaten. Raped."

"No!" Mike said. "What?"

Jack didn't repeat himself. "My father just called a little while ago. Mel and I are packing—we'll get on the road as soon as we can. Listen, I need someone who knows law enforcement, criminology, to walk me through what's happening with her. They don't have the guy who did this—there's got to be an investigation. Right?"

"How bad is she?" Mike asked.

"My dad didn't have a lot of details, but she's out of emergency and in a room, sedated and semiconscious, no surgery. Can you write down a couple of numbers? Can you keep your cell phone turned on so I can call you? With questions? That kind of thing?"

"Of course. Yes," Mike said. "Gimme numbers."

Jack recited phone numbers for the hospital, Jack's father, Sam, and Mel's old cell phone that they'd charge on their way to Sacramento and then carry with them.

"Do they have a suspect? Did she know the guy?"

"I don't know anything except her condition. After we get on the road, get the phone charged and we're out of the mountains and through the redwoods, I'll call my dad and see what he can tell me. Right now I gotta go. I gotta get down there."

"Right," Mike said. "Okay. My phone will be in my pocket twenty-four-seven. I'll call the hospital, see what I can find out."

"Thanks. Appreciate it," Jack said, hanging up.

Mike sat on the shoulder, staring at the phone for a long minute, helpless. Not Brie, he thought. Oh God, not Brie!

His mind flashed on times they'd been together. A couple of months ago she'd been in Virgin River to see her new nephew, Jack and Mel's baby. Mike had taken her on a picnic at the river—to a special place where the river was wide, but too shallow for fishermen to bother. They'd had lunch against a big boulder, close enough to hear the water whisper by as it passed over the rocks. It was a place frequented by young lovers and teenagers, and that big old rock had seen some wonderful things on the riverbank; it protected many secrets. Some of his own, in fact. He'd held Brie's hand for a long time that day, and she hadn't pulled it away. It was the first time he'd realized he was taken with her. A crush. At thirty-seven, he felt it was an old man's crush, but damned if it didn't feel awfully like a sixteen-year-old's.

When Mike met Brie for the first time a few years back, he'd gone to see her brother while Jack was on leave, visiting his family in Sacramento right before his last assignment in Iraq. Mike was oblivious to the fact that his reserve unit would be activated and he'd end up meeting Jack over there, serving under him a second time. Brie was there, of course, recently married to a Sacramento cop. Nice guy, so Mike had thought. She was a prosecutor for the county in Sacramento, the state capital. She was small, about five-three, with long, soft brown hair that flowed almost to her waist, making her look like a mere girl. But she was no girl. She put away hardened criminals for a living; she had a reputation as one of the toughest prosecutors in the county. Mike had immediately admired her brains, her grit, not to mention her beauty. In his past life, before the shooting, he'd never been particularly discouraged by the mere presence of a husband, but they were newlyweds, and Brie was in love. No other man existed for her.

When Mike saw her in Virgin River right after Jack's son was born, she was trying to recover from a painful divorce— her husband had left her for her best friend, and Brie was shattered. Lonely. So hurt. Mike immediately wanted to take her into his arms and console her, for he was hurting, too. But Brie, crushed by her husband's infidelity, was determined not to put her heart on the line again, and she wanted nothing of a man, especially another player who'd had more than his share of women. A further complication—this was Jack's baby sister, of whom he was so protective it verged on ridiculous. And Mike was no longer a driven, devil-may-care Latino lover. He was a cripple. The body just didn't work right anymore.

It had been only a couple of weeks since he'd last seen her. She had come back to Virgin River with the rest of her family to help erect the frame of Jack's new house. Preacher and his bride, Paige, were married in that framed structure the very next day. For a man who could barely walk six months ago, Mike had given Brie a fairly decent twirl around the dance floor at the wedding. It was a fantastic party—full of that good old country food, barbecues flaming, the chairs pushed back and the band set up on the foundation of Jack's unfinished house, the frame strung with floral garlands. He grabbed her, laughing, into his arms and whirled her around with abandon, and whenever the tempo allowed, pressed his cheek close against hers, whispering in conspiratorial amusement, "Your brother is frowning at us."

"I wonder why that is." She laughed.

"I don't think he wants you near a man so like himself," Mike speculated.

That seemed to amuse her a great deal. She tipped her head back and laughed a little wildly. "Don't flatter yourself," she said. "It has nothing to do with your great success with women. You're a man, near his baby sister. That's enough."

"You're no baby," he said, pulling her closer. "And I think you're having too much fun with this, getting him riled up. Don't you realize he has a dangerous temper?"

Unmistakably, she held him tighter. "Not toward me," she whispered.

"There's a devil in you," he said, and looked death in the face by kissing her neck.

"There's a fool in you," she said, tilting her head just slightly to give him more of her neck.

In years gone by he would have found a way to get her alone, seduced her, made love to her in ways she'd dream about later. But three bullets had decided a few things. Even if he could spirit her away from her brother's protective stare, he wouldn't be able to perform. So he said, "You're trying to get me shot again."

"Oh, I doubt he'd actually shoot you. But I haven't been to a good old-fashioned wedding brawl in ages."

When they'd said goodbye he had hugged her briefly, her sweet scent like a cinch around his mind, feeling her cheek against his, his arms around her waist, pulling her close. A bit more than just a friendly gesture—a suggestive one, which she returned. He assumed she was having fun with the flirtation, stirring things up a little bit, but it meant far more than that to him. Brie held his thoughts in a disturbing way that suggested if he were capable of giving her love, she would capture his heart and mind in that powerful way that wipes all other women out of the past. He really didn't have that to offer anymore. Although that didn't keep him from thinking about her, wanting her.

He could not bear to think about all that mischief and sass lying broken and violated in a hospital. His heart was in pieces, aching for her. Dying to know that she was going to be all right.

He put the SUV into Drive, looked over his shoulder and got back on the freeway. He gunned the engine and veered across two lanes of fast-moving traffic to make the exit to Sacramento.

★ ★ ★

When Mike got to the county hospital a couple of hours later, he called Sam's cell phone number and left a message to say he'd arrived and wanted to know where they were. A prosecutor, the victim of a crime, was not going to be with the general population—she would undoubtedly have security.

Sam came to the hospital entrance, extending his hand. "Mike. Good of you to come. I know Jack will appreciate it."

"I was on my way south and was almost here anyway. Brie's a special friend. I'll do anything I can."

Sam turned and headed for the elevators. "Unfortunately, I'm not sure what you can do. She's going to be all right. Physically. I have no idea what a woman goes through after something like this...."

"Tell me what you know so far," Mike said. "Did she know her attacker?"

"Oh, yes. Remember that terrible trial she had about the same time Jack's son was born? The serial rapist? The media circus? It was him. She identified him for police."

Mike stopped walking and frowned. "She's sure?" he asked. That was such a sick, bold move for someone who'd just gotten a free pass. Brie had lost that trial and it was a hard loss, especially coming on the heels of her divorce. It was as if the sky was falling on her. Also, it wasn't something men like that did. Typically, they bolted. Got away from anyone who had the balls to go after them, as Brie had.

"She's sure," Sam said.

Mike couldn't help but wonder—was she hit in the head? Hallucinating? In and out of reality because of the trauma? "Her injuries?" he asked.

"Her face is battered, there are two broken ribs and the usual..." He paused. "The usual injuries incurred during a rape. You know."

"I know," he said. Tearing, bleeding, bruising. "Has she been seen by a rape specialist and police?"

"Yes, but she wants Mel. Understandably."

"Of course," Mike said. Jack's wife, Mel, was the nurse practitioner and midwife in Virgin River and had had years of experience in a huge L.A. trauma center. She was an expert in battery and sexual assault and if she could be the medical eyes and ears, maybe Mike could cover the police angle. "I heard from them at seven this morning. They should be here in two or three hours, depending on how fast they got out of town."

Mike noticed a uniformed Sac PD officer standing at the entrance to a room; undoubtedly that's where Brie was. "Well, let me talk to some people, see if I can find out anything at all. But first, I'll say hello to the family." He moved to a large clot of people in the waiting area just down the hall. Jack's three other sisters, their husbands, a few of his nieces. Mike was embraced and thanked. Then he got about the business of talking to nurses, got the number of the detective on the case from the officer guarding the room. All the detective could tell Mike at this time was that the suspect was still at large. The doctor would discuss her injuries, that was all. But it appeared that apart from being horribly assaulted, she would recover physically.

It was almost three hours later that Jack, Mel and baby David arrived. Jack embraced his father, then looked in surprise at Mike. "You're here?"

"I was already close," he said. "I thought I'd come over. If I can help, it's better for me to be on-site."

"Oh, man, I didn't expect this," Jack said.

"Hell, you've done more for me," Mike said. "And you know I love Brie. Mel," he said, reaching for baby David, "she said she wants to see you the minute you get here."

"Of course," Mel said, handing off the baby.

"I think she needs Mel's opinion of how the rape evidence was collected," Mike said to Jack. "Go hug your sisters. By that time you'll be able to see her."

"Have you seen her yet?" Jack asked.

"No. It's family only. But I've talked to some people, trying to gather whatever facts they'll share."

"God," Jack said, gripping Mike's biceps hard. "Thanks. Mike, I didn't expect this."

"You should have." He laughed, jostling little David a little. "That's how it is with us. Right?"

Jack sat by his sister's bedside at the county hospital for almost twelve straight hours. He had arrived at eleven in the morning and it was now 11:00 p.m. Outside her door, in the hallway, the family had gathered for most of the day, but as evening had descended they'd drifted home because she was out of danger and sedated. Mike had taken Mel and the baby back to Sam's, but Jack hadn't wanted to leave Brie. Brie was close to her entire family, but it was Jack with whom she had the deepest bond.

Jack was torn to pieces as he looked down on his little sister. Her face was horrific; the bruising and swelling was terrible. It looked much worse than it was, the doctor promised. There was no permanent damage; she would regain her former beauty. Every few minutes Jack would reach over, gently smooth back her light brown hair, touch her hand. She wrestled in her sleep now and then, despite the sedatives. If not for the ribs, he might have taken her into his strong arms during these struggles. Instead he would lean over her bed, touch her face where there was no swelling, drop a tender kiss on her forehead and whisper, "I'm here, Brie. You're safe now, baby."

At almost midnight he felt a hand on his shoulder and turned to look up into Mike's black eyes.

"Go on home, Jack," he said. "Get a little rest. I'll sit with her."

"I can't leave her," Jack said.

"I know you don't want to. But I had a nap," he lied. "Sam gave me a room at the house. I'll sit right here in case she wakes up, which she probably won't, and we've got the cop in the hall there. Go. Get a little rest so you can be here for her tomorrow."

"If she wakes up and I'm not right here…"

"They're putting heavy-duty bug juice right in the IV to get her through the night," Mike said softly. "It's okay."

Jack laughed a little. "I sat by your bed through a week of nights when you were shot."

"Yeah," Mike said. "Payback time. Go home to your wife. See you first thing tomorrow."

It surprised Mike that Jack actually left. He was the kind of man who went days past exhaustion to be there for someone he cared about. Mike took his place on a chair beside Brie's bed and sat vigil. Her battered face didn't shock him—he'd seen worse. But it hurt him inside. He couldn't imagine the kind of monster who could do that.

The nurses came and went through the night, checking her IV, taking her blood pressure, sometimes bringing Mike coffee from their break room—and it tasted a whole lot better than what the machines dispensed. If he asked, a nurse would sit with Brie while he ran down the hall—a result of the coffee. But Brie didn't move except for some occasional disturbances that caused her to stir fitfully.

Mike had carried fallen soldiers out of harm's way; he'd sat by the side of dying men while sniper fire whizzed past his head. But nothing compared to what he felt while looking down at Brie, beaten like this. Thinking of her violation filled him with a kind of rage that had never been visited on him before. Although she was a beautiful woman and strong, his vision kept mixing her up with the vulnerable woman he'd taken on a picnic a couple of months ago. A pretty, young woman who'd just been left by her husband, and was crushed by the betrayal. And what fool would give her up? he thought. It was beyond him.

The rape trial had been one of the toughest of her career. It had taken her months to prepare a case against the suspect for serial rape. The forensic evidence had been strong, but in the end the only witness who hadn't failed her was a prostitute with a bad record, and the guy walked. Brie had identified him to the police as her rapist when she'd regained consciousness.

In the early hours of the morning she turned her swollen face toward Mike and opened her eyes—or tried to. One was partially shut because of the swelling. He scooted closer. "Brie," he whispered. "It's me, Brie. I'm here."

She put her hands over her face and cried out. "No! No!"

He took gentle hold of her wrists. "Brie! It's me. It's Mike. It's okay."

But he couldn't pull her hands away from her face. "Please," she whimpered pitifully. "I don't want you to see this…."

"Honey, I saw you already," he said. "I've been sitting here for hours. Let it go," he said. "It's okay."

She let him slowly pull her hands away from her battered face. "Why? Why are you here? You shouldn't be here!"

"Jack wanted me to help him understand what was happening with the investigation. But I wanted to be here. Brie, I wanted to be here for you." He brushed her brow gently. "You're going to be okay."

"He… He got my gun…."

"The police know, honey. You didn't do anything wrong."

"He's so dangerous. I tried to get him—that's why he did this. I was going to put him away for life."

Mike's jaw pulsed, but he kept his voice soft. "It's okay, Brie. It's over now."

"Did they find him?" she asked. "Did they pick him up?"

Oh, how he wished she wouldn't ask that. "Not yet."

"Do you know why he didn't kill me?" she asked, a tear running out of her swollen eye and down over the bridge of her purple nose. He tenderly wiped it away. "He said he didn't want me to die. He wanted me to try to get him again, and watch him walk again. He wore a condom."

"Aw, honey…"

"I'm going to get him, Mike."

"Please… Don't think about that now. I'll get the nurse. Get you another sedative." He put the light on and the nurse came immediately. "Brie needs something to help her go back to sleep."

"Sure," the nurse said.

"I'm just going to wake up again," she said. "And I'm just going to think the same things."

"Try to rest," he said, leaning over to kiss her brow. "I'll be right here. And there's an officer outside your door. You're completely safe."

"Mike," she whispered. She held his hand for a long moment. "Did Jack ask you to come?"

"No," he said, gently touching her brow. "But when I found out what happened, I had to come," he whispered. "I had to."

After having a sedative administered into the IV, she gently closed her eyes again. Her hand slipped out of his and he sat back in his chair. Then, his elbows on his knees and his face buried in his hands, he silently wept.

Jack was back at the hospital before dawn, not looking particularly rested although he had showered and shaved. He had dark circles under eyes that were lit by a very scary inner brightness. Mike had sisters he cherished; he could imagine the rage that burned inside Jack.

Mike stepped into the hall outside Brie's door to quietly talk with Jack, explaining the night had been quiet and he thought Brie had rested. While they stood there, the doctor making rounds went into the room, his nurse in tow. Mike used that opportunity to visit the men's room. He stared in the mirror; he looked far worse than Jack. He needed a shower and shave, but he didn't want to leave her. Family members would be returning soon, but Mike didn't think they'd be keeping Brie in the hospital for long.

On his way back to Brie's room, he saw Jack talking to a man outside her door. In fact, Jack was right up in his face. The officer providing security was stepping closer to them, making a gesture with his hands that they should separate. Then Mike realized it was Brie's ex-husband, Brad, and that probably within seconds Jack was going to kill him just on principle.

Mike made fast tracks. "Whoa," he said, separating them first with an arm between them, then with his entire body. "Whoa," he said again. "None of this. Come on."

From over Mike's shoulder, Jack demanded of Brad, "What the hell are you doing here?"

Brad glared meanly. "Nice to see you, too, Jack," he said.

"You don't belong here," Jack said too loudly. "You left her. You're done with her."

"Hey," he said, bristling. "I never stopped caring about Brie. Never will. I'm going to see her."

"I don't think so," Jack said. "She's in no shape to have to deal with you right now."

"You're not in charge of the guest list, Jack. That's up to Brie."

"Come on," Mike said sternly. "Let's not do this here."

"Ask him if he wants to take it outside," Jack snapped back.

"Yeah, I'll—"

"Whoa," Mike said yet again, widening the space between the two men. "This isn't happening here!"

Brad moved closer, pushing up against Mike, but lowered his voice cautiously. "I know you're angry, Jack. In general and at me. I don't blame you. But if you get tough with me, it's going to be worse for Brie. And this officer is just going to hook you up."

Jack ground his teeth, pushing up against the other side of Mike. Mike was having some trouble holding them apart. "I really want to hit someone," Jack said through clenched teeth. "Right now, you'd do as well as anyone. You walked out on your marriage. You left her while she was building a case against that son of a bitch. Do you have any idea what you did to her?"

Oh, boy, Mike thought. It was going to happen between these two any second, right in the hospital hallway. Mike was a good six feet and pretty strong, but Brad and Jack were both taller, broader, angrier and not a shoulder injury between them. Mike was going to get hammered when they lost it and started pummeling each other.

"Yeah," Brad said. "Yeah, I do! And I want her to know that I still care about what happens to her. We're divorced, but we have history. A lot of it good history. If I can do anything now…"

"Hey!" Mike said to the cop. "Hey! Come on!"

The police officer finally got in it, putting himself between Brad and Jack along with Mike. "All right, gentlemen," the cop said. "I have my orders. No scuffling outside Ms. Sheridan's door. If you want to talk this over calmly, I'd like you to move down the hall."

Oh, that was not a good suggestion, Mike thought. If they moved down the hall, they wouldn't be talking. Mike cautiously backed Jack up a few steps. "Take a breath," he said quietly. "You don't want to do this."

Jack glowered at Mike. "You sure about that?"

"Back off," Mike said with as much authority as he could muster.

Just then a nurse came out of Brie's room and Brad snagged her too fast for Jack to intervene. "Ma'am, I'm Ms. Sheridan's ex-husband. Brad. I'm also a police detective," he said, badging her. "Off duty. Will you ask her if she'll see me? Please?"

The nurse made a U-turn and went back into the room.

"What's he doing here?" Brad asked, indicating Mike with his eyes and a jut of his chin.

Oh, mistake, Mike thought instantly, stiffening. Was Brad crazy? Pissing off the guy who was keeping Jack from killing him? He felt his own fists begin to open and close. The ex wants to know why another man is here? He dumps his wife for another woman, but no guy is supposed to pick up where he left off? Mike actually smiled, though coldly. Balls, he thought. I should just let Jack beat him up.

"He's a cop," Jack said, stretching the truth somewhat. "I asked him to come. To help."

"He can go," Brad said. "We don't need his help."

That did it. Mike took one fast step in Brad's direction, but was stopped by a strong hand on the bad shoulder, pulling him back. That was all it took to get his attention; he wasn't going to put Brie through this. But if they all ran into each other somewhere else, like the parking lot, he couldn't make any promises. Right now he wanted a piece of Brad as much as Jack did.

The nurse returned from the room and spoke to Brad. "When the doctor is finished, you can go in."

Brad had the good sense not to take on any superior airs. He didn't avoid eye contact with the other men, however.

"Let me ask you one question," Jack said to Brad, trying to keep his voice under control to avoid being ejected by the uniform. "Were you at work the night it happened?"

"No."

Jack ground his teeth. "Then if you hadn't walked out on her for another woman, you'd have been at the house that night. Maybe waiting up for her to get home. Maybe right inside where you could hear her scream. So much for your good history."

"Hey," Brad began, clearly wishing to argue the point. But Jack turned away from him and took several steps down the hall. Right then the doctor came breezing out of the room, looking down at the chart as he walked by all three men. Brad lifted his chin, glared briefly and entered Brie's room.

Mike let out his breath. "That was gonna be so ugly," he said. He went to the chair outside Brie's door and sat. Jack paced, fidgeting. He took several steps down the hall, away from the door.

Mike rested his elbows on his knees. He scratched his itchy beard. He noticed the cop was standing beside him.

"This has got to be tough," the cop said to Mike, indicating Jack just a few feet away, his jaw pulsing and his hands in fists at his sides.

Mike turned his head, looked up at the young officer. He glanced at his best friend; Jack was tortured, helpless. "Nothing can prepare you for something like this to happen to a woman you love," he said softly. "Nothing."

Brie was released from the hospital that afternoon and she went home to her father's house. Sam and Jack drove her while Mike followed in his own car, watching with concern. He hadn't been around very many sexual assault victims in his police career, but certainly he'd come into contact with some.

He had never seen a woman so stoic, so removed. Once they all arrived at Sam's, she went directly to the room that had been hers when she was younger. She called Jack to come, to cover the mirror.

Brie took her dinner on a tray in her room that night. Her sisters stopped by one at a time, visited with her in her room, but didn't stay long. There were five Sheridan siblings, all married but Brie. Two of the sisters were older than Jack, one was a couple of years younger and then there was Brie, the caboose, eleven years younger than Jack. Her three older sisters had brought to the family eight daughters, and Jack and Mel had provided the only boy in little David. So when the family was all together, it was an almost unmanageable crowd. A teeming throng filled with noise and laughter—Mike had seen that for himself on earlier visits. It was not unlike the Valenzuela household. Not so now. The house was still, like a mausoleum.

Mike had a quiet dinner with Sam, Jack and Mel.

"You should probably head for L.A.," Jack said to Mike when the table was cleared.

"Whatever." He shrugged. "I can stay a day or so, see if anything develops."

"I don't want to hold you up," Jack said. Then he walked out onto the patio and Mike followed. "I can call you if anything happens."

Sam came outside holding a tray with three glasses. There was a short shot of amber liquid in each and he put the tray on the patio table. Without conversation, the men each took one, sipping in silence. The June air was sultry in the Sacramento valley, humid and almost oppressive. After a few minutes Sam got up and said good-night. Then Jack finished his drink and went into the house. One by one, the lights inside began to go out, leaving only the kitchen light for Mike. Exhausted as he was, he didn't feel like sleep. He helped himself to another short shot and went back to the patio, lighting the candle on the table.

The whole family is in shock, he thought. They move around silently; they grieve Brie's lost innocence. Everyone under this roof is in terrible pain; they feel each physical blow for which she bears the marks.

"You should probably go now."

He lifted his head and saw Brie standing in the open patio doors, wearing the same clothes she had worn home from the hospital. "Brie," he said, rising.

"I've talked to the detectives several times. Jerome Powell, the rapist, was tracked as far as New Mexico, then the trail was lost," she said, very businesslike. "I can tell you from experience, the odds are at least ninety-five percent he's gone—pulled a territorial. I'm going to start counseling and group therapy right away—and I've decided not to go back to work for a while. Jack and Mel insist on staying the rest of the week, but you should go. Visit your family."

"Would you like to come and sit with me?" he asked.

She shook her head. "I'll talk to the D.A. every day, see if he turns up anything new. Of course I'm staying here. If I need any assistance in the police department, I have an ex-husband who's feeling very guilty. And very helpful." She took a breath. "I wanted to say goodbye. And to thank you for trying to help."

"Brie," he said, taking a step toward her, his arms open.

She held up a hand, and the look that came into her eyes stopped him where he was. She shook her head, kept her hand raised against him. "You understand," she said, warning him not to get too close, not to touch her.

"Of course," he said.

"Drive carefully," she said, disappearing into the house.

2

One week later Mel and Jack returned to Virgin River to resume their routine. Mel went into Doc's every morning, the baby with her for the day. If something urgent came up, she could always take the baby over to Jack at the bar, or if Jack wasn't there, Paige or Preacher or Mike were more than willing to babysit. For the most part, David could be counted on to remain content for the half hour or so Mel needed to see a patient as long as she had the bouncy seat with her and he was neither hungry nor dirty. He still took two long naps a day—one in the morning and one in the afternoon.

Mel had been back from Sacramento less than two weeks when a teenage girl from Virgin River came to Doc's and asked to see her. Carra Jean Winslow was fifteen and Mel had never seen her before. In fact, even though Mel had lived and

worked in Virgin River for just over a year, she didn't know
the girl's parents. Taking note of her age and obvious anxiety,
Mel took her to an examining room before asking her what
she needed. When a fifteen-year-old girl who didn't cough or
wheeze or bring her parents came in to see the nurse midwife,
the possibilities seemed pretty limited and obvious.

"I heard there was a pill that could keep you from getting
pregnant if, you know, you had sex," she said. She said it very
quietly, looking at her feet.

"Emergency birth control. But it's only effective if the intercourse has been very recent."

"Two nights ago," she said weakly.

"That's recent enough," Mel said, trying to put her at ease
with a smile. "Any problems? Pain? Bleeding? Anything?"

"Bleeding. There was some bleeding."

"First time?" Mel asked, smiling kindly. The girl nodded.
"Have you ever had an internal exam before?"

She shook her head and looked down again.

"I'd like to check you, make sure everything is okay. It's
not as terrible as you think," Mel said, touching her arm gently. "How much bleeding?"

"Not too much. A little… Getting better…"

"How do you feel? There?"

She shrugged and said, "Still a little sore. Not bad."

"That's good. I assume, if you're interested in emergency
contraception, you didn't use a condom.…"

"No," Carra answered.

"Okay, we can handle this. Can I get you to undress and
put on a gown for me?"

"My mom… No one knows I'm here."

"That's all right, Carra. This is between you and me. I'm
only interested in your health. Okay?"

"Okay," she said.

"I'll be back in a few minutes. Everything off, just the gown."

Poor thing, Mel thought. She ached for young girls who had just stumbled into this sort of thing without planning, without being sure. And that described almost all young girls. But at least she was here, avoiding yet another disaster. She gave Carra plenty of time to get undressed, but didn't leave her waiting long enough to tangle up her nerves, then returned to the exam room.

"Let's get a blood pressure and listen to your heart first," she said briskly.

"I have to pay you myself," Carra said. "I don't want my parents to know about this."

"Carra, confidentiality is important in this office—you can trust that," she said. "This is all going to work out." She applied the blood pressure cuff, noting there were a few small bruises on the girl's upper arm. "You have a couple of bruises here," she said.

"It's nothing. It was…volleyball. It can get a little rough sometimes."

"Looks like someone grabbed you," Mel suggested.

The girl shrugged. "It happens."

Mel got the blood pressure, which was normal. She listened to Carra's heart, looked in her eyes, checked her pupils. Except for the nervous pounding of her heart, she seemed to be in good shape. She showed her the speculum, explained the procedure and eased her carefully into position for the pelvic. "Nice and slow, feet right here, slide down for me. That's it. Try to relax, your knees apart, honey. Thank you. This isn't going to be bad at all, so take some deep breaths and try to relax."

"Okay," she said, and began to softly cry.

"No crying now," Mel said gently. "Everything is going

to be all right, because you came to see me right away." She gently parted the girl's knees and was frozen. Her labia were bruised and swollen; there were bruises on the insides of her thighs that bore a striking resemblance to the bruises on the girl's upper arm. An unmistakable thumbprint and fingers. Oh, God damn. Mel stood from her stool and looked over the drape at Carra's face. "Carra, I can see that you're very sore. Bruised and swollen and a little torn. I'd like to proceed, take a closer look to be sure everything is all right. But only if you're up to it. Are you okay?"

She pinched her eyes closed, but nodded.

"I'll be as gentle as I can," Mel said. She put on her gloves but set the speculum aside. "I'm just going to check your vagina and uterus, Carra—I'm not going to use the speculum because you're sore. I'd like you to take a deep breath for me, then let it out slowly. That's it," she said. "It'll just take a minute. Don't clench. Relax your muscles, Carra. There you go, very good. Tell me, does this pressure hurt?"

"Not so much," she answered.

Why do these things always come in batches? Mel thought. I'm not over Brie! Carra's vaginal wall was torn, ragged. Raw. Her hymen was ripped open and looked like so many little fingers. She completed her exam quickly, and while she didn't have a rape kit handy, she did have a sterile swab with which she took a vaginal specimen, although it could be too late for any DNA recovery.

"Okay, Carra, let me help you sit up." Mel snapped off her gloves and helped Carra get herself settled, legs dangling off the table. "I'm concerned about what happened to you, Carra. It looks like you've been hurt. Want to tell me about it?"

She shook her head and a couple of big tears spilled over. Carra was a plain girl with an oblong face, bushy, unshaped brows and a small problem with acne. And right now, a really bad case of regret and fear and nerves.

"It will be confidential," Mel said tenderly. "It's not just the bruises, Carra. Your vagina looks ragged. Torn. The damage isn't serious. It'll heal. But from everything I can see—"

"It was me. It was my fault."

"Something like this is never a woman's fault," she said, and she used woman purposely, although this was a mere girl. "Why don't you tell me what happened, and we'll go from there."

"But you'll give me that pill?" she asked desperately.

"Of course. We're not going to let you get pregnant. Or sick."

She took a deep breath, but it brought the tears harder. "I just changed my mind when it was too late, that's all. So it's my fault."

Mel touched her knee. "Go back to the beginning. Nice and easy."

"I can't," she said.

"Sure you can, honey. I'll just listen."

"We decided we were going to do it. He got all excited about that—he said he was sorry after. We'd already started.... He couldn't stop."

"He could," she said. "I can see the bruises from his fingers, like he held you down, held your legs apart. I can see the marks, the tears. Let me help you."

"I wanted to, though."

"I know, Carra. Until you didn't. And you told him no, didn't you?"

She shook her head. "No. I wanted to."

"If you said no at all, that's rape, Carra. Date rape."

Carra leaned forward, her position pleading. "But I've done things with him. Lots of things. And I wanted to."

"Have you ever had intercourse before?" She shook her head. No. "You can say no right up to the last minute, Carra. That's the law. And it doesn't matter what you did with him before. Tell me—is this a boyfriend? Or someone you've only known a little while?"

"I've known him a long time from school, but he's been my boyfriend a couple of weeks."

But they've done a lot? Mel was asking herself. "Carra, he moved pretty fast. I want you to think about this. A couple of weeks. This is one determined guy. How old is he?"

"No," she said, shaking her head. "No, I'm not telling you any more. I'm not getting him in trouble. It wasn't his fault. It was my mistake, but he's sorry."

"Okay, listen—don't get yourself all upset. If you change your mind and want to talk about this, you just call me. Or come to see me. Doesn't matter when. Let's get you on a dependable birth control and—"

"No. I'm not doing it again," she said, holding her mouth in a tight line while tears wet her cheeks.

Oh, she'd been raped. Sounded as if she didn't even have much of a date, Mel thought. "Carra, if you continue to see this boy, this man, it's going to happen again."

"I'm not doing it again," she said firmly. "I need that emergency pill. That's all."

"That's all for right now," Mel said. "I want you to come back in a week or two, so we can test for STDs and be sure you're healing up. It's too soon for anything to turn up today, this soon after exposure. But this is really important. Will you do that?"

In the end she agreed, but she wouldn't accept birth control. In a very businesslike tone she asked Mel, "How much?"

"Forget it, Carra. This one's on the house. Call me if you need me. Anytime. I mean it—anytime. Night or day. I'll write down the number here and my number at home for you. Okay?"

"Thanks," she said meekly.

After all that, the thing that really tore at Mel's heart was seeing her patient ride away on her bicycle. The girl wasn't even old enough to drive a car. And she pedaled while standing up—her tender bottom couldn't handle the seat.

Mike Valenzuela called Brie. He couldn't help himself. It had been two weeks since he'd heard her voice. Jack was more than happy to keep him up-to-date on her recovery, how she sounded, but Mike needed more. "How are you feeling?" he asked her.

"Pretty rugged. Kind of edgy and nervous," she answered. "But then, it hasn't been that long."

"Physically?" he pressed.

"I… Ah… I guess the worst is over. The bruises are beginning to fade. But it's amazing how long it takes a couple of ribs to heal."

"Jack says you took an extended leave of absence from the prosecutor's office," Mike said.

"Did he tell you why?" she asked.

"No. And you don't have to tell me. Don't make yourself uncomfortable."

"Doesn't matter," she said coldly. "Because I can't work like that—when I can prosecute a suspect for rape and he gets off." She laughed bitterly. "On me!"

"Oh, Brie," he said, sympathetic. "God, I'm so sorry."

"If I get a chance, if they find him, I'm going to bury him. I'll put him away for life. I swear to God."

Mike took a deep breath. "You're one of the bravest women I've ever known. I'm proud of you. If there's anything I can do…"

"It's nice of you to call," she said more softly. "Not many people besides family are brave enough—I guess they're afraid of what they might hear. Does Jack know you called?"

It wouldn't be long before Jack found out, Mike thought. Sam had answered the phone, asked who was calling before putting her on. "I didn't call you because you're Jack's sister, but because you're my friend and I wanted to know how you are. I don't really care if Jack's okay with it, only if you are."

"I'm okay with it. His protective nature usually just amuses me. Or annoys me. But not at the moment," she said. "It feels kind of like a shield, just knowing how he is."

"I'd be protective if you were my sister, too," Mike said. "I'm feeling protective myself, though there's not much I can do but call and talk. I think this is what happens to everyone around the crime, Brie. We all have our responses—from the victim to her friends and family. It's all part of the healing process. I watched my friends and family go through that, too. It's one of the reasons I came up here—it was becoming oppressive. Their need for me to heal so they could feel better."

"I keep forgetting that," she said. "That's how self-absorbed I've become. You're a crime victim, too."

"You're supposed to be self-absorbed right now. Self-protective. Focused."

"And that's how you were?" she asked him.

"Ohhhh." He laughed. "I wish you could've seen my routine. I started out the day by crawling out of bed crippled, the pain terrible. I dosed up on the anti-inflammatory, iced down my shoulder and groin, drank Mel's protein supplement drinks that would gag a maggot, and then started my exercises with one-pound weights—so light, so nothing. And it would make me almost cry. Then I'd have to lie down. It took me two months to do a sit-up—and Mel would help me with the physical therapy on my shoulder every day, but not until afternoon, not until I could drink a beer first to take the edge off. She's little, you know, but you shouldn't let that fool you—she can pull and push and grind on an injured muscle until you beg like a baby. My life was all about getting my body back."

"I wish this was just about my body," she said softly.

"There were also nightmares," he said quietly, almost reluctantly. "I'd like you to know—I'm not having them anymore." And he thought, you just don't realize yet how much of this is going to end up being about your body. He had at least a passing knowledge of what rape and assault victims went through. It was going to be a long time before Brie would have a healthy sexual relationship.

Afterward, Mike was pretty astonished that Jack made no mention of his call to Brie. It could mean only one thing—neither Brie nor Sam had mentioned it, and he wasn't sure why. He gave brief consideration to bringing it to Jack's attention himself. He could explain his concern easily—he had a few things in common with her at the moment and might be able to offer support. But in the end, he said nothing. He didn't feel like an odd three-way, checking in with Jack about his feelings for Brie. Nothing had changed in the way he felt toward her, except that at the moment they were both crippled.

The middle of July was steamy and wet, and Mike called her every couple of days, and still Jack said nothing. It seemed to Mike that she took his calls as if looking forward to them a little bit. They rarely talked about the crime and her recovery, but about mundane things. His fishing, what she was reading or watching on TV, weather, Sam and her sisters and nieces, letters that Ricky—a kid from town who had been Jack's and Preacher's young protégé and helper in the bar—was writing home from USMC basic training.

She told him about her new phobias—the dark, public places, noises in the night that she'd probably never even heard

before. She put her house on the market—she had no inten-
tion of living there alone again. She thought she might eventually be strong enough to live on her own, but not there,
where it happened.

"Are you getting out at all?" he asked her.

"Counseling, group sessions. The occasional trip to the store
with Dad," she said. "I don't really want to leave the house.
I'll have to find a way to change that soon, but for now, I just
want to feel safe. That's a tall enough order."

He could hear the growing strength in Brie's voice despite
her new fears; she laughed regularly, and the sound of her
voice brought him great peace of mind. He teased her, told
her jokes, even played his guitar for her over the phone so she
could tell him he was improving.

Jack, however, was too quiet. Mike confronted him, asked
him how he was doing. "I just want her back, man," Jack said
somberly. "Brie—she was always such a goddamn life force."

Mike gripped Jack on the upper arm. "She'll be back. She's
got the stuff."

"Yeah, I hope you're right."

"I'm right," Mike said. "You need me for anything tomorrow? I'm thinking of driving down the coast, having a look
around."

"Nah, enjoy yourself," Jack said.

Ordinarily, Mike wouldn't have given even a second
thought to going to Sacramento without mentioning it to
Jack, but these circumstances were different, and he wasn't an
idiot—Jack would want to know. Still, he said nothing and
in fact had covered his tracks, acting as though he was out for
a day of poking around. He rose before Jack began splitting
logs behind the bar in the early morning—his ritual even in
summer, when there was no need to lay a fire. He hit the road

south through Ukiah in the predawn hours, arriving in the
city by ten in the morning.

After he rang the doorbell, he saw a shadow cross the peephole, then the locks slid and the door opened. "Mike?" Sam
asked. "I didn't expect to see you."

"I decided not to call ahead, sir," he said. "I thought—"

Brie appeared from around the corner, standing behind her
dad. "Mike?" she asked in equal surprise.

He smiled. "You look good," he said, relieved. "Great. You
look great. I was saying I didn't call ahead because I thought
if I just came here, maybe I could lure you out of the house
for a while. If I'd called, you'd think of a million excuses."

She actually took a step back. "I don't know…"

"How about Folsom," he said. "Enjoy the mountains, walk
around the shops, have a little lunch, maybe stop at a vineyard
or two. Just a few hours, just for some fresh air and maybe a
little practice at facing the public. You have to get out in the
world eventually."

"Maybe not this soon…"

"It's only soon because you haven't done it. You'll be safe,
Brie."

"Of course, but—"

"Brie," Sam said. "You should take advantage of this. Mike
is a trained observer, a cop with years of experience. You
couldn't be in better hands."

Mike gave his head a slight bow in Sam's direction, respect-
fully. "Thank you, sir. You're welcome to join us."

He laughed. "No, I think I'll pass. But this is a good idea.
Brie," he said, taking her hand and rubbing it between his, as
if warming it, "you should go out for at least an hour, maybe
two. Mike's come all this way…."

She looked at him pointedly. There might have been a glare

in her eye. "You didn't tell Jack you were doing this, did you." It was not a question.

"Of course not. He would have tried to talk me out of it. If you needed someone to pry you out of the house, he'd want to be the one to do it." He grinned. "I couldn't risk that."

She seemed to think about this momentarily. Finally she said, "I'd better change."

"Nah, you're fine. Folsom isn't any fancier than your shorts. Let's just do it. You won't be out longer than you're comfortable."

"Dad…?"

"This is a good idea, Brie. Go out for a while. Have lunch, a glass of wine. I'll be right here when you get home."

Mike got her into the car and started to drive. Brie was predictably quiet, which was what he expected. "You might be stressed for a little while, but I think it'll ease up," he said. Another few minutes of quiet reigned in the car. "We internalize when we've had a trauma. Grow very quiet, very private with feelings." Again, no conversation. She looked straight ahead, tensely, holding the shoulder strap with one hand, her other crossed protectively over her belly.

"I was the fourth of eight children and had three older brothers," Mike said as they began to drive into the foothills of the Sierras. "By the time I went to kindergarten, I had three younger sisters as well, so my mother, she was very busy. A lot of old-world traditions and values in my house—my father had trouble keeping us all fed, yet he still thought he had the world by the balls with all those sons, and I'm sure he wanted more. But it was a loud and crazy house, and when I went to school for the first time, my English wasn't so good—we spoke only Spanish and some very bad English in my home, in my neighborhood. And although my father is successful now, at that time we were considered poor." He glanced over at her briefly. "I got beaten up by some bigger kids my first week in school. I had bruises on my face and other places, but I wouldn't tell anyone what had happened." He concentrated on the road. "Not even my brothers, who offered to add to the bruises if I didn't tell them who had done it and why. I didn't talk at all for a couple of months."

She turned her head toward him, looking at him. He met her eyes. "From working with kids who were victims of abuse, I learned that's not unusual. To go silent like that. I also learned it's all right to get your bearings before you start talking."

"What made you talk?" she asked.

He chuckled to himself. "I don't know if I remember this correctly, but I think my mother sat me at the kitchen table, alone, and said, 'We have to talk about what's happened to you, Miguel. I can't let you go back to that school until I know.' Something like that. It was the not being allowed to go back, even though I was afraid of getting beaten up again, that made me more ashamed of those boys thinking I was a coward. Empty-headed machismo even then." He laughed.

"Did your mother tell the authorities?" she asked.

"No." He laughed again. "She told my brothers. She said, 'If he comes home with one bruise, I will beat you and then your father will beat you.'"

"Well, that's pretty horrible," Brie said.

"Old World. Tradition." He grinned. "Don't worry, Brie. There were a lot more threats than there were beatings. I don't remember beatings. My father whipped us across the bottom with his belt, but never injured anyone. For my mother, it was the wooden spoon. Not your pansy gringo wooden spoon, but a spoon as long as her arm. Christ, if the belt was unbuckled or the spoon plucked off the shelf, we ran like holy hell. The next generation of Valenzuelas has given up that form of child raising. By the way, it's not Mexican by genesis—it's that generation. It was not against the law to beat your child if he misbehaved."

She was quiet for a moment. Then she asked, "Did you marry Hispanic women?"

He looked at her curiously. "I did," he said. "Both times. Well, mixed Mexican."

"You're drawn to that culture.... Very strongly drawn..."

"I love the traditions of my family, but I don't think that had anything to do with the marriages. I dated a lot of women who weren't Hispanic. My marriages were brief failures of my youth."

"What happened?"

"Well, the first time I was too young, and so was she. I was in the Marines, and she worked for my father. I wrote to her, married her while home on leave, returned after my tour of duty to find she was interested in another young man. I could have been outraged, but the truth is—I wasn't faithful either. I was married and divorced by the time I was twenty-one. My mother was completely ashamed of me."

"And the second wife?"

"Just a few years later. An employee at LAPD. A dispatcher." He chuckled. "Time-honored tradition—cops and dispatchers. It lasted six months. My mother has completely lost hope in me."

"I guess you didn't cling to all the traditions...."

"You know what I miss about my family's traditions? My mother's cooking, my father's skills and ingenuity. My mother and father did most of their cooking for large tribes on the patio—on the grill and in huge pots over slow burners. Mole, the old family recipe, tamales wrapped in banana leaves, enchiladas, carne asada. My mother's salsa and guacamole would make you pass out, it's so good. She makes a fish with sliced olives that's amazing. Her shrimp in tomatoes, avocado and Tapatío is astonishing."

"Tapatío?"

"Hot sauce. Pretty hot hot sauce. And my father could do anything—he built a room on our house, a gazebo in the yard, poured concrete, put a wall around the yard, rewired the house, built a freestanding garage—and I'm sure he did all that without building permits, but I had the sense never to ask. And the landscaping was incredible. That was his business, landscaping. He started out trimming hedges and mowing lawns, but later he started his own little business. It's now a pretty good sized business with a lot of corporate clients. He has a million relatives and sons—he never runs out of employees. My father was an immigrant, but he didn't have to naturalize. My mother is a first-generation American, born in Los Angeles—marriage to her validated him. But interestingly, she is the one to uphold the old traditions in our family. He wanted to acclimate himself to the U.S. quickly, so he could get about the business of making that fortune poor, hungry Mexican boys dream about. And he did, though he worked damn hard to do it." He pulled into the town of Folsom, found a place to park and went around to Brie's side to open her door.

"Tell me about your growing up," he said.

"Not nearly as interesting as yours," she said.

"Let me be the judge," he said, taking her elbow and walking her across the street toward a gift shop.

As he maneuvered her through shops, galleries, antique stores and bakeries, she told him about life with three much older sisters who babied her, and Jack who fussed over her till she was about six, then again when he was home on leave. Her household didn't sound terribly different from his, except that her mother didn't cook outside, use oversize cooking pots and implements, and her father was a whiz at numbers and investing, not building or landscaping. Otherwise, their childhoods were similar—large families filled with noise and laughter, loyalty and blistering sibling fights. "The girls fought like animals," she said. "They never fought with me—I was the baby. And Jack was threatened with certain death if he ever struck a girl, so they went after him with a vengeance, knowing he was helpless."

"Any chance there's a video of that somewhere?" he asked, laughing.

"If there was, Jack would have it destroyed by now. They were terrible to him. It's amazing he loves them now. Of course, he had his revenge in small ways. He played tricks on them constantly—but to his credit, he never fought them physically. Fought back, I should say. Until he returned from his first hitch in the Marines, I believe he wished them dead."

Mike stopped walking outside a corner pub and looked at his watch. "I'll bet you're getting hungry."

"There's a Mexican place down the street," she said.

"Nah, there's not a Mexican restaurant in the world that can satisfy me now. I'm a mama's boy. How about a hamburger?" he asked.

She smiled. "Sure. This has been easier than I expected."

"We're taking it nice and slow and you've been distracted by conversation," he said.

"That sounds so professional," she commented, entering the pub. "And here I thought you were having fun."

He laughed at her. "Surely you can tell I'm completely miserable," he said. "Of course I'm having fun. But I'm here on a mission—getting you out. If I happen to have a good time while I'm doing it, even better."

He directed her to a corner booth, moved her into the seat from which she could see the whole restaurant so she wouldn't feel vulnerable, and told her to order a beer or glass of wine. There were only a few people in the pub, so she could easily see everyone having lunch. Then they ordered hamburgers and continued the discussion into the teenage years—their grades, dates, trouble they'd been in. Here they were opposites—Brie was an exceptional student, had a couple of very polite boyfriends, never any trouble. Mike couldn't concentrate until he was over twenty, dated anyone who would have him, got into plenty of trouble—even trouble with the police, who brought him home late at night more than once, waking his parents. By the time they were halfway through their hamburgers, there was a slight disturbance in the pub. A man shouted at the waiter, "It's unacceptable!"

Brie's eyes grew round and Mike looked over his shoulder. There were two couples across the room at a table; they looked to be middle-aged married couples. One of the men was irate, while the other tried to mollify him, placing a hand over his forearm and speaking quietly. Both women drew back, if not just embarrassed, then concerned. The waiter leaned down and said something to the angry man, and he reacted. He picked up his glass of beer and hurled it toward the bar, smashing the glass, beer splattering and shards of glass flying. If the pub had been more crowded, it could have been dangerous. "Not good enough!" he shouted.

Brie gasped and stiffened, terror in her eyes. Mike glanced at her, glanced over his shoulder again, back at Brie. Panic was showing on her face.

Then the owner or manager came rushing into the room and to the table, speaking quietly first to the waiter, then to the disgruntled customer. The angry diner talked back, though his words were impossible to make out. The other man at the table clearly tried to quiet him, but he stood abruptly and shoved the manager, causing him to take a few steps backward.

Mike looked at a terrified Brie and thought, this is all she needs. Bullshit like this her first time out in the real public. He put a hand over hers. "Stay right here and breathe deeply." Then he got up and strode purposefully toward the table. Already kitchen staff were peeking out the window in the swinging door to the kitchen.

Mike placed himself between the waiter and manager, directly in front of the offender, and was grateful that he was taller than all of them, younger and more fit than the pissed-off man. He looked into the manager's eyes and said calmly, "Call the police, please."

"Thank you, sir. I believe we can handle the situation now."

"Then if you'll allow me the use of your phone, I'll place the call."

The angry customer tried to shove Mike out of the way and said, "I'm getting the hell out of this shit hole."

Mike simply straightened, grabbed the wrist of the man's hand to ward off his shove, blocked his passage and raised the palm of his other hand. He used an authoritative voice to say, "Please sit down, sir. I don't believe you've paid for your meal and drinks." He was firm but polite. Though Mike was only a couple of inches taller, he was younger and the expression on his face very determined. The man sat. Then Mike looked at the manager and said, "The police, if you please."

"Here," said the friend, standing, opening his wallet. "Let me just pay for it and—"

"I'm sorry, sir, but your angry friend is going to settle up with the police now. Throwing glassware, assaulting the management is against the law." Then he looked over his shoulder, lifted his eyebrows to the manager and gave a nod.

"Call the police," the manager instructed the waiter, and the young man fled.

Twenty minutes later the local police took the angry client

away, still sputtering about his terrible meal. It turned out that his dissatisfaction with his lunch had been met with an offer of a replacement meal or discount from the waiter, but the man had wanted his entire foursome comped, despite protests from his wife and the other couple. It also turned out he was a little drunk and unmanageable. Handcuffs were not necessary, but the police decided it would be best if these visitors were escorted out of town and everyone exited calmly. The little pub returned to its quiet atmosphere.

The manager brought Mike a beer and Brie the wine she'd had with lunch. "With our compliments," he said, smiling.

"Thank you very much," Mike said. Then, turning to Brie, he placed a hand softly over hers and said, "God, I'm so sorry that happened, Brie. I hope you're not too upset."

Brie's eyes were actually twinkling. She smiled. "Talk about baptism by fire," she said.

"Of all the days for that clown to get tanked and cause trouble—"

But Brie answered him with a laugh. "God. For a minute I had all kinds of hysterical fears—and then it was over. The police were called, he was escorted away and it was over. Plus," she said, lifting her glass, "free drinks."

Mike's brows drew together, concern that she'd become hysterical. "I'll cover the drinks in the tip. I guess you're not hopelessly traumatized?"

"No." She laughed again. "I'm reminded. I've been up against some scary individuals, but ninety-nine percent of the time, they're all bluster. They threaten, make a lot of noise, show off and then when they're picked up by police, they cry." She leaned across the table. Her voice sank to a whisper. "I've been reciting a mantra to myself for weeks—it's been over ten years since an officer of the court was actually hurt by a defendant, and that ADA was not seriously injured. I'm not fixed, but I'm reminded—what happened to me was very unusual. What happened today was more typical."

"You deal a lot in percentages, I guess," he said.

"Ninety-three point five percent of the time," she answered with a smile.

Every week, like clockwork, Jack received a letter from Ricky, the boy who'd been his shadow for a few wonderful years until joining the Marines immediately following his high school graduation. The letter was always addressed to Jack, opened with "Dear Jack, Preach, Mike and everyone." It was the best part of his week.

When Jack first came to Virgin River, he bought the cabin because of its size and location, right in the middle of town. It had spacious rooms. He slept in one room while he worked on the other, then shifted his pallet. He was building the bar, not quite knowing if it would work in a town of only six hundred. He added the room upstairs and the apartment behind the kitchen, where he lived until Mel came into his life.

Ricky was a kid from down the street, a gregarious, freckle-faced youngster with a bright smile and the disposition of a friendly puppy. When Jack found out it was just Rick and his elderly grandma, he pulled him in, acting as something of a surrogate older brother or father. He had the privilege of a few years with the boy, watching him grow into a fine young man—strong, decent, brave. Jack taught him to fly-fish, to shoot and hunt. Together they'd gone through some fun times, some heartbreaking times. The day Rick left for the Marine Corps at the tender age of eighteen had been a day of both admiration and grief for Jack. There was a part of him that swelled in pride that Ricky would take on the Corps, and another part that worried, for no one knew better than Jack how challenging, how dangerous it could be.

When the letters came, he would share them with Preacher and Mike, then walk down to Lydie's house—Rick's grandmother. They would exchange news, for Rick wrote at least two letters a week during basic training—one to the bar where he had worked since he was fourteen, and one to his grandma. Lydie's news was always censored, Rick keeping the rougher and tougher parts of his experience from her. But Jack read his letter aloud and Lydie laughed and gasped and shuddered, but loved hearing the unabridged version.

People started showing up at the bar when they heard there'd been a letter. Connie and Ron, the aunt and uncle of Ricky's teenage girlfriend, always came around, hungry for news. Doc Mullins was as anxious as anyone, as were Mel and Paige. The Carpenters, Bristols, Hope McCrea... Everyone missed Ricky.

"They run us through the rain and mud with a thirty-pound ruck on our backs for miles and miles and miles, screaming and yelling about how we have to pay our dues, get tough—and it makes me want to laugh," Rick wrote. "I keep thinking, brother, this is nothing. I paid my dues in Virgin River...."

Ricky and his young girlfriend, Liz, had had a baby together six months ago. A baby who hadn't lived. They were too young, too fragile to be having a baby in the first place; too young and tender for such a tragedy. Being a father himself, Jack had no trouble imagining how the rigors of the Corps could seem like child's play by comparison.

Jack missed the boy. Missed him as a father misses a son.

Mike stepped up his phone calls to Brie to almost every day and it reminded him of how he'd fallen in love when he was a boy. So much phone time. So many hours given to idle conversation about the day, the activities, the family. They'd occasionally drift into tenuous territory—religion and politics. At one point Mike asked her if she was driving yet and she said, a little bit. Over to her sisters' houses, once in a while to the store, really quickly. "How are you doing in the car?"

"I don't have a problem driving. It's when I get where I'm going that I feel vulnerable. Unsafe. I have a new gun," she informed him. "To replace the one I lost."

He was silent a minute. "Uh, Brie… I wouldn't want your confidence in the car to come from the fact that you plan to shoot the first Good Samaritan who pulls over to help you change a flat."

"That isn't exactly what I meant. But…"

"Never mind. I don't want to know any more."

She laughed at him. Her laugh seemed to come a little more easily these days, at least with him. "It makes me feel safer, even though it didn't do me any good before."

"I was wondering—do you want to have lunch again? Meet me this time? Provided you don't have far to go and agree to leave the gun at home…"

"Where?" she asked.

"Maybe Santa Rosa," he suggested. "I'd be happy to come to Sacramento, but it might be good, you driving somewhere that's not just around the corner."

"It's a long way to go for lunch," she said.

"Practice," he said. "Expand your boundaries. Get out there."

"But what's in it for you?" she asked quietly.

"I thought that was clear," he said. "There are a hundred reasons I want to help you in recovery, not the least of which is, I like you. And… I've been there."

It worked. Lunch in Santa Rosa at a small Italian restaurant where they had pasta and iced tea and talked and the patrons behaved themselves. He held her hand across the table for a little while.

It was strange to Mike that he'd first become attracted to a feisty, tough character and now, even though most of the time she was soft-spoken and had trouble maintaining eye contact, his feelings toward her hadn't changed all that much. He would welcome the old Brie back if she could fully recover—but he realized that even if she remained this vulnerable, he was feeling something strong. Something he wasn't going to be able to let go of easily.

"Where did you tell your dad you were going?" he asked.

"Out to lunch with you," she said, shrugging. "I made sure he knew which restaurant and when I'd be home. He was thrilled. Of course he wants me to get back into circulation. He has no idea how far I am from that. This is something… Well, it's not getting back into the world, but it's lunch with a friend. And that feels good."

Two weeks later they met in Santa Rosa again, this time at a French restaurant in a vineyard, again small, where Brie could see every patron. And two weeks later, again Santa Rosa. When he first saw her, he wanted to rush to her, grab her up in his arms and hold her for a while, but he always put his hands in his pockets, smiled and nodded hello. By the sixth week and fourth lunch, she hugged him goodbye. "Thanks," she said. "I think this helps."

In between lunches, there were the phone calls. When they talked, he was constantly reminded of the spunky, smart-ass woman he'd fallen for. But he was faced with an uncertain woman; her confidence had been shattered. Yet in her core, this was the same woman—honest, humorous, brave.

Mike was faced with a first-time challenge. He was gentle with her, and kind—not difficult for him, because if anything he was a gentleman. But he had to work at making it seem he wasn't worried about her; that he held no pity for her, when in fact there was nothing quite as hard as knowing a woman he admired so profoundly, cared for so deeply, had been brutalized in such a way. He couldn't have her add his pain to her agenda—her recovery was difficult enough. It wasn't easy to keep his concern from showing in his eyes, his smile. She needed strength now, not weakness. He would not be the weakness in her life.

Neither of them ever mentioned Jack in their conversations, except when Brie talked about the family, about growing up, how she'd missed him after he'd left for the Marines. So far Jack had not mentioned the phone calls or lunches.

Summer was growing old. Mel and Jack had been back from Sacramento since June and the summer had been fraught with tension for Mel. Her fifteen-year-old patient was very much on her mind, as she had not returned to the clinic to be tested for STDs. She had two pregnant women in her care, not to mention the other patients who wandered into Doc Mullins's little clinic.

And her husband had not touched her in weeks.

Jack's routine was to go to his business early, chop wood, look at the schedule for the day, confer with Preacher and do what work was needed at the bar—inventory, supply run, help serve at mealtime. Then, if he could get away, he would go out to their new homesite to work on the house in progress.

The latter seemed to occupy him more, because there he could be alone. And Jack suddenly seemed to need a great deal more time alone than he had before his sister's assault. He didn't talk about Brie's rape; he was stonily silent.

Sometimes when there was nothing going on at Doc's, Mel would drive out to her new homesite with the baby and watch Jack driving nails into the wood, planing, leveling, hefting huge boards on his broad shoulders. Ordinarily, he stopped work immediately upon seeing her, spent a little time with her. But these days, these weeks, silence consumed him.

Brie called almost every day, because if she didn't call Jack would call her. She was improving both physically and emotionally, but Jack wasn't. Mel was painfully aware that this was the reason he hadn't made love to her in so long, and for them it might as well be an eternity. Their lovemaking had always been frequent and satisfying; sexually, they were a matched set. It was one of the driving forces in their marriage. Jack had strong urges, powerful urges, and Mel had learned to depend on the amazing fulfillment he brought her. Nothing could make her feel adored the way Jack did when he put his hands on her. She reciprocated, doing everything in her power to show him the depth of her love.

Knowing that it was the assault on Brie that was deeply troubling him, crippling his desire, she had exercised patience and understanding. But it was hard to lie beside him every night and not receive his usual advances. She understood his pain, his anger, but she also understood that she couldn't let her man brood forever.

She had to have him back.

A usual custom of theirs was to spend an hour or two at the bar at the end of the work day, perhaps having dinner, perhaps just a beer or cup of coffee with some of the patrons before going home to their own dinner. On this particular day, Mel simply went home. She hadn't even stopped by the bar to say goodbye. She fed the baby and put him down, showered, put on one of Jack's shirts and sat on the couch with the cool evening breezes drifting through the screen door. She could smell his scent on his shirt—his special musk mixed with the wood and wind and river.

He called and asked where she was and she said, "I decided to just come home tonight."

"Why?"

"Because there was no one to talk to at the bar," she said.

"But I'm here."

"Exactly," she said. And then she said goodbye.

Of course it took him only about twenty minutes to make his excuses to Preacher and get home. Mel knew that to have confronted this any sooner might not have given Jack the time he needed to work through it. In fact, she worried that it might still be too soon, but she was hell-bent to try. It had been a long time. Too long. The health of her marriage was everything to her.

"What's wrong?" he asked, coming in the cabin door.

"I'm lonely," she said.

He sat down on the sofa beside her and hung his head. It was that hangdog look along with his silence that was eating at her. "I'm sorry, Mel," he said. "I know I should have snapped out of it by now. I would have expected it sooner myself. I'm not a weakling. But it's Brie…"

"Jack, Brie needs you, and I want you to be there for her. I couldn't be married to any other kind of man. I hope you have a little left over, that's all. Because I love you so. I need you, too."

"I know I've disappointed you. I'll do better…"

She knelt on the couch beside him, facing him. "Kiss me," she said. He leaned his lips toward her, pressing his mouth against hers. He even made a noble effort to move his mouth over hers, opening and admitting her tongue. But there was no passion in it, no desire. He didn't put his hands on her, didn't draw her near, didn't moan with his usual hunger.

She was afraid she was losing him.

"Come with me," she said, taking his hand and leading him to their bedroom. "Sit," she said.

She knelt in front of him and worked at taking off his boots.

Then, rising on her knees, she began to unbutton his shirt. "This may not turn out the way you expect," he said.

"Shhh. We'll see." She opened his shirt, pushed it off his shoulders and began to rub her hands over the soft mat of hair that covered his chest. She kissed his chest, running a small tongue over his nipples, one at a time. She pushed him back on the bed and slowly opened his belt, the snap on his jeans, the zipper. She kissed his belly. She hooked her small hands into his jeans and tugged, bringing them down over his hips. Down off his long legs. It did not escape her that he was barely rising to the occasion, and for Jack this was astonishing. He was known to spring to life at the mere suggestion there might be sex coming his way. But she wasn't discouraged. Down came the boxers and she caressed a little life into him, then put her mouth on him in exactly the way he loved.

And there was that moan that she had longed to hear. That deep groan. He couldn't remain passive during this, one of his very favorite treats. There. He responded, perhaps in spite of himself, but she didn't care. It was a start.

Jack had never in his life had a problem that kept him from wanting sex. In fact, during the worst stress of his life, he found sex to be a wonderful escape. But not this time—this time he'd been numb. He was barely aware it had been happening to him, and then his wife let him know when she came after him, demanding a response, and he suddenly realized that he hadn't deprived only himself in some pattern of grief. He felt her small mouth take him in, and his body allowed him blissful separation from his mind. He closed his eyes in luxury. She climbed on him, hot and sweet, and he ran his hands around her bottom and under the shirt she wore, up to her full breasts, and heard her hum in pleasure, "Oh, Jack— I have so needed your hands on me." It hit him, how much they depended on each other. They should be helping each other through the difficult times, not closing off.

He lifted the shirt over her head and brought her breasts down to his mouth, tasting their sweetness. Then he rolled with her, bringing her beneath him, filling her, listening to her pleased sighs and purrs. "Baby, I'm sorry," he whispered. "I never meant to neglect you." He moved and she bent her knees, lifted her hips to bring him deeper and deeper, her hands on his shoulders and arms, her mouth on his mouth.

This is what he loved about his woman, his wife—that she was as driven sexually as he. In this they had been beautifully paired and it had taken boldness on her part to bring him back to life. He'd never before suffered so long a dry spell, and it meant the world to him that she wouldn't allow it, that she was desperate for him, that she was determined to have this back in their marriage. Thank God for her, he thought. Anyone else would have become moody, angry, taken offense or even ignored the drought. But not Mel; she was committed to him. Committed to this passion they shared. She would not give it up easily.

He grabbed her small, tight fanny and held her to him, making it good, making it right, the perfect friction that caused her to gasp and cry out his name. He chuckled, a deep raspy laugh, for he adored this about her—that she couldn't be quiet, that when he did the things he knew she loved, she was swept away, helpless.

When she heard that lusty laugh, the sound he made when he was again in control, focused on nothing but bringing her pleasure, making her body soar, she wrapped her legs around him and blasted him with an orgasm so hot and strong, he trembled. As she weakened beneath him, she knew immediately he had held himself back. Saved himself. He was going to do it to her again before he let himself go.

She touched his beautiful, sculptured face with her hands, saw the smile on his lips and the dark smoldering fire in his eyes, and said, "Welcome home, darling. Welcome back."

Brie had to forcibly pry herself off the couch. She'd rarely left her dad's house since it had happened. Most of her outings were to her counselor or support group and a lunch once in a while with Mike. Lunches she looked forward to with anxiety and delight. Sam, so afraid of making things worse, rocking her already rocky boat, hadn't said anything to her about it, but he knew. And she knew he knew.

Brad called almost every day, and while Brie wasn't really interested in talking to him, she knew he'd tell her the truth about what was going on with the investigation. That was one of the things they'd had in common from the beginning— casework. Right now, if Brad could deliver the news that they had taken Powell into custody, it would make a huge difference in her life. But of course that had not yet happened.

Another person who called regularly was Christine, her former best friend and Brad's new woman. Those were calls Brie refused to take, but even Sam's advice that Christine stop calling had no impact. "She says that eventually you'll talk to her, let her tell you how worried she's been and how much she loves you," Sam reported to Brie.

Brie gave a huff of laughter. "She just loves way too many people, doesn't she?"

With every call, she'd revisit that drama in her mind, still amazed by the way the whole thing had unfolded. They'd been couple friends since before Brie and Brad married; Christine's husband was also a Sacramento cop, Glenn. Glenn and Christine had danced at their wedding. Christine was a surgical nurse who worked for a private practice surgeon; she and Brie had become close. In fact, besides her sisters, Christine had been the closest woman in her life. They'd talked almost every day, seen each other at least a couple of times a week, with husbands or without.

Brie was aware that Christine and Glenn had some marital problems. They bickered over the usual things—sex, money and parenting. With two demanding jobs, two little kids and a too-big house, it seemed to Brie they were destined to have certain squabbles until the kids got older, until they could mellow out and get ahead of the bills. But Brie was wrong— a couple of years after Brie and Brad married, Christine and Glenn separated and divorced. They were almost more amicable than when they had been married. It wasn't too tough to sit on the fence on that one—Brad saw Glenn at work and he'd drop by the house for a beer occasionally, and Brie and Christine remained friends. After the shock of Glenn's moving out settled a little, it seemed to Brie that her best friend was in many ways calmer and happier on her own, managing her own money, getting a break from the kids a couple of days a week when Glenn took them.

There were signs that Brie had taken no notice of. Christine didn't date or talk about men; a year after her divorce, their phone chats had become fewer—but Christine was very busy. It wasn't easy being a single, working mom. And Brie's job was demanding, her hours long, so she was usually the one unavailable for girlfriend time. If she were honest, she could admit Christine had always done most of the phoning, inviting. What was still impossible for Brie to grasp was that Brad's behavior had never seemed to change. They talked on cell phones several times a day, were together every night Brad wasn't on duty, making love as often as before. Up until the time he told her he was leaving, that he needed some space, she had no idea anything was wrong.

Brie didn't know how it started between them, but Brad

admitted it had been going on about a year. "I don't know," Brad said with a helpless shrug. "A couple of lonely people, I guess. Glenn was gone, you were always working and Christine and I were pretty close friends to start with."

"Oh, you are so full of shit!" she railed at him. "You never once asked me to take time off! My hours were just what you needed to pull this off!"

"If that's what you have to believe, Brie," he had said.

It had knocked the wind out of her. The only thing worse than the pain was the shock and disbelief. Six months after the divorce was final, she'd thought she'd made some important headway in dealing with it, but it was as though the rape brought it all back; her depression over the divorce seemed suddenly brand-new. Robbed, again and again, she kept thinking.

Most of the time all she did was watch TV, snack, sleep, tidy up the house. Her concentration wasn't good enough to read a novel—something she had craved when work had been so consuming. Working a crossword puzzle was out of the question—she couldn't focus; she used to do the Sunday-morning crossword in ink before Brad even got out of bed. She couldn't even go to the mall. But she made it to those lunches with Mike. She came to think of them as her secret lunches, almost the only thing that brought her away from herself, away from all the blows of the past year. Her father's silence on the matter intrigued her; she hadn't even whispered of these meetings to her sisters. It was as if that would take the magic away.

She didn't even recognize the woman she'd become. She'd been so tough. Some people—mostly men—thought of her as hard. At the moment she was limp and frightened. She was paranoid and afraid it would never pass. She'd been dealing with the victims of crimes for years now, and a number of them had been rape victims. She had watched them wither, paralyzed, unable to act on their own behalf. As she cajoled and coached them for their testimonies, she would become frustrated and angry by the reduction of feeling that seemed to weigh them down, overwhelm them. The helplessness. The impotence. And now she was one of them.

I'm not giving in, she kept telling herself. Still, it had taken her weeks. Months. "I need some exercise," she told Mike during one of their lunches. "I can't seem to get out of bed or off the couch if I don't have a specific appointment or lunch with you."

"Have you asked anyone for an antidepressant?" he asked. "I thought it was pretty routine after a crime."

"I don't want to go that route if I can help it. Up to now, I've always had so much energy."

"I went that route," he admitted to her. "I didn't think I needed to, but it became clear I was depressed—a combination of major surgery and being the victim of a violent crime. It helped."

"I don't think so…"

"Then you're going to have to think of an alternative or this thing can swallow you up," he said. "Brie, fight back. Fight back!"

"I am," she said weakly. "I know it doesn't look like it, but I am."

He touched her hand gently and said, softly but earnestly, "Fight harder! I can't lose you to this!"

Well, she couldn't jog anymore—she was afraid to be out there alone, even in broad daylight. It couldn't be a gym or health club—she couldn't have men looking at her right now. She remembered with some longing how she had loved being looked at. She had a small, compact, fit little body and lots of long, silky hair that she braided for court but let swing freely down her back the rest of the time. It made her heady with power to garner the stares of attractive men. Now if a man looked at her, it threw her into panic.

But she wasn't going down without a fight—so she joined a women's gym and started running on the treadmill and lifting weights. If she couldn't have a full life, she was at least going to fake one.

The joke was on her—a couple of weeks of vigorous exercise and she was sleeping better and eating better. She felt it put her into the next stage of recovery, every day a tiny bit easier than the day before.

There were times she thought that if not for Mike's attention right now, she'd be lost. Oh, her family was amazing—the way they managed to hold strong for her, encourage her and make themselves constantly available should she want to talk. But Mike, the very man she had vowed would never get near her when she recognized his flirting last spring, was the only thing in her life that allowed her to feel like a woman. For that she would be forever grateful.

Tommy Booth was the new kid in town, just checking in for his senior year at Valley High School. His father, Walt Booth, had just retired from the Army and had given Tommy his choice—a military academy, a nonmilitary private academy or Valley High. Tommy chose to live with his dad for a couple of reasons—he'd lost his mom in a car accident a few years ago and it had just been him and his dad since, a couple of bachelors who got along fairly well for father and son. And his older sister, married and pregnant and separated from her husband by the Marine Corps, was going to come to Virgin River to live with them until Matt, his brother-in-law, got back from the Middle East. She was going to have her baby there—and Tom was secretly a little excited about that. Plus, there were his horses, which he couldn't take to a private school.

Tom's father, a retired three-star general, had found this property a couple of years ago; the general had a younger sister and niece a few hours south in Bodega Bay and had looked all over California for the right spot, not too far away from them. Aunt Midge was sick; she had been sick several years, bedridden the past three. She was worse than sick—she was terminal, with Lou Gehrig's disease, and her daughter, Shelby, was her full-time caregiver. Walt Booth had been ready to settle in Bodega Bay to be there for her even though he was more of a forest and mountains than beach kind of guy. But Midge had convinced him not to choose Bodega Bay because of her presence there—she wasn't going to last more than a couple of years. She might be gone by the time Walt retired from the Army and if she was not, he could visit. Thus, Virgin River—close enough to see Midge and Shelby as often as he could, but the kind of place Walt wanted to put down his final roots. It had begun to look as if Aunt Midge was right— she couldn't possibly have much longer. By the time Walt and Tommy got to Virgin River, Midge needed twenty-four-hour care, and Hospice was on the scene.

While Walt finished his last assignment at the Pentagon, he'd had the house renovated via long distance and the new stable and corral constructed. Tommy had seen it only once before actually moving in, but he loved the land—the enormous trees, the rivers, the coast, the mountainsides and valleys through which he could ride.

Classes started in late August. He wasn't that jazzed about the high school. The kids sure weren't as sophisticated as the D.C. kids. And Tom was a little bit on the shy side until he got to know someone. This being a small-town high school, all the cliques had been established ages ago, so fitting in was going to take a while. He was a big kid, athletic, but he'd been too late for football.

He met a kid in first period right off—Jordan Whitley, a funny guy. Kind of skinny and hyper, but really friendly. He hung out with him a couple of times after school. Jordan lived pretty close to the school, while Tom had to drive his little red truck all the way from Virgin River every day. Also, Jordan's parents were divorced, he was an only child and his mom worked—which freed up Jordan's house until about six. As long as Tom got home before dinner, in time to take care of the horses, it was no big deal to go over there for a little while after school.

Tom also learned that there were frequent keggers at an abandoned rest stop area right at the edge of Virgin River. Weekend parties that Jordan really wanted him to attend, but Tom always had an excuse. He didn't know anyone but Jordan. And he was quiet about the fact that he had a house to himself for a few days every other week or so while Walt went to Bodega Bay. He wasn't about to be overrun by Jordan and his tribe—if Walt ever found out, he'd be dead meat.

Jordan somehow managed to score beer at his house. After-school beer. Tom was very careful about that because if the general smelled it on his breath he was toast. But the other thing Jordan had going on was girls. He seemed to always have a different girl. So far Tommy hadn't seen one that got him excited—Jordan didn't seem to draw the really pretty ones. But it was kind of fun to go over to his house and get all the flirtatious attention bestowed on him, being the new kid and not that bad looking.

"Come on over to my buddy Brendan's Friday night," Jordan invited. "We're gonna get lucky."

"Yeah?" Tommy grinned. "Who you gonna get lucky with?"

"I've got this girl who wants me so bad she can't hold herself back. And she's on the pill."

"So you want me to come over and watch you get lucky? I might have to pass on that," he said with a laugh.

"She's bringing a girlfriend," Jordan said.

"I might come by for a beer," Tommy said. "Let me think about it. I don't know this Brendan guy."

"He's cool," Jordan said. "He graduated a couple of years ago, and when his mom goes out of town, which she does a lot, the house is his. And if we get lucky, we can get lucky all night long, if you get my drift."

"Oh, I get your drift," he said. And he was thinking, you idiots. You don't go banging the local girls who advertise they're on the pill. He wasn't stupid—that's how you got stuff. Bad stuff. An image of telling his dad he had the drip sent shivers up his spine.

But he went. He popped the top on two beers, total, without finishing either one; he knew better than to drink anything out of a keg or punch bowl. There was a little pot floating around, though not everyone indulged. Tommy didn't get near that shit. Too risky for a kid planning on West Point; too risky for a boy with a father like Walt, who would dismember him before killing him.

The girlfriend who was earmarked for Tom if he was interested was way too aggressive and ready for anything, and he just couldn't see it. Plus, Jordan and Brendan were busy getting everyone as shit-faced as possible, as quickly as possible, and there was nothing quite as funny to watch—but inevitably boring. He finally slipped away about nine without anyone really noticing he was gone.

The next Monday morning at school Jordan excitedly asked, "Where'd you go, man?"

He shrugged. "I had to get home. My dad is pretty strict."

"Yeah, but we had beer and girls!"

"I had a couple of beers," he said. "And the girls… Well, I didn't meet one I really liked."

That made Jordan laugh almost hysterically. "Well, so what? You're not…? You don't still have your cherry, do you, man?"

In fact, he did. "'Course not," he said, because what do you say to something like that? Tom hadn't made it with a girl, but not because he couldn't. Because he was very careful and he and the last girlfriend back in D.C. had barely graduated to some petting before he moved away. He was in a desperate hurry to find a great girl, but she'd have to be a great girl, not just someone who'd put out. In fact, a girl who put out was kind of a put-off. And if he found a great girl, he was going to be a great guy to her, not someone out for himself.

"Come over after school," Jordan said. "Maybe we can hook you up."

"Listen, Jord, I know you're just trying to be a good friend and get me laid, but how about you worry about you and I'll take care of myself. Huh?"

"Aw, man, you don't know what you're missing!"

But Tom had seen the girls, the beer and pot, and he thought—actually, I think I do know what I'm missing. He hadn't met anyone through Jordan who interested him. So far. "You take care of you—I'll take care of me."

Still, Jordan was one of the few friends he'd made. And Jordan loved coming out to the ranch and hanging around the horses sometimes. The general didn't like him, but didn't have a really good reason. Tom found himself a little torn—grateful to have a friend at all, but hopeful that someone a little more substantive would show up before too long.

A young man came into the bar and claimed a stool right in front of Jack. He was clearly under thirty. Jack eyed the polo shirt, khaki pants and loafers—not the mountain attire most commonly seen around here. This guy was not hunting, fishing or splitting logs. He gave the counter a wipe and said, "What can I get you?"

"How about a beer?"

"That's our specialty," Jack said, serving him up a cold draft. "Passing through?"

"No, as a matter of fact. At least I hope that's a no—I just started teaching at Valley High School. I thought I'd get to know some of the folks around here." He took a pull on his beer. "You have any high schoolers?"

"Brace yourself," Jack said, lifting his coffee cup. "I have a new baby. By the time he gets to high school, I'll have a walker."

The young man laughed. He put out a hand. "Zach Hadley."

"Jack Sheridan. Welcome aboard. How do you like it so far?"

"A little out of my experience, to tell you the truth. I'm used to a bigger school, city kids. But I wanted to give a rural community a try." He grinned. "The kids find me real interesting—they laugh at my clothes."

Jack grinned. "Lotta ranchers, farmers, vintners and that sort of thing around here. That, and hunting and fishing." He nodded at the young man. "Not a lot of golf."

"Is that what I look like? A golfer?" He chuckled. "Figures."

Mel came into the bar, the baby on her hip. She passed the baby right across the bar to Jack. Jack hefted the baby and said, "Mr. Hadley, meet David, your future student." David laughed, put a finger in his mouth and farted, bringing a big laugh out of Jack.

"Yeah, he's just warming up. He's going to be one of the fun ones, I can tell."

Jack reached underneath the bar for the backpack. He very deftly slipped David into it and then the straps over his shoulders. "Mel," he said, while getting David comfortable. "Meet Zach Hadley, new high school teacher in town."

They shook hands and Zach explained he was renting a small place outside Clear River and was just getting around, meeting neighbors and parents of his kids. "Well, you're here at the right time," Mel said. "The locals will start turning out for a beer or cup of coffee."

"Excellent," he said. "Do you run this place with your husband?"

"No. I'm a nurse practitioner and midwife. I work across the street with Doc Mullins in his clinic."

"Is that a fact?" he asked, intrigued.

"It's a fact no one around here gives birth in daylight," Jack said, serving his wife a short beer.

"My very able helper," Mel said. "When I have a delivery at Doc's, Jack usually sits up through the night in case I need him for anything."

Mike came into the bar, took his place beside Mel. Jack introduced him as a former LAPD police officer who'd served with him in the Marine Corps. Next was Doc.

"You know, there's a lot of interesting experience in this little bar. I bet it would be good for some of the kids to hear about your career choices. How about it?"

Mike said, "I've done that, actually."

"You have? How'd it go?" Zach asked.

"Hmm," he said, shaking his head. "They wanted to know two things—have I ever shot anyone and have I ever been shot. My answers were yes, and not yet. Shortly after that I was shot. I don't think that'll get the department any recruits."

"I'd be happy to talk to the kids about birth control, sexually transmitted disease and sexual assault," Mel said. "I've been looking for a way into the school—this is pretty conservative country."

"Mel," Jack said, "Zach was just saying he's new and hopes he's not just passing through." Preacher came into the bar with a rack of clean glasses. "Preacher, meet Zach, new high school teacher in town. He's looking for some volunteers to talk to his students about their career choices."

"Hey, man," Preacher said, shoving his rack under the bar, wiping a big meaty hand on his apron and sticking it out. "Nice to meet you."

"You could talk about being a chef," Jack said.

Preacher looked at Zach, smiled and said, "No way in hell. I barely talk to my own wife. Welcome to town." Then he went straight back to the kitchen.

Zach leaned over the bar and looked past Mike and Mel to Doc. "Dr. Mullins?" he questioned hopefully.

Doc lifted his one whiskey of the day along with a bushy white eyebrow. He sipped, put the whiskey down and said, "In your dreams, young man."

Zach picked up his beer and said, very good-naturedly, "That went well."

"You know what you got yourself here, young man," Jack said. "You got yourself an excellent place to have a beer."

"How about you, Jack? You'd do it, right?"

"Sure, Zach. I'll go tell the kids all the advantages of own-ing your very own bar. Right after that, Mel can teach them sexual responsibility. Kind of a little family business."

"That's it," Zach said. "An excellent place to have a beer."

3

Sue and Doug Carpenter and Carrie and Fish Bristol—best couple friends—had been having an after-work beer at Jack's a couple of times a week since he opened, so Mel knew them well. And Sue had called Mel to make an appointment for her sixteen-year-old daughter. On the phone she had said, "The girl is pregnant and we have to do something." Well, this was Mel's job—to give medical attention to pregnant women, whatever their age or marital status. And Sue was a bit put out that Mel insisted on seeing her patient alone first.

"What have we got, Brenda?" Mel asked, looking at the chart.

"I guess I'm pregnant," she said. "Figures."

Mel looked up from the chart. Brenda was a high school junior. From gossip between the Carpenters and Bristols at the bar, Mel had gathered that this girl was an honor student, cheerleader, student council officer—a leader. College bound; scholarship material. Nature certainly doesn't discriminate, Mel thought. "Do you know how many periods you've missed?"

"Three. Can you get rid of it?"

Mel tilted her head, surprised by the caustic edge to the girl's question. Brenda had always been soft-spoken, on the sweet side. The tragedy was usually that these young girls were ready to throw away their lives, their promising futures, based on some immature romance with a young boy. Didn't sound as if Brenda was suffering from that syndrome. "You have lots of options, but first things first—how about I examine you to be sure that's what's going on."

"Fine," she said shortly. "Whatever."

"Okay, let's get you in this gown. Everything off. And I'll be back. How's that?"

Rather than answer, Brenda snatched the gown and didn't even wait for Mel to leave before she began undressing.

Mel went to the kitchen, had a sip of her diet cola and ran this over in her mind. Maybe Brenda was just mad at her mother for finding out. Maybe the boy had taken off. Maybe a lot of things, she thought. She reminded herself to stick to the facts for now.

She gave Brenda a few minutes, knowing better than to stretch this out for too long. Brenda didn't need to settle her nerves; she needed to get this over with.

"Have you had a pelvic before?" Mel asked her.

"No," she said shortly. "Just do it."

"Sure thing," Mel said. "But let me get your blood pressure and listen to your heart first, if you don't mind."

"Whatever."

"Brenda, excuse me, but are you angry with me?"

"I am angry in general," she said.

Mel sat on her stool and looked up at the girl. "Because...?"

"Because this sucks."

"Well, people make mistakes. You're human..."

"Yeah? I could live with that if I knew I was making a mistake!"

"Okay, let's back up a little. Want to tell me about it?"

"Why bother? Do it, okay? You'll just think I'm as stupid as I already think I am."

"Try me," Mel said, crossing her legs, resting her arms on her knee.

"I went to a party. A kegger. I got drunk. I woke up sick. Puking sick. The guy I was with said he passed out and nothing happened. But obviously someone is lying if I'm pregnant."

Mel couldn't help herself—her mouth dropped open. "Brenda, you told your mother about this?"

"Not until two periods didn't come, because how was I going to know? I did one of those home test things. I never thought it would be...positive...."

"Were you sore? In your vagina?"

"I was sore everywhere! Like I'd fallen down a flight of stairs! And so sick I wanted to die. My vagina was about the last thing on my mind!"

"When you woke up—you were dressed? Any evidence of rape?"

"Completely dressed. Right down to the vomit on my shirt. And in my hair," she added with a shudder.

"And you were with friends? Anyone see anything?"

"I was with a couple of girlfriends and one useless guy. They were all as drunk as me. We'd never... It was like the first time for something like that. I've had maybe one or two beers, but I've never been to a kegger before. I'm obviously not much of a drinker."

"Do you remember drinking a lot?" Mel asked.

"I don't remember much of anything. A couple of the guys said I was totally shitty. Drunk out of my mind. And one of my girlfriends swears my date really did pass out right away."

"Ever think there could have been a drug involved? Slipped into your beer?"

"What kind of drug?" she asked.

"What do you think happened?" Mel asked her.

"I think I got hammered and let some guy— Obviously I wasn't in a position to make a good decision. Plus, these are my friends. Well, the girls I went with are my friends—they wouldn't lie to me. I don't hang out with the other ones who were there."

"All of them were your friends?"

"Someone's not—unless there was a guy there who also doesn't remember."

Mel leaned forward. It was in her mind to ask Brenda if she'd ever heard the term, whiskey dick. "An unfortunate reality for most males is that too much alcohol inhibits erection or ejaculation. Whoever did this remembers."

"And is lying…"

"Well, somebody's lying—and if you're pregnant and can't remember getting that way, it probably isn't you. Brenda, you could have been raped."

"Or—I could have been so stupid drunk I didn't know what I was doing."

"Same thing, in my mind," Mel said with a shrug. "Have you talked to the police?"

"Yeah." She laughed bitterly. "Right."

Mel reached out a hand to touch her knee and Brenda flinched. Mel's mind immediately flashed on Carra and she cringed inwardly. "You have DNA in you, Brenda. The person responsible can be revealed."

"Uh-huh. That should be interesting." She laughed again. "Real interesting."

"Listen, Brenda…"

"I don't want to know. Whoever it is will just say I wanted it. Why wouldn't he? And I would never be able to say otherwise, since I don't fricking know. Meanwhile not only the whole school, but the whole town would know Brenda is a whore. Brenda's knocked up, Brenda would like everyone to believe she was drugged." She laughed at Mel. "Who are we kidding? Huh?"

"Is that likely? Let me tell you something—girls who aren't sexually active don't usually have one occasion of getting drunk and waking up pregnant because they wanted it." Brenda looked away. "Have you been sexually active? Not that it matters in this case."

Her eyes came back and the anger had seeped away. "I had a boyfriend last year who… I really liked him a lot. But we didn't go all the way." She looked down. "I wouldn't give it up. I wanted to be sure, wanted it to be special. You know?" Now there were tears in her eyes, but they vanished as quickly as they had come.

Mel touched her hand. "It'll still be special, honey," Mel said, standing up. "When you're ready, it'll be special. Let's do an exam, test you for sexually transmitted disease, get a blood workup for HIV."

"H-I-Vee?" she asked, stricken. "Oh, fuck!"

"One thing at a time, Brenda. Are you up-to-date on the hepatitis B vaccine for school immunizations?"

"Hepatitis B?" she asked. "What's that got to do with anything?"

"It's also an STD," Mel said.

"Oh, God," Brenda said weakly.

"Take it easy, sweetheart. Feet here, in the stirrups, slide down for me, that's it." She put on her gloves. "Take a deep breath, let it out slowly and relax your muscles as much as possible. There you go." Mel took a look and noted some inflammation, tenderness. She did her pap slide, then inserted a swab in the cervical area to test for chlamydia and gonorrhea. "I'm going to let that swab sit for a moment. Listen, do you remember the people who were at that party? And where it was?"

Brenda put the back of her hand on her forehead and her chin quivered. "All I want to do is get it out of me and get on with my life. School already started and everything...."

"I understand that, but I'm worried. This isn't a situation we should ignore. What if some other young woman is attacked like this, made pregnant without even consenting to sex?"

"Or remembering that she consented?"

"Do you remember any bruising? On your arms, pelvis, hips? Buttocks?"

"My chest was really sore, and so was my throat. I thought it was from throwing up."

"Where?" Mel asked. Brenda put her palm against her upper chest, on her sternum, right above her breasts. "On the outside? Like you'd been hit in the chest by a...by a basketball or something?"

"Yeah," she said, apparently surprised by how well the analogy fit.

Mel finished her exam and helped Brenda sit up. "Would you be willing to talk to someone about this? Like maybe one of the nurses at the family planning clinic? Give whatever details you can remember?"

"What for?"

"For the future protection of some girl who doesn't know what dangers lurk at a kegger?" Mel said.

Brenda looked down miserably. "I don't know."

"No one's going to expose you. No one's going to confront

anyone without charges being filed. But for right now—you deserve better than to have no idea what happened to you."

"I don't know. Maybe. I'll have to think about it."

"Okay. Get dressed. But first—will you tell me one thing? The party. Was it here? In Virgin River?"

"Yeah," she said. "Right here."

Mel had a long chat with a nurse in the family planning clinic in Eureka. She agreed that it was very important to interview this patient, but before that could even happen, Brenda miscarried. Less than a week later the test results came back positive for chlamydia.

Mel immediately got in touch with Carra Winslow. She was a little past caring if a parent answered the phone, but fortunately for Carra, it was she who picked up. Mel was straightforward—she told her there was a venereal disease making the rounds and it was imperative that Carra return to the clinic for testing.

She also tested positive for chlamydia. Mel fixed her up with antibiotics and made her promise to return to the clinic in a couple of months to follow up. Carra still refused birth control; she was no longer seeing the two-week boyfriend. And even though he had given her an infection, she still wouldn't blame him or name him.

But this weighed on Mel's mind mightily. She was afraid they might have a serious problem in her town.

September and October brought a time of year that Mel disliked, though it was good for the bar. Bear-and deer-hunting season. Since there was no hunting inside the Virgin River town limits, the hunters they saw were those who passed through town en route to and from the lodges and camps in Shasta and the Trinity Alps where some of the best hunting was found. As a rule, these were a decent lot of men and even a few women, many of whom had been seen at Jack's in previous years and made it a point to stop by to enjoy Preacher's cooking. And Preacher went to a little extra trouble, knowing they'd bring their money and high expectations. They didn't change the pricing of their food and drinks for the hunters—it was all sold on the cheap, catering first to the town. But Jack did lay in some of the finer liquors, like Johnnie Walker Blue, because this was a monied crowd who liked their drinks. And they always left a lot more money on the bar and tables than they were charged.

City girl that she was, Mel abhorred the sight of a beautiful buck tied to the roof of an SUV or tossed in the back of a truck. Having already been through one hunting season and being married to a man who happened to enjoy the hunt, she'd learned to say very little.

Jack and Preacher had always catered to the hunters and fishermen—it was one of the reasons Jack had built the place. During the season, the bar stayed open a little later if there were people around, and still opened at the crack of dawn. Jack usually stayed to help out until at least nine, sending Mel home to get David settled for the night.

At a time of day when Mel might already have been and gone from her dinner hour, she had a call to make with Doc, and brought the baby to Jack. Being over five months now, husky and strong, David was most often seen riding happily in Jack's backpack as opposed to the front sling he had occupied in earlier months. As Mel slipped the straps over Jack's shoulders, she said, "He's fed and changed and I shouldn't be too long."

Mike was having his dinner at the bar when six hunters came in. Since Jack didn't greet them as men he'd seen before, Mike assumed this might be their first time through town.

These were young men, all in their twenties, and obviously having a good time. All six went up to the bar, made a few jokes about the bartender being part-time babysitter, which Jack took in good-natured stride. They eschewed dinner, opting for some drinks. Once Jack had set them up with beer and shots, they retired to a table, where they enjoyed rehashing every aspect of their hunt.

"Who do you think is the designated driver in that crowd?" Mike asked Jack.

Jack was watching, but said nothing. And Mike was watching Jack, because the latter had a good sense for things. Getting a little loud and rowdy was not frowned upon here, so long as you could keep your head. These boys were hanging in there, though they were ordering up more beer and shots; they wanted a pitcher and a bottle and were getting a little louder by the shot.

It wasn't long before Paige came out of the kitchen. "Have you asked them about dinner?" she asked Jack.

"Last time I offered, they weren't interested," he said.

"Okay, let me just check before we close the kitchen." She went to their table to ask them if they wanted anything to eat. "My husband has a great lasagna and garlic bread, but also some broiled, stuffed sturgeon fresh off the river and steamed vegetables, if you're interested."

"Husband?" one of them chortled. "Damn, my hunting sucks no matter where I go."

She instinctively retreated a step and the man reached for her hand, pulling her back. "You can get rid of the husband, can't you, sweetheart?" His buddies laughed at his brazenness and Mike thought, shit. This is not a good thing; you don't want to mess with Preacher's woman. He looked across the bar at Jack's narrowed eyes. Oh, boy.

Paige simply pulled her hand back, smiled politely and

didn't grapple with them any longer over food. As she would have gone back to the kitchen, Jack stopped her and asked her to take David. He slid the backpack off his shoulders and into her hands and one of the hunters yelled over to Jack, "That the wife, buddy?" And Jack's mouth curved in a slow smile as he shook his head—no, you don't really want to meet her husband.

Now, what none of these idiots knew was that Jack hadn't had a nice summer. His sister's trauma was not that long past and he'd been in a real mood. There was a side of Jack that was all soft, crushed concern and a side that wanted to kill someone. This was not a great time to screw with him. Since Jack had shed the baby, a telling move, Mike thought it might be worth it to try to head this off. He stood up from his meal at the end of the bar and walked over to their table. He flipped around a chair from a neighboring table and, straddling the back, he said, "Hey, boys. You have a good hunt?"

They eyed him suspiciously. One of them said, "One buck—young. Not much to brag about. Who are you?"

"Name's Mike—how you doing? Listen, I just thought I'd mention—you don't want to overdo it. Especially if you're driving out tonight."

They started to laugh, meeting eyes with each other as though sharing some kind of private joke. "That a fact?" one asked. "And who put you in charge?"

"I'm not in charge of anything," he said. "But gee—I'd hate to see anyone get hurt. These roads," he said, shaking his head. "Sometimes pretty tight around the curves going down. And real, real dark. No lights. No guard rails."

Right then, Mel came into the bar, hung her jacket on the peg inside the door and jumped up on a stool in front of her husband, elbows on the bar, leaning toward him for a kiss.

"Holy shit," one of the men said. "Look at that one. Talk about a doe I'd like to bag."

Jack straightened before meeting his wife's lips. The look on his face wasn't a pretty one.

"You know," Mike said, laughing uncomfortably, "about our women. You boys don't want to be giving the women around here any trouble. Trust me on this, okay?"

That set up a round of hilarious laughter at the table of hunters and one of them said, unfortunately too loudly, "Maybe the girl wants to get bagged. I think we should at least ask her!" But oops—glancing over his shoulder, Mike saw Jack had heard that. And probably so had Mel. And after what those two had been through earlier in the summer, comments like that were not taken lightly.

And that's when Mike became convinced that these guys had been pretty well oiled before they hit Virgin River. They had absolutely no judgment. Hunting and drinking was a thing he disliked—frowned on by him and his brothers, both the Mexican brothers and Marines. Drinking after the hunt— that was another story. Especially if the shooting was done, the guns unloaded and stowed, and all you were going to do was walk out back to your camper.

He looked back over his shoulder in time to see Jack whisper something to Mel. Mel jumped off the stool, disappeared into the back and Mike thought, oh fuck. He stood. "Okay, boys. Settle up for your drinks and hit the road. While you can still see straight. Okay?"

"Relax, chico. We're not quite done here."

Chico? He hated it when people did that. You don't want to call a Mexican man a little boy.

Out of the corner of his eye Mike saw him. He'd known he would. Preacher had come out of the kitchen and stood behind the bar next to Jack, arms crossed over his massive chest, those big, black eyebrows drawn together in a frown that only Preacher could effect with such a look of menace. The diamond stud in his ear seemed to twinkle. Jack had sent Mel for him. They were ready to mix it up with these guys, defend the place.

Mike absently worked his shoulder a little bit, loosening it up. He couldn't remember hearing about a bar fight around here. Certainly not since Preacher had come on full-time. You'd have to be drunk and stupid to get into it with him.

These guys looked pretty fit. Lots younger by average than Jack, Preacher and Mike. But they'd been doing a lot of drinking, whereas that evening shot before closing had yet to be poured for the crew running the bar. The home team had been on coffee.

As Mike knew, Jack hated it when his bar got messed up. It was a sacrifice he'd make if threatened, but it made him very unhappy. Maybe he'd stay behind the bar and just let them wander off. Or maybe he'd enjoy a little fight, having had the kind of summer he'd had.

"Come on, boys. Get going. You really don't want to mess this place up..." Mike said.

The hunters exchanged looks, then slowly stood. They began to move away from the table, having left no money to pay for their drinks, which was a sure clue trouble was coming. The one in the group closest to Mike whirled suddenly, landing a blow right to Mike's face. It sent him skittering backward, his hand to his lip, ending up against the bar. He said, "Oh, you're going to hate yourself."

He wound up and hit back, left-handed, sending his assailant flying into his boys, knocking two of them off balance.

It started. Preacher and Jack were around the bar before Mike even delivered his first blow. Preacher knocked two heads together, Jack landed a blow to one gut, another jaw.

Mike grabbed up his attacker, decked him again and then sent him into another guy, downing them both. Someone came at Jack with a ready fist, which Jack caught easily, twisted his assailant's arm around his back and shoved him into his boys. In less than two minutes, six partially inebriated young hunters were on the bar floor, spread over some broken glasses and amidst toppled chairs and two tables. All of them were moaning. Besides that first blow to Mike's face, they hadn't even managed contact. The heartiest of the bunch got back on his feet and Preacher grabbed him by the front of his jacket, lifted him off the floor and said, "You really wanna be this stupid?" He instantly put up his hands and Preacher dropped him.

"Okay, okay, we're out of here," he said.

"It's too late for that, guys," Mike said. He yelled, "Paige!" She stuck her head into the bar. "Rope!"

"Aw, come on, man," someone said.

"Just get 'em the hell out of here," Jack said, disgusted.

"Can't," Mike returned. Then to the hunters, "Hell, I tried to warn you. You don't want to mess with the women. You don't want to fight. Not around here. Jesus," he said in disgust. "Shit for brains."

Mike explained to Jack that not only were these boys too drunk to drive down the mountain, they might get down the road and claim they'd been jumped. Since they had all the bruises and the home team had only sore knuckles, it just wouldn't be smart to take that kind of chance. Better to let the police handle things now. Fifteen minutes later each one of them was tied to a porch rail out front, and a half hour after that three sheriff's deputies were standing around the front of the bar, assessing the damage.

"Merciful God," Deputy Henry Depardeau said. "Every time I turn around, somebody's getting beat up or shot around here!"

"Yeah, Henry, we're awful sorry," Jack said. "We hardly ever have any trouble."

"And what was it this time?" he asked impatiently.

"That one," Jack said, pointing. "He threw the first punch. That was so frickin' rude, don't you think? You can see, it was just out of line. You know?"

"You're taking up way too much of my time!"

"I'll buy you dinner one of these days, how about that? You and your boys just drop in anytime."

"Yeah, yeah. All right, let's load 'em up. I sure hope you boys have yourselves licenses and your deer tag." By the droop of one hunter's head, it looked as if there were going to be more fines. It made Jack laugh. "Aw, man," Henry said. "Poachers are usually quiet and polite so they can slip in and out of here unnoticed. I should book you for stupid."

Hope McCrea, a feisty old widow, was almost a daily visitor at Jack's. She liked to have a Jack Daniel's and a cigarette at the end of the day. She'd often sit up at the bar next to Doc, but there were times Mike talked with her a while.

"You know I hired Mel to come up here, right?" Hope asked Mike one night.

"I heard that, yeah," he said.

"I'd like you to come out to the house to talk about something. A proposition."

"Well, Hope." He grinned. "That sounds real interesting...."

"A job, you young fool," she said, pushing her too-big glasses up on her nose. But she had a toothy smile for him just the same.

"I don't want a job, Hope," he said.

"We'll see. Jack will tell you how to get there. Tomorrow. Four o'clock." She stamped out her cigarette and left.

Mike drove out to Hope's house the next day because Jack

had said it might be at least worth listening to. Hope was seventy-seven and had been widowed for over twenty years. She had given Mel a contract for a year, paid her out of her own accounts plus the cabin she was living in, now with her husband and child. After that one-year contract was exhausted, Doc had pulled Mel into his practice and they'd managed a modest salary for her without help from Hope, which was exactly what Hope had intended. Mike had learned this from Jack.

Now, according to Jack, what she wanted was a town cop, and she hoped the same thing would happen—that she would pay him a salary from her savings for a year and the town would realize it was a positive addition and manage to pull together enough for his salary.

Hope lived about five miles out of town in a big old Victorian home that she and her husband had bought fifty years ago. They'd never had children and so had filled the place up with junk. "I've never been inside," Jack had told Mike, "but the rumor is that Hope hasn't thrown away a thing in seventy years." After her husband died, Hope had sold off the acreage to her neighbors for farming and grazing land.

He pulled up to the remarkable old house and found her on the porch with her coffee and cigarettes and a folder full of papers. When he stepped up on the porch, she greeted him with a victorious smile and said, "I knew I would get you eventually."

"I don't know what you'd be getting, Hope. I have no idea how to be a small-town cop."

"Who does? But you have lots of law enforcement experience, and clearly we can use it. Lately we seem to have had our share of problems."

"Not from Virgin River people, however."

"What's the difference? If it happens in Virgin River, it becomes our problem."

"What have you got there?" he asked, indicating the folder.

"Just paperwork. I had to get a little legal help from a county attorney. Here's what I can do—I can hire you as a local security officer, a constable. Even though you've graduated from one of the toughest police academies in the country, you wouldn't be recognized by the state as an official law enforcement officer, but that really doesn't matter. If you run across a lawbreaker, you detain them and call the sheriff, just like you've been doing. You're not prevented from investigating. Hell, any private investigator can do the same. You should visit the sheriff's department, Fish and Game, California Department of Forestry, the Highway Patrol and some of our neighbor towns who have their own local police departments. Introduce yourself. Believe me, they'll all appreciate any help, with all the territory they have to cover in these rural towns."

"And what do you expect me to do?" he asked.

"Well, you don't have to worry about speeding tickets." She laughed. "You'll figure it out. Assess the needs of the town. It's a law-abiding place—there shouldn't be too much stress. But, as has happened a couple of times too recently, if we get some real trouble, I want an experienced police officer around." She lit another cigarette. "You don't have to keep a jail. You shouldn't need flashing lights or a bulletproof vest."

"When would you expect me to be on duty?" he asked.

"I expect, if you're around, you're on duty. I understand everyone needs time off, needs to get out of Virgin River sometimes. If you're around five or six days a week, that's five or six more days a week than we've had. Let's just hope our crime sprees fall on your work days."

All that came to mind was a trip to Santa Rosa for lunch every couple of weeks. Something he hoped would become even more frequent. "Sounds like a paid vacation," he said.

"With any luck," she said. Then she opened the folder and showed him a one-year contract that displayed a pathetic salary.

"Not exactly a paid vacation," he said. But then, he'd been looking for something to do, and it wasn't necessary that he find work. He had his retirement and disability income, plus a little savings. "Why do you do this?" he asked. "First Mel, now me?"

"Hell, someone has to mind the needs of this town. This town is disorganized—I have to think what to do about that. And we're growing, if only a little." She took a drag. "I'm not going to last forever, though sometimes I'm afraid I might."

She slid a badge across the table to him. It said Virgin River Constable. "I had that made five years ago. Nice, isn't it?"

"You expect me to wear this?"

"You want to keep it in your pocket until you need it? You don't have to wear a uniform or anything. You wouldn't be the only guy in town carrying a sidearm or rifle. But I recommend you generate some forms so you can write up reports when you actually do something. There ought to be records. Want me to buy you a filing cabinet?"

He grinned at her. "Yeah. That would be nice. It doesn't have to be big. And business cards, please. So I can be sure anyone who might need to call me knows my number."

"Done." She smiled back at him, holding out her pen. "For now, just drive around. Sit on the porch at the bar and talk to people. Fish a little and think. Think what your job is going to be—you'd know more about that than me."

What a kick, he thought. The constable. Hah. For six hundred completely law-abiding citizens. "I feel like Andy of Mayberry," he said.

"That's a damn good place to start," she said, pointing the pen toward him.

He didn't take it. "Not just yet," he said. "Let me get the lay of the land, then we'll talk about this contract."

"You planning to try to negotiate?" she asked suspiciously.

"Oh, I have a feeling that would be useless. But before I make a commitment to you, to the town, I'd like to find out how receptive my fellow cops are to having someone like me in the mix. Let me visit around a little. Lotta type A's in law enforcement, Hope. Some wouldn't take a rope from a guy like me if they were in quicksand. If that's going to be the case, I should just save you the time and money."

"I don't really care what anyone else thinks about a guy like you."

He stood up. "Well, you should. I could probably help out a little, but cops don't work alone. You might not have local police, but you don't want this new idea of yours to drive away the coverage you have. One thing at a time."

Mike borrowed Preacher's computer to fashion a pretty informal résumé and letter of introduction. Because Preacher's printer wasn't top quality, he put the information on a disk and drove over to Eureka to have both printed. He chose a simple format that merely listed his experience and gave plenty of phone numbers to check references.

If Mike had been applying for a job, he would have gone into more detail about training, awards, special assignments. In fact, he felt boastful about his accomplishments at LAPD, about his experience. He couldn't see the advantage in downplaying what he knew about law enforcement and criminal justice, but when trying to fit in with the local cops, he didn't want to appear arrogant. It was a very fine line. His goal was to become one of them, and he was curious if they would accept him. He was from the city, he was Mexican, he'd been around the block. Around a lot of blocks. One thing the local guys never appreciated was some hotshot hitting town, acting as if he knew it all—whether that happened in L.A. or Eureka. A lot of ex-cops were boastful, eager to play on their war stories. A lot of times their war stories were bullshit.

His first stop was the Fortuna Police Department. The chief, Chuck Andersen, was a big guy with meaty hands, bald, and he wasn't smiling. Mike got the immediate impression he reserved his smile, kept it inside so it would never appear he was playing around. Mike shook his hand and introduced himself. "Thanks for seeing me, Chief," he said, handing him a couple of pages. "I've been asked to take a job in Virgin River—town cop, more or less."

"Sure," the big guy said. He indicated a chair but didn't sit behind his desk, so Mike continued to stand. The chief looked over the résumé quickly. "How long you been here?"

"Since just before Christmas. Couple of my best friends live in Virgin River."

"Why didn't you apply to one of the departments around here?"

"I wasn't looking for work," Mike answered. "This was a surprise. I guess the woman who put together a contract for a constable has been looking for someone, but I didn't come to Humboldt County to work. I came here to fish. Hunt."

"Not too many people can do that at..." He looked through the résumé briskly. "At thirty-seven."

Mike took a glance around the office. Family picture, good-looking wife, two handsome kids, a dog. He smiled with a little envy. "I don't have a family. I was retired from LAPD with a disability."

The chief's eyes came up to Mike's face. "How'd that happen?"

"I got shot," Mike said without self-consciousness. "During that last assignment on the résumé," he added with a nod toward the paperwork.

"Gang Unit," Andersen said. He looked as if he might have memorized the page by now. "Patrol, narcotics, gangs, robbery, gangs again."

"I worked gangs, then after passing the sergeant's exam, was reassigned there with my own squad. I loved gangs. I hated narcotics," Mike said unnecessarily. "I was always good with Patrol. Grassroots policing suited me."

Finally the chief sat, so Mike took his seat. When he did so, the chief lifted his eyes slightly, maybe surprised. "Marine Corps," he said.

"Yes, sir. Active for four, reserves for ten." Then he laughed. "I got through a lot of stuff, then got picked off by a fourteen-year-old." He shrugged. "No accounting for luck." As the résumé described, when Mike had finished his first tour with the Marines, he'd started college on the GI bill, and got his degree in criminal justice while working LAPD.

The chief read awhile. Then he lifted his eyes again. "What's your mission here?"

"Here? In your office or in Virgin River?"

"Okay, my office."

"I just want to say hello. I'm going around to the departments. If the meter reads No Help Wanted, I'm not signing that contract. If the local cops think they can stand having a guy like me helping out in Virgin River, I might go with it, see what I can do."

"A guy like you?"

"Ex-cop," he said. "I know at least as many ex-cops as cops. I realize most of us come with a lot of baggage, a lot of stories. I used to get real bored with 'em, real tired of all the drama. And here I am—one of them. With drama. With a big story." He shrugged. "I'm checking out how that goes over. It's only fair. To you guys."

"This department doesn't have any presence in Virgin River...."

"There's always the chance a problem in Virgin River could connect to your town, your department—in which case I'd like to think there's someone I could talk to over here."

The chief seemed to think a moment. He almost smiled. "And the disability?"

"I'm as close to a hundred percent as a guy can get. It was mainly the shoulder," he said, working it a little bit. "It's all good. I can shoot straight, angle just fine. I've got a left arm that's getting better all the time."

"But you're taking the comp, the disability."

"Damn straight," Mike said with a nod. "I paid into it for fifteen years and it wasn't the first time a weapon was fired my way. I'm just a working guy. But you know, I'm so damn lucky—the head works, the brain seems okay. I'd like you to know something—if I'd had a chance to talk my way out of that shooting, I might have tried, but it wasn't like that." He nodded toward the paperwork. "There's a report available, if you want it. I was kind of... I was ambushed. That's all. It was a jump into a gang, and picking off the sergeant was a coup. So... That's it. I thought I'd come up here and—"

"You could get a good job with a résumé like this. There are lots of places—private industry, corrections, small departments..."

"Yeah, thanks," he said, chuckling. "That's nice, I appreciate it. Go ahead and call some folks for references. There are lots of names on that résumé there—and you can get all the numbers of people not on the résumé. If I can help out in Virgin River, great. If it's a problem—I got a lot of fish to catch."

"How much can there be to do in Virgin River?" Andersen asked.

"Hopefully, not a lot," Mike answered. He nodded toward the pictures on the credenza. "Beautiful family," he said. "Good-looking dog," he added.

"She's yours," the chief said. Then he smiled. "The dog."

It was Mike's turn to smile. "You wouldn't give away that dog," he returned.

"Nah, but I might trade her for enough dirt to fill the holes in the yard. Try me."

Mike laughed and stuck out his hand, which Andersen shook. "Thanks, Chief. Enjoyed it." He gave a nod, the chief gave a nod and Mike left.

To be met with some suspicion and reluctance was not unexpected, but it didn't make the experience very inviting. Mike was damn glad he wasn't looking for work. He had to fight himself to keep from being a little insulted; he was a decorated police officer from a big...no, huge department. But he reminded himself this was their turf. He was an interloper.

Despite the fact it was intimidating and difficult, he visited the Eureka department, the sheriff's department, Garberville police, Grace Valley, a few other small towns that had local police, sometimes just one or two cops. The initial reaction was always the same. Yeah, you're this big-shot guy? What're you doing up here, poking around? Why not go after a real job?

A few days later Chief Chuck Andersen called him. "I thought you might want to spend a little time over here," he said. "Do a ride along, look at a couple of things. See how it's different in a small city. Maybe give us a perspective..."

"That would be good, sir. I'd like that," Mike said.

"I called a couple of people at LAPD," Andersen said. "You have a pretty good reputation there."

He had an excellent reputation there. "Thanks," he said. "I was better at some things than others. I did okay in police work."

"Seems like," Andersen said. "Good to have you helping

out. Do a ride along with one of our guys. And Valenzuela? Bring a pillow."

Mike laughed. "Thanks, sir."

The sheriff called, then the Eureka chief. Tom Toopeek, the chief from Grace Valley, weighed in, but there were towns that never got back to him. No matter, the consensus was that he would be welcomed as a constable. By state regulation he was not an official law enforcement officer, but more or less one of the team as far as most of the local guys were concerned. He'd be happy to help out anyone who asked, but what mattered was that he could go to them if there was a problem in his town. And he'd be happy to have a purpose again.

He signed the contract. The first person he told about it was Brie.

Tom Booth met a girl in physics who he thought might fill the bill. Brenda. Gorgeous Brenda. Soft, shiny, light brown hair that curled under on her shoulders, blue eyes, drop-dead figure, long legs, a smile that could put him in a trance. She was more beautiful than any girl he'd seen in D.C., which was some kind of miracle—the D.C. girls were pretty awesome. Fortunately, she seemed almost as shy around guys as he was around girls, which could work to his advantage. He struck up a conversation with her in class and learned that she was only a junior, in accelerated math and science programs, and he thought, hot shit. Pretty, smart, nice. Yup, this was a winner.

They talked about her plans for college, his horses. He asked her if she'd like to go out sometime and she said maybe. "Not right now. I'm kind of just getting over a really bad flu. Had me flat on my back right as school was starting and I'm still on medication, so my mom is a little overprotective."

"That's okay," he said. "Maybe we could do homework together sometime, when you start feeling better." Then he smiled his most engaging smile and said, "If you don't mind me saying so, you sure don't look sick."

"I'm feeling lots better than I did, believe me."

"So—maybe I could call you sometime? You feeling well enough for that?"

"Yeah," she said with a smile. "That would be okay."

"What do you like to do? When you're not—you know—feeling bad?"

"I don't know." She shrugged. "Games. Dances. Movies."

"Great," he said. "That sounds great. I'll give you a call one of these days." And he thought, maybe this isn't going to be such a boring place after all.

He called her that night. Why waste time?

4

The fall air was crisp and refreshing and Mel, still troubled by a couple of her cases, wandered over to the bar in the afternoon as David napped in Doc's care. She found Mike sitting on the porch, feet up on the rail, his hat, his Rio Concho, pushed down on his forehead to shield his eyes from the sun, taking in a relaxing autumn day. She sat in the Adirondack chair next to him, scooted forward on the edge.

"Looking for your man?" he asked.

"Actually, I was looking for you," she said. "What's going on in there?" she asked, giving her head a toss toward the inside.

"Preacher and Paige are getting dinner ready."

"Are we alone?"

"Yeah." He shoved his hat back, took his feet off the rail and put them on the wood planks of the porch, turning toward her. He rested his elbows on his knees and leaned forward. "What's the matter? You don't look too happy."

"Let me ask you something. Just how much of a cop do you intend to be around here? What if I suspected a possible problem? Could you look into it? Maybe investigate?"

"Well, I have detective experience, but I'm used to having a crime lab to back me up." He grinned. "I used to belong to the biggest gang in L.A."

"Gang?"

"LAPD. Lotta backup there. Want to lay it on me?"

She took a breath. "Understand, I can't give you names or evidence—just a real strong intuitive hunch. And I've been doing this awhile."

"Shoot."

She looked into his coal-black eyes. "I'm worried that we have a date raper. A kid, I think. I've had two girls who were clearly forced—neither willing or able to admit it. The scenarios were different, but there were some alarming similarities."

"Go on," he said, encouraging her to continue.

"The first came to me for emergency birth control. She said that she and her boyfriend of a whole two weeks had decided to have sex and at the last minute she lost her nerve, but he couldn't stop. She was bruised. Held down. Her vagina was ragged and torn. She was visibly upset. But she absolutely insists she was not forced.

"The second one went to a kegger somewhere around town—her first drinking party, though she admits to having a beer or two before. She passed out and didn't remember having sex, but missed two periods and took a home pregnancy test and told her mother what had happened. The kids at the party were all drunk, she said, and no one remembered anything...."

"Yeah, right," he said.

"I explained that to her—that in order to have successful intercourse, it was very likely one of them wasn't too drunk."

"Very likely? I thought that was a law of nature," Mike said.

"I thought it was, too," she said. "It was obviously too late to detect damage or bruising—but she said she'd been very sore all over, especially on her chest." She laid her hand on her own sternum. "As if hit in the chest with a basketball."

"Possibly held down as she struggled," he supplied. "What about bruising on the inside of her thighs?"

"She didn't recall anything like that, but she was distracted by the fact she was real hung over and sick. The first one, however, had unmistakable finger and thumb prints on the inside of her thighs. Both tested positive for chlamydia. The pregnant one miscarried and, understandably, wants to forget the whole thing. If she can. Neither of them would give me a name or even an age of the boy or boys."

He winced visibly, inhaled deeply and rolled his eyes briefly skyward. "Jesus," he said.

"I can't go anywhere with this. I don't even have grounds to report it without at least one of them relenting and saying it could have been rape. In the second case, the girl didn't remember drinking much—I'm wondering if there was a drug involved."

"Roofies?" he asked. "GHB? That could have made her really sick."

"She woke up covered in vomit."

"She's lucky she woke up. A side effect of GHB is a suppressed gag reflex. She could have aspirated and died," he pointed out.

"This really eats at me, Mike. There's nothing I can do. Well, I did do one thing—I got a vaginal swab from number one, but intercourse was a couple of days old and I'm sure she bathed a couple of times before coming in. Even if it turns out there's DNA present, we might never get that far."

"But still, good thinking. Any chance you got pictures of the bruising?"

"No. I have nothing. She was nearly hysterical and insisted she wasn't raped. If she had relented, even once, and said that she'd been held down and forced, I would have reported it. As it stands, all I have is this big ache in my gut that tells me there's a teenage boy out there who's out of control."

"Sounds like it's time for me to get to know the youth of Virgin River."

"Whew. I hoped I could dump this on you. I feel a little lighter already."

"You tell anyone else?"

"Yeah—I did. I called June Hudson in Grace Valley—she and her partner, John Stone, will be watching their patients for similar symptoms. And the family planning clinic in Eureka is aware of my concerns. But Mike—what sickens me most is that my second girl said this happened in Virgin River."

"Either a teenager whose testosterone popped or a new kid in town. Worth looking at."

"Thank you."

"Obviously, if any more girls come into the clinic—"

"Of course. I'll be sure to let you know."

"I'll start looking around, talking to people."

"Thanks," she said, leaning back in her chair, relieved.

"I've been meaning to talk to you about something else, Mel. I'm ready to discontinue the antidepressant you prescribed after the shooting, during my recovery."

She smiled at him. "Feeling pretty good?" she asked.

"Stronger, yes. I agree, it was a good idea at the time. But—"

"Sure, sure. We said a few months, right? Sounds good," she said. "Let's take you down slowly. I'll write up a dosage schedule for you. We'll have you off in a couple of weeks. How's that?"

"Perfect."

John—Preacher to his friends—was thirty-three years old and knew a lot about war and about cooking, about hunting and fishing. He'd served in the Marine Corps for twelve years and followed Jack to Virgin River, where he'd turned himself into one of the best cooks in the region, if little known. But his knowledge of women was recent.

When he met and married his wife, that was when his education began. He'd been a man who knew few women up to that point, and he'd never considered himself much of a lover. In fact, he'd been scared to death of Paige—she was so petite and feminine and he was six-four, muscled, with huge, strong hands and shoulders so broad he had to turn sideways to pass through some doorways. He had been terrified that he'd hurt her, leave a bruise on her.

But she had worked him through it, confident that he was the gentlest man she'd ever known. In her arms he had been transformed. Now he not only understood the female body, but worshipped it. Things he hadn't known existed were now second nature to him, and his wife was his treasure, the most awesome gift he could ever have received. To make her feel wonderful was one of his greatest obsessions. He knew every erogenous spot to touch, to kiss, and the better he could make her feel, the more he enjoyed his own experience.

She was his partner by day in the bar, working beside him in the cooking and management, and his angel by night in his arms. Between them they parented her son, Christopher, now four years old, and Preacher had the kind of happiness he'd thought existed only for other men. There was one small problem—he and Paige wanted to have a baby together, and while they'd been married only a few months, she'd stopped taking her pills over six months ago and nothing had happened.

He might be disappointed, but she was beyond disappointment. She'd been pregnant when she stumbled into the bar a year ago, and, as a result of a horrific beating from her then husband, had miscarried. Paige was afraid that there might be some kind of damage to her reproductive organs that would prevent her from having a baby with John—and sometimes it caused her deep sadness.

At the end of every day he would clean his kitchen at the bar, turn off the Open sign and lock the door, read to Christopher after he'd had his bath, then retire to the little apartment he shared with his wife, and love her. Born again in her arms, night after night.

He found her in the bathroom, wearing one of his huge T-shirts, and he caught her softly crying. It had been a very long time since he'd seen her tears, and it knocked the wind out of him. He couldn't bear it. "Here, here," he said, pulling her into his strong embrace. "You're crying."

She wiped the tears off her cheeks and looked up at him. "It's nothing," she said. "I got my period again. I didn't want it to come. I wanted to be pregnant."

"You weren't even late," he said, for he knew everything about her, about her body. You could set a watch by her.

"Not even an hour late," she said, and a big tear spilled over.

"Is it a hard one?" he asked tenderly.

"No, it's nothing at all. Except, I thought maybe finally…"

"Okay, it's time," he said, wiping away the tear. "You should talk to Mel. Maybe to John Stone. See if we should check something out."

"I get the impression that could be expensive."

"Don't you worry about that," he said. "Never mind

money—this is about us being happy. We want a baby. We should do what we have to do. Right?"

"John, I'm sorry—"

"Why are you sorry? You're not in this alone. Everything is both of us. Right?"

"Month after month…"

"Well, now we're going to face it and ask for advice. We'll get some help. No more crying."

But she dropped her head against his chest and wept anyway, and it tore his heart out. He couldn't stand Paige to be in any kind of pain. He lived for her happiness; she was his world. His life.

"Are you crying because you're PMS-y?" he asked.

"No. I don't think so."

"Cramps? Want me to rub your back?"

"No," she said. "I feel fine. Really."

He lifted her chin and kissed her deeply. Lovingly. Lustfully. "Want me to make you feel a little better? I know how."

"That's okay, John. There's no need."

"You don't have to be shy with me. There's no part of your life, your body, that puts me off. I love every bit of you."

She sighed deeply. "I should just take a shower and crawl into bed. I'm feeling sorry for myself."

He reached behind her and started the water. Then he ran his hand up the back of her thigh, over her bum and under the large T-shirt she wore, caressing her back, pulling her close to kiss her some more. When he released her lips, he slowly pulled the T-shirt over her head. He loved the way she stood so erect and comfortable when she was naked in front of him, when he filled his eyes with her. He lowered his lips to her naked breast and drew gently on a nipple, causing her to let her head drop back and sigh deeply. If there was anything about his life with her that was past magnificent, it was the fact that she was as easily turned on by him as he was by her. Their love life gave her a constant glow. And he knew exactly how to make the tears go away.

He pulled the shower curtain wider for her to step inside, but then he quickly shed his clothes and got in with her. He pulled her into his arms again, his mouth on hers, his hands on her body.

"You don't have to do this," she whispered against his lips.

"I never do anything I don't want to do," he said. "I'm going to give you something happy to think about." He kissed her forehead. "Baby, I love you so much."

Mel and Jack had just finished having dinner together at the bar when Paige approached their table. "Mel, do you have a minute? I wanted to ask you something. Something medical."

"Sure," she said. "We can kill two birds with one stone—I have to nurse the wild one. Maybe we can go to your place."

Jack handed over the baby. "I'll take the bar," he said.

Mel didn't have a lot of occasions to be in Paige and Preacher's room behind the bar, but those few times she was, warm memories flooded back to her. This was where Jack had lived when she came to town; this was where David was no doubt conceived. She remembered the night so well—she'd had a major emotional meltdown, standing in the rain crying over her dead husband on the anniversary of his death, and Jack had held her. Then he'd dried her off, given her a brandy, put her to bed. Sometime later he'd joined her there and showed her a life and love she'd never known could exist for her.

Now the room held the influence of Paige—pictures of Christopher, some toys in the corner, flowers on the table. Paige had drifted into their lives almost exactly a year ago, a battered wife on the run, and with Preacher's strength behind her, had divorced her abusive husband and seen him sent to prison.

Paige sat on the sofa and Mel took the big chair, settling David on the breast. He curled around her comfortably, gently kneading her breast with his chubby hand.

"John wanted me to talk to you—I'm sorry to bother your evening, but you weren't around Doc's much the last couple of days."

"No problem. You're not bothering my evening. He's bothering my evening," she said with a smile. "He's crabby tonight. Too much running around, I think. Not to mention cookies. What's on your mind?"

"I'm not getting pregnant," she said. "It's only been six months or so that I've been off the pill, but in my previous life it was as though I couldn't keep from getting pregnant. What do you think I should do?"

"Well, let's see—are your periods regular?"

"As clockwork," she said.

"The assumption is that you're ovulating regularly, then. Usually, if you're going to do any kind of infertility workup, you start with Dad—make sure you're dealing with an adequate sperm count. It's the cheapest and quickest test, plus you don't want to do a complete workup on Mom until you rule out Dad. And after all, we know you can get pregnant."

"Well—I could before," she said.

"Still, there was no indication any damage was caused beyond the miscarriage," Mel said. "Bleeding stopped right after the D & C and you haven't had any peculiarities—like real heavy or weird periods, have you?"

"No, not at all."

"And you have relations on a regular basis?"

Paige rolled her eyes. "You have to remember, John has just discovered sex," she said. Then she smiled a bit shyly.

"Oh," Mel said. "I take that to mean—?" But she stopped herself.

"He can't get enough," she said. "But then, I haven't had a loving partner until now, so I'm not complaining."

"Well, that might be the problem. Having a lot of sex is a bad way to get pregnant. It depletes his sperm count. Before you try any fancy tests, you should drive to Fortuna, buy yourself an ovulation testing kit at the drugstore and ask Preacher to save up. It takes at least forty-eight hours to replenish the count. Make him wait. No more often than every couple of days. Every few days would be better and then only once— no marathons. And you want to make sure he's been on ice a few days before the big day." She smiled. "You get a reprieve on ovulation day, of course. Knock yourselves out."

"Oh, brother," she said, looking a bit stricken.

"How much do you want a baby?" Mel asked. "In fact, you might not hit pay dirt that first month. You might have to keep that kind of schedule for two or three months. Just because you're both fertile doesn't mean you get pregnant on one try."

"Oh, boy," she said. "I can just imagine how happy John's going to be to hear this. I'll have to remind him it was his idea to get your input."

"If you like, we can do a sperm count before you put him through all this—but if it's low, the prescription is going to be wait it out, see if it gets better. On the other hand, if it's really high after all that sex, he's good to go. No reason to cut him off. Are you a betting woman?"

"I have a feeling how this is going to turn out," Paige said. "He'll want to do what matters, but…"

Mel laughed in spite of herself. "Yeah, he's been so happy for just months now. I guess I can expect those frowns and scowls back. My advice—try this for three months and then begin the infertility routine—starting with sperm count. Sure you want to do this?" she asked, taking the baby off the breast and putting him over her shoulder for a burp.

"I want a baby, yes," she said. "But John was the first one to say he wanted children with me."

"You can always wait until next year," Mel said. "Spend the rest of this year seeing if you can get tired of it."

"I'll talk to John," she said, noncommittal.

A few days later Mel ate a late lunch at the bar as Jack stood behind it. He filled her water glass. "I want to ask you something," he said. "I have absolutely no idea how you're going to answer this."

"Sounds scary," she said, taking a spoonful of Preacher's delicious chicken soup into her mouth.

"Depends on your perspective. Ricky's USMC graduation from basic is just around the corner and I want to go. I want us to go."

She shrugged and said, "Of course, Jack."

"I want us to go alone," he said.

She swallowed. "Alone?"

He nodded. "I think it's important, Mel. We have to carve a little time out for the two of us, just you and me."

"Are you feeling neglected?" she asked.

"Not at all. In fact, I feel pretty spoiled. But I still think we should make a habit of taking some time now and then, when we can be away from the town, the baby, the bar, the patients, everything. Regularly."

She gave him a seductive half smile and lifted one brow. "Why, Jack..."

"It's not even about that," he said. "Well, it can be about that." He grinned. Both hands braced on the bar, he leaned toward her. "You're my wife, my lover and best friend. I want you all to myself once in a while."

"What am I going to do about nursing David?"

"You'll manage. You pump for extra bottles anyway, and he's certainly not dependent on the breast anymore—he has bottles regularly. There are lots of people who'd be more than happy to keep him a couple of nights, but I thought about calling Brie. She's still not working and loves an excuse to come up here. Plus, I haven't seen her in so long. I'd like to see her again—just to see how she's doing. Looking. You know." He leaned forward and kissed her forehead. "Come away with me, Mel. Just a couple of nights."

"I would love that. I'll call Brie this afternoon."

Mel left the baby napping at Doc's and drove out to her homesite. She parked and got out of the Hummer. Leaning against the hood, she watched Jack driving nails into Sheetrock inside the frame of their house. Momentarily he stopped and came to where she stood. He opened his arms to her and she filled them. Thank God, she thought. My man is mine again. Those silent, distant days seemed to be behind them.

"What are you doing out here?" he asked her.

"I wanted to tell you something," she said. "Brie is coming. She's thrilled to come and babysit. She'll stay at least a week, probably two. In fact, she said there was nothing in Sacramento to demand her quick return."

She looked up at him and could see the struggle in his eyes. He wanted Brie—he wanted her near if she felt that it was good for her. He wanted to take care of her in any way he could, but he also wanted a private life with his wife. A private life reclaimed not all that long ago. And there was absolutely no privacy in that little cabin; every sound was shared by all.

"This is good, that she's coming," Mel said. "I think she needs to get out of Sacramento for a while—it'll do her good. And when we get this house finished, I think we should try to buy the cabin from Hope. It'll be a good place to have when we're bursting at our seams. You have a very large family."

He smiled at her. "Well, Mrs. Sheridan, you're certainly throwing money around today, aren't you?"

She shrugged. "We have plenty of money. We should think about hiring subs, get this house moving. If you get bored, we'll find you something else to build."

"I wanted to do it for you," he said. "I wanted to show you how much I would do, how far I would go. How hard I would work."

"You can't possibly think I don't already know all that."

"You're not serious," Preacher said to Paige. "That can't be right."

"That's what Mel says," she told him.

"Wow. Who'd ever think that the way to get pregnant is by not having sex." It seemed as though he might've hung his head.

"John, it's up to you. We don't have to do this. Right now, anyway. I'm not insisting..."

"No, we'll do it. We want a baby. I want a baby as much as you do and getting your period makes you cry. So we'll do it." He shook his head. "How'm I gonna know when it's okay?"

"Well—a few days between. You know? And just once, John, on those days. Except on ovulation day." She grinned at him. "You can go crazy on ovulation day."

"Damn, I'm going to miss it," he moaned.

"John, I don't have any facts to support this, but I don't think everyone is having as much sex as we are...."

He had a confused look on his face. "Well, why not?"

She laughed at him. "Oh, John..."

"Did you get your little thing? Your little ovulation thing?"

"I'm going to run over to Fortuna later for some supplies for the bar and I'll pick up a couple of kits, exactly the kind we need, because Mel said it could take longer than just a couple of months for us to make this work—if that's the problem."

"More than a couple of months?" he asked weakly.

Don't laugh, don't laugh, Paige was saying to herself. "We try this for two or three months," she said. "If it doesn't work by then, we'll get you tested, maybe try something else."

He put his head in his hand. "Wow," he said. Then, lifting his head bravely, he said, "It's okay. We can do it."

She put a hand on his arm. "John, ovulation day is just around the corner. A couple of weeks. That's your reward."

"I promise you, Paige. I'm going to make it your reward. I promise."

Oh my, she thought. This was going to be interesting.

"I think we're going to have to get a sitter for Christopher and close the bar on ovulation day," he said.

Before Mel and Jack could leave for Ricky's graduation from basic training, a newcomer appeared in Virgin River. The lunch crowd had cleared out and Jack was behind the bar when a young woman came in. She had reddish-blond hair and that golden complexion that suggested freckles. Her lips were peach colored and she was smiling so brightly that Jack tilted his head, returning the smile, wondering who this might be. She came right up to the bar and leaned on it. "Jack Sheridan?" she asked.

"That's me."

She put out her hand. "I'm Vanessa Rutledge. Matt Rutledge's wife. We have some people in common."

He grabbed her hand. "You bet we do, one being your husband. How's he doing?"

"He's back in the Middle East, I'm afraid. He's been gone a few months. I'm staying with my dad while he's there, but

Matt told me I'd better come here right away, look you up, find out when your boys are coming around, because Matt's best friend and our best man is Paul Haggerty."

"That's right," Jack said. "I remember, now that you mention it. I had those two boys in my squad way back—they were just kids. Paul, Matt, Preacher, Mike Valenzuela. Then Paul and the others were in my platoon on my last assignment in Iraq, and we're still tight. Paul was here not very long ago, and due back again soon. We always try to catch some of hunting season, however many can make it."

"Paul and Matt went to school together," she said. "They enlisted together, went into basic and served a couple of tours together. In fact, they were together the night I met my husband."

"Oh, Preacher and Mike are going to love this," Jack said. He turned away from her and hit the wall that separated the bar from the kitchen to bring Preacher out.

"I've heard all about Preacher," she said. "Paul talked about you guys and this little bar a lot. It was such a weird coincidence that my dad found this place to settle."

"Where is your dad?"

"He bought an old ranch on the edge of town a couple of years ago, right before his last assignment. He was having some work done to renovate it before he retired, then brought my little brother and their horses out here from D.C. over summer."

"Last assignment?"

"He retired from the Army. Major General Walter Booth."

Amused surprise registered on Jack's face. "A grunt general let his daughter marry an enlisted jarhead?"

She lifted one pretty eyebrow, aquamarine eyes sparkling, and said, "I don't take orders from anyone." And they both laughed.

Preacher came out of the back, frowning at having been summoned by the pounding. He met with the gleaming smile of the pretty redhead at the bar and he softened his expression somewhat, curiously.

Vanessa was not startled by the big man's size or surly expression. Neither was she surprised when his features softened into a curious smile. "You must be Preacher," she said. She put out a hand. "I'd know you anywhere, except I heard you were big and bald. Now you're just big. Vanessa Rutledge—Matt Rutledge's wife."

"No way!" Preacher exclaimed, reaching for her hand. "I heard he got married. What's he doing these days?"

She shrugged and made a half smile. "Guess. Iraq. Baghdad, last I heard."

"Oh, kid," Preacher said sympathetically. "And you're here?"

"My dad just moved here—he's out on the edge of town. A nice place for him and his horses. And my little brother, Tommy."

"My lord," Preacher said. "I can't believe it. Right here!"

"The world just gets smaller," she said, stepping back from the bar and pulling open her jacket to reveal a pregnant tummy. "I'm on my way to see Jack's wife. I'm going to need her services."

"Wow," Jack said. "Look at you. First?"

"Yep. Just a few months to go."

"Is Matt going to get back for the baby?" Jack asked her.

"No, but if we time this right, he should get a nice long leave when the baby's a couple of months old." She looked around, taking in the bar, the animal trophies on the walls, the rich dark wood. "So this is the place, huh? Boy, I've sure heard a lot about this place."

"The boys love this place," Jack said. "When Matt's out, we'll make sure he gets up here with the rest of them."

"When he's out? Hah! You think that's going to happen? Matt's a career Marine." But she smiled, clearly proud of her man. And being a general's daughter, she would be more than familiar with the rigors of military life.

"No rush," Jack said. "We'll be around a long time."

Paige was summoned to the bar to meet Vanessa. Before long Mike made an appearance and was delighted to make the acquaintance of Matt's wife. An invitation was extended for the general to stop by the bar for one on the house and Jack promised to get in touch with Vanessa and her father before Paul joined the next Semper Fi gathering, coming up soon.

"Whatever you do, don't tell Paul we're here," Vanessa said. "I'd love to surprise him."

5

Mike Valenzuela became aware that beneath the surface of a perfect small town there could be crime, some minor and predictable, some of an insidious nature. He thought often about the two patients Mel had presented as he visited casually with neighbors, with the high school in the next town attended by the Virgin River kids, asking what people did for fun around these parts. Most of the time he got the expected responses—adults had their own gatherings, parties, picnics, cookouts. They frequented restaurants, galleries, wineries and nightspots in and around the coastal towns, and of course just about everyone hunted and fished. Most of the community socializing surrounded school functions, from sporting events to band and choir activities, after which there would always be big gatherings among the parents.

Zach Hadley dropped by Jack's once or twice a week for a beer and Mike took the opportunity to get to know him a little better—his link to the high school kids paid off almost right away. He said the teens had their school functions from games to dances, but they also had a few haunts. Parties, both with parents home and away, keggers in the woods. He'd overheard some talk about an isolated old rest stop back off highway 109 where there were a few ancient barbecue pits, bathrooms and picnic tables. Highway 109 had been heavily traveled before the newer freeway was finished and now was more of a daytime road, left to the teens by night. A perfect place, when the weather allowed, to bring a keg or a case of beer. Where Mike grew up in L.A. the kids had desert keggers or beach keggers—but out here, they had the forest.

"As long as they don't get way back in the woods, far from the towns, they're probably safe from problems with wildlife or marijuana growers," Mike said. But were they safe from each other? Mike wondered.

"That's true, then?" Zach asked. "All that illegal growing they talk about?"

"It's true," Mike confirmed. "Listen, if you ever have any concerns that I can help with, I wouldn't let on where I got the information."

"Actually," he said, keeping his voice low, "I happened to see something—a half-written note—that startled me. Got my attention—but I wouldn't have the first idea where to go with it."

"I'm your first idea," Mike said.

"It's just gossip, you know. Sometimes things kids that age say can be shocking—and entirely fictional. But the note said something like stay away from those parties. There was a rumor about a girl ending up pregnant, though she couldn't remember having sex."

Mike's eyebrows shot up. "How'd you come across that?" he asked.

"A student left a notebook in class." He shrugged. "I looked through it."

Mike smiled. "I like your style. Nosy. Whose notebook was it?"

"I have no idea. I left it where I found it and it disappeared after lunch. Never saw it again, and I watched the kids, checked out what they were carrying into class. It belonged to a girl, I can tell you that. The doodles were all female."

"You keep an eye on that, huh? Listen carefully," Mike suggested. "That could be important information."

"I know kids are going to drink some beer," Zach said. "But if there's any truth there, that's some real hard drinking."

"Yeah," Mike said. And he thought—I bet it wasn't the beer. "Keep me posted. I'll never let on that we talked."

Mike hung around the school, introducing himself, trying to cozy up to the kids, being as friendly and cool as possible. He knew he'd find some pot as he looked deeper. There was whispering of some methamphetamine, but no one breathed a word of roofies. Having Zach on his team was a big plus, but he was hoping to nab himself a teenage confidential informant, a CI who would feed him some names. The local police and sheriff's department would already be looking into any underage drinking or illegal drug use when it turned up. But he wanted to know if any of his Virgin River girls were getting raped, and unless someone had filed a police report, local law enforcement wouldn't know about it. And he already considered them his girls, his town.

He took a swing by the rest stop on 109 and found some beer bottles and condoms in the trash. He decided he might visit this spot with regularity, see who turned up. What turned up. He might even try a little woodsy surveillance. But winter came early in the mountains and he suspected that his window of opportunity was nearly closed for the season.

There was only one new guy on the block, as far as Mike could determine—seventeen-year-old Tom Booth, Vanessa's younger brother, the general's son. Tom hadn't been in town very long, not long enough to effect any damage. Booth, who invited Mike to call him Walt, was a widower and introduced him to Tommy, who seemed bright and affable. Polite and sincere. He would probably be popular with the girls, but he didn't know many people yet. If Tom were well acquainted at school, he'd make a good source, but that wasn't the case. When Mel's second patient had awakened pregnant after a party, Tom had still been back in D.C.

And then there was a host of boys who had passed the age of fifteen, sixteen, seventeen—and perhaps come into some serious hormonal brain damage. A little testosterone and a lack of values could do the trick.

Unsurprisingly, the one person he wished he could talk to about this was Brie. But if he was any judge, she wasn't up to that conversation. It was still too close to her own violation.

Mike didn't expect to find himself back at the sheriff's department quite so soon, but he felt compelled to let him know what he was sniffing around for. Since he had no victim, no suspect, no evidence, he really expected the sheriff to thank him politely and ask Mike to keep him informed. To his surprise, the sheriff called a detective named Delaney into his office and introduced him as their representative to a multiagency drug task force, comprised of law enforcement from each local, state and county agency. "We have a detective working sexual assault, but it sounds like that would be getting ahead of ourselves. I'll check with him, though. Ask if he's heard anything about this," the sheriff said.

"Thank you, sir," Mike answered. "I understand this is big marijuana country," he said to Detective Delaney.

"We have a lot of that, yeah. But we have a growing problem with white dope and really want to get ahead of that," he said. White dope would be meth, cocaine, heroine.

"Gotcha," Mike said. "Heard any rumblings about ecstasy? Roofies?"

"Ecstasy, though rare. Roofies—no. But Jesus, if you chase that down…"

"You'll keep us up to speed?" the sheriff interrupted.

"Absolutely," he said. "With this reluctance on the part of possible victims to report this, it could be a long process."

"Even more reason I'm glad you're willing to look further," the sheriff said. "Without a victim or charge, no way I could free up a deputy to look into this. I appreciate the help." He stuck out his hand. "That little town upriver is lucky to have you around."

"Thank you," Mike said. What he didn't say was that in this case his motivation went a bit deeper than simply finding a bad guy. This was hitting a little close to home. There was Brie…

The next day he drove to Eureka and bought a laptop and printer. It was time to get online, use the Internet and his contacts for research.

When Brie arrived in Virgin River she had a couple of days with Jack, Mel and the baby before her brother and sister-in-law got off to an early start on the third day, headed for San Diego to the graduation. Then she changed the linens on the bigger bed in the room next to David's and looked forward to a peaceful couple of days in the cabin. She bathed and fed her nephew, read while he had his morning nap, then took him into town at about lunchtime.

David was a baby used to being taken everywhere. While

his mother and father worked he was either at Doc's clinic or at the bar, being looked after by a variety of people. He was a flexible baby, but because of the hectic schedule his parents kept, easily bored. Sitting around at home wouldn't do it for him. So Brie went visiting.

She spent some time with Paige, hearing about the new quest to make a baby. She had lunch at the bar and David had finger food from the tray in his stroller. She spent a little time at Doc's, where they played gin while David had his afternoon nap. She visited with Connie at the corner store and watched the afternoon soap opera with Connie and Joy, finding the starring hussie was doing yet another guy on the air, much to the delight of the older women. It was nearly dinnertime by the time she got back to Jack's and people started wandering in. Brie had herself a beer while Preacher warmed up some finger veggies for David and a little skim milk for his special cup with the spout. Everyone who came into the bar gave her a friendly hello but then went immediately to David to kiss him, snuggle him, nuzzle him, make faces at him and entertain him. This was one of the most loved residents of Virgin River, and if it was not because he was charming and handsome, then it was because he belonged to Mel and Jack.

By five, Mike came in, and of course he went immediately to Brie. He had a beer while she finished hers and then they had their dinner together. He talked a little about driving around to the surrounding towns, trying to get to know people, learning how they spent their time and whether they had any concerns with which he could assist. He was beginning to get a sense of what they needed in a community policeman and found it to be like having any neighborhood beat in a city. It was not long after dinner that David began to fuss, needing that bedtime change and bottle.

"I have to go," she said, getting up and taking the baby's stroller in hand.

He stood, as well. "Would you like some company tonight?" he asked.

"Thanks, but I think I'm going to concentrate on my job." She smiled. "When Mom and Dad get back, maybe we could do something."

"We'll find something fun," he said with a smile. "It might not be too early to see the whales—they should be migrating south pretty soon."

"Maybe we should try that," she said.

When Brie took David home, the first thing that struck her was that it was very dark. She hadn't left any lights on at the cabin and although it was only about seven, the night was quickly descending. The towering trees that surrounded the clearing cast long shadows. This place had always given her such a sense of peace and safety, it surprised her to be set on edge like this. She tried to ignore the anxiety it created in her and talked to the baby, as if he were company enough. "Come on, buster. Let's get you settled. You had a good day, didn't you? Yes, you did."

Then there was that matter of the door having been left unlocked; she felt her heart skip a few beats. But she went inside, flipped on lights and locked the front door. She went to the back door and locked it. Her first two nights there had been so restful and tranquil, it had never occurred to her she'd be nervous tonight. Then, despite the fact that David fussed unhappily, she put him in his bed and retrieved her 9 mm handgun from her purse. Gun in hand, she searched the cabin, anxious to put her mind at ease. Inside closets, under beds, up in the loft. It didn't take long to find it empty of threats, thank goodness, because her nephew was getting loud and impatient in his crib. She put the gun on the nightstand beside her bed and tended to his needs. She changed him and warmed the breast milk that had been left for her by Mel.

It bothered her that there were no blinds or shutters to close over the windows. But why would Mel and Jack have bothered, out here in the forest? Who was to peek in the windows besides a bear? This hadn't bothered her last night or the night before. Still, it caused Brie to fidget and continually glance around at the uncovered windows. Then she realized she had not spent a night alone since June.

"You have to do it sometime. You have to get beyond this," she said aloud to herself.

Once David was changed, fed and put in his crib, she couldn't imagine what she was going to do with herself, sitting in the little living room of that cabin, feeling as if anyone could look in, the TV fuzzy because Mel and Jack had never bothered to get a satellite dish. So she turned off the lights, and in the dark she undressed for bed. She put on a lightweight but concealing sweat suit, remembering with some longing the days when she'd slept in the buff, confident and unafraid. She hadn't slept in the nude since that night. Even though it wasn't yet eight o'clock, she got into bed. Her heart was beating too fast and she talked to herself—there's no one out here who wants to hurt you. You're isolated in the woods—no one even knows you're here.

Brie lay on her back, her arms folded across her stomach, her gun on the bedside table. She forced her eyes closed for a minute, then two minutes, then longer if she could. It seemed forever before her pulse slowed and she relaxed a little; every sound the wind made caused her to tremble. If I can just make it through one night, I can make it through another, she told herself. She looked at the bedside clock at eight-fifteen, eight-thirty, eight forty-five.

At some point she dozed off, but later she was jolted awake by a fright. She gasped, sat straight up in the bed and realized she was sweating, panting, her heart hammering. She grabbed up the gun and held it out in front of her, pointing it toward the bedroom door. She listened intently. There was a whistling and soft moaning; the wind through the pines. There was a slight muffled sound coming from David's bedroom and she got out of bed, gun in hand, muzzle pointed to the ceiling, and crept into his bedroom to be sure there was no one there. David squirmed around in his sleep, nestling into the bedding, dreaming.

Oh, God, she thought. I'm creeping around my baby nephew with a loaded gun! Tears stung her eyes. I'm a basket case, she thought.

She went into the dark kitchen, picked up the phone and called Mike. When he answered, she said in a breath, "I'm sorry. I'm scared."

"What's happening?" he asked, alert.

"Nothing. Nothing that I know of. The doors are locked, I've checked the house, but I'm prowling around here with a loaded gun in my hand. I'm completely nuts."

"Can you put that gun down, please," he said calmly. "I will be there in ten minutes."

"Okay," she answered tremulously, feeling that she had somehow failed. Failed her brother and Mel, failed herself.

"Please, put it aside, and I will come."

"Okay," she said again. But she didn't put it aside. She slipped down onto the kitchen floor and sat there against the cabinets in the corner, from where she could see the rest of the kitchen. If anyone came at her, she could shoot him. And then she thought, my God, it's a good thing David can't walk! Right now she would shoot anything that moved; she was wired enough to shoot at nothing and a ricocheted bullet could hurt or even kill the baby! She tried to keep her finger relaxed along the barrel and away from the trigger, repeating in her mind, do not act unless you're sure. Do not.

Ten minutes is an eternity when you're afraid. And there is nothing worse than fear, whether or not there is an object. There was a metallic taste in her mouth from the adrenaline and her pulse beat dangerously fast. Finally, after what seemed like an hour, her knuckles white from holding the grip so fiercely, she heard the sound of an engine as a car came into the clearing, then a small toot as he honked the horn to let her know it was him.

She pulled herself to her feet, put the gun on the kitchen counter and unlocked the front door. When she opened it, she saw him standing there in a heavy suede jacket, wearing a sidearm. It somehow made her feel better, him having that gun. It was as though he had taken her seriously. As if her fear, though unfounded, could have had some basis.

"God," she said, falling against him gratefully. "I'm afraid of nothing!"

"Take it easy," he said, gently touching her back. He held her a bit, very careful not to hold her too tightly. "These things take time."

"I feel stupid."

"Well, don't. It's so understandable as to be almost predictable." He pulled back from her, his hands on her upper arms. "Your first night alone?"

"Yes," she said. "Honestly, I didn't see this coming. I've felt so great since I got here. I've never slept better."

"Would you like me to check the house for you?"

"Even though I've checked it," she said, nodding. "And maybe outside."

"I'd be happy to. Sit down. Take a few deep breaths and try to relax."

He saw the gun on the counter and touched the grip. It was still warm. She'd been so afraid, she hadn't been able to put it down.

He walked around the house and up into the loft, turning lights on and off as he went. He took a flashlight from his car to check the grounds outside, where he found everything to be undisturbed—no footprints or mashed grass or shrubs. When he went back into the house, he locked the door behind him, took off his sidearm and holster and put it on the counter next to her gun. He took off his jacket and draped it over a kitchen chair. Then he went to the tiny living room, where he crouched in front of the cold hearth. He stacked a few logs over some starter pine cones, lit them and watched the flames rise. He rubbed his hands together in front of the fire, then went to sit on the sofa beside her.

"Thank you," she said meekly.

"It's nothing, Brie. You should feel safe so you can take good care of David. That's all that matters."

"But I called you out in the middle of the night. You must be so annoyed."

He grinned handsomely. "Brie. It isn't even ten o'clock."

"Oh, my God! I didn't even sleep an hour!"

He chuckled and, leaning over to pull off his boots, said, "You'll get a good night's sleep now. I'm staying the night."

"Oh," she said nervously. "I don't think that's such a good idea...."

"Relax, mija. Don't I know everything you're going through trying to get your life back? You can't honestly think I'd do one thing to make you feel threatened."

"Well..."

"Don't insult me," he said. "I've done a lot of unforgivable things, it's true, but I've never been unkind to a woman. I am a gentleman. And you need sleep."

She thought about it for less than a second. "I know if you go, I'll crack up. For God's sake, when does it end?"

"I'm not sure, but I know it does. It turns out this is just a little too soon for you. There's no need for you to feel self-conscious about this. We just won't mention it. No one watches my comings and goings. No one watches this cabin to see whose car is parked outside."

She gave a sigh and leaned back into the couch cushions. "I hate what this has done to me. I thought I was tougher."

"Jesus, don't do that to yourself," he said. "It's bad enough what's been done to you without adding that. It's not a small thing to get over, Brie."

She drew her feet up, massaging her temples with her fingers. "Headache?" he asked her.

"Just a little tension," she said. "It'll pass." Then she laughed a little. "I was looking forward to coming back here for some fun. Before this happened to me, I'd been planning all the many ways I could break your heart."

He cocked his head and smiled at her. "Had you, now? That sounds interesting. Now I have something to look forward to."

"I was thinking you'd be devastated. Wiped out," she told him.

"Ah. Are you willing to share any details?"

"Not a chance."

"I'm already devastated." He stood up and went into the kitchen, dug around in the refrigerator and came out with two bottles of beer. He popped the tops and handed her one, keeping one for himself, and took his corner of the couch again. He hoped it didn't show on his face that just looking at her in the dim firelight was a treat, a delight. Her hair all mussed from bed, her feet bare, her cheeks pinked up from anxiety, she almost took his breath away. He knew she was skittish around men to the point that she couldn't even go to a coed gym to work out, and he didn't delude himself that he was exempt from that category, not even after all the time they'd had together. Oh, perhaps at the moment, as they shared a couch with a couple of feet separating them. But if he tried to get too close right now, she would freak. Bolt. Melt down.

"Maybe you should think about going back to work," he said.

"I've thought about it, but I've lost interest in prosecuting felons. I haven't lost interest in the law, but I don't know in what field. My experience is all criminal, and I just don't feel like going back into any kind of criminal law."

"How about working with rape victims?"

She sighed deeply. "I'm trying not to be a rape victim anymore. I'm trying to move on from that, even though I realize some of it will be with me forever." She shook her head and said, "I've been prepping rape victims for years, and now I am one. I just don't want to stay in that cycle. God, I want to move past that if I can!"

"That's reasonable. Maybe there's some way you can use your prosecutorial expertise on the defense side."

Her expression was shocked. "I can never defend a criminal against prosecution. Especially now."

"There has to be something," he said. "Human rights? Discrimination cases? EEOC? Women's rights? ACLU?"

She shrugged.

"You're used to having a mission, some injustice that needs you. You've always worked hard. I'm not sure all this time to think is such a good thing."

She stretched out her legs and put her feet on the coffee table to warm them from the glowing fire, and he put his up as well, not touching. And she found herself wondering, not for the first time, if all the women he had so greatly wronged had been his friend like this at first. Had he spent long hours, months, talking to them in sensitive, nonthreatening ways before having sex with them, marrying them and then betraying them? It would have taken such a lot of time. Such an investment. She further wondered if she could be tricked the way they were. She took a pull on her beer.

"After Mel and Jack return, if you're not in a hurry to get back to Sacramento, how about if we take a day and go over to the coast. I don't know if we'll catch the whales, but there's a lot of stuff over there. Art galleries, wine-tasting rooms, trails to the headlands and beach, nice restaurants. We could just be tourists for a day."

"Would you be thinking of that as a...date?"

He grinned. "I would," he admitted.

A smile tilted her lips. "I could do that," she said. "Were you good friends with your wives before you married them?"

"I shouldn't really answer any more questions about that. About them," he said.

She sat up a little. "Why not?"

"It could give you an unfair advantage in staging my heartbreak. I want to level the playing field."

It made her laugh. Or the beer made her laugh. But this was one of the things that was working on her—he didn't take her too seriously, and yet he took her very seriously. And she trusted him, which both reassured and worried her. She pulled her feet back, tucking them under her, and turned toward him. "Were you?" she demanded.

"Nah. I told you—I was always hunting."

"There's more to the story," she said.

"Not very much more," he said.

"I'm trying to figure out some things," she said. "The rape—that's not hard. Impossible to believe, but completely understandable. It was revenge."

"An ambush," he supplied.

"Ambush," she repeated thoughtfully.

"That's what happened to me," he added. "The one thing you really can't protect yourself against."

"Of course," she said, leaning back. "Of course."

"That was the hardest part of the equation for me to reason out—that there wasn't really anything I could have done differently. Or smarter. Have you struggled with that?"

She thought for a moment, holding her bottom lip between her teeth. "I've struggled with every part of that. But the thing that still gnaws at me is how I screwed up with Brad. For some reason, since the rape, it's like the pain of the divorce is fresh."

"What makes you think you screwed up?"

"I had no idea he was the kind of man who could do what he did. I never saw it coming. I've thought back to the beginning—to the first date. To every day of the marriage. Maybe I worked too hard—my hours were so long. I could have paid closer attention. Maybe my commitment to my career was stronger than my commitment to Brad. I never—"

Mike took his feet off the trunk, planted them on the floor and said, "Brie, it might've been his screwup, not yours. When I met you for the first time, years ago, what I saw shining in your eyes was trust and commitment. And love. God, you were so in love with him. And on top of that you were a brilliant achiever, a woman of strength and power and courage. And you couldn't get close enough to him, giving him all your attention. If that wasn't enough for Brad, you can't blame yourself."

"Tell me about them. Tell me why you married them, why your marriages failed."

He cautiously reached out a hand to gently touch her hair. "Honey, it's not that interesting. It won't help you understand Brad. The only thing I have in common with Brad is we were both idiots."

"Tell me," she demanded softly.

He took a breath. "Carmel was nineteen years old when she went to work for my father as a novice bookkeeper and sec-

retary, and we met while I was on leave. We wrote letters—
lonely, sweet letters that became more romantic. Six months
later when I was again on leave, we made love, and after that
she needed to be married. So that's what we did—married,
and then I was sent to Iraq. When I came home, she was ready
to move on. She broke my heart and saved my life all at the
same time, because I wouldn't have left her, and I would have
continued to be a terrible husband to her. I lived in the moment. I was too easily distracted. Always thinking of myself."

"And the next one?" she asked.

He shrugged. "We married out of guilt. She was with another man when I began to see her and she broke it off with
him to be with me. That was her choice—I didn't ask her to
do that. But like Carmel, she needed to be married after that.
Maybe neither of us could handle what we'd done—I have
some pretty large Catholic guilt. So we married. We tried to
turn a sexual fling into true love and it didn't work. Within
six months she was gone. It was a mistake from the beginning,
but I didn't learn my lesson about that kind of thing for quite
a while. If a woman was warm and willing… I was still living in the moment, thinking of myself. There's no defense for
what I did to either of them, but I was only twenty-six years
old when my second marriage was over and still a young fool.

"And the other thing was, I didn't take marriage seriously. I
thought I'd just find a wife automatically. I'd just aim, fire and
bang—I'd be married and have a bunch of kids." He shrugged.
"That's what my brothers did. And my sisters. They dated
someone, married 'em, the rest is history. They're all happy.
It never occurred to me they knew what they were doing."

"You wanted kids?"

"Certainly. Thank God that didn't happen. I'd hate to have
kids caught up in my miscalculations. Before the shooting, I
had no patience, hardly any scruples. I might've hit on you

four years ago if you hadn't been obviously in love with your husband."

"What about that shooting changed you?"

"You're kidding, right? I almost died. I had a lot of time—downtime—to think about how I'd misspent my life. About all the people I must have disappointed—not the least of whom was myself. I wasn't unlike Brad—the kind of guy who'd take too many chances, risk things a person with a brain would never risk. And it cost him everything. Cost me everything." He took a drink from his beer. "My ex-wives—they might not have been perfect, but I can't blame anyone but myself."

"You see?" she said, sitting straighter. "Your heart has to be broken!"

"Yeah. I'm sure it will be."

"But what I can't get past," she said, "is what if I face that again? What if I'm in love with some man, want to have a life with him and it seems everything is okay. Wonderful. Perfect. And then...?"

"Aw, Brie, there aren't any guarantees in this life—you know that better than anyone. After you take your time, know as much about him as you can and use your best judgment, it might be you who has a change of heart." His dark eyes glowed in the firelight. "Or maybe you're right about everything—about your feelings and his—and it's destined to last forever, to be perfect forever, and something you couldn't have foreseen happens. He slips off the mountain or falls off a boat." He touched her nose. "If you find yourself in that wonderful temptation, believing in someone enough to take that kind of chance, the person you'll have to trust most is yourself."

They talked until almost midnight and Brie began to yawn. And yawn and yawn. Finally Mike said, "You're driving me crazy. Go to bed. I'll be right here on the couch. I'll hear every sound, so you can just fall asleep and leave me in charge."

"You're sure?"

"I'm sure. First of all, this is a solid cabin—all locked up tight. Second, if anything stirs, I'm up like that," he said, snapping his fingers. "It's not even a choice. It comes from years of nodding off while sitting surveillance. And that's nothing to how light a sleeper you become in Iraq."

"Hmm. I could buy that. It's true, isn't it?"

"It's true. I haven't lied to you yet."

She thought about all the things he'd told her about himself—totally uncomplimentary things guaranteed to keep her from getting further involved with him, and decided that he hadn't lied to her. "Okay, then," she said, standing. "Thanks. I mean it, really. Thanks. I don't think I can do it yet—alone. You want a pillow or something?"

"Nah. I'm comfortable."

Brie went off to bed. He heard the sound of her brushing her teeth. Moving around. Snuggling in. He lay down on the sofa; his legs were too long and he propped them up on the arm. His feet would be asleep before morning, but it was okay. He wanted to do this for her.

Not much time had passed when he opened his eyes to find her standing over him. "Umm," she said nervously. "Can you...? This is awkward. I'm still very squeamish about a man even seeing me on the treadmill, but could you share the bed, in your clothes, and manage not to do anything? I mean, even in your sleep?"

"I'm okay right here, Brie. Don't worry about me."

"I'm not worried about... I just thought, that couch isn't big enough. And there's a bed in the loft, but I just don't want you way up there. And I... Could you lie beside me on the bed without—"

"I'm not going to try anything with you, Brie. I know you can't handle that."

"I don't think I can sleep unless you're…closer," she said very softly.

"Aw, honey…"

"Then come on," she said, turning back to the bedroom.

He didn't move for a moment, thinking. It didn't take long. He wanted to be next to her, but he didn't have to be. But if she needed him, he was there. He stood and got rid of his belt because of the big buckle, but everything else stayed on. And he went to the bedroom.

She was curled up under the covers, her back facing out, leaving him room. So he lay down on the bed on top of the covers, giving her that security. "Okay?" he asked.

"Okay," she murmured.

It wasn't a big bed, just a double, and it was impossible to keep a lot of space between them. He curved around her back, spooning her, his face against her hair, his wrist resting over her hip. "Okay?" he asked.

"Okay," she murmured.

He nestled in, his cheek against the fragrant silkiness of all that loose hair, his body wrapped around hers, though separated by layers of clothes and quilts, and it was a long, long time before he found sleep. By her even breathing, Mike knew she rested comfortably and that made him feel good.

When he woke in the morning, she had turned in her sleep and lay in the crook of his arm, snuggled up close to him, her lips parted slightly, her breath soft and warm against his cheek. And he thought, Oh damn, she's right—this is going to just break the hell out of my heart.

Jack and Mel drove to Eureka and picked up a couple of connecting flights to San Diego, arriving a night before Rick's graduation. That gave them a little time alone together at a nice hotel. They had a swim, something they never did in

Virgin River. Then a nice dinner and a long, wonderful night as man and wife. That first night away they managed to concentrate only on each other, but first thing the next morning Mel called Brie to make sure the baby was all right.

"I miss him so much," she complained.

"I know you do," Jack said. "So do I. Thank you for doing this for me," he said, pulling her into his arms.

"It wasn't just for you. It was for me, too. But I miss him so much."

"Just two nights, baby. Then we'll be home. And we won't leave him again for a long time."

Watching Rick stand at attention while being inducted into the Marine Corps sent pride spiraling through Jack's breast. He graduated at the top of his class, a young leader, a powerfully strong and smart young man. When the company was dismissed by the commanding officer, the young Marines all took a step back, did an about-face and shouted, "Aye, sir!" Mel grabbed Jack's arm, leaned against him, moved to tears. Out on the field it was handshakes and hugs, the young men thanking the drill sergeant, big grins and laughter. Jack put an arm around her and held her close. They stood at the edge of the field and waited for Rick to find them.

When he did, Jack grabbed Rick's hand in a firm clutch that brought them chest to chest, "Hoo-rah, man," Jack said. "Good job. I'm proud of you, son."

"Thanks, buddy." But Mel just leaned against him, hugged him and cried. "Hey, Mel," he said, laughing, patting her back. "Easy does it, huh?"

"Oh, Ricky, you are so handsome. Look at you. You're so beautiful."

"Here are some options, Rick. We can get your things," Jack said. "We've got a couple of rooms, not barracks. We can have a nice dinner out and catch our flights early tomorrow

morning. Or maybe you have some plans with your boys before you check out of here and I can get you in the morning,
take you home."

"I've had about enough of these boys."

"There has to be some stuff going on tonight. To celebrate?"

"Yeah, I'm sure. But I'm just ready to get off the base. I
like your first idea."

Jack suspected some of the young Marines would be getting
hotel rooms as well, but they'd be wanting to get drunk and
find girls. After what Rick had been through last year with
his girl, he was probably less than interested. So Jack checked
them in, took them out to a nice steak dinner and heard all
the stories about basic. After dinner he tucked Mel into bed
and went to Rick's room with a cold six-pack. He tapped
on the door and was admitted by a freshly showered kid in
sweatpants, bare chested. "Hey, you're my best friend," Rick
said, spying the beer.

Jack was somewhat taken by the boy's physique, which
had been honed by basic training. He'd been strong and lean
when he went in, but now he was cut and powerful looking.
His beard was getting heavy; the hair on his chest had grown
thick. Jack laughed and shook his head. "Damn it, boy. You
sure don't look eighteen anymore."

"I don't feel eighteen, either. I feel about a hundred and
ten." He took a bottle of beer and touched the neck to the
one Jack held. "Thanks for coming down, Jack. It meant a
lot to me."

"Meant a lot more to me," Jack said. Jack sat on one of the
chairs by a small table in the room while Rick sat on the edge
of his bed. "Some of the boys are coming up next week to
catch a little of deer season. We'd like you to join us."

"That'd be great. There are a couple of things I have to do
first," he said. "I have to spend a little time with my grandma.

And I have to drive over to Eureka," he said, dropping his gaze. "I want to check on Liz."

"Did you hear from her?" Jack asked.

"Yeah, a little bit. But usually it was only when she was having a hard time. I'm telling myself that she's not having a hard time every day or I'd have gotten more letters. What does Connie say?"

"Not a lot. That she's getting by, that's about it. How are you doing?"

"It was the right thing to do, Jack. Signing up. It took me out of my head a little. Made me way too tired and most of the time too scared to think."

"How are you feeling about things now?"

He shrugged. "I'm getting closer to living with myself. But Lizzie's still just a kid. Sixteen now—she's getting older in spite of herself. She's been through an awful lot for a girl her age."

Jack couldn't help but think that Ricky was only two years older, yet taking on all the blame as though he was the only one responsible. And he'd been through a lot, too. "I'm going to say this again, son. It wasn't your fault that baby didn't make it."

"Just my fault there was a baby," he said. He took a long pull on his beer.

"We're men, Rick. We're idiots. Ask Mel," he said.

"Yeah." He laughed.

"You take care of your business, then hunt with us a little. Might as well get a lot of unasked-for advice from the boys. They think of you as one of them now—there won't be any holding them back."

"Yeah. You going to hunt?" he asked.

Jack puffed up a little. "I am. I am going to defy my queen and take a rifle into the woods. But if I hit anything, I'm blaming you."

6

When Mel, Jack and Rick got back to Virgin River, the dinner hour was approaching. This boy was one of the town's favorite sons and everyone would be anxious to see him again, so Rick was dropped off at his grandma's house merely to scoop her up and take her to the bar. Lydie was a rare patron of the bar, but this was a special occasion.

It was early, but there were plenty of people already there, waiting to see Rick. Brie and the baby had been in town most of the afternoon already and when David saw Mel, he sent up an alarm, waving his arms at her, squealing with excitement. She couldn't fill her embrace with him fast enough and couldn't wait to nurse him. She slipped back into Paige's little living room to spend some quality time with her boy.

Preacher had made a big sheet cake with a remarkably good

Marine medallion iced onto the center. He'd also put out a lot of snack food and made a huge pot of barbecue with a big basket of buns, potato salad and baked beans, all Rick's favorites. It wasn't long before the place started to fill up with friends and neighbors. Mike arrived just minutes before Rick and Lydie, and when the young Marine walked into the bar, a cheer erupted. There were lots of hugs, backslapping, an air of celebration.

This was the kind of night that always made Jack glad he'd opened this place—surrounded by friends and neighbors, the walls throbbing with happy noise. On a night such as this, there was no charge for the food—a jar was put on the bar for people to drop in whatever they could afford, but no one would be turned away. There was plenty of free beer and sodas—the only things he sold were mixed drinks.

Once David had had a private reunion with his mother, he held up pretty well during the party, being passed from person to person. Rick took his turn with the baby, astonished at how big he'd gotten in such a short period of time.

While Brie was up on a bar stool and Jack was at his favorite place behind the bar, he asked her, "How'd it go, Brie?"

"David was an angel. We stayed very busy, running around visiting people."

"And you were all right?"

"Sure," she said, smiling. "I had a nice time. Anytime you need an auntie, I'm your girl."

He leaned across the bar and put a kiss on her forehead. "Thanks."

"How was your escape?" she whispered.

"Perfect. My wife missed her baby too much, but then, so did I."

After a big dinner and lots of visiting, the farmers, ranchers and business owners began to disappear—that time of night was upon them. Livestock didn't give days off; people around here got up very early. Rick jumped up on a bar stool, grinning. "Fantastic, Jack," he said. "It sure is good to be back. I'm going to get my grandma home—she turns in pretty early. Then I'm heading to Eureka."

"Tonight?" Jack asked, surprised.

"Yeah," he said, a slight stain on his young cheeks. He gave a lame shrug. "Gotta see that girl. You know."

"You'll get there kind of late," Jack pointed out.

"I bet she'll wait up," Rick said. He put out a hand. "Thanks for everything."

"Sure thing," he said. And he wanted to add, Please be careful. He followed Rick with his eyes as he walked Lydie out of the bar.

Mel was beside him, the baby on her left hip while she circled his waist with her right arm. "Rick's on his way to Eureka tonight," he said.

"They'll be all right, Jack," Mel said.

He shook himself and looked down at Mel. "Damn, I'd feel so much better if they'd just get about ten years older, real fast."

"I know. You're such a mother hen. But I just spent two days with Ricky and I'm not worried about him. He's paying attention. I think I'll go ahead and take David home, get him settled in his bed. I'm exhausted—it was such a long day. You stay as long as you like."

He leaned down and gave her a kiss on the head. "I'll see you a little later."

Brie jumped off her stool. "I'll take you, Mel," she said.

And then Jack noticed another thing. A lot had been happening around here, he guessed. While Mel went out the door with David, Brie took a slight detour, finding Mike, who was in a conversation with Paige across the room. She reached for his hand and, holding it, said something to him. Something that made him smile. He leaned toward her and put a peck on her cheek, gave her upper arm a brief squeeze and out the door she went.

That might not be a good thing, Jack thought. Brie didn't know Mike the way he did.

Once the guest of honor was gone, the bar emptied of partiers. Paige had gone to settle her son into bed in the room upstairs, leaving the three men in the bar alone. Jack got down three glasses. He poured Preacher a shot of his favored whiskey while he chose a single malt scotch for himself. "Mike?" he asked.

"Sure," he said.

"How were things while we were gone?" Jack asked Mike as he poured.

Mike shrugged. "Everything seemed fine," he answered. "Preach?" Mike asked.

"Yeah," the big man said. "Far as I know. Fine. The boy looks good, Jack. The Corps doesn't seem to have beat him into mush."

"I think he takes to it a little," Jack said.

"No doubt," Preacher said. He threw back his drink. "Can you boys lock up behind yourselves?"

"Sure thing," Jack said.

Preacher went through the kitchen to his quarters and Jack tipped the bottle again, giving himself and Mike a splash. "I didn't plan this," Jack said. "But since it's you and me—tell me about Brie."

"Tell you what, Jack?"

"When she was leaving… It looked like there was something…."

"Spit it out."

"You and Brie?"

"What?"

Jack took a breath, not happily. "Are you with my sister?"

Mike had a swallow of his whiskey. "I'm taking a day off tomorrow—taking her down the Pacific Coast Highway through Mendocino to look for whales, see the galleries, maybe have a little lunch."

"Why?"

"She said she'd like to do that while she's here."

"All right, but you know what I'm getting at—"

"I think you'd better tell me, so I don't misunderstand."

"I'd like to know what your intentions are toward my sister."

"You really think you have the right to do that? To ask that question?" Mike asked him.

"Just tell me what was going on between the two of you while I was gone."

"Jack, you'd better loosen your grip a little. Brie's a grown woman. From where I stand, we're good friends. If you want to know how she sees it, I think she's the one you have to ask. But I don't recommend it—she might be offended. Despite everything, she tends to think of herself as a grown-up."

"It's no secret to you—she's had a real bad year."

"It's no secret," Mike agreed.

"You're making this really tough, man…"

"No, I think you are. You spent some time with her tonight. Did it look to you like anything is wrong? Like she's upset or anything? Because I think everything is fine and you worry too much."

"I worry, yeah. I worry that maybe she'll look to you for some comfort. For something to help her get through. And that you'll take advantage of that."

"And…?" Mike prompted, lifting his glass but not drinking.

"And maybe work a little of your Latin magic on her and walk away." Jack drank his whiskey. "I don't want you to do that to her."

Mike put down his glass on the bar without emptying it. "I would never hurt Brie. And it has nothing to do with whose sister she is. Good night, Jack." He left the bar.

Mike had to do a memory check, remember how he felt about his own sisters, try to get it straight in his head that some of this behavior was beyond Jack's control. If Jack had looked at one of his younger sisters the way Mike was probably looking at Brie, he might have gotten his back up. Big brothers like me and Jack, we can get proprietary. It wasn't right, but it was there.

It pissed Mike off. But more than that, it worried him. He didn't really think he had much of a chance with Brie for a lot of reasons, but he didn't want one of those reasons to be his best friend.

He wished he'd finished that whiskey.

It was a long time before Mike was able to sleep, even though he hadn't slept much the previous two nights. He kept wishing Jack and Mel had stayed away a little longer. He'd lain beside her for two wonderful nights. She'd slept right up against him. Platonically, but it had been luxurious. In her sleep she would move closer, snuggle up against him, let him cradle her in the safety of his arms. Trusting him. Believing in him. Her scent still lingered in his mind, real enough so that every once in a while he would catch a whiff so memorable it was almost as though he could reach out and touch her.

But he was alone tonight. And when sleep finally did come, it was restless and fraught with dreams, the kind he hadn't had in a long time.

He saw their bodies as if from above—her pale, ivory skin against his tan Mexican hide, his large hands pressed against her perfect white bottom, holding her tight. Close. Although he watched from above, he could feel every sensation—the light touch of her fingers threading through his black hair, her lips on his neck, his chest, his shoulder. He tasted her skin, crumbled handfuls of her soft honey hair against his face. He was inside her, her knees raised and her pelvis tilted to bring him deeper, and he rocked with her in a gentle but intense pace. Her sighs filled the room; he whispered love words in her ear, encouraging her, telling her how much he wanted to please her.

He saw her small hands running up and down his back, his shoulders broad once again, restored. And as he told her he loved her, adored her, could never have a life if she was not part of it, she returned his words of love in Spanish. "Estas en mi corazón." You are my heart. "Te quiero." I want you. "Te quiero mucho, Miguel." I want you so much Miguel... Mike.

He heard her cries, felt her close around him with a hot, tight power so awesome his whole body shuddered convulsively. As she called out his name again and again, he exploded into a climax too grand, more fabulous than he remembered from his earlier life.

He woke suddenly, panting, his heart hammering, sweat drenching him so that the sheet clung. Alone. But not alone; she'd been with him, beneath him in that nocturnal fantasy turned bliss. And he thought, Oh God! I'm not dead after all!

His immediate next thought was that he was so grateful that hadn't happened to him while he slept with her at the cabin. It would have scared her to death.

Brie rose extra early; three people jockeying around one shower had its challenges. By the time she was toweling off, she could hear Mel and Jack in their bedroom, talking softly in response to the baby's gurgles and giggles. While she was in the loft dressing, the shower turned on again and again—Mel and Jack getting up for the day. David was back in his bed for an early-morning catnap when she met Jack at the coffeepot. Brie already had a steaming cup in her hand.

Jack looked her up and down, taking in the skirt, blouse and vest—not her usual country attire. She was dressed for a date. It ate at his gut. He slowly poured a cup of coffee. "Mike mentioned he was taking you over to Mendocino," he said.

"Yes," she said. "We're going to be tourists for a day."

"Listen, Brie, there's something you should know about Mike. He's been married twice."

"I know," she said.

Mel migrated into the kitchen in time for that last exchange. She plucked a cup off the counter, lifted the coffeepot and glared at her husband with a deep sigh. Jack completely ignored her.

"He's known for... Well, for being on the move a lot. Where women are concerned."

"I know that, too," she said.

Jack put down his cup. "Listen to me. I've known the man forever. He has a reputation with the women."

"Oh?" She laughed. "Has he been hustling the good women of Virgin River and breaking their hearts?"

Jack scowled at his sister. "He's been on hiatus healing up. He's healed now."

"Jack, stay out of this," Mel warned.

Brie just laughed at her brother. "Relax, Jack. I'm fine with Mike. He's been a good friend. We've talked a lot since June. We even met for lunch a few times. He's been very supportive through some of this mess I've been through."

The look on Jack's face was one of pure shock and it appeared as though the air was briefly sucked out of him. "What?" he asked.

"He called to see if I was doing all right, we talked, we talked some more, he drove down to the city to get me out of the house for an afternoon, and believe me—it made a difference. We have some things in common, you know. We're both victims of violent crimes."

"And no one told me this?" he asked, clearly stricken. Betrayed.

"There were things about what I've been going through that Mike understood. That it would be hard for anyone else to understand," Brie said.

"Why would no one tell me about this? He's my friend. You're my sister."

She shrugged. "Maybe no one wanted to deal with one of your outbursts."

"Dad knew?" he asked, disbelieving.

"Jack!" Mel warned again. "Leave this alone!"

"Of course Dad knew," Brie said. "I wouldn't leave the house without telling him exactly where I was going. And God knows, I don't answer the phone!"

"Brie, listen, I'd trust the man with my life, but not necessarily with my sister," he said earnestly, desperately.

"You wouldn't trust the pope with your sister," she said. "What do you suggest, huh? If it weren't for Mike, I'd still be lying on the couch, watching the soaps, scared to go out of the house in the middle of the day!"

"I told you if you needed anything, anything at all…"

"That my big brother would come racing down to Sacramento to rescue me," Brie shot back. "What makes you think I knew what I needed? I'm pretty grateful Mike had a clue!"

Mel wandered onto the porch with her coffee cup and stood there, not entirely grateful she could hear the argument going on inside. In five minutes they'd have the baby awake. And in thirty minutes or less, she was going to kill Jack.

"He has a knack for that," Jack blustered. "He seems to know exactly what it is a woman's looking for."

"Looking for? You jackass, I'm not looking for anything! I'm trying to get on with my life!"

"Great, that's great, but if you'd at least talk to me about the ways you're considering doing that—"

"I know you've been to war with him a couple of times and hunting with him a bunch of times, but what do you think you know about Mike that I can't figure out in a few months?" Brie asked rather too loudly. "And how the hell is he any different around women than you were for about twenty years?"

Mel took a sip of her coffee and tried, desperately, to remind herself that siblings fought. She and Joey hadn't had a good knock-down-drag-out since Mel's first husband had been killed, but growing up, becoming adults, hadn't exactly put a total end to all disagreements.

"I was never married!" Jack fired back.

"Probably through no wisdom of your own!" Brie retorted loudly.

Mike's SUV came into the clearing and Mel smiled and gave him a wave. Then she walked into the cabin. "Brie, your ride is here," she said more calmly than she felt.

Brie glared at her brother and plucked her purse off the counter.

"You have that new gun in your purse?" Jack asked sarcastically.

"No. It's upstairs in my suitcase. If it had been handy, you might be bleeding through a hole in your stupid head by now." And she whirled away from them, storming out the door.

Left alone in the kitchen, Mel stared Jack down for just a second before he turned away from her, presenting his back. He'd just been beaten to a pulp by his little sister; he wasn't in the mood to go a round with his wife.

The baby fussed.

"Asshole," Mel said, leaving the kitchen to see about David.

When Brie got into Mike's SUV she was clearly flustered. "Whew," Mike said. "Wanna talk about it?"

"No!" she snapped. Then, taking a deep breath, "We had… Words, we had words, me and Jack. About my new gun, which I do not have with me, so relax."

He put the car in gear and smiled at her. "I will if you will."

"I'll need about five minutes," she said. She took a couple of deep breaths. Then it slowly dawned on her—she'd fought! She wasn't weak and sniveling, wasn't scared, wasn't sheepish— she'd gone right back after him! Sure, it was only Jack, not a homicidal predator, but still… She'd always looked for Jack's approval, and this once she'd stood right up to him, the jerk. A slow smile spread across her lips. Maybe all was not lost. Maybe she could get her life back. She relaxed back onto the seat. "Ah," she said. "I need a day off. A day away." From my buttinsky brother, she thought.

Mel had decided to give Jack some time to cool off and get his head wrapped around the idea that Brie had gone away with Mike for the day, but in the end it was really she who needed the time. Her husband had made her furious. She was spitting tacks.

When David was down for his morning nap in the crib Mel kept at Doc's, she left the Hummer at the clinic and took Doc's old truck out to their homesite. If Doc had to leave, he would call Paige to babysit. When she got to their property, Jack was inside the house where she couldn't see him, but she could hear the power saw as she pulled up. She drove right up to the front of the house, parked within a few feet and jumped out. She gripped a solid board to hoist herself up onto the foundation and stood there, facing his back. He didn't turn around and her blood started to boil; he knew she was there. He always knew. When the saw stopped whirring she yelled, "Don't you dare pretend you don't know I'm here!"

He slowly turned around, and he had the audacity to still be wearing that stubborn frown. His eyes were narrowed to slits.

"Jack Sheridan! Knock it off!"

"She's my sister. She's been through a lot," he said, his voice gravelly and impatient.

"That's right—and she's entitled to enjoy herself. Make her own choices. It's important she make her own choices! If she wants to spend time with Mike, she doesn't need your permission."

Jack stepped toward her. "You don't understand. I've seen him with women!"

"Yeah, I bet! At about the same time he was seeing you with women!"

"That's different! That was over when I met you!"

"Maybe it's over for him!"

"Hah! You don't get it! That guy ran through women real quick, never even gave it a thought—"

"And this is different from you how?"

"He screwed up two marriages! Brie's already been through a painful divorce, not to mention the other horrible crap she's endured! I don't want her hurt!"

"Then you better butt out before you're the one who hurts her!"

"I would never hurt her! I want to keep her safe!"

Mel put her hands on her hips and lifted one finely arched brow. "The way you wanted to keep Preacher safe from Paige and almost cost the man the most joy he's had in his lifetime?"

"I admit—I was wrong about that."

"You're wrong about this! No matter what the outcome is, you cannot get in the middle of the relationships that people choose." She stepped toward him. "Jack, she's lonely and hurt—let her be. Let her go. If she finds a little sliver of happiness, it's not your job to take its temperature."

"If he hurts her, I don't know what I'll do. I'll kill him, that's what I'll do!"

"Then let's tell her she has to leave. Let's get her out of here before we have to watch her face hurt one more time. Forget giving her a chance to make herself happy, make herself well. Let's tell her the truth—you can't take it while she stumbles along and tries to figure out what's right for her." She took a breath; he looked down at his feet. "Like I did," she said more softly. His head snapped up. "Just like me, Jack. I came into this town so blissfully stupid about the fact that you'd been with a hundred women and never committed to one of them. If I'd had a big brother handy to clue me in—I could have escaped all this happiness." Tears ran down her cheeks.

"Mel," he said, stepping toward her.

She waved him back, shaking her head. "I haven't ever been raped," she said, "but I've been emotionally bruised pretty bad." Her voice dropped to a whisper and she was shaking her head miserably. "It should never have worked with you. You of all people! Jesus, you had to have been as bad as Mike, probably worse! You had your women—quick and dirty and back on the road. No commitments. You never loved any of them. It should've been like that with me. A couple of months and then you're bored, you're moving on...."

"Mel," he said. This time he wouldn't be held back. He reached for her, took her into his arms. "God, baby. Where is this coming from?"

"But I got pregnant! You couldn't get out of it, could you?"

"Oh, for God's sake, Mel..."

She looked up at his face. "This is Mike," she said in a whisper. "This is a man whose bed you sat by for ten long days, waiting for him to wake up, sit up, speak. He kept your squad safe from insurgents in Fallujah. He came to Virgin River to be near us to get well—do you really think he's going to treat

Brie with disrespect? Do anything bad to her? My God, he sees you as his brother! Where is your brain?"

He pulled her close, held her against him. "At this moment I have absolutely no idea." He kissed the top of her head. "Tell me something. Do you think I'm going to get bored? Stray? Do you think we're only together because of David? Tell me."

She looked up at his face, tears wetting her cheeks, and shook her head. "But if I'd known about you what Mike knows about you—I'd have run for my life."

"But I told you, Mel. I never lied to you. It all changed the second I saw you. Tell me you believe me. Tell me I showed you that."

She reached up to lay a hand along his cheek. "I believe you. You've never given me any reason to doubt you."

He let out sigh of relief and pulled her tighter. "God, don't do that to me. Don't throw my shitty past at me like that— you know I can't talk my way out of it."

"But I'm going to talk you off this ledge if it kills me. You can't do this to your sister. This is up to her."

"I understand. It's hard, but I understand what you're saying."

She put her arms around his waist, laid her head against his chest and cried. He stroked her hair, kissed her head, held her and rocked with her as they stood inside the unfinished structure. He said things like, "It's okay, baby. You know you're everything to me. You and David." But what he was thinking was that this was very unusual for his wife. She wouldn't hesitate to go after him, but she didn't become distraught. She cried from time to time, but over events that would bring the strongest woman to tears—the loss of a baby, the anniversary of a loved one's death. And he thought, oh-oh. Something about this isn't quite right.

At length she stopped. She looked up at him and he brushed

the tears from her cheeks. "Sorry," she said. "You made me so frickin' mad I thought I was going to kill you."

"Yeah, join the party. Brie threatened my life." He smiled down at her. "Thank you for not killing me," he said. "You're right—I have to stop smothering her, questioning her. She's a grown woman. She's smarter than me. I'll try harder."

"No trying," she said. "Let go. When she comes to you, open your wonderful arms to her, but when she's trying to get on with her life, toast her. Celebrate her. Let her go. And for God's sake, please remember that you can trust Mike."

"You're right," he said. "I learned my lesson. I'll listen to you now."

"It isn't easy being the wise one in the marriage," she said.

"I imagine the pressure is terrible," he said with a smile.

She reached her fingertips up to the hair at his temples. "You're showing a little gray here. Not much, but a little. I suppose I did that to you."

"Probably. But I'm very tough—I can take it."

"Oh, Jack," she said, leaning against him again. "Please, I don't want to ever fight with you."

He lifted her chin with a finger. "Don't be a candy ass. You fought good. You won, as a matter of fact."

"But it was awful. There have been times since this thing with Brie that you've been so far away. It just… It frightens me."

"You should never be afraid. Not while you're my wife. It's my job to make sure you're never afraid."

"Then know this—all I want is to die in your arms. I can't live a day without you. Do you get that?"

He nodded, but he said, "No dying allowed. We're going to get old and very wrinkly together. I insist on it."

Tommy knew he was pretty obvious—he called Brenda every night. When she walked into their physics class he couldn't suppress a huge grin—he could feel it all the way to the soles of his feet. He scored a homework session with her at her house in Virgin River and it might as well have been a date at the Ritz, he was so pumped. When she walked him out to his truck, she held his hand for a few minutes.

The girl moved really slowly, and he liked that. One of these days he was going to get his arms around her, kiss her. She had to be about the prettiest girl at school. Maybe the world.

He'd like to be walking her to her classes, but the second physics was over she was surrounded by her girlfriends and whisked away, so he made do with those phone calls and after-school homework sessions. "We should go out," he said. "You seem to be all over that bad flu."

"There's a dance coming up in a few weeks," she said.

"You have a date," he promised. "But I hate to wait that long. Maybe there's something we can do before that. As a warm-up date?"

She laughed at him. "You're too funny. Stop looking at me and look at your physics homework."

Brenda's mother stayed awfully close while he was at her house, so there was no potential for getting snugly. But he was completely okay with this, because when Brenda walked him out to his little truck there was a moment on the front porch that she let him get close. He slipped an arm around her waist. And she kind of leaned against him, so he let his lips brush softly against her cheek. "That's nice," he said. "Do you know your hair smells like vanilla?"

"Of course I know that," she said.

"You sure do make homework a lot more fun than it used to be."

"I'm glad to be of help," she told him.

"Hey, you want to go to a party?"

"Where?"

"I heard there's something going on out at this rest stop—"

She jumped away from him so fast, he was startled. The look on her face was one of sheer horror.

"What's the matter?" he asked.

"I don't go to those parties," she said.

"Okay. That's fine. I just thought—"

"Do you go to those parties?" she asked angrily.

He shrugged. "I haven't been to one yet. I just heard about it. Why? Are they bad?"

"A lot of beer. A lot of kids get drunk. Puking drunk."

He made a face. "Ew. Sounds like loads of fun. Okay, how about a movie in Fortuna?"

"Maybe," she said.

"Hey, what's wrong? Did I say something wrong?"

"It's just… Those parties out at the rest stop, they have a real bad reputation. I don't want a reputation."

He smiled at her. "As far as I can tell, you already have one, and it's totally good. So—" he shrugged "—we'll skip the rest-stop parties."

"You drink beer?" she asked him.

"I've been known to have a beer," he said. "But I don't overdo it. You have to meet my father, Brenda." He laughed. "Then you'd know right away that I don't want to piss him off."

She seemed to relax a little. "I might go to a movie with you. But we should have another couple along."

"Like who?"

"Maybe one of my girlfriends and her date?"

"Whatever makes you happy. But I want to go out with you sometime—because all this homework is making me so smart I almost can't stand myself."

She smiled and said, "Okay, Tommy. Call me later."

7

Brie couldn't believe she had lived in California all her life without ever visiting the Mendocino coast. It charmed her at once—the breathtaking vistas, the Victorian villages, the art, the food. She recognized Cabot Cove, the filming site for Murder, She Wrote. They lunched in an adorable little restaurant with an ocean view, binoculars on the tables. Before they had finished lunch, they were sharing binoculars to view a fleet of whales, migrating south. The mammals were so far out to sea, the binoculars were necessary.

"In the spring, during the migration with their new calves, they come much closer to the shore. We'll come back," Mike said.

The excuse to come over here had been seeing the whales, but there was much more to the coast than that. They dropped into galleries, tasted wine in tasting rooms, walked along the ocean bluffs, down the trails to the tide pools and private beaches. They visited botanical gardens, climbed to the top of a lighthouse and sat under a tree in the park, eating popcorn. They laughed, played, held hands. Too soon, the day had aged.

"We should at least stay for the sunset," Mike suggested. "There's nothing like a Pacific sunset. Would you like that?"

"I would. Do you think I should call Jack? Let him know?"

Mike shrugged. "I don't know what kind of arrangement you two have. Would he be worried if you're not home before dark?"

Remembering her brother's dark mood in the morning, the way he'd tried to warn her off Mike, she almost said that Jack would be especially worried tonight. But instead she said, "As a courtesy, I'll give him a call. I'm really having too much fun to go back yet."

He touched her cheek with the back of a knuckle. "Are you, Brie?" he asked softly.

"You don't have to ask." She smiled.

"There's a phone," he said, pointing across the street. "Do you have plenty of change?"

"Lots."

"I'll get us some drinks. We can take them to the bluffs and watch from there."

Jack came to the phone in the bar and Brie told him she was having a wonderful time and they planned to watch the sunset over the ocean before heading back. Although she tried to keep her voice passive and not defensive, she really expected some kind of argument. Instead, her brother said, "I'm sorry about this morning, Brie. I was out of line. That wasn't my place—I want you to enjoy yourself. I mean that."

"Gee, Jack," she said, amused. "You sure came around quickly."

"I know," he said. "I'm a genius that way."

"Mel must have really lit into you," she said.

"That always increases my intelligence about tenfold."

"I love you." She laughed. "We'll be home later." She was still chuckling to herself when she crossed the street to meet Mike.

"What did he say?"

"Have fun," she said, laughing again.

"What's funny about that?"

"Well, as I was leaving this morning, he warned me about your irresponsible ways with women—but now he's docile as a lamb, apologizing, telling me to have a good time."

"He's starting to get on my nerves when he does that thing about the women," he said, taking her elbow and steering her toward the bluffs. "We've been all over that. He can give it a rest anytime. He had a million women before Mel. Two million."

She laughed at him. "You never mentioned to him that we spent a lot of time together over the summer," she said.

"I told you—it wasn't because you're Jack's sister. I met you because of Jack—I care about you because of you."

"Did you tell him you spent the nights he was away in his bed?"

Mike laughed. "Would I be walking around today if I had? You know that would put him in a black mood."

"You could have explained—I asked you to come, to stay."

"This would be Jack Sheridan's little sister. He would've expected me to sit guard out on the porch."

"You didn't tell him I got scared?"

He slipped an arm loosely, cautiously, around her waist. "You would have told him if you had wanted him to know."

"Which one of us are you protecting?" she asked with a laugh.

He was conscious that she didn't pull away from him. "You and me, our privacy. What goes on with us just isn't his business. If you want to know—he asked. I don't know how he picked up the scent, since apparently no one clued him in. I must be losing my touch—I've become obvious. I used to be slicker than that. But he wanted to know if there was something going on between us."

"And you said...?"

"I said that I would never do anything to hurt you and if he wanted to know anything, he should ask you. I suggested he be very careful about that because you consider yourself a grown-up."

That made her laugh rather happily. "Oh, I bet you really pissed him off."

"He'll get over it. He pissed me off."

They walked the headlands trail to the bluffs and found a place on the grassy knoll to sit. The sun was already making its downward path and Brie found herself hoping it wouldn't go quickly. They were hardly alone there—lots of people strolled, children ran around, lovers paused to embrace, kiss.

Mike sat with his legs stretched out in front of him; Brie curled her legs under her and braced herself on an arm, close to him. "Here," Mike said, gently pulling her back to recline against his chest. "Be comfortable."

Leaning against his broad chest, she felt herself relax in a way she hadn't in months. With this interlude coming at the end of day like this, she was as close to carefree as she'd been in too long. Feeling the strength of him behind her was like a foundation. It didn't hurt that she'd slept beside him for two nights and he had been perfect. And she began to think, I was wrong about what I can feel. I can feel things. Closeness and trust, for one thing. Security. He made her feel safe, and not just safe from danger. She had absolutely no worry that trusting him was foolish.

The sun set very slowly, the number of people dwindled

as it darkened and soon it was almost as if they were alone.
They reclined on the bluffs in silence for a long time, until it
was nearly dark. The dark no longer seemed to bother her,
because she was with Mike.

Finally she said, very softly, "Is there anything between us?"

"Oh, I think there's much."

"Tell me..."

"Well, I am determined to do anything I can to be there for
you, and you are determined to break my heart. That heart-
breaking business, it's very serious."

She laughed at him. She felt his head drop forward to her
shoulder and nuzzle her hair. A hand on her upper left arm
gently squeezed and he said, "Brie... Tu creas un fuego en mi
corazón." Brie, you create a fire in my heart.

She straightened a bit, but didn't pull away. "What did you
say?" she whispered.

"You are lovely. You touch my heart," he answered, pulling her back against him again. He slipped an arm around
her waist gently, tenderly, cautiously holding her against him,
very careful that she not feel confined. "Tu debes sentir estas
manos amorosas así a ti." You should feel loving hands on you.

Her heart beat a little faster and she knew that it was not
fear she felt. She wanted to say, "Deja a que sean sus manos."
Let them be your hands. But she wasn't ready. Instead, she
said, "Your language is beautiful."

"Te tengo en mis brazos," he said. I will hold you in my
arms.

"Tell me what you said," she urged him.

"Nothing, really. Just an endearment. It is a very romantic language."

She could tell him now she spoke his language fluently,
that she knew he lied. But she didn't want to break the spell
he had created in thinking she couldn't understand him. He

spoke his heart while he thought she was innocent of his desires. "Say something to me—something heartfelt," she said, not turning around.

He touched the hair at her temple, threading his fingers into it. "Te querido más te de lo tu hubieras." I have wanted you for longer than you know.

She let her eyes close. "What did you say?" she asked in a whisper.

"You deserve all happiness," he said—he lied.

A small smile floated across her face. She was on to him.

"No te merezco." I don't deserve you. "Te quiero en mi vida." I want you in my life.

"I think you seduce women with your language."

"When you are with me, you should know that I care about you as much as I care about any of my sisters. Or my mother, who is queen of the world."

She laughed a little. "I'm not sure that was entirely flattering."

"I want you to believe you are completely safe and protected when you're with me. I promise you, you have nothing to fear from me. Not ever."

"I think you're manipulating me."

"Do you, now?" he asked, humor in his voice.

"You're luring me into a false sense of security, trying to trick me so I forget my plan to break your heart a hundred times."

He laughed, stroking that long mane of hair that floated down her back. "I know you're a very determined woman, and if breaking my heart is your goal, you won't rest until it's done."

"I'm going to make mincemeat out of you," she said.

"I have no doubt."

She pivoted to face him. It was dark enough so that it was hard to see the light in his eyes. She leaned toward him and put her lips softly against his. Her kiss was very tentative.

Brief. Cautionary. "I suppose I'll have to lure you into my confidence first."

"A good idea," he said, aware that his voice had become husky. "Tienes labios que gritan besame." You have lips that scream kiss me. And he slowly, carefully, leaned toward her. He touched her mouth, drawing her lower lip between his lips sweetly, sensuously. He wanted to put his hands on her, but he was unsure what she could tolerate. He let one large hand touch her waist delicately, but he didn't apply pressure and didn't pull her to him. "I think I like this—being drawn into your confidence. I knew the heart-breaking would be something to look forward to."

"I didn't know I could do this," she said a little breathlessly.

"I knew," he said. "I told you. It was just a matter of time."

"You're going to get us into trouble...."

"No, Brie. There's no trouble here, no problem. Everything is all right."

"You sound overconfident."

"I'm not worried about anything," he said. "I won't let anything happen to you."

"You're not trying for an upset? Trying to break my heart before I can break yours?"

"Estas en mi corazón." You are my heart. "Go ahead. Do your worst. I'm strong. I welcome the pain."

"Kiss me," she said. "Kiss me one time, as though you don't find me breakable."

"Oh." He chuckled, a husky sound. "Are you sure you mean that?"

"Just once," she said, her voice a breath.

He circled her waist with his arms and drew her forward, pulling her across his lap and against his chest. Her hands rested lightly on his shoulders, waiting. He hovered over her lips for a moment. He let the flesh of his lips touch hers.

Slowly, giving her time to change her mind, he pressed against her mouth. Her hands slowly drifted upward, circling his neck, a hand reaching up to the back of his head, holding him against her mouth, and with a groan of desire he moved over her mouth passionately, opening his lips. Hers opened as well, admitting his tongue. He wanted to die, the taste of her was so sweet, so delicious. He pulled her harder against him, feeling her firm breasts bore into his chest.

And it happened to him. He became aroused. It was the first time he had responded this way in so long that for a second he wanted to grasp her to him, lower her to the ground and press himself against her. But the hell of it was, he couldn't proceed with her. She was just testing these waters and was still so unsure, so easily frightened. This kiss, this deep and wet and wonderful kiss, was a huge step for her. It was possible, lying across his lap as she was, that she felt his desire rising beneath her. And he didn't want her to be afraid.

He heard her sigh, her breath soft against his face, and he withdrew from her lips. "Brie, I'm sorry. I can't," he whispered.

"Can't?"

"I can't kiss you like this. You tempt me. And you're not ready to be with a tempted man. I have to take you home."

She sat back, sliding off his lap and, a little rattled, brushed at her skirt. "Whew," she said.

He ran a hand from her shoulder down her arm. "Okay?"

"Hmm," she said. "Okay."

"We have to go. It's dark now. And we've had a full day."

Jack was splitting logs in the early morning when Mike came from his RV. His hands plunged into his pockets, heading toward the bar for coffee, he said, "Morning" as he walked by.

"Mike," Jack called after him. Mike turned and Jack leaned

the ax against the stump. "I should probably say something about the other night," Jack said. "I can't figure out what."

Mike grinned in spite of himself. "That's too bad. I'd love to hear what you come up with."

"How about—I'll stay out of your business."

"I don't believe it, but I like it."

"You have sisters. You know where I'm coming from."

"Yeah," Mike said, taking a step toward him. "I understand."

"I care about her. Worry about her."

Mike stepped toward him. He put a hand out to shake. When Jack took it Mike said, "I'm not talking to you about her. Period."

"The boys will be here to hunt in a couple of days," Jack said. "I'm going to Eureka for some supplies."

"Need a hand with that?"

"Nah. Need anything while I'm there?"

"I'm good," Mike said.

Jack nodded. "Thanks," he said.

"For?"

"For refusing to talk about her. Says something." He put a hand on Mike's shoulder, directing him ahead toward the bar. "Let's get a cup of coffee."

An hour later Jack was gone to Eureka and Mel's Hummer was parked in front of Doc's. Mike drove out of town. He thought it was possible Brie was at Doc's with Mel, but he didn't stop to check, didn't want to tip his hand. He pulled into the clearing at the cabin and gave the horn on his SUV three short toots. Then he stepped out and leaned against the driver's door. In just a couple of moments she appeared on the porch, her damp hair pulled over one shoulder as she patted it dry with a towel. She wore slim jeans and moccasins on her feet. She looked so young, so vulnerable. She smiled when she saw him. "What are you doing here?"

He pushed his Rio Concho back on his head. "Checking in. How are you this morning?"

She tossed the towel onto the Adirondack chair and came down the porch steps toward him. "Fine. Very fine."

"You look fifteen," he said, feeling every one of his thirty-seven years. She took a step closer and he put his hands on her waist; she put her hands on his forearms and looked up at him. He twisted his hands at her waist, wiggling her a little closer. Then his arms went around her waist and he lifted her up so that her face was level to his. Her hands rested lightly on his shoulders. "I missed you," he said. "I was thinking about you."

"Is that so? Are you coming on to me?"

"Brie, I've been coming on to you for six months," he said. "How'm I doing?"

"You're pretty obvious."

"I can't help that. I have no savoir faire."

She laughed at him and plucked the hat off his head, holding it behind him. "I think you have more than you deserve. Enough to be dangerous."

"With you I'm an innocent." He touched her lips lightly with his. Tentatively. "My days of being dangerous to women are over."

"Is that so? And when did that happen?"

He gave a shrug. "A few months ago I began to lose interest in other women. A few weeks ago, it was over. There is only one."

"You're wooing me."

"I'm trying, yes."

"If you mean business, you should kiss me," she said.

"Oh, I was hoping you would say that." He covered her mouth with a passionate kiss, holding her close against him.

Her mouth opened under his lips at once and he probed with his tongue. She not only let him in, she welcomed him in, moving over his mouth with lips that were hot and urgent, holding him tightly. From what he could taste, she was enjoying the kiss very much; she moaned softly and grew breathless. He couldn't remember when he had last kissed a woman before Brie. A thousand years ago, surely. She tasted like honey, so sweet and pure.

He hated for it to ever end and when it did, she whispered, "Would you like to come inside?"

"No." He smiled. "You're not really ready for me to come inside."

"You make me wonder what I'm ready for." She kissed him again. Deeply and passionately.

"When you no longer wonder, we'll talk," he whispered against her lips.

"You could take advantage of my weakness," she said.

He put her back on her feet and put a soft kiss on her forehead. "There will be no taking, mi amor. Only giving."

"Oh, my. I can see why women would marry you so easily."

He touched her nose. "Brie, it was never like this."

"I don't believe you," she said.

"I wouldn't believe me either, but it's true."

He pulled her to him and she leaned into him, resting her head on his chest, her arms around his waist. He held her like that, both of them quiet for a long time, just enjoying the closeness. He stroked her back and dropped soft kisses onto her damp hair, feeling more alive than he had in such a long, long time. It filled him with pride that she didn't tense or tremble while he held her. She had slowly become accustomed to his touch, his embrace, and knew that she was safe and loved in his arms. Even if nothing more ever came, he felt he had already won the prize.

"You know the boys are coming to hunt?" he asked her.

"Yes. Jack's getting ready for them. Will you hunt?"

"Of course. Which means I won't be around town much during the day. If you need me for some reason, you'll have to let me know beforehand."

"I'm helping Mel with a big project she has going on. Something about free mammograms for the women around here."

"Then I'll see you later?"

"Yes. Later."

He gave her a peck on the lips and pushed her gently away, taking his hat out of her hand, then got back into the SUV and drove away. He watched in his rearview mirror and saw that she stayed outside in the clearing in front of the cabin until he was out of sight.

When Mel went into the bar for her morning coffee, David contented in the stroller after his breakfast, she found Paige sitting at one of the tables with the newspaper spread out in front of her. "How's it going?" Mel asked, parking David by the table while she went for a mug and some coffee.

"Good," Paige said. "Hi, coochie," she said to the baby, making him smile. She automatically took a toast crust from her nearly empty plate and gave it to him to teethe on. He was delighted by it.

Mel brought her coffee to Paige's table and sat with her. She noticed David gnawing on the toast and smiled. "Isn't that good?" she said to the baby. "Where is everyone?" she asked Paige.

"Hmm. I think Jack has gone to Eureka for supplies. I offered to do that—the boys are going to be here pretty soon. He said he'd get it, then next thing I knew he wasn't around. John's in the back, setting up lunch, with Christopher under-foot as usual."

"How about Mike?" she asked.

Paige shrugged.

Preacher came out of the kitchen with a tray of glasses. He put them under the bar roughly. "Hey, Preach," Mel said. "Where's Jack?"

"Eureka."

"How about Mike?"

"It's not my day to watch him," he said gruffly, going back to the kitchen.

"Jeez," Mel said. She looked at Paige and met twinkling eyes. "Something funny?"

"John appears to be a little tense. Amazing he got through so many years without sex every day."

"Every day?" Mel asked. "Well, holy shit, his count must be down to nothing!" She looked over her shoulder to make sure they were alone. "How's he handling the drought?"

"He's a little testy," Paige said, amused. "I keep telling him this is entirely up to him. If it's too much, we can make a few adjustments. But he wants to do it right."

"Hope he doesn't explode," Mel said absently.

"He asked if we can close the bar on ovulation day."

Mel's eyes widened in surprise and they both melted into laughter.

Jack hadn't seen Rick in a couple of days. He hadn't been back from Eureka for long when Rick showed up. A couple of hunters were having a late breakfast at one of the tables, so Rick jumped up on the bar stool and Jack fixed him up with a cup of coffee. "Welcome back," Jack said.

"The party was great, Jack. Thanks again for everything you did."

"I didn't do anything. This town has a habit of turning out for important people."

"I've been checking on Liz," he said. "She's doing great. You can't believe how good she looks. Beautiful, in fact." He laughed. "I didn't think she could get more beautiful."

"That checking business seems to work out for you pretty well," Jack said, lifting his cup. "Your complexion looks a little clearer."

Rick laughed and ducked his head a little. "Here's how it is, Jack. Me and Liz—it's not cut-and-dried. I'm going to finish my hitch, alone. We're not going to make any promises to each other until that time's up." He shrugged. "We're gonna let Liz get a little older, finish school, see where we are. I want her to have a chance, you know. If this isn't right for her—hooking up with me—then I want her to have the space and time to move on. In the meantime, for right now, we're still a little too locked in to each other. You can understand that, can't you? After everything... Well," he said, lifting his mug and taking a sip, "we have a pretty strong bond. I'll be there for her as long as she needs me—it's the least I can do. I'm not going to tell her she can't feel it, that she has to try to get over it."

"How about you?"

"Oh-ho." He laughed. "I feel it pretty good. That girl really does it to me. She always has. It's just going to take some time to know if it's permanent or just something that happened to us."

"You're not taking any chances, are you?"

"Of course not. And I mean, absolutely not. I don't want you to worry. I don't want you to think I'm a total idiot who never heard a word you were saying."

Jack put his hand over Rick's forearm. "I don't think that."

"Thanks." Rick was quiet for a minute or so. "It's nice, Jack. When there isn't a lot of pain. When there aren't any tears. Nice."

"Yeah," Jack said. "You hunting with us? Or you just going to spend your whole leave working on your complexion?"

Rick grinned. "I'm hunting," he said. He drank a little of his coffee. "We're not doing that much hunting, are we?"

The whole town of Virgin River looked forward to the visits of the Marine brothers—they brought such an air of camaraderie and celebration when they came. The first to arrive in his truck with camper shell was Zeke, who came from Fresno. He was in town by early afternoon. Just a couple of hours later came Joe Benson and Paul Haggerty together, pulling a fifth wheel behind a truck—they were good friends who often worked together, Paul building Joe's houses whenever possible. Then came Corny, who drove in from Washington State but hailed from Nebraska—thus the nickname. Next, Phillips and Stephens—Josh and Tom—both from Nevada, right on the other side of the Sierras. By 6:00 p.m. everyone was present, even Rick, and the din in the bar was raised to an all-time high.

Doc Mullins was in the midst of the throng, enjoying his one whiskey of the day with the guys, David was being passed from Marine to Marine, jostled as if being weighed, Rick was getting an awful lot of free advice and Mel, Brie and Paige were hugged so much they felt their bones crunching. Of course, others from town made brief appearances, wanting to be a part of the reunion for at least a little while, but not wanting to get in the way. Connie and Ron and their friends Joy and Bruce put in appearances. Harv dropped in for a beer after work, as did Doug Carpenter and Fish Bristol.

Paul dropped an arm around Mel's shoulders and asked, "Why the long face? Aren't you having fun?"

"I hate hunting. I can handle ducks, but not deer. I mean,

I don't want to pass judgment—I just wish my husband didn't shoot deer."

"Oh, Mel, don't worry. I've been hunting with your husband—the deer are completely safe."

"Melinda, we'll have venison all winter. You'll love it," Jack said.

"Don't worry, Mel," Paul whispered. "He'll never get a thing. They can smell him coming."

Some people came into the bar and Mel immediately recognized Vanessa, her newest patient. The older gentleman with her must be her father. She left Paul's side and went to her immediately, embracing her in welcome, and was then introduced to Walt, her dad.

Paul just stood where he was, glassy-eyed with a faraway smile on his lips. Vanessa! His best friend's wife. Then Vanessa spotted him and went to him instantly, arms open wide. He hugged her, rocking her back and forth a little. Then he held her away from him and stared approvingly at her belly, which was growing nice and round. "I had no idea you'd be here," he said, refusing to take his arms from around her.

"I wanted to surprise you. My dad's retirement ranch is just down the road and I'm staying there while Matt's in Iraq. Mel's going to deliver my baby."

"When?"

"A few months. Gosh, it's so good to see you. I haven't seen you since—"

"The wedding," he answered. "God, Vanni—you're gorgeous." He touched her belly. "Jesus, he kicked me."

"We don't know what it is yet."

"Gotta be a guy," Paul said.

She was joined by her dad, his hand out to Paul in greeting. "General, good to see you, sir," Paul said. "Let me introduce you two around," he said.

Several of the guys knew Matt, but the only person in the room to have already met Walt, General Booth, was Mike. Because of his investigation of teens, he'd been to the Booth household. And although the general invited them all to address him by his given name, only the women seemed so inclined. For these Marines, rank had its privileges. General Booth declined the offer to join the hunting party, saying he might take them up on that the next time. After about twenty minutes of introductions and conversation, Paul grabbed Vanessa's hand, dragged her off to the table nearest the hearth and sat her down there to talk, to catch up. He wanted to hear all about Matt, about her little brother Tommy, about how she liked living way out here, so far from everything.

And she wanted to know everything that was going on with him. Paul, thirty-five like Matt, had left the Marines after four and remained in the reserves while Matt stayed active. Paul had finished his degree and joined his family's construction company in Grants Pass, Oregon, not far from the California border. "And are you seeing anyone?" she asked him, grabbing his hand across the table.

"Nah, not really. Until someone as pretty as you comes along, I'll just keep looking."

"You've always been too shy for your own good. You should be married and have a ton of kids. You'd make such a great dad."

"Yeah, I should," he agreed.

"I've missed you, Paul," she said. "Will I be seeing more of you now? While I'm here?"

"Sure," he said. "Yeah, I get down here sometimes."

At about eight o'clock the crowd thinned out a little bit. Mel and Brie took the baby home, giving Jack strict orders to sleep in the RV on the pullout if he had too much to drink with his boys. Paige had already gone upstairs to bathe Christopher and get him into bed and the general took his daughter home, promising to drop in the next night for a beer and a debrief on the hunt. Rick went home to his grandma's and promised to be back at 4:00 a.m. for the trek back into Trinity to hunt.

When it was down to Marines, the cards, money and cigars came out. Poker ensued. At about ten Paige swam through the smoke and tapped Preacher on the shoulder. He folded his hand, having nothing anyway, and said, "Be right back."

"God, it's weird, seeing Preach act like the little husband," Stephens said.

"Little husband?"

"You know what I'm saying. All Paige has to do is lift her pinkie finger and he's on his knees."

"How are your eyes, man? She can lift that little finger my way and I'd get on my knees," Joe said.

"The little husband might pound you into sand," Jack said.

"I meant if she weren't married. You old farts are starting to act real whipped."

"That's because we are," Jack said. "And it's good. It's very, very good."

Preacher came back, lifted his cigar and took a pull. "I'm not hunting tomorrow," he said. "I'm going to have to stay here."

"Why?"

"It's ovulation day," he said with a straight face.

"It's what?" three men asked in unison.

"It's frickin' ovulation day, jag-off. We're trying to make a baby and if I miss ovulation day, who knows how long I'll have to wait. I don't feel like waiting. I've been waiting."

His explanation was met with completely nonplussed silence—no one at the table knew about this quest, including Jack. And after a moment of stunned silence, laughter erupted that was so loud and wild, the men were nearly falling off their chairs.

When the group got a little under control, Preacher asked, "Is there something funny about ovulation day? Because I don't think it's funny."

"Nah, it's not funny, Preach," Joe said. "It's cute, that's what it is."

"But really, Preach, you should hunt and leave me home— I'd probably make a better-looking baby than you, anyway," Zeke said.

"You've made enough frickin' babies, jag-off," Preacher said. "Your wife sent you up here to hunt so she can catch a break. Whose deal is it anyway?"

While they dealt a few more hands, Jack noticed that Paul didn't seem to be laughing as much as the others, but he was drinking more. Paul folded his hand, left the game, poured himself a shot from the bottle on the bar and sat up on a stool. Jack had them deal him out and went behind the bar. Paul turned pinkened, watery eyes toward him. "Oh, boy," Jack said. "You're going to hate yourself."

"Don't I know it," he agreed with a slight slur, drinking another shot nonetheless.

"Want to tell me about it?"

"About what?"

"I'm thinking it has something to do with Vanessa," Jack said.

"Matt's my best friend. That would be wrong."

"What happened?"

"Nothing happened. For me, anyway." He put his empty glass on the bar.

Jack was sure Paul had already had too much, but he poured. "Okay, now I'm just taking advantage of you," Jack said. "Because I'm curious. She said you and Matt were together the night you met."

"Yeah. I should've stopped going out with him years ago. I spotted her first."

Jack kind of lifted his brows. "How'd he get her, then?"

Paul threw back his drink. "I think the son of a bitch said dibs." And then he put his head down on the bar and passed out.

So that's how it went. Because if Matt was the first one to get to her, talk to her, and if she was impressed enough to go out with him, a Marine doesn't mess with a brother's woman. Not even Valenzuela would do that. That was a line even he had never crossed—not his Mexican brothers and not his Marine brothers. Because he liked living....

Whoa, damn, Jack thought. And now she's married, pregnant and Paul is still miserably drawn to her. That bites.

"I'm going home," he said to the boys. "Back here at four. Someone has to put Haggerty to bed." He shrugged into his jacket. "Try not to burn the place down, huh?"

8

Mel had asked Brie to help with a pet project she'd been working on since David was born. While Brie was happy to help Mel in anything she asked, she was a bit surprised by how much she enjoyed this particular project.

While Mel had been at home with her newborn, she'd had time to go online on her laptop, plus she could make phone calls while he slept. The women in her town were mostly uninsured. They would pay whatever they could afford for medical care, often in goods and services. Some of the ranchers and farmers had insurance to cover catastrophic illness or accident, but that left nothing for the cost of well visits, like pap smears and mammograms. Mel had been able to step up the annual pap smears by offering to charge only for the lab costs, and by doing a little bit of hounding. But when it came to mammograms, which she believed her patients over the age of forty should have every year, most of her women were making do on breast self-exam. She had ninety-two women over the age of eighteen in town, and forty-eight of them were over forty. At least forty of those women were not getting annual mammograms.

She had tracked down a mobile unit that was operated by a foundation—and with the help of Dr. June Hudson in Grace Valley, they were trying to put together a visit from this unit to their towns. They could hold a mammogram event day, turn it into a party and get everyone x-rayed. "We can get them to come on the cheap, but we'll still have to come up with some money—probably more than most of my patients can afford," Mel had said.

June had had a perfect idea for subsidizing the cost. The fall festival in Grace Valley was coming up soon—the second weekend in October. They planned to set up a booth and sell homespun small-town items, from needlework to baked goods. There were lots of city folks who flocked to the festival looking for some of that small-town mystique. Mel's mission was to go around Virgin River, from farm to ranch to neighbors in town, requesting donated items they could sell at the mammogram booth.

Recruiting Brie was not only a great help, but fun for Mel to introduce her sister-in-law. On the days the Marines were off hunting, Mel and Brie drove the back roads of Virgin River, visiting all the women Mel knew—those who had attended her baby shower and parties at the bar, women who had been patients over the past year. Brie was meeting many of them for the first time and was instantly charmed by their welcoming natures, the way they drew her in as if she'd been around for years. Every stop they made involved at least a cup of coffee, usually cookies or thin slices of cake, so that by the time the day was drawing to a close, they were too stuffed to even think about dinner. And of course David was with them all day long, which amounted to a lot of cuddling all over town. Snuggling and sugar, since country women couldn't stand it if they couldn't put a cookie in his fat little hand.

The Virgin River women were fantastic—little surprise. They promised everything from pies to quilts—stock that would be picked up the day before the festival or brought to Grace Valley by the women themselves.

When they got back to town the hunters had returned and Mel was delighted to see no evidence of murdered wildlife in the truck beds or tied to roofs. But her elation was short-lived, because once inside the bar she learned that they had bagged two bucks, four-by-fours, both of which had already been taken to the meat processor to be butchered. "Oh," she whined emotionally. "Who did it?"

Jack looked at his feet. But he made an attempt. "I think Ricky did it."

Mel met Rick's eyes and the boy put up two hands, palms toward her. It wasn't him. Mel leaned against her husband and, unbelievably, started to cry. Jack shook his head, put an arm around her and led her away from the gathering, back toward the kitchen. As he did so, David was bouncing up and down on Mel's hip, waving his arms wildly and reaching for his dad. "Melinda," Jack said. "You knew we were going hunting. We didn't torture the deer. We're going to have venison."

"I hate it," she sniveled.

"I know you hate it, but it's not a cruel thing. It's probably more humane than the way cattle are slaughtered."

"Don't try to make me feel better about this."

"Jesus, I wouldn't dare," he said. "What's wrong with you?"

"I don't know," she whimpered. "I'm weepy."

"No shit. Here, let me have him. He's out of his mind."

"Sugar," she said. "I should go nurse him."

"He's going to be riding his bike up to the breast before long."

"He doesn't want to give it up."

"Understandable. But you're worn out. Maybe you should go home and go to bed."

"I don't sleep till he sleeps. And he isn't going to sleep until he detoxes."

"All right," Jack said, taking his son. "Go cry or wash your face or nap or something. I'll hang on to the wild one until he calms down a little." He kissed her forehead. "This really isn't like you. Not even over deer."

"By the way, you smell really bad," she said.

"Thank you, my love. You smell really good. I'll wash this off before I smell the rest of you, how's that?"

She let go of her son and went to the bathroom while Jack took David back to the gathering.

"Is she all right?" Brie asked.

"She'll be fine. She loves the deer."

"Want me to take him?"

"Nah, he's fine. He needs to work off your afternoon. Let me guess—you stopped at every farm and ranch in Virgin River and he's had fifty cookies."

"Maybe not fifty…"

He looked at his son's face. His eyes were wild, his smile bright and drooly, his arms flapping. "Someone should have been in charge," he said. "Have a beer, Brie. In fact, we should probably give this one a beer—he's electric. Jeez."

Just as he made that suggestion, Mike brought Brie a beer and when she took it, he draped an arm around her shoulders with familiarity. There was really no need for Mike to talk about her with him, Jack thought. He was working on celebrating her, as he had been instructed to do. But whatever was going on between Mike and Brie, it was putting a light in both their eyes. He was trying to relax about that.

"So—you make that baby today?" someone yelled at Preacher.

"I believe I did," he said, sticking his chest out.

Paige brought a big platter of wings out to the bar and said, "John, shut up."

"Well, I believe I did. Don't you?"

She looked up at him, shook her head in disgust and said, "You certainly did your best," and turned to walk back into the kitchen.

Mike pulled Brie aside and said, "You're the only woman on the premises who's not just a little pissed off at her guy. Wanna run away with me right now? Before I do something stupid?"

She grinned at him. "You think you're my guy, huh?"

"Well, that's what I'm hoping...."

A total of three deer were bagged, but no bear. The Marines left Virgin River, Ricky went back into active duty and the next weekend brought the Grace Valley fall festival. A sign was posted on the bar door—Closed. And below it a map, giving directions to Grace Valley.

Trucks, cars and SUVs were loaded with items for the mammogram booth. Mel, Brie and Jack left early with the baby and a truck packed with donations. They met Paige, Preacher and Christopher there to set up. Through the day, women from Virgin River arrived with even more wares to put out and everyone took their turn at working the booth—and items were disappearing like crazy. Mel didn't have to sit there the entire day, but she stayed close to keep an eye on their growing funds.

The day was filled with visiting old friends and meeting new.

By the time darkness was falling and the booths were mostly shut down, Mel was growing so tired she thought her very bones ached. They had absolutely nothing left to sell on Sunday. "I'll keep the banner and a donation jar out here tomorrow," June said. "Even if we get just a few dollars more, I'm sure we're close to what we need to bring the mammo RV out here."

"Are you sure you don't mind?" Mel asked. "I'm so shot."

"I have to be here anyway—we keep the clinic staffed during the fair. It won't be any trouble."

When the sun went down, the band set up behind the café and there was dancing and fireworks. The raffles were called out, and someone had rented a dunking booth that seemed to keep everyone in Grace Valley entertained as their local hotshots took their turns on the seat.

While Mel held David and watched the dancing, Jack came to her, slipped his arms around her and gave her a fairly decent twirl around the asphalt, baby and all. "Who would take you for a dancer," she said.

"That was barely dancing, but you're a good sport. You're exhausted," he whispered. "As soon as you're ready, we're heading home."

"It was a long day. Maybe we should find Brie."

"I found her," he said. "I'm trying to celebrate her...."

Mel followed his gaze and saw that on the other side of the asphalt dance floor, she was twirling around with Mike. "When did he show up?" she asked her husband.

"Just a little while ago. He stayed in Virgin River most of the day, looking after the town while so many people were here. I think he might have come for one reason only."

"That could work to our advantage," Mel said. "He might give her a ride home."

"I'll give her a few minutes, and ask," Jack said.

On the other side of the asphalt, Mike held Brie closer than necessary for a little country dancing, moving her around with more skill than she showed, making her laugh. And then to his pleasure, the pace of the music slowed and so did they. He tried not to, but he was helpless and lowered his face to her neck, taking in the intoxicating fragrance of her soft hair. "Ah, mija," he said against her neck. He kissed her cheek, her lips. She put her palms against his cheeks and pulled him closer, opening her mouth under his, sending him reeling with desire.

"Mike," she said softly. "I'm going home tomorrow."

He pulled back, stunned. He stared at her, a million questions in his eyes. "Were you going to say goodbye?" he asked.

"I am saying goodbye," she answered. "I have to spend some time with my family, and Mel and Jack need some family time—without a visitor."

"Will you be back?" he asked.

"Oh, I'm sure I will, eventually." She shrugged. "I don't know yet where I want to be. Or what I want to do."

"I had tricked myself into thinking it might be here," he said. "It was nothing you did or said, my love, just crazy hope. Is it all right that I call you while you're there? Maybe visit once or twice?"

"I'd be disappointed if you didn't. Hardly a day has gone by that we haven't talked."

He touched her hair. "You've gained such beautiful strength while you've been here. Your laugh is a little wilder, a little more alive. Your cheeks are flushed and charged with good health."

"A lot of that has been you. Your kisses. Your tenderness. I'll miss that."

"You know it will be right here, whenever you like. Before very long, I hope. In the meantime, if you want me to come to you, all you have to do is tell me."

Jack, holding his son in his arms, interrupted them. "I'm

going to take Mel home. Do you want to come later?" he asked his sister.

"No," she said, pulling out of Mike's arms. "I'll come with you. I'll be right there." As Jack walked away from her, she leaned forward and, up on her toes, kissed Mike's cheek. He held her waist for a long moment, his eyes closing. But then she pulled out of his embrace and said, "I'll miss you," and turned away from him to follow her brother.

"Not nearly as much as I'll miss you," he whispered to her departing back.

Jack woke a few mornings later to the sound of David's fussing, but instead of hearing his wife's usual cooing and cajoling as she took care of his early-morning needs, he heard a very different sound. A very unpleasant sound. Retching. He sat up, found his boxers on the floor and shrugged into them. He went to his son's room and lifted him out of the crib. "Morning, pardner," he said to his boy, hefting him onto the changing table to get off that all-night diaper. "Whew," he said as he removed it. "That's gotta be ten pounds of pee. I don't know how you do it." He gave David's bottom a wipe, diapered him and carried him to the bathroom doorway.

Mel was kneeling in front of the toilet holding her hair back with one hand.

With David on his hip, Jack wet a washcloth with the other hand, squeezing it out. He handed it to her. "Come on, Melinda. You can't avoid it forever. We both know you're pregnant."

"Ugh," she said, accepting the cool, wet cloth. She pressed it to her face, her brow, her neck. She didn't have any more to say.

But Jack knew. There had been tears, exhaustion, nausea. She turned watering eyes up to him. He shrugged and said,

"You eased up on the breast-feeding, popped an egg and I nailed it."

Her eyes narrowed as if to say she did not appreciate the explanation. He held out a hand to bring her to her feet. "You have to wean David," he said. "Your body can't completely nourish two children. You'll get weak. You're already exhausted."

"I don't want to be pregnant right now," she said. "I'm barely over being pregnant."

"I understand."

"No, you don't. Because you haven't ever been pregnant."

He thought this would probably be a bad time to tell her that he did so understand, since he had lived with a pregnant person and listened very attentively to every complaint. "We should go see John right away, so you can find out how pregnant."

"How long have you suspected?" she asked him.

"I don't know. A few weeks. It was a little tougher this time...."

"Oh, yeah?"

"Well, yeah. Since you haven't had a period since the first time I laid a hand on you. God, for a supposedly sterile woman, you certainly are fertile." Then he grinned, fully aware it would have got him smacked if he hadn't been holding the baby.

She whirled away from him and went to sit on their bed. She put her face in her hands and began to cry. Well, he'd been expecting exactly this. There'd been a lot of crying lately and he knew she was going to be mighty pissed off. He sat down beside her, put an arm around her and pulled her close. David patted her head. "It's going to be okay," he said. "I'm not delivering this one. I want that understood."

"Try not to be cute," she said through her tears. "I think my back already hurts."

"Can I get you something? Soda? Crackers? Arsenic?"

"Very funny." She turned her head to look at him. "Are you upset?"

He shook his head. "I'm sorry it happened so soon. Sorry for you. I know there are times you get damned uncomfortable and I wanted you to get a break."

"I should never have gone away with you."

"Nah. You were already pregnant. Wanna bet?"

"You knew before that?"

"I wondered why you were so emotional, and that was a possible reason. I never bought your whole sterile thing. But I don't have a problem with it. I wanted more kids. I like the idea of a larger family than the three of us. I come from a big family."

"There will not be five, I can guarantee you that," she said. Then she bored a hole through him with her eyes. "Snip, snip."

"You're not going to blame this on me, Mel. I suggested birth control. A couple of times, as a matter of fact. You were the one said it could never happen twice. And then explained that whole business about not ovulating while you're nursing. How's that working for you so far? Hmm?"

"Screw you," she said, not sweetly.

"Well, obviously…"

"I'd like you to understand I wasn't relying on that breast-feeding thing. I'm a midwife—I know that's not foolproof. I really didn't think it possible that… Shit," she said. She sighed deeply. "I just barely got back into my jeans…."

"Yeah, those jeans. Whoa, damn. Those jeans really do it to me. No one wears a pair of jeans like you do."

"Aren't you getting a little sick of having a fat wife?"

"You're not fat. You're perfect. I love your body, pregnant and unpregnant. I know you're trying to get me all worked up, but I'm not going there. You can try to pick a fight with me all day and I just won't play. It wouldn't be a fair fight— you're out to get me and we both know it. Do you have appointments this morning?"

"Why?"

"Because I want to go to Grace Valley for an ultrasound. I want to know when I have to have the house done."

All the way to Grace Valley, she ragged on him. She threatened him with dire consequences if he got all puffed up and studly about this. It was easy for him to take it in stride—exactly how many eight-pound babies had he pushed out? And if he joked about this even once, she was going to make him pay. Perhaps for life.

Jack had some premonitions. His patience was going to be severely tested for the next several months. He was not going to be having much sex. John Stone, her OB, was going to think this was hilarious. He might have to kill John.

"Well, Melinda, you little devil," John said, grinning.

She rested the back of her hand over her eyes while John and Jack studied the ultrasound, examining that little heartbeat in a barely moving mass. John pointed out small buds where arms and legs would be growing.

"When was your last period?" John asked her.

She took the hand off her eyes and glared at her husband. "Um, she hasn't exactly ever had one."

"Huh?" John said.

"That I know of," Jack said with a shrug.

"A year and a half ago, all right?" she said crisply. "Approximately. I've been nursing. I've been pregnant. I've been cast into hell and will live out my days with sore boobs and fat ankles."

"Whew. Going right for the mood swings, huh? Okay, looks like about eight weeks to me. That's an educated guess. I'm thinking mid to late May. How does that sound?"

"Oh, duckie," she answered.

"You'll have to excuse my wife," Jack said. "She was counting on still being infertile. This might cause her to finally give up that illusion."

"I told you if you made one joke—"

"Melinda," Jack said, his expression stern, "I was not joking."

"I would just like to know how this is possible!" she ranted. "David is like a miracle pregnancy, and before I even get him off the breast, I've got another one cooking."

"Ever hear the saying, pregnancy cures infertility?" John asked her.

"Yes!" she said, disgusted.

"You know what I'm talking about—probably better than me. I guess you didn't think it would apply to you, huh?"

"What are you talking about?" Jack asked John.

"A lot of conditions that cause infertility are made better by pregnancy—endometriosis being one. Often when you finally score that first miraculous conception, the rest follow more easily. And when you change partners, you change chemistry. You're going to want to keep these things in mind," he said. And he grinned. "You want to continue nursing?" John asked Mel.

She got tears in her eyes. "I wasn't quite ready to quit," she said.

"Mel was going to breast-feed right up to basic training," Jack said.

"I thought he'd be my only baby and I didn't want to rush

him," she said, a tear spilling over. She got a very pathetic look on her face.

On that note, Jack leaned down and scooped her up from behind, holding her. He had a unique sense for when it would work and when it would get him smacked. Right at that moment, she needed a little human contact, support from her man.

"Then how about let's evaluate your vitamin program, add some supplements and maybe you can get David down to a couple of meaningful feedings a day—the ones that comfort you and him most. You'd better add lots of water to your regimen—you have to keep the fetus in fluids, too." John grabbed her hand. "Easy does it, Mel. You're in good health, you had a very successful delivery and at one time you would have said this was the answer to your prayers. Try not to make Jack feel like shit."

That night, lying in her husband's arms, she asked, "Did I make you feel like shit?"

"Only a little bit. It's not like I tricked you. As I recall, you were an incredibly willing accomplice." He sighed. "Incredibly."

"I'm just in shock. Stunned. Not quite ready."

"I know. Do you have any idea how gorgeous you are pregnant? You shine. There's light around you. Your eyes are brighter, your cheeks rosy, you smile and feel your belly all the time—"

"You smile and feel my belly all the time...."

"I can't believe I'm getting all this," he said wistfully. "You and a couple of kids. A few years ago I thought I'd be alone the rest of my life."

"Do you know how old you're going to be when David graduates from college?"

"What's the difference? Does Sam look old to you? I think I can hang in there."

"Snip, snip," she said.

He rolled onto his back and looked at the ceiling. "Everyone around me is in a mood," he said.

"Is that so?"

"Well, there's Preacher—he's pretty prickly when it's not ovulation day, which you might have warned me about...."

"That would have been confidential."

"Well, not anymore. I think Paige might be a little put out that he told all the boys he was staying home to have sex."

"You think?" she asked, laughing in spite of herself.

"And Mike is past moody. I think that's because my sister isn't here—and believe me, I don't know how to take that. I want Brie to be happy. It would be nice to have Mike happy, but not if he's getting happy on Brie, if you get my drift. I'm celebrating, I'm celebrating," he said before she could scold him. "And this little surprise has had an effect on your mood, if you don't mind me saying so."

"I mind," she informed him.

"I just wish things would get back to normal," he said.

And Mel thought—when has anything been normal for us?

The notebook Jack had been using to make all his building calculations was getting worn and bent. He had been folding it in half to stuff into a back pocket while he worked on the house, and some of his numbers were wearing thin and faint. But he was attached to it and that was what he had out, along with his calculator and pen, while he was on the phone. He had pulled up a stool to the kitchen counter and gone down a list of general contractors, all highly recommended and all men whose work he had seen at one time or another.

Everyone, it seemed, was pretty busy. Booked.

He called Paul Haggerty in Grants Pass, Oregon. "I know this is a shot in the dark, Paul, but is there any way you can help me with this? I'm on a real deadline here and I can't find any general contractors or crews."

"What've you got?"

"Well, the house is framed, drywall is up, it's plumbed, wiring is mostly done, the roof is on—and Melinda has a bun in the oven."

"Whoa! How about that! Congratulations, my man!"

"Thanks, buddy—but she's very pissy. She needs a house."

"Gotcha. Let me make some calls, see what I can do. Maybe we can get this done for you before the weather turns."

"I'll pay overtime. I'll sell my soul."

Paul laughed. "Take it easy. I wouldn't take your soul—I'm pretty sure it's tarnished. Overtime might cut through some tight schedules, however."

"I'd sure appreciate it. I'll wait to hear from you."

When he hung up the phone, Preacher turned from his chore of chopping vegetables for his soup. "What's going on, man?" he asked.

"I have to get that house finished."

"Mel getting impatient?"

"No. Mel's got another one cooking."

"Oh?"

"She's pregnant again, Preach."

"Oh! Wow, that's great, man!" he said, sticking out his hand.

"Thanks. But just so you're warned, she's not too thrilled yet. Watch your step."

"Oh? Why not?"

"David's still a baby, and she feels like she just finished being pregnant. Plus she's moody, she's exhausted, she's puking and she thinks I did it to her on purpose."

"Ohhh," he said. "Okay. But you? You okay?"

"Hey." He grinned. "I'm great. I'd have five more. But I wouldn't live to tell about it."

"This ever make you feel... You know. Old?"

"Oh hell, no. Every time I get her pregnant, I feel about ten years younger. And if you tell her I said that, we're both gonna die."

"Okay then, we go easy with Mel. But hey. Good for you, man."

When police officers are assigned a new area or beat, one of the first things they do is get intimate with it. Learn all the roads, houses, vehicles and people. In the city, where the population is dense, it takes a while, but eventually every yard and alley, every building and business, every suspicious character becomes part of a familiar landscape.

In the country, in the mountains, there's a lot more ground to cover, an awful lot of back roads and hidden trails, but the people, buildings and vehicles are a little more sparse. Mike spent as much as a few hours every day driving and hiking the countryside surrounding Virgin River and the neighboring towns. He made frequent runs by the old rest stop, but nothing much seemed to have changed there—he'd expect to see a lot of trash if the place had been used recently for a party.

As he roamed closer to the countryside and mountains surrounding Clear River he saw a couple of structures he chose not to get too close to—one appeared to be a very small prefab house and the other a storage shed. Both had recent tire tracks leading to them—off-road vehicle tracks, probably quads or Jeeps. Neither was in plain sight, though it wasn't certain they were hidden in the trees and growth; it could be the owner's preference to be unobtrusive. But on the chance one or both were illegal grows, he kept his distance—sometimes such enterprises were booby-trapped. And besides wanting to know what was out there, this wasn't really his business. It was all just part of knowing the lay of the land, and it was lonely work.

There was a lot of interesting signage out this way. No Trespassing and No Hunting were pretty common, but now and then he'd see Trespassers Will Be Shot, Guard Dogs Patrolling and Hunters Will Be Hunted. They didn't sell such signs at the hardware store—they were hand stenciled or spray painted. One sign that said Firearms Prohibited In This Area was riddled with buckshot.

Quite often he ended up at the place he'd begun to think of as Whispering Rock, the place he'd shared with Brie last spring. He'd park his SUV upstream and walk along the riverbank. From time to time there'd be a fisherman or two, though the water here was too shallow for a good catch. He'd seen a young couple sharing a blanket on the ground, doing what appeared to be homework. When he'd walked into the clearing they'd looked up in surprise, maybe a little nervous by his sudden presence—so he'd smiled, waved and walked back upriver, leaving them alone.

He liked to be there in the late afternoon when the sun was shining. He could almost see Brie leaning against that big boulder, eyes drifting closed, smiling her secret smile. He stayed a little later than usual one day, through the setting of the sun. He'd just been thinking how nuts it was to do that without a flashlight when he heard a car engine. He assumed it would be young lovers, for this was not a place to be in the dark—there were no lights and it was far off the main road. Before he could be seen, he started up the river, back toward his vehicle. Something made him stop; the car had pulled into the clearing, the lights remained on, but he didn't hear the sound of a car door. He stood and just listened for a moment.

Young lovers would kill the lights. What other business was there at this isolated bend in the river, after dark?

He waited; the engine continued to run, the lights shone. Mike walked the short distance back to that spot, looked through the trees and saw the form of a single man inside the truck. Waiting. Now his curiosity was stirred and he watched.

It was probably ten minutes before a second vehicle pulled up to the clearing, another truck. The engines of both vehicles remained on, headlights illuminating the clearing, but when the second vehicle arrived, one man emerged from each truck.

Then it got interesting. From the first truck stepped Detective Delaney and from the second, a man Mike recognized as a well-known illegal grower. He was a big guy, just over six feet, and wore his signature Shady Brady hat. Over the past year Mike, Jack and Preacher had all had a little unexpected traffic with him. The first time was before Mike got to Virgin River—the man took Mel out to an illegal grow to deliver a baby. Most recently, the man showed them where to find Paige when her abusive ex-husband abducted her; it was very probable the guy had saved her life. He was an enigma—clearly a criminal, but apparently with a humanitarian side.

The men faced each other; Delaney leaned on the hood of his truck, and the grower kept his hands in his pockets. They didn't shake hands or greet each other as friends, and no money or goods changed hands—it was not a drug buy. In less than five minutes they got back into their respective trucks and left the area.

There were a number of possibilities, but the most likely was that Delaney had himself an informant inside the cannabis trade.

9

Paul Haggerty would help Jack anytime he could—that went without saying. It being a profitable venture for him as well made it even more palatable. But when he got right down to it, the deal maker was the fact that Vanessa was now residing in Virgin River.

He found six men who were ready to sign on immediately, so he had a contract drawn up for Jack and faxed it to the bar. Next he leased a large mobile home and had it delivered to the homesite, along with a portable toilet and commercial Dumpster for the grounds. His crew could drive down and sleep in the trailer during the week, going home weekends if they so chose. He'd haul his own small trailer for himself. He'd change out and add crews as progress was made on the house. Jack would have to double as a foreman because Paul couldn't stay in Virgin River all the time. He was leaving his dad and two brothers to run their construction company while he took on this project and he'd have to spend some time back in Grants Pass trying to pull his own weight.

While the structure was being completed, Paul would scout around the area for painters, carpet layers, tilers, paperhangers, cabinetmakers. Jack would have no trouble having light and plumbing fixtures and appliances installed, once Mel chose them. The house had been started last spring and great progress had been made, but alone, it would take Jack another year. Together, with crews, they might be able to finish it in a few months. If the weather didn't hamper them too much, by early spring at least.

And during that time he would see Vanessa. The idea threatened to give him hives. He loved being around her, went nuts with her effervescence and buoyancy. The problem was that he found her just as sexy and distracting pregnant as he had that very first night Matt put the moves on her. He wondered if he was just setting himself up for a lot of long, troubling nights of thinking about her and feeling sorry for himself because he would never, under pain of death, touch his friend's woman. He felt guilty that he even wanted to.

But this would be his secret, that he desired her, worshipped her. And while Matt was at war, Paul would look in on her from time to time, be sure she was holding up.

He and Matt were like brothers. They had gone to the same Oregon high school, had a couple of years of college together, joined up and went into the Corps together. But Matt was the one who was confident with the girls, while Paul had always been the reluctant one, a little shy. It was hard for him to make that first move; he'd always had to think it through for a long time before he could work up to approaching a woman.

He'd overcome a lot of that by now, but not enough. He'd never have the speed, finesse and confidence of his best friend.

He remembered that night just a few years ago as if it was yesterday. Matt was on leave and they met in San Francisco to do the town. They were out drinking when they spotted a group of flight attendants on layover at one of the bars. Paul had said, "Oh, my God, would you look at that! Would you look at her!"

"Which one?" Matt asked.

"The leggy one with the red hair and gold skin. I'm going to pass out."

"I'll go get her for you."

"No! God, don't do that. Wait till I figure out something...."

And Matt grinned and said, "Three, two, one... I'm gone."

But he didn't bring her back. Instead, he waved Paul over and tried to hook him up with one of Vanessa's friends. And Paul went along with it, because what else was he going to do? If he'd had an ounce of courage he would've said, "Stop! I saw her first! She's mine!" To this day, he regretted that.

Before that weekend was over, Matt and Vanessa were in love. Since she had airline travel privileges and he was stateside, she spent every weekend with him for a year. A year after that Paul was best man at their wedding. He swore if he ever again saw a woman he was that drawn to, he would tackle her on the spot, probably knocking her off her feet, and never let her get away.

As far as he could remember, that hadn't ever happened to him before. And it sure hadn't happened since.

When Paul got to Virgin River he went directly to the job site to be sure everything was in place. The trailer had made it just fine and stood ready for his crews. His best supervisor, Manny, would be bringing materials on the big truck and the others would follow. He unhooked his fifth wheel, leaving it at the site, and drove his truck to the Booth household. When he pulled in, he immediately had second thoughts—he should have called her. But wouldn't calling her indicate that she had some play in his coming here, doing this for Jack? That wouldn't be good. So he just knocked on the door.

Walt answered, his glasses pushed up on his head and his newspaper in his hand. "Paul! Damn, boy! What are you doing here?"

"I'm here on a job, sir," he said, laughing. "We're going to have to keep it on the downlow for now—I don't think it's out yet."

"That so?" he asked, pushing open the door. "Come in, come in! You can tell us all about it. Vanessa! You won't believe this!"

Paul stepped into the foyer of the house and looked around appreciatively. It wasn't much from the outside—just a long, narrow ranch. But inside it was spacious with vaulted ceilings and lots of windows facing the stable and corral so they could watch their horses from the house. It looked as though the general had probably gutted it and had it completely remodeled. The foyer opened up into a great room with an impressive fireplace and lots of soft leather furniture. As Paul stepped into that room he saw that the dining room was to his right and he leaned slightly to peek into a huge modern kitchen. Down the hall, he assumed, were bedrooms. Out the greatroom windows he could see horses in the pasture, the new stable and a view of the mountains and river. It wasn't hard to tell why the general had chosen this place. He was a hunter, fisherman and sportsman who loved his horses.

Out back, a foot up on the corral fence, looking at the horses, was a young man. That would be Tommy. He couldn't wait to get a closer look at the kid. At the wedding a couple of years ago he'd really enjoyed his sense of humor. He was an intelligent, handsome teen who was funny but with the kind of careful manners that would come from being raised in a strict household, by an Army general's firm hand.

Vanessa came down the hall toward him. Her face lit up in pleased surprise. "Oh, my God!" she said, grinning widely. "What are you doing back here so soon?"

"Well, I'll tell you in a minute. How are you? You look fantastic!"

"I'm starting to get really fat," she laughed.

"You look perfect. I think you're more beautiful than ever. Are you taking lots of pictures for Matt?"

"Every week I have Dad take a new picture of my belly. Time-lapse photography."

"That's great."

"How about a beer, Paul?" Walt asked.

"Sure, why not? Is that Tommy out there?"

"Yeah. He's having a bad day. Let me get that beer. Go sit down."

"Come on," Vanessa said, taking his hand and pulling him into the great room. She led him to an overstuffed chair with an ottoman near the windows that overlooked the corral.

Before Paul even got comfortable in the chair opposite Vanessa, the general appeared with a cold beer poured in a tall glass. He had one for himself as well and said, "Vanni, I didn't get you anything, honey. I didn't even think."

"No problem, Dad. I'll go get some water in a minute. Boy, doesn't that beer look good! I have to admit—I can't wait."

The general was at least six feet tall, broad shouldered and silver haired, with black brows, square face, about sixty years old; he had had a magnificent Army career that spanned over thirty-five years. A few years ago his wife had died, and when that happened he wrapped it up with the Army. Without that great partner of his—a woman lauded often but whom Paul had never met—he wasn't interested in any more military challenges.

"What's up with Tommy?" Paul asked, taking a drink of his beer.

"Aw, teenagers," the general said. "He's hanging with this kid I just don't like. He got himself in a little trouble—went out to some forbidden kegger in the woods. I found out there's been a little beer after school and noticed his grades slipping in a couple of his classes. And I think it's this one kid."

"That's not all of it. Dad doesn't like his face."

"Huh?" Paul asked.

The general shook his head. "This kid, he's got that shifty look, that manipulative little grin. I mean, we were all seventeen, right? Had a couple of beers, drove our cars too fast, tried to pick up girls? Huh? But this one's different. I think he's a little fucker, and I don't want him fucking with my kid. Sorry, Vanni."

She laughed. "Well, that's the first time I've ever heard those provocative words."

"I can just tell," the general said.

Paul thought, he probably just can. The general had spent an awful lot of years looking at the faces of young soldiers and he'd learned to read them pretty well. He kind of nodded to the general. "So? You ground him or something?"

"Yeah, he's grounded, but I told him I want him to make better friends, because if he lies to me again, he's history. I'll send him to another school—a private school. I thought this place would be quiet—the kids would be docile. I think they're wilder than the city kids. At least, this one he's been running with. This kid's a bad influence. Now, never mind our family troubles—what are you doing here?"

Paul looked at Vanni and said, "I told your dad we have to

keep this quiet until I understand how much of this is out—but I'm here to help Jack finish his house. I rounded up a crew, installed a trailer out on his homesite and we're going to try to get it done as quickly as possible. Because your midwife is pregnant—they need more room."

"Really? Wow."

"My intel says she's very annoyed by this development—she wasn't quite ready for another one yet. So Jack, being the Prince Charming of a husband he is, is paying all my boys overtime to get that house finished."

"Aw. That's sweet. Are you saying the pregnancy hasn't been announced?"

"I'm not sure, but I don't want to be the one to announce it. So let's not say anything. And I don't know if she knows what Jack has done."

"But where are you staying while you're in town?" she asked. "Won't she wonder why you're here?"

"Oh, I'm sure Jack's going to tell her about my crew real quick because, as I understand it, she goes out to the site fairly often just to look around. She's going to notice the people, the trailer—and I brought down my fifth wheel."

"No!" she said. "Stay here! With us!"

"Absolutely," the general said. "We have lots of room."

"I couldn't do that," he protested. "I'll be coming and going, my hours will be weird, I'm sure I'll spend some time with Jack and Preacher in town...."

"Who cares about that? Come and go as you like! We'll just fix you up with a key." She laughed. "Not that anyone remembers to lock a door around here."

"I'm going to have to commute—I left my brothers with the company in Grants Pass. I'll be going back and forth, but honestly, it's going to be—"

"I can't stand to think of you in a fifth wheel for weeks—

and I don't care what kind of hours you keep!" Vanessa protested.

"To tell you the truth, Paul, I could use a hand," Walt said. "I'm making a run down to Bodega Bay almost every week for a couple of days. Every other week at least. Do you remember Vanessa's cousin Shelby, from the wedding?"

"Of course," he said, sitting up straighter.

"Her mother, my sister...she's disabled. Bedridden now."

"I'm sorry, sir—I had forgotten. ALS, isn't it?"

"That's right. Frankly, none of us expected her to last this long, but she's still with us. The bravest soul I've ever known. But since I can't convince Shelby she'd be just as well off in a nursing home, I go as often as I can. To help, to visit. To offer moral support. Vanni goes now and then, as well. It sure would ease my mind if there were someone around here to keep an eye on things when I have to be gone."

"Keep an eye on Tom, he means," Vanessa said. Then she grinned. "I'm sure he'd prefer your mothering to mine."

"Any way I can help, sir," Paul said. "I'm awful sorry about your sister."

"Thank you—she's not in any pain. The hardest part about this is that my niece has taken it on, full-time, and she's just a girl."

"Shelby's doing exactly what she wants to do," Vanessa said. "She's very stubborn about it. If it were my mother, I'd do the same as my cousin."

"I'm sure we can work out our schedules, General," Paul said. "If you make your trip down the coast while I'm working on the house and not back in Oregon, I'd be glad to hang around here. Make sure no one's going wild." He smiled, but inside his pulse picked up a bit. Being under Vanessa's roof while her father was away wasn't going to do much for sleeping soundly.

"You're a good man, Paul," Walt said.

Paul thought, if I were a good man, I wouldn't be having these thoughts, these feelings.

Jack showed up at Doc's at about eleven in the morning and found Mel at the computer, David in his playpen not far away. "Hey," he said. "What's going on?"

"Not so much," she said. "I'm scheduling our mammogram unit to visit town. What's going on with you?"

"I have something to show you—if you can take a break."

"What?"

"Can't you be surprised?"

"I'm so bad at surprises," she said.

"Yeah. I know. You should work on that. Where's Doc?"

"He's around here somewhere."

"Well, find him and tell him you're stepping out. I'll get David. Let's take a ride. I think you're going to like this."

"Jack," she said, standing up, "I hate when you do this."

"I haven't given you one bad surprise yet," he said, lifting his son out of the playpen. When she glared at him he said, "I haven't! I make excellent babies and if you're surprised, I think that's your fault!"

"Yeah, you don't have to rub my nose in it."

It took Mel only a few minutes to get herself together, find Doc to excuse herself, grab her medical bag, which went with her everywhere, and shrug into her coat. Jack put David in his car seat—he was delighted to be going somewhere. Anywhere.

When they were turning off the road onto the drive that had become her drive, to her new home, she got a little keyed up. Happy, if you dared. "What's going on?" she asked.

"Wait till you see. You're going to like this. You're going to like me again."

"I love you—I'm just not thrilled about how potent you seem to be."

As Jack pulled up to the top of the hill, coming through the trees, she sat up straighter when she saw all the activity around the house. It was a full-fledged construction site, complete with trailers, vehicles, portable toilet, men at work. Right in front of the largest trailer, wearing a hard hat, she recognized Paul.

"What's going on?" she asked again.

"We're getting your house done, Melinda. Paul brought a crew down from Oregon and we're finishing up. We're going to have to go over to Eureka to pick out our fixtures, paint, carpet, tile, cabinets. It's going to go fast now."

"Jack," she said in a breath, turning toward him. She put her hand over his.

"We're going to get you in and settled before the baby. I'm going to do everything I can to make this easy for you." He shrugged. "If I could carry the baby for you, I would." He grinned. "Thank God I can't. But after this little one is born, I'm going to do whatever I have to do to be sure you have time to enjoy your kids. We'll try my method of birth control instead of yours next time. I miss your joy. Your smile."

"I smile," she protested.

"You've been pretty cranky."

"Jack, I'm sorry, darling. It's not you.... It's me. I feel like an idiot. I feel like one of those teenage girls who come to me already five months pregnant without a clue because they didn't want it to be so. It's pretty embarrassing, given my profession. I really, really thought David was a miracle, and the only miracle I'd have. People like me shouldn't have that kind of denial. I don't know what possessed me...."

"Do you have any idea how much I love you? Mel, I'd

never do anything to hurt you, make you uncomfortable." He smiled. "I just can't keep my hands off you."

"I know, Jack," she said. "The hell of it is, I can't resist you."

"So—the only problem we have is that you're way more fertile than you thought. We can work with that. Kiss me."

She leaned over to him and put a hand around the back of his neck, pulling him against her mouth, which she opened passionately, treating him to one of her lustiest kisses. He put his arms around her and moaned appreciatively. Kiss at an end, he said, "Now, that's what I'm talking about. You just taste so good. Come on, let's go see what Paul's got going on."

Mel got out while Jack pulled David out of his car seat. The second Paul saw them getting out of the truck, he came to them, opening his arms to Mel, hugging her close. "What do you think? Your man make you happy today?"

"I can't believe it—this is wonderful of you!"

"Nah, I'm not wonderful—he's paying through the nose. But it's going to be beautiful, Mel. I guarantee it. You have work to do, too—you have to appliance and accessory shop right away. Some things take a long time to be delivered."

"We'll get right on it. Will you stay with us while you're here?"

"I've had nothing but offers, and I've got my trailer. Which, believe it or not, I happen to like. I think when I'm not out here with the boys or back in Grants Pass, I'll be spending some time at the general's house."

"Well, that's perfect," she said. "We'll pick a night this week to have you, Vanessa and her family and all your guys for dinner at the bar. Right, Jack?"

"You got it. Anything you want."

She grinned. "I like it when he says that. Did he happen to tell you the news?"

"What news?" Paul asked dumbly.

She gave him a playful whack on the arm. "Stop it—I know you know. It's why you're here."

He put an arm around her shoulders. "If I know, it's because you're glowing. Again."

"I'm not so sure about that," she said. "I'm pea-green until about nine in the morning."

"Right after which, she glows," Jack agreed.

"Nothing more beautiful than a pregnant woman," Paul said.

"Oh, brother," she said.

"You do good work," Paul said to Jack.

"Yeah… And if I ever find out who gave her those shoes…" Jack added with a laugh, which earned him a dirty look that amused both men beyond good sense.

The mammogram RV showed up in Virgin River on a Monday morning and was set up in Doc's clinic. All the women Mel had contacted came in early in a big crowd, some dragging kids along and all bearing food and drink. They gathered in the waiting room and held an all-day party, leaving one at a time for their mammograms. It was a long, exhausting and fulfilling day for Mel, and for Doc, too—if you looked closely enough his grimace almost looked like a smile.

The next day the truck went to Grace Valley to June Hudson's clinic, where mammograms were provided for those women over forty and younger women who were at a high risk for breast cancer.

The following day was appointment day and Mel had three prenatals—the third being Vanessa Rutledge.

Mel wasn't surprised her first two patients favored home births even though a hospital and epidural were available to them—they came from rural families that had been having home births for generations. But the one who really surprised her was Vanessa, who was by all accounts a city girl. She planned to have her baby in her father's house, naturally. "Just three months to go," Mel told her. "And you're in absolutely perfect health. Now, how about a little trip to Grace Valley for an ultrasound? We should be sure right now that we don't have any obvious complications. Do you want to know the sex of the baby?"

"That would be great—then I can tell Matt. He feels so left out."

"How about next week?"

"There isn't anything on my schedule," she said with a shrug.

"It must be hard, having him so far away when you're pregnant."

"It is, but this seems to be the history in the Booth family. My dad wasn't around for either me or my brother's births. The military can really screw up the best of plans."

"I don't know how you do it," she said.

"Wasn't Jack in the Marine Corps for twenty?" Vanessa asked.

"A little over twenty—but I didn't find him until recently. I came up here from L.A. to work with Doc Mullins when I met and married Jack. He was already retired."

"And you had a baby right away!"

"Boy, howdy," Mel said. She touched her still-flat tummy. "And guess what? He got me again." She shook her head. "I'm going to have to put him in that little guesthouse out back."

Vanessa laughed at her. "Listen, there's something pretty special going on at our house tomorrow night—and we'd like you and Jack, Preacher, Paige and Mike to all be there if possible. Of course, Paul will be there, too. My dad got us signed up for some kind of program called 'Voices From Home.' We're going to get an Internet call from Matt—real

time, video cam from Baghdad. We'll make a party of it—
and after we all get a chance to talk, we'll have a big dinner.
Can you come?"

"Vanessa," she said, touching her hand, "don't you want
him all to yourself?"

"There's a part of me that does, but I'm thinking of Matt—
he's all the way over there and right here are some of his favorite people. You have no idea how much he talked about
Jack, Preacher and Mike. And it will be almost as big a deal
for him to talk to Paul as to me. I'm going to walk across the
street right after leaving here to ask the boys. Say you'll come."

"Are you absolutely sure, honey? Because it's understandable if you—"

"I'm sure! I just wish I knew the sex of the baby for that
video conference. That would really top it off."

Mel smiled. "Well, girlfriend, I can hook you up. I have
some connections. Can you drive over today or tomorrow
morning?"

Her face lit up. "I can! Can you really make that happen?"

"You bet. It's the least we can do for you."

On the day of the video conference with Matt, Tommy was
on his way to his truck in the high school parking lot when
Jordan snagged his arm. "Hey, man, where you been?"

"I've been around," he said, not very happily. He'd been
avoiding Jordan. After what Brenda had said about those rest-
stop parties, he'd been curious. So he'd dropped in on one
when she had other plans with a girlfriend. It was, as she had
said, pretty out of control. There weren't too many kids and
the weather was cold, but stuff had been going on that he
didn't like. Jordan and his buddy seemed to be taking kids
away from the crowd briefly; he couldn't see what was happening, but they weren't gone long enough to smoke a joint and

there was a little too much delight in their expressions when they returned. He suspected some kind of score. Ecstasy, he thought. Or something a little more high-powered, like meth.

Tommy had a beer, headed for home...and his dad had waited up for him, smelled his breath. And he was in trouble.

"I haven't seen you. Wanna come by the house? We got beer, we got fun times."

"Nah, I'm not into that."

"Since when?"

"Since I took a run out to your little party at the rest stop and got into trouble with my old man. I gotta go—I got something going on."

"What is your deal? You cut me off like that without saying anything? I know a girl I want you to meet."

"I have a girl, Jordan. I have to go."

"Wait a minute. What girl?"

"I've been seeing someone. A junior. Girl named Brenda. We've been out. And stuff."

"Brenda? Carpenter?" he said, his eyes lighting up. "Yeah, I know Brenda." He waved his hand in front of his face as if to cool a sudden fever. "I know Brenda real good. Real, real good."

Tommy's expression closed off. Dark. "No, you don't."

"Yeah." He laughed. "Oh, yeah. She's a hottie. A real hottie."

Tom went instantly unconscious. Brain dead. Steam started to pour out of his ears. He moved on Jordan, getting in his face. "What are you talking about?"

"Nothing, man. It was a long time ago. No big deal. We partied together a little bit."

Tommy grabbed him by the shirtfront. "No. You didn't."

"Okay." He laughed again. "Whatever you say."

Tommy drew back and landed a blow to his face, knocking

him down. But Jordan sprang right back up and delivered his own blow, surprisingly hard for the skinny runt he was. And it was game on. They were hitting, rolling around, crunching, swearing—and then they were pulled apart by two teachers.

In the principal's office Tommy admitted immediately what had set him off and Jordan confessed as fast that he'd just been mouthing off and it wasn't true. That was one thing about the country as opposed to the city—they kind of expected you to handle something like that with a punch or two. The principal said to Jordan, "Sounds like you were just asking for it, son. If you'd said that to me about my girl, I'd have given you a lot worse than what you got. Now I want you boys to stay away from each other, because if this happens again, you're both suspended."

The problem was, it took a long time to get to that point and Tommy wanted to get home. He didn't want to miss a chance to talk to Matt.

There was a definite air of excitement at the Booth household as the hour for the contact through the Internet approached. The general had moved the computer into the living room with a camera installed above the screen. For this special night he had purchased a larger, flat-screen monitor, as an image of Matt's face would be projected onto the screen, just as the faces of the people who talked to him would be videoed to him for the conference. Vanessa was running around nervously, worrying about her hair and makeup, while Jack and Mike went immediately to the kitchen to help the general serve up drinks and hors d'oeuvres. Jack's bar had been closed for this event and Paige and Mel spent all their time trying to reassure Vanessa that she'd never been more beautiful. Preacher held Christopher on his lap, keeping him under control at this gathering while David slept peacefully in the playpen in a bedroom down the hall.

As the time for the contact approached and the general got the computer online, tension rose about tenfold in the house. Long, stressful minutes passed as the time for the video conference came and went. And then, suddenly, a voice rang out in the room. "Hey! Anybody home?"

Vanessa rushed forward. She was momentarily speechless, staring at the face of her husband on the screen. Her hand reached out toward him.

"Hey!" he said again. "Vanni? You there?"

"Matt," she said, too softly. Then, turning on the camera and pulling herself up internally, louder, "Matt! Darling!"

"Aw, Vanni—look at you! Let me see it—your belly."

She turned sideways in front of the small camera.

"Whoa, Vanni! You're getting big! You're growing me a great big baby!"

"Matt, I have so many surprises for you. First of all, I just found out this morning, it's a boy. A son, Matt!"

There was deafening quiet. "Aw, Vanni!" he said in an emotional breath. "I love you, baby. I love you so much."

"I love you, Matt! Are you okay? Is everything okay?"

"Fine, Vanni, it's all good. We're working hard, but that's what we came here for. It won't be too much longer. You're beautiful, baby."

"Have you lost weight?" she asked him.

He laughed. "Baby, everyone loses weight over here. I don't think I'm going to have any trouble putting it back on. I just can't wait to hold you."

"Me, too, Matt. By the time you get home, you can hold both of us. You should be thinking of a name, okay?"

"I will. How are you doing there? You feeling okay?"

"I feel great, darling. And I have more surprises for you. Guess who's here. Jack, Preacher, Mike—come over here!"

One at a time they put their faces in the line of the camera. "Hoo-rah," Jack said, grinning. He was joined quickly by the other two men. Preacher scowled into the camera and said, "What's up, Marine?" Mike smiled and said, "Buy you a beer when you get back, buddy."

"Oh, man!" Matt said, laughing, slapping his forehead in surprise. "Damn me, you boys look good! You must not have to work for a living, you look so good! God, I'm glad Vanni's there—I told her she'd love it there! How's the general doing? You looking out for him?"

Walt pushed his way in. "Who says I need looking out for?"

"Hey, man! How you doing, sir? You watching over your grandbaby?"

"By the time you get home, I'll have him standing at attention!"

Matt laughed, clearly enjoying the small reunion. "Tommy around?" Matt asked.

"I'm afraid he's late, Matt. I can't imagine why—he's been looking forward to this. There's someone else here," Walt said, pulling Paul into the frame.

"Haggerty! What the hell? What are you doing there?" Matt asked.

"I'm finishing up Jack's new house for him. He's got a kid and another one on the way...."

"Jack's got a kid?"

"Yeah, can you think of anything crazier? He needed some help. How's it going over there, bud?"

"Aw, it sucks. Big surprise, huh?"

"You making any progress?"

"Slow, miserable progress. You going to be around there a while?"

"Couple of months maybe, on and off. But I'm never very far away, you know that. When you get back here, I'll just come—"

"Hey, Paul… Buddy… Listen, if anything happens…"

"We don't talk that way, come on."

"Paul, if anything goes wrong, you look after Vanni, huh? I think she always liked you best anyway." Then he laughed. "We're going to kick some ass here, don't you worry."

"I'm not worried. Hey, we don't want to steal this time from your wife. We're going to step out, leave the two of you alone, okay?"

"Thanks, buddy. Paul? Buddy? Hey, you know I love you, man."

"Hoo-rah," Paul said. "You hang in there. Give 'em hell! Vanni—get back here," Paul said.

And like an exodus, everyone left the great room for the kitchen so that Vanessa and Matt could have what was left of the air time alone. From the kitchen they could hear the voices in the background. Walt quietly passed out drinks while they whispered. "He looks good," Jack said.

"For a jarhead," the general joked. "Tommy was supposed to be here. Late again." Then to Mel he said, "That was perfect, what you did. Getting the ultrasound before this video conference."

"They didn't have anything like this when I served," Preacher said. "This is good, this Internet conference. Too bad they can't talk every day or every week." He draped an arm around Paige's shoulders, pulling her near. Clearly he wouldn't be able to bear being away from her, separated like Matt and Vanessa.

After a few minutes had passed, there were no more voices coming from the other room. Paul had seemed to be on alert and it was he who first poked his head around the corner. The screen was dark and Vanessa sat in front of it with her head lowered to her folded arms, crying.

Paul approached her. "Vanni, come on, Vanni," he said, down on one knee, his arms enfolding her. She turned in his arms and with her head on his shoulder, she just wept. "Oh, honey, that was hard, wasn't it? But he's okay—you saw that! He's tough, Vanni. He's going to be fine. He'll be home before you know it."

She lifted her head and met Paul's eyes. "At least I held it together while he was online," she said.

"Yeah, you did good. Come on," he said, pulling her to her feet. "Let's get your face washed. I don't want you all upset. We don't want to get the little critter upset. Come on," he said, arm around her shoulders, leading her away from the computer, down the hall toward the bathroom.

Walt was the next one out of the kitchen. "It's probably going to take her a few minutes," he said. "I knew the whole thing would be good and bad all at the same time. But with all of you here, she'll come around quicker, enjoy herself, have some good feelings just from seeing him again, seeing he's okay."

The front door crashed open and Tommy rushed in. "Did I make it?" he asked, eyeing the gathering.

"You missed it, son. Where've you been?"

"Aw, man, I'm sorry, Dad. I tried to get back…."

Walt walked toward his son, frowning. The boy was as tall as his dad, though leaner. He had a split lip and some dirt on his clothes. "What's this? You've been fighting?"

"Not really," Tommy said. "Maybe a little bit. Dad, I'm sorry I missed him. I'll explain later, but I promise, I'm not going to let you down again. I promise."

"Just tell me one thing—did this have anything to do with Jordan Whitley?"

Tommy grinned. "Yeah. And he looks worse than me. I'm through with him, Dad. Honest."

"Well, that's something, I guess."

Paul was spending a few nights at the general's house following the video conference while Walt was in Bodega Bay, and he decided to do little big-brothering. He found Tommy in the stable, mucking the stalls. "Hey, pal," he said. "How's it going?"

"Okay. What's up?"

"I'm staying out of the kitchen. Believe me, Vanessa doesn't want my attempts at food preparation. I was wondering something…"

"Yeah?"

"I don't want to pry, so you tell me if it's none of my business. You having any trouble at school?"

"Like…?"

"Like the kind that gets you into fights?"

"Oh, that. What did my dad tell you?"

Paul shrugged. "He said you were hanging with a guy he didn't like. That's all I know."

"The second he saw him, it was instant hate, and I don't have that one figured out yet. I don't know how you can take one look at a guy and know he's an asshole."

"Well, the general has looked at a lot of young guys over the years. Did he turn out to be right?"

"Yeah," Tommy said with a grin, then touched his split lip in sudden pain. "Don't tell him I said that. He already thinks he knows everything."

Paul returned the grin. "Your secret's safe with me, pal. How'd you get hooked up with him?"

"New-kid syndrome," Tommy said, leaning his shovel against the wall of the stall. "I got here too late in the summer for football and didn't have anything better to do. I thought he was a little weird, but you know—he always managed to have a couple of beers or a place lined up for a party." He shrugged. "You know how it goes."

"I guess," Paul said, though his senior year had been pretty tame. "So what kind of an asshole did he turn out to be?"

"The usual kind. He's a liar. Likes to brag about the girls he's nailed."

"Lot of that going around the locker room."

"I always learned a real man doesn't brag about it. Plus, I don't have anything to brag about."

"No shame in that, Tommy. This is a good time to be real careful, if you know what I mean."

"I know exactly what you mean, Paul," he said, smiling more cautiously. "Don't worry. My dad has had this talk with me a hundred or so times. But Jordan really pissed me off good—he was talking about a girl I've been dating. I've only been out with her a few times, and there's school and home-work at her house, and she's a nice girl. A good girl, you know? She moves real, real slow. The way that asshole talked, it was like he was saying he'd done her. There's no way he'd even get to hold her hand. I had to slug him. You know?"

"Whew," Paul said. "You finished with him now?"

"Oh, yeah. Every time I see his face, I just want to mess it up."

"How's it going with the girl?"

"It's good. You should see her—she's beautiful. And you would never believe how smart she is. I think she kind of likes me."

"Who wouldn't?"

"Surprises the hell out of me," Tom said, glancing away.

Paul laughed at his modesty. He was already six feet tall with some good-sized shoulders and arms on him from playing sports and taking care of a stable and four horses every day. Tossing around heavy bales of hay was better than lifting weights. "Hey, you have any time on your hands? Any need to make money?"

"I could always use a little money."

"Yeah, if you're gonna date beautiful girls, you need money." Paul laughed again. "There's work out at the job site, if you're interested. It's dirty and it's hard—clean up around the site. But Jack's paying overtime. I could give you a few hours after school or on weekends."

"I'll take it," Tom said, smiling.

10

Brie's routine in Sacramento lacked challenge, but she still had no desire to go back to the prosecutor's office. All she did was exercise every morning, clean up her dad's house and cook dinner for the two of them. She read when she was relaxed and could focus—not law text or nonfiction, but escapist novels. Finally there were a few places around town she was comfortable going to—if only in the light of day. She felt safe at the grocery store and the women's gym, but not the library; those narrow aisles of tightly packed books gave her claustrophobia. So she bought her books online and had them delivered. There was still enough anxiety in her that she even varied the time of morning she went to the gym for her workout, conscious that criminals who watched their victims studied their habits to use against them.

She went to her sisters' homes and sometimes the girls would come to Sam's. Sunday dinners with the whole family at Sam's were pretty typical. Everyone had noticed that even if Brie's routine hadn't changed much, her mood had. She was lighter of spirit; she smiled and laughed more easily.

"I think Virgin River gets you right," her oldest sister, Donna, observed. "This isn't the first time you've gone there after a crisis and come home better."

"It's not the town," she admitted. "And it's not Jack." When she'd gone to Virgin River after the trial and David's birth, she'd been empty inside. Hollow. A brand-new divorcée having just lost the biggest trial of her career, she'd felt as if she was nothing. A zero, a nonperson; a woman who couldn't hold her man, a lawyer who couldn't win her case. But a picnic, a little wedding dancing, some flirting, and she'd begun to feel female again. Then the rape had set her back a year; she was broken in a million pieces. But some phone calls and lunches, some strong arms around her and lips on hers, and she'd started to feel like a woman. In fact, that was the only place she felt like a woman and not a victim—in his arms.

Since being back in Sacramento Brie had seen Mike only twice in several weeks—Santa Rosa lunches, holding hands across the table. There were long, deep, wonderful kisses at parting. She talked to him almost every evening, taking the call in her room, and for about an hour they would share the events of the day. He caught her up on all the news, from the video conference at the general's to who'd been at Jack's for dinner. She was amazed by how hungry she was for every tiny piece of information about that little town.

Then as the conversation would draw near its end, their voices would grow lower and softer and their words more intense. "I miss you, mija," he would say, his voice husky. "I can't wait until you threaten me with a broken heart again. I think you're all talk and you've lost interest in my heart."

And she would say, "Not at all—breaking your heart is still a huge priority with me. I'll be back."

"Not soon enough."

"I miss your kisses," she told him.

And he said, "Te tengo en mis brazos." I will hold you in my arms. "Te querido más te de lo tu hubieras." I have wanted you for longer than you know. "I will kiss you as much as you allow," he translated incorrectly. It sent shivers through her.

November arrived, bringing crisp days and cold nights to the Sacramento valley, and she heard on the news that snow had fallen in the mountains. The pass from Red Bluff through the Trinity Alps to Virgin River could be closed now and any trip made to that part of the country would have to go from Sacramento to Ukiah and up the Mendocino valley. Just as well—highway 36 was treacherous and slow even in the best weather, but it was spectacular. Brie spent a lot of time thinking about which route she would take when she eventually decided it was time to return to Virgin River.

She told her sisters about him, but only one at a time, and sometimes in hushed tones that she knew became a little breathless. "He speaks to me in Spanish, in low, sexy Spanish, and then he lies about what he's said, thinking I don't know."

"What does he say?" Jeannie asked her.

"He'll say something like, 'I want to hold you and make love to you,' and pretends he has said he would like to kiss me."

"Do you think you can have this in your life again? Intimacy of that kind? Are you ready for that?"

"I'm very nervous, but I long for it," she said. "I want him."

"You trust him enough?"

"When I'm with him, I feel completely safe. Nurtured. Protected. He doesn't hurry me—he's very kind. Very cautious.

He's the only kind of man I could deal with right now, and he knows that." She shivered and said in a low breath, "But there's a fire in him. I can feel it." She took a deep breath.

She'd been home from Virgin River for a month and was beginning to think in terms of going back after the holidays. But then Brad came to see her with an agenda that turned her world upside down again. It was afternoon and Brie had been thinking about what to prepare for dinner when she heard her father go to the door. It always gave her a little tremor when the doorbell rang, even in broad daylight, afraid of who it would be standing there, and that Sam would forget to check through the peephole.

Sam came into the kitchen and said, somberly, "It's Brad."

She dried her hands on a dish towel. "Here?"

Sam nodded. "I'll go to my office."

When she went into the family room, he was standing there, still wearing his leather jacket, the one she had given him two Christmases ago. His hands were in his pockets, his head down. He was as tall as Jack; as broad shouldered with a wide, hard chest. Looking at his back, she realized it could almost be Jack, and for a split second she wondered if she had married him because he resembled her brother in so many ways. That sandy-brown hair, square jaw, long legs, powerful physique.

Mike wasn't anything like the Sheridan men—he was six feet, quite tall to her five foot three, but not towering like her brother and father, like Brad. His shoulders and arms were strong, but he was lean. There was that soft, coal-black hair, high cheekbones, black eyes, tan skin, his teeth so white they were almost startling. His hands were soft and his fingers long and graceful. She hadn't seen him without a shirt, but she knew his chest and belly were muscled and hard, almost hairless. She found herself imagining that below his waist was more of that black hair, swirling downward. His legs were the strong, sculpted legs of a runner—she remembered the feel of his thighs as she lay across his lap to be kissed.

She had to shake herself, focus on the moment.

"Brad, what are you doing here?"

He lifted his head and turned, smiling when he saw her. He reached for her as an old friend might, his arms open. She allowed these brief hugs, but then extricated herself quickly. "I have to talk to you, Brie. Is this a good time?"

"It's fine. Here, sit," she said, indicating the couch. When he had taken a seat, she chose the love seat, not beside him but facing him at an angle.

"This is hard," he said, dropping his chin, looking down. "I've been trying to figure out how to do this for months." He stared at the floor for a moment.

"What is it, Brad?" she asked impatiently.

He took a breath. "Me and Christine," he said. "We're not together anymore. We split up. A few months ago. Not long after your... The incident."

It took her a second to absorb that. Then she gave a short huff of laughter and said, "I don't know what you expect me to say. I'm sorry?"

He reached for her hands, but managed to snag only one. "Brie, I was a fool. I made a terrible mistake. I don't know what I was thinking. I'm a screwup. But I still love you. I never stopped loving you."

She pulled her hand away, and the look on her face was one of incredulity. "You're not serious."

He reached again, but she pulled back. "I know—it's crazy. We split up months ago, but for months before that, we weren't getting along at all. We tried to keep it together, if for no other reason than we'd put our spouses, our families through so much. Brie, it was never the answer, but I didn't see it for a while. God, I'm so sorry."

Her face held the shock of what he'd just said—more than he even realized he'd said. Put our spouses through so much…? "She wasn't divorced when it started," Brie said softly. "She wasn't, was she?"

"I don't know," he answered. "Not really, no. You know they were having trouble anyway. They weren't going to make it. Glenn didn't know about us," he said with a shrug. "There wasn't much to know. Really, there was all that other stuff."

"Christine and Glenn split up because of you!" she said. She stood up and backed away from him. "It was more than a year," she said. "God, you took your best friend's wife! And he doesn't even know?" She turned sharply, presenting her back.

He approached her and put a hand on her shoulder. "No, it wasn't exactly like that," he said. "There were feelings, maybe. Temptations, I guess. A kiss or two. But I told you the truth about when we got involved. Physically…sexually… I just didn't go all the way back to the beginning because honest to God, I didn't know where the beginning was, or where it was going. Jesus, Brie—"

She turned around and faced him. "You left me a year ago. You were sleeping with her for a year before that. But you were fooling around with her for even longer, lying to me with every kiss good-night, every touch…."

"There was something physical… I can't describe it…. It was like I couldn't stop myself."

"Something physical?" She laughed. "Oh, God! You were sleeping with both of us! At least she threw Glenn out, but not you! You had two women! Two women who loved you, wanted you!" She laughed at him, a cynical and mean laugh. "You must have been in heaven! You think that's something I'm going to get over?"

"I'm sorry. There's no good explanation. I was an idiot."

"I've been paying you alimony. Even while I've been unemployed."

"I have it all. It's not spent."

She shook her head in disbelief. "I never thought this could get worse."

He took another step toward her. "If you'll give me a chance, I'd just like a chance to show you that I— I'm sorry, Brie. Can't we—? Can't we try again? See each other? See if we can rekindle some of what we had? I know it'll take time…. If we can't, I have no one to blame but myself, but can we just—"

She gave a huff of laughter. "Poor Brad," she said. "You went from two women who couldn't get enough of you to no one. You're not getting laid, are you? You're pathetic!"

"I know you're angry—you should be. I'll make it up to you somehow. Just give me time, give us time—"

"No!" she yelled at him. "No!" And then she started to laugh again. "God, you don't know how long I waited to hear you say that! Even while I was hating you, I might have taken you back!" She shook her head in disbelief. "Jesus! Thank God you didn't pull this sooner."

"Brie—"

"For God's sake, do I want anything to do with a man who can cheat on his wife because there's some kind of physical thing? Something you can't even explain? Forgive me, but I thought we had something physical!"

"We did. We will again."

"No. No. Go. Get out of here. You left me for my best friend and now you'd like to see if we can rekindle something? Oh, you are such a fool. What did I ever see in you? Why didn't I know this about you? Go!"

"No, Brie, there's more."

"I can't take any more," she said.

"They found him."

She was stunned for a second. She couldn't breathe. "What?" she asked. "What did you say?"

He took a deep breath. "They found him—Jerome Powell. He's in Florida. They have him in custody there. They're working on the extradition. I think you'll get a call tomorrow from the D.A. I heard it at work."

She took a step toward him. "Why didn't you tell me this first?" she asked in a furious whisper.

"Because I wanted you to know that I love you. I'd like to be with you through this. With you when they bring him back. I want to take care of you."

"Oh, my God," she said in a breath. "You thought I'd take you back out of fear? Helplessness? You're an idiot, that's what you are! A big, stupid, goddamn idiot!"

He hung his head. "Don't you think I feel pretty terrible about what happened? Haven't I been around since it happened? Don't you think it's killing me? Hell, Brie—that's probably what broke me and Christine apart."

She started to laugh again, but tears smarted in her eyes at the same time. "It's all about you, isn't it, Brad?" There was a sweet voice in her head. *There will be no taking, mija. Only giving.*

"I want a chance to try to make it right," he said.

"Well, you can't. No one can make it right, especially you. You made your choice, Brad. You're stuck with it." Then she ran out of the room. She went to her bedroom and slammed the door.

Brad was about to follow her when he came face-to-face with Sam, who blocked the hallway. "I think you'd better go, son," he said patiently, but firmly.

"You heard?"

"Every ludicrous word. Goodbye, Brad," he said.

Brad turned to leave and Sam followed him, locking the front door behind him.

In her bedroom, Brie was already folding clothes into neat little piles on the bed. She was thinking of Brad's lame suggestion that he take care of her through this. He didn't know the meaning of taking care of his woman.

There was a light tapping at the door. "Dad?" she asked.

"Yes, Brie."

"Come in, Daddy," she said. When he opened the door, she filled his arms. "Oh, Daddy."

"It's okay, Brie. We'll get through this."

"Daddy, I'm going to Virgin River." She looked up at him. "I'm going to Mike. I want to be there. I'm going right now."

"Do you want me to take you?" he asked, smiling down at her. "I wouldn't have to stay around, but I could take you, so you wouldn't be alone on the drive."

She shook her head, but smiled back. "No, I'm okay in the car. But if I don't go right away, I might lose my nerve. Dad, tell me the truth—do you think I'm making a fool of myself? Going to him? Trusting him?"

Sam looked nonplussed. "Mike? Why would I worry about Mike?"

She shrugged. "Jack has warned me of his fickle, roving ways with women. A player, he says."

Sam chuckled. "Ah, Jack, who was as pure as the driven snow. Hah. I guess they know each other pretty well, Mike and your brother. Brie," he said, running his big hand along the hair at her temple, pushing her hair behind her ear, "I could be wrong. I've been wrong before, but I can't think of any reason not to believe Mike, not to trust him." He smiled into her eyes. "Your brother trusted him for many years—for that he has to be a good man. And obviously he cares about you."

"He makes me feel like a person," she said softly. "Like a woman. I haven't felt like a woman since Brad... And then..." She stopped. "I have to go before they bring that monster back here for trial. Before I face him and can't imagine a loving touch."

"Do you think that's what's waiting for you in Virgin River?" Sam asked.

She nodded. "I think so. I hope so. If I'm wrong..."

"You're packing," Sam said. "You don't feel like you could be wrong." She shook her head. "You're my baby, and you're thirty-one," he said in a whisper. "I don't want you to be alone and afraid. I want you to have love in your life. It's the natural order of things. And I think Mike gives that to you. You go," he said, kissing her forehead. "I think you've had enough of the tough side of life. Time for a little bit of the tender side." He pulled her close. "Don't be gone too long. I'll miss you."

When Brie pulled into Virgin River, there were still trucks and cars surrounding the bar, though it was nearly the time of night Jack and Preacher would close. She pulled her Jeep right up to the front of the RV, parking beside Mike's SUV. She could talk to Jack in the morning; she needed Mike's arms around her. Jack would not misunderstand her presence here, though he might not be happy about her decision. She even left her suitcases in the back of the Jeep when she went to the RV's door.

Mike opened the door and saw her standing there, looking up at him. He gasped and jumped out of the RV. "Brie!" he said in a breath, grabbing her up in his arms, lifting her clear of the ground, burying his face in her neck.

Her whole world tilted and warmth spread through her

from deep inside; just feeling his arms around her made so much right. Everything was suddenly as it should be. She held on to him, held him tight, feeling his lips, his breath on her neck. "Brie," he whispered. "What are you doing here? Why didn't you tell me you were coming?"

She looked up into his black eyes. "It was sudden," she said. "I came to be with you, if that's all right."

He ran a knuckle down her cheek to her chin, lifting it. "Anything you want is all right. You have only to tell me what it is."

She'd been thinking about this through a five-hour drive, and had planned a hundred ways to approach it delicately. But in the end she said, "I need you to make love to me."

Instead of looking shocked or excited by the prospect, he asked, "What's wrong, honey? What happened?"

She shook her head, looking into his eyes with moist ones of her own. "Brad," she said in a breath. "He came to ask me for another chance. And in the same conversation, told me they'd found the rapist and would be extraditing him to California for trial."

He was quiet a moment, a half smile on his lips. Then he asked, "And you think I can make that go away?"

"No," she said. "But I knew if I didn't come here soon… Mike, I'm not whole, you have to know that. It's been so long, and there's been so much…. I just learned my husband was with two women for a long, long time before he chose her. And what Powell did to me… I can want you, but truthfully, I'm not sure I can ever feel again."

"Shhh," he said. He gently touched his lips to hers. "You already feel, or you wouldn't be here," he whispered.

She said, "Quiero que me abraces. Para amarte durante la noche." I want you to hold me. To love me through the night.

A slow smile grew on Mike's face. "I haven't had any secrets, have I?"

"Nada," she said. Not one.

Mike laughed softly. "It serves me right. I didn't know you spoke Spanish," he said. "Tu debes sentir estas manos amorosas así a ti." You should feel the touch of loving hands.

"Deja a que sean sus manos." Let them be your hands.

"Brie, are you sure you're ready for this? Are you sure you want it to be me?"

She shook her head. "I'm only sure I want to try, to feel complete, to feel like a woman again before it's too late, before that bastard is brought to trial and facing him turns me to stone again. But you? Sí. Te quiero mucho." Yes. I want you so much.

"Have you seen Jack?" he asked, his hand on the back of her neck under her hair, kneading gently.

She shook her head. "I didn't even go into the bar. I don't think he'll have any trouble figuring out why I'm here when he leaves tonight and sees my car."

"Do you want me to take you to him? Be there when you tell him you're back?"

She shook her head again. "I'll see him tomorrow." She laughed nervously. "I'm not sure what I have to offer. I'm absolutely certain, and still… Maybe you should give me a beer," she said.

"Tu no necesitas eso. Nada malo te pasara en mis brazos." You won't need that. Nothing frightening will ever happen while you're in my arms. He pulled her to him with the hand at the back of her neck.

"What if I'm really dead inside?" she whispered.

"You know better than that. You've never been dead inside, just frightened. You trusted yourself enough to come here. Leave the rest to me." He touched her lips softly. "You have

to know something while there's still time for you to change
your mind about this. I'm not a Good Samaritan, Brie. Not
just a man willing to help a good friend get in touch with
her feelings again. I'm in love with you," he said, hovering
over her lips. His breath was hot and sweet on her face, then
slowly he descended on her, covering her mouth in a kiss that
was powerful and hot, a kiss that seared and demanded. He
moved over her parted lips hungrily and she clung to him with
a whimper. "I'm so in love with you."

When he released her lips, he pulled her up and into the RV
and locked the door. She slipped out of her jacket and asked,
"Will he come pounding at the door?"

Mike chuckled low in his throat. "Not a chance. I think
even Jack knows when he'd be taking his life in his hands."
With his hands on her face, he pulled her lips onto his, de-
vouring her. He kissed her again. And again. Holding her
against him with arms that had ached to hold her like this for
too long. He felt her small tongue in his mouth and it made
him weak in the knees, it was so delicious, so sweet. All he
hoped for was that he could make her comfortable with his
touch, soothed enough so that she would welcome more of
him. He wanted her to relearn, in his arms, the beauty of
what could happen between a man and woman. The joy and
ecstasy. After what had been done to her, she should know
that in this, the love that he had for her, there would never be
fear or pain, but only pleasure. Pleasure so wild and wonderful, it would fill her life for many days and nights to come.
These thoughts combined with the sensation of her against
him made him erect at once and he sprang to life, folded almost painfully inside his jeans. With a hand on her bottom,
he pulled her against him to show her what holding her did
to him, and a deep and beautiful moan escaped her.

"Everything is up to you, Brie," he said. "If you want to change your mind…"

"No," she whispered against his lips.

"There's no hurry, baby. Tell me when to slow down, when to stop…."

She shook her head. "I trust you. I need you."

He drew her through the RV, past the full kitchen and a shower big enough for two into a small bedroom. There were only a couple of feet on each side of the queen-size bed and the walls were lined with closets, drawers and shelves, but it was all beautiful and modern, and plenty big enough.

His hands went to the bottom of her soft sweater and he drew it slowly over her head, leaving her in only her bra. He was on her mouth again, bruising her lips with the passion of his kiss. He pulled her hands from around his neck and, looking into her eyes, placed her fingers on the buttons of his shirt. She didn't need to be told—she tugged his shirt out of his pants and worked the buttons quickly, then with her hands against his chest, spread the shirt over his shoulders to bare his chest. She touched the scar on his right shoulder, then caressed his chest with her small soft hands. "I love the way your skin feels," she whispered. "You're so smooth. So silky." She kissed the hollow place at the base of his neck.

With one deft movement, the bra disappeared and he pulled her against him, her breasts on his chest. Flesh to flesh. Her arms encircled him and held him close. The feeling of her small hands running up and down his back stirred his blood just as the sensation of her nipples against his chest bored through him with heat. One of his hands found and cupped a full breast, his thumb running over that erect nipple, stimulating it. Then he lowered his lips to gently draw on it, and she moaned softly, sweetly, whispering his name.

Mike was aching for her. He brought his mouth back to

hers, and while kissing her, he backed her slowly and carefully to the bed until the backs of her legs were against it. Then his hands went to the snap of her jeans. "Okay?" he asked against her lips. "Do you need a little more time?"

She shook her head. "I'm ready," she whispered.

He undid them carefully, slowly. Then, sliding his hands gently along her hips, moved them down. He sat her down on the bed and knelt to take off her shoes, pull off her jeans. When he stood and put his hands on the buckle of his belt, he hesitated, waiting for her to tell him if it was too much, too fast. But she brushed them away and replaced his hands with her own. She undid the buckle, the snap and zipper, and tugged the pants down. Freed, he leaped out at her and her eyes widened briefly. She glanced up at him, then, her eyes closing, she leaned toward him. But he stopped her by putting his hands on her shoulders. "Another time, mi amor. Tonight is about you." He gently pushed her back onto the bed while he freed himself from his boots and trousers so he could get in beside her.

Both of them naked, he took her into his arms. She was so small and compact against him. He closed his eyes and in his mind he could see them against the white sheets, her ivory body against his tan, his dark hand on her hip and her small pale hand on his. He filled his hands with her satiny flesh, covering her body with long, smooth, calming strokes from her shoulders to her knees while he kissed her deeply. He caressed her gently for several minutes, giving her time to get used to the sensation of their naked bodies together, entwined. She slipped a leg over his and her hands on him became bolder as she moved down his back and grabbed his butt, pulling him closer, harder against her. He slipped his hand between their bodies and moved it lower, inching his fingers down over her flat belly and farther, finding, with some surprise, that she parted her legs for him. He found the prominent little knot he was looking for and gave it a little attention, rubbing her gently, bringing a deep, lusty moan from her. Then he moved lower still, gently dipping a finger into her to find she was ready—this was a passionate woman who had been too long without a man to love her. But he wasn't going to rush her; he was going to bring this to her sweetly, slowly. The last touch she'd felt had been brutal. He would erase that with gentleness and love so that she would never again fear it.

He rolled her gently onto her back and rose above her. "Let me look at you, Brie," he whispered. He ran a slow hand down her body from her neck to her pubis and over, letting his fingers slip into her damp softness for just a second, causing her to writhe against him. "I don't think I've ever seen anything this beautiful," he whispered. He put his hands on her hips and gently squeezed. She was soft and lush. He began a line of gentle kisses from her neck to her shoulder, her chest, her breast, her belly. Then he rose to kiss her neck again and with his lips against her ear, he whispered, "Trust yourself, Brie." Then he resumed his kisses, less gentle as he lowered his mouth until he was at the center of her body. He parted her legs and put his mouth on her, delicately at first, and then with more pressure. She moved her hips against his mouth; he heard her groan and cry out, then felt her hands on his shoulders, gripping him fiercely, and he pulled on her carefully with his lips, massaging with his tongue until he could feel her tremble, open up, clench, vibrate against him. It was glorious, the way she let it go, let him take her to that pinnacle and beyond. This pleased and surprised him; he had prepared himself to have to coax her into pleasure, into orgasm, but she was quick and hot, consuming him, her fingers digging into his shoulders. As she relaxed, he drew away, rising slowly, kissing her belly, her breast, her neck, her mouth. "Brie, you are wonderful. Delicious. You honor me."

She had trouble catching a breath. She said, "Oh, God. Oh, my God."

"I don't think you're going to have trouble feeling...."

"God," she whispered, weak and spent in his arms.

"That's better, isn't it?" he whispered, gently pecking at her lips.

"I want more of you," she said.

"Are you sure?" he asked her.

"I'm sure," she whispered.

But he took his time again, allowing her to recover, slowly arousing her with slow hands, sweet lips. There was a fierce ache in him that wanted to dive into her and experience her quickly, bring his own release, but he ignored it. He concentrated on her responses, sure that she was rising to that ultimate pleasure again. And then, because he was honor bound, he whispered against her ear, "Brie... I have a condom."

She froze. "No," she said emphatically, shaking her head. "Please, no."

"Very well, my love."

"I'm sorry, I can't..."

"It's all right, Brie. We'll do without...."

He gave her a little time to forget about that, spreading his kisses over her once more, lingering at her breasts, her neck, her lips. Then finally he rose over her and with a knee placed carefully between her legs, he gently moved them apart again. He looked at her face; her eyes were closed and her head turned away from him. She held her bottom lip between her teeth, tensely. With a hand on her chin, he turned her back to face him and kissed her tenderly, lightly. Then harder, opening her lips with his. Her hands went to his hips, whether to hold him back or draw him in, he wasn't sure. He lowered himself to her and the moment he touched her where he might enter her, she flinched. Stiffened. "Brie," he commanded softly. "Look at my face. Look at me, baby. It's me. Say my name, mi amor."

In a breath it came. "Miguel."

"Put your hand on me, Brie. Show me the way. You're in control."

She wrapped her small hand around him, and at the merest touch he was ready to lose it. He wasn't sure he could last long enough to please her again, but he was hell-bent to try. Slowly, cautiously, she led him into her. "My love," he said, "focus on my face, Brie. It's you and me, and I love you. I'll never give you anything but love."

"Miguel," she said softly.

"Brie," he whispered. He slid into her slowly, filling her, and she tilted her head back, her pelvis up, and with her hands again on his hips, pulled him deeper. Being inside her like that, he thought he might die, it was so good. He pulled up her knees and balanced on them, moving within her, rocking, stroking, making sure to create the friction that he knew from experience worked, while pushing himself deeply inside, which also worked. It was so important that she reclaim the joy of this. It wasn't just feeling again, but feeling to her very core; feeling that was so shattering, it would leave her consumed. She was straining against him, bucking, losing herself in the moment, reaching for another orgasm, and this time from the feared penetration. This was what he wanted for her, that she could have success now, like this, with a man who wanted only to please her, with a man who adored and respected her and loved her more than life itself. He knew she would have to trust him completely for her release to come.

When her orgasm came, it closed around him with a powerful grip and he felt her fingernails dig into his butt. He moaned in deep appreciation while he pushed harder against her, deeper into her. She clung to him and cried out. He held her fast, held her close, still, his body her body, as one. "Brie," he gasped. "Dios." And when he sensed that she was almost complete, the storm nearly past for her, he moved inside her again, deep and strong and quick, and that was all it took to bring her up and over the top once more. She gasped and rose against him, pulsing around him all over again. When it stole her breath away and she was again at the peak, he let himself go. He went off like a rocket inside her. The strength of it overpowered him and caused him to tremble.

"My God," she whispered, astonished by him. By herself. "Oh, God."

He nearly collapsed, but held his weight off her. A fine mist of perspiration covered them. Recovery was a long time in coming for both of them; she lay weak and spent beneath him, her hair scattered across the bed in disarray, her eyes closed, a small smile curving her lips. "Brie," he finally said in a breath. "You're smiling."

"Hmm," she said, not opening her eyes, her lips curving a little more.

He chuckled. "I think we have it back, love."

She shook her head slightly, eyes still closed. "No, we don't," she said, groggy.

"We don't?"

She shook her head again. "I never had anything like that before…."

He laughed at her, smoothing the hair back from her brow. "You're incredible. Like a shooting star."

"Hmm." Her arms lay spread wide, limp, on the bed above her head. "Thank you," she muttered.

He kissed her tenderly, tugging at her lips with his. "Feel

better?" He kissed her again, small, delicate kisses. "You seem pretty relaxed," he teased.

"Hmm. I never give good sex enough credit," she said. "You didn't slip me a Valium, did you?"

"Not Valium, no." He laughed. "I wanted you to feel good. I didn't know you were going to give back so much."

"Hmm. Neither did I."

He sucked gently at the lobe of her ear. "I didn't know it could be like this," he whispered. "You didn't turn into stone."

"No kidding," she said softly. "I was hoping to feel nice." She opened her eyes, but only a little. "Warm and cuddly. Feminine. I didn't know you were going to blow my brains out two or three times...."

He lifted a black brow. "Two or three?"

She shrugged. "I'm not sure, but that's okay—I'm fine now. Better than fine. Do you think you can remember how you did that?"

"I could go write it all down."

"I just wanted to feel like a woman again...."

"Oh, baby. You did—trust me. Congratulations. They just don't make any more woman than that. Now I'm doomed," he said. "Now I can't live without you."

"All right, then," she said with a weak little chuckle. "I'll hang around awhile." She ran her hand along his hair at his temple. "Thank you. I couldn't have done that without you."

He rolled onto his back. "Well, if you figure out how to do that without me, we'll get a patent. Retire in the Swiss Alps. Eat caviar for breakfast."

She giggled again. "Really, that was so good...."

"Really. I know."

"I think you fixed everything. It seems to be working fine."

"Hmm," he answered. "That doesn't touch it. There are no words..."

"You said you were in love with me," she reminded him.

"I am over the moon, I'm so in love with you. But right now, after sex like that, it might sound insincere. Because I've never had sex like that in my life."

She rolled to her side and propped herself up on an elbow. "Really? You haven't? How is that possible?" she asked him.

"Can we worry about that tomorrow?" he asked her. "I'd hate to screw this up."

"If you insist."

"We're going to try this again before tomorrow. See if we know what we're doing…"

"If you insist," she said again, laughing.

"I want you again," he said. "Already. I think you have a magical effect on me."

"Oh." She laughed. "Poor you."

"By morning, you might regret this."

She sighed. "Betcha I don't…"

And he began with soft kisses on her lips…

When Jack got home, the baby was asleep and Mel was sitting up, comfortable in one of his shirts, the laptop on her knees in front of her, either researching something on the Internet or writing e-mails. It always made him smile to see her like that. She said she liked to wear his shirts right after her shower, smelling his musk on them. He liked to wear those same shirts the next day, a reminder of her body inside, the faint memory of her fresh scent apparent. "I have a surprise for you," he said.

"What?"

"Brie is back in town. She's with Mike."

"Really?" Mel said, suddenly giving him her attention. She closed the laptop and put it aside.

"I haven't seen her. When I was leaving the bar, her Jeep

was parked next to Mike's car. She came to Mike. Not to us—to Mike."

She shrugged. "Well, that makes sense. He loves her."

"How do you know that?" Jack asked.

"How could you not?" she asked.

Jack sat back on the couch. "I thought he was just trying to get laid."

"That's pretty irrelevant," she said, laughing. "You're all trying to get laid. Some of you actually love the women you're trying to get close to."

"You act like we're all just a bunch of bulls being led around by our dicks."

She laughed at him, gleefully for a woman who was annoyed to be pregnant, and moody to boot. "Do I? I wonder why?"

"So you think this makes sense?"

"Extraordinary sense. It even makes me nostalgic."

That caused him to smile devilishly. "Nostalgic enough to take me to bed?"

"Tell me something—are you letting go of this weird control thing you have over Brie?"

"Yeah," he said, almost tiredly. "It's not like I haven't wanted her to have a full life. I thought she was going to have that with Brad, the shit. It was Mike who worried me—he's been such a frickin' tomcat." He glanced at his wife's disapproving expression. "Yeah, yeah, let's not go over that again. We all made our rounds."

"I doubt he made any more rounds than you," she said.

"It was just the marriages that got under my skin," he said. "So help me God, if he marries her and walks away from her, I am going to kill him."

"Looks to me like he's totally sunk," she said. "A complete goner."

"Fine," Jack said shortly. "I'm out of it now—she's staked her claim." Then he reached out a hand, threaded it under her hair and around the back of her neck, pulling her toward him. He kissed her deeply. "How are you feeling?" he asked.

"Pursued. How are you feeling?"

"Lucky."

11

In the cool light of morning Mike rose on an elbow to look
down at the beautiful pale body of his love. Brie slept on
her stomach, and the curve of her back and small, round bottom was exquisite. Irresistible. He hated to disturb her, her
rest was so peaceful, but he couldn't help himself—he touched
her. He ran his hand tenderly from her neck, down her spine,
over her bottom. She hummed in half sleep and he pressed a
gentle kiss into the small of her back.

There was a soft knock at the door. She lifted her head;
her hair cascaded over her face. "Shhh," he told her. "Don't
move. I'll be right back."

While he sat on the edge of the bed to retrieve his jeans
from the floor, she saw the tattoo on his back for the first
time—a large sunburst right between his shoulder blades.

Very sexy on that broad, brown back. She'd seen the other one earlier, an armband in the shape of a chain. He shrugged into his pants, pulling them up over his hard, compact butt.

When Mike opened the door he saw that someone, Jack or Preacher, had left a breakfast tray on the ground just outside the door. He looked around; there was no one there. Mike brought the tray inside. There were two covered dishes and a thermal pitcher of coffee. He put it on the table. His kitchen was fully equipped with dishes, utensils, pots and pans—but he hardly ever used it. He took all his meals at the bar.

Then he realized something else was missing—there was no log splitting this morning despite the fact that the weather was perfect. Jack was giving them more than just privacy—he wasn't even making his presence felt on the property.

Mike took off his jeans again, letting them drop. He got back into his bed and continued the pleasurable study of Brie's smooth, silky back. He scrunched up her tangled hair and pulled it to his lips. She hummed contentedly.

"Who was at the door?"

"Room service," he said with a chuckle. "Breakfast has been delivered."

"Are you hungry?" she asked.

"Not for food," he said. He stretched out over her back, careful not to put all his weight on her. He moved her hair away from her neck, kissing her there, and began to grow firm against her soft bottom.

"Breakfast can wait," she said, breathless, tilting her hips upward, wriggling softly against him.

It occurred to Mike that he'd had a lot of sex in his life, but it had never been like this. There was an intimacy he shared with Brie that went beyond the coupling; they'd been through so much together, emotionally, before the loving. He felt as though there had never been a woman before her; no one had ever taken him into her body in the free, wild, trusting way she did. After that first tentative and hesitant touch, she'd held nothing back from him. She gave her body completely, insatiably. She welcomed his hands, his lips, every bit of him, relying on him to do right by her, showering him with her pleasure over and over.

He had nearly forgotten that for the better part of a year he hadn't thought he would enjoy this aspect of life again. Pleasing her, re-creating the joy and safety of sex for her again had put his own burdens so far from his mind that he was completely removed from worry as to whether he could perform. It not only worked well, it worked again and again and again. She created a fire in him that he couldn't put out. And from her reaction, her response, she had fire of her own. For him. She wasn't the only one who needed blissful release from a troubled past; Mike needed to be brought back to life, as well. Until that moment he had been focused only on helping her heal, not realizing that she had done the same for him.

He slipped a hand beneath her, creeping down over her belly, lifting her pelvis slightly. He gently parted her legs with his knee. "Is this okay? Like this?" he whispered, pressing toward her again.

"God," she said. "Oh, yes."

He slipped in, moving inside her yet again, rocking her, pushing smoothly against a deep, erotic place inside. A slow, even pumping of his hips brought deep sighs from her; she moved against him, meeting him with each stroke. There was a special place inside a woman that was secret, sensitive, and he'd made a study of her body and knew exactly where to go. He thrust against that secret spot, rhythmically, gently but firmly, relentlessly. Finally she pushed back against him, eager for the pressure he applied, craving it with sighs and whimpers, and after a while a startled gasp escaped her and she lunged into him, hard. He held her against him as she was sent soaring into a pleasure so hot and bold it seemed she couldn't breathe for a long moment. He enjoyed success; he felt the hot spasms surround him, a flood of liquid heat that poured from her and drenched him, and then he joined her in a moment of fulfillment that left them both weak, content.

When she began to recover, he slipped out of her and gently rolled her over onto her back.

"Dear heaven," she gasped. "I've never felt anything like that in my life...."

He rose on an elbow to look down at her beautiful face, her lips crimson from love, her cheeks in high color. "You like that?"

"Good lord!" she said, her voice still quivering. "What in the world did you do?"

"Magic," he said. "A treat. For both of us. The G-spot."

She stared at him in stunned wonder for a moment, then surprised him with a laugh. "I thought that was a myth! A legend!"

"Completely real," he said. "Obviously."

"How can you know more about my body after one night than I've known in my life?" she asked.

"It's you," he said, running a hand over her shoulder and down her arm, entwining his fingers in hers. "It's the way you trust me. Let me in."

"Can you do that again?"

He laughed at her. "Not for a while, I'm afraid."

"You amaze me." She ran a hand over his chest. "The things you know."

"I've been with too many women, Brie. I apologize. I can't undo that. But I have never felt as much a part of a woman as I do with you. It's like I was never really intimate before now. I can't explain it any better than that."

"Hmm," she said, letting her eyes drift closed.

"It blows my mind. Do you feel it?" he asked her.

She laughed. "I feel it, Miguel. What are we going to do about it?"

"Do you think it would be frowned on if we just stayed here, naked, and had a couple of meals a day delivered, for maybe a month or two?"

She giggled. "How long do you really think Jack will stay out of our business?"

He shrugged and smiled. "I guess we'll have to get dressed eventually...."

"Do you remember when I came here after Davie was born? I would listen to you practice your guitar in the early mornings."

"I didn't know you were there."

"I used to pretend you were playing for me. I was so moved by the music, I imagined you playing for me late into the night. You tempted me even then."

He chuckled. "I never knew. At that time, you wouldn't give an inch."

"I was pretty sure all men were dogs."

"We are. We deserve nothing. But we beg just the same." He touched her face. "I'm not the same man since you came into my life."

"I wasn't sure I'd ever be able to make love again," she said softly. Then, smiling, she said, "Now I'm not sure I can stop."

"Tell me," he whispered. "Last night, the first time—you froze up, you tensed. You didn't want the condom."

She closed her eyes and shook her head. Then she opened her eyes, met his and said, "I couldn't. I couldn't feel that latex inside me because he—"

"I know, my love," Mike said sweetly. "It's all right. A little flashback?"

"For a second, but you brought me into the present and it was all right then." She smiled. "Way more than all right."

"There's something you should keep in mind," he said softly, stroking her hair. "No matter how perfect things seem, you could find yourself—"

"I know. Back there, in that terrifying moment," she finished for him. "I've had a lot of counseling. They try to prepare you for that. It happened to me once before, that first night at the cabin. It snuck right up on me." She ran a finger along his ear, down his neck. "Talk about baggage…"

He smiled into her eyes. "Everyone has something, Brie. Everyone has a haunt, a relentless ghost. The best way to scare it off is to look it square in the face."

"You're so good," she whispered.

"There's no danger of disease," he said. "I haven't been with a woman since before the shooting, and in the hospital every cell in my body was screened. But there is another matter…. Are you taking pills?"

She shook her head, but her eyes were clear.

"Ah," he said. "Mel can help with that. There's something she can give you to prevent a baby."

"What if I didn't do that?" she asked. "What if I didn't go to Mel?"

That caused him to straighten a bit. "I assume you passed biology 101," he said.

"There's no telling what would happen." She shrugged. "Probably nothing."

"If the amount of pleasure we have correlates to conception, there will be a hundred babies by the end of the week."

"If you'd like me to see Mel, I will. This is probably just crazy. I wouldn't push you, rush you."

"Brie, you can't rush me. I want to give you everything. If you wanted me to give you a baby, I would die trying, but only if it was our baby. Together. Maybe you should think about it a little longer, until you're sure."

She smiled at him. "Ah. I knew I forgot something. It's the reason I came here, to you—it wasn't just because I needed your touch to help make me stronger. It was so much more than that. I couldn't be away from you a second longer. I think you're the best friend I've ever had. In fact, we became so close in the last six months, I didn't think we could get any closer." She put her fingers on his lips. "The joke's on me—this goes beyond my wildest expectations. If you're only pretending, you're a gifted actor."

"No acting, Brie. I love you. Endlessly."

"And I love you."

Her admission fulfilled his deepest desires. "You mean this?"

"Sí, Miguel. I can't imagine being without you. Not now. You've been everything to me for months. I love you so much."

"Nunca soñe que yo pudiera tener esto en mi vida." I never dreamed I could have this in my life.

"I didn't even know it existed."

"And this is what you want? To let nature take its course?"

"Betting on nature probably isn't very risky. Before I knew..." She took a breath. "I stopped taking my pills while I was married to Brad. We'd been talking about a baby and I thought I'd surprise him. I didn't know he was brewing a romance with my best friend.... A long time before... Well," she said. "It wasn't just a year before he left me. It was longer."

"Is that what he told you yesterday?" Mike asked. "At the same time he was explaining Powell had been found?"

"I think he let it slip," she said. "I guess she booted her husband on the excuse of their many little fights, but it was really because she was in love with Brad. And he knew it."

"Oh, man..." Mike said in a breath.

"But he never stopped sleeping with me. I was clueless, try-ing to surprise him with a baby. Nothing happened, though. I didn't get pregnant."

"Aw, honey," he said, stroking her arm. "Maybe it's best that didn't work for you, under the circumstances. But this could be different. Your eyes should be wide open. I'm told you shouldn't trust the water around here. It might be wise to do some planning, for your sake. I live in a trailer in Vir-gin River."

"Details." She smiled. "I've never felt more at home." She touched his handsome face. "If last night made a baby, it will be a beautiful baby. I don't want Mel's help to make sure it doesn't stick. If it's there, it's yours—and I want it."

"Then that's how it will be," he said. He kissed her deeply, passionately. "Whatever you want."

"I don't want this to end."

"There's no end in sight, mi amor. Trust me."

Jack hadn't been watching the RV during the morning, even though it had been on his mind. It was a pure accident that he happened to see the door open and Brie step out. He glanced at his watch—eleven. Almost lunch. Right behind her was Mike. Probably he should have turned away, but he didn't. His sister looked so small and girlish in her jeans, moc-casins, suede jacket with fringe and all that light brown hair cascading down her back almost to her waist.

She stood in front of Mike and he lifted her chin, pressing an intimate kiss to her lips. Even from this distance it was easy to see they were not anxious to be parted. But in a moment Mike pulled himself away and went to his SUV to leave while Brie walked toward the back door of the bar.

Jack went behind the bar quickly so as not to get caught watching. He picked up a perfectly clean glass and began to wipe it with a towel. The door opened and Brie walked in, and he almost took a step back. He had never seen her look this way. She was radiant. There was an expression on her face, a glow in her eyes, a secret smile on her lips that said volumes. She didn't hesitate—she walked behind the bar, right up to him, and put her arms around his waist. He got rid of that glass and towel and wrapped his arms around her, hugging her close.

All Jack had wanted since June was to have his sister back, well and whole, restored. Happy and alive, without that fuzzy blotch of fear and uncertainty around the edges of her aura like a smudge. He wanted his Brie back, renewed and a force in the world once again. Jack hadn't been able to give that to her—none of the family had been able to do it. And yet the young woman in his embrace nearly vibrated with joy. It wasn't as though the old Brie was merely back, but this was a new Brie—a woman reborn. A woman experiencing love and life as if for the first time.

Sometimes it took him such a long time to accept the very things that he knew intimately for himself. The very things he had discovered in his wife's arms. What Brie needed in her life, what everyone needed, was perfect love. He'd found that with Mel, Preacher had found it with Paige and now… He kissed the top of her head.

She lifted her head to look up at him. In a voice soft and sincere, she said, "You are never to doubt him again. Never."

He put his hand along the hair at her temple and smiled tenderly into her eyes. He gave his head a very slight shake— never again, he was saying to her. Brie had chosen her mate. And for all Jack's previous doubts, it appeared she had chosen well.

Jack had resisted when he should have trusted his sister to know what she needed in her life, and he should have trusted

Mike, as much a best friend as Preacher, to treat her like the precious jewel she was. Whatever had happened between them had clearly surpassed a physical fulfillment.

My wife, Jack thought, is always right about everything.

For Mel, a nightmare had come to roost in the form of sixteen-year-old Sophie Landau. She thought something might have "happened to her." Mel had a sinking feeling in the pit of her stomach even before more of the story came out. "Me and my girlfriend Becky went to a party that we weren't supposed to—I said I was staying over at Becky's and she said she was staying over at my house. Brendan Lancaster invited us. Brendan's older—he graduated a couple of years ago," she said with red lips that looked as if she'd been chewing on them.

"Okay," Mel said, encouraging her.

Sophie sat on the exam table, still dressed, while Mel leaned against the cabinet, listening, dreading. Sophie was on the chubby side with straight brown hair that fell limply onto her shoulders. She had a little problem with acne, her teeth were crooked and she was clearly nervous in a general way—nails bitten down, a hair-twisting habit, an occasional twitch of her cheek.

"So you went to a party. Big party?" Mel asked.

"Small. Six or seven kids."

"Brendan lives alone?"

"No, he lives with his mom, but she's gone a lot. She was gone over the weekend. And he's out of school now—you know—working over in Garberville, pouring concrete with his uncle. So there wasn't anyone there but kids."

"Okay…?"

"So there were a few kids and we drank beer, smoked a couple of joints. And got drunk and a little high. I passed out. Becky thinks she did, too."

"Becky thinks she did?"

"She doesn't know, because she got wasted and went to Brendan's mother's bedroom and lay down and woke up at about three in the morning. Me—I think I must have passed out, because I was just waking up in the morning, in Brendan's room. There were only a couple of kids still there—Becky, Brendan, a couple others sleeping in the living room."

"And…"

"And I felt really awful. Like I'd been hit in the head with a brick and my stomach was all upset. I couldn't wait to get home and sleep it off. When I got home I told my mother I thought I'd got the flu while I was at Becky's, and I went to get into bed, and undressed, you know? My underpants were inside out and backward."

Ew, Mel thought. I have another one.

"So—I didn't think anything about it—figured I did that to myself drunk."

"Big drinker, are you?"

She hung her head. "Not really," she said. "I've been to a few parties with these guys. Maybe three. I never got so trashed before."

"Ever pass out and put on your undies inside out and backward?"

"No. Nothing like that. But I realize I was pretty drunk."

"But you didn't think anything about it? Let me ask you something—did you have any soreness anywhere? Bruises or anything?"

"I was a little sore, down there," she said, glancing into her lap. "I just thought it was impossible. You know? Because I thought if anything had happened, I would've woken up. But then later when I heard this girl in the locker room at gym class telling one of her girlfriends to never go to one of those parties—those beer parties. And she said something like, 'I'm not even going to tell you what happened to me! You just wouldn't believe it!' And right away I knew. Don't ask me how I knew—I just knew."

"You think you might have been raped?"

"I might've been, yeah. I don't know. It just doesn't seem like those guys... They're just friends. They don't seem like the kind of guys who..."

"Have you missed periods or anything?"

"I'm on the pill. I'm on it for my periods, you know? Because they're awful. I got my period on time about a week later, but now I'm starting to worry about other stuff. Like what if something happened to me and I got something?"

"Straight thinking, kiddo. We can check for everything and put your mind at ease. But, Sophie—I've heard something similar to this before and I'm concerned. I have no idea if anything happened to you besides a little too much beer, but I seriously need you to talk to a friend of mine, a police officer, who—"

"Wait a sec," she said. "I don't want to get into trouble."

"Sophie, you're not in trouble. My advice is to stop going to unchaperoned parties where alcohol is served and joints are available, but that's just advice. My friend might want to ask you who was there, just to see if there are any similarities between your experience and... And other things I've picked up just talking with people."

"And if there are? Will the people who were there get in trouble? Because I don't want to do that."

"Sophie, I can assure you no one's going to get into trouble for drinking beer. I'm not even interested in the pot. Everything you say will be kept in confidence. But seriously—we need to know what's going on, if something like assault is going on."

"What if nothing's going on?"

"Then nothing more will come of it," Mel said. But in her gut, she knew. "My friend, he has a lot of detective experience, he's worked with a lot of kids—and he's been looking into this stuff already. He'd be very interested in talking to you. And he will never divulge where he got his information without your complete permission. Will you, Sophie? If it could help keep this from happening to anyone else?"

"I might," she said, ducking her head shyly. "Let me think about it."

Mel did the requisite pelvic exam, tested for STDs and convinced Sophie to talk to Mike. Mel asked Sophie to wait at the clinic for a little while, just long enough to see if she could find Mike. They could have their conversation in private at the clinic—the safest place she could think of, away from Sophie's friends and parents. If Mike wasn't around, she would have to ask Sophie to come back the next day, and cross her fingers that the girl would.

Mel felt terrible all over. She hated hearing Sophie's story, because she was convinced there was a date raper in town, maybe even a group of boys, young men, possibly using drugs on unsuspecting girls.

It was early afternoon when she left Sophie in the clinic and went to the bar. It was quiet, as was usual for the midafternoon. Jack's truck was gone—she assumed he was out at the house, getting in everyone's business. In the kitchen she found Paige and Preacher getting things started for the evening meal. "Hi, guys. Anyone seen Mike?"

"His car's out back, but I think he's locked in with his... You know Brie's in town, right?" Preacher asked.

"Yeah," she said, picking up the phone in the kitchen. She punched in Mike's land line. "Hi, Mike. I hate to do this to you. I need you. It's about a situation we discussed a while ago—it's business." Then she said, "Thanks. I owe you one."

She went behind the bar and fixed herself a sparkling water, waiting for Mike. The speed with which he appeared gave her a little peace of mind. She hadn't interrupted anything too complicated or private, and for that she was grateful.

"What's up?" he asked.

"Let's step out on the porch," she said.

Once outside, she explained in hushed tones what she'd just heard, and the girl's willingness to talk to him. Then she took him across the street and introduced him to Sophie. She should have expected Mike to be a pro, yet she was pleasantly surprised by the tenderness and finesse with which he handled Sophie, putting her at ease at once, gaining her confidence and trust. He took her into Doc's kitchen, since there were no patients in the clinic. A few moments later he came out, asking for a tablet and pen, then went back behind closed doors.

Mel really wanted to go see Brie, but she felt she had to stay at the clinic while Mike interviewed her patient. David had been napping in the reception area in his playpen and she heard him start to rouse. Before long he sent up an alarm and she had to go pick him up, change him, cuddle him quiet. Over an hour passed before Mike walked Sophie out of the kitchen. He had a hand on her back, solicitously escorting her, thanking her in soft tones for helping him so much.

By the moony eyes Sophie turned up to Mike's face, not only had he won her over, she adored him. Trusted him completely.

When Sophie had gone, Mike looked at Mel and gave her a somber nod.

"We have a bad one on the loose, don't we?" she asked.

He nodded. "Or ones. Now I have names. Now I can talk to some other youngsters, one of whom I suspect is one of your other girls—because the name didn't come from you."

"What'll you do?"

"Interview. Right away. And I'm going to have to round up some support for Sophie—she's going to need to talk to a professional."

"Family Planning might help with that. And the county has a sexual assault response team."

He shook his head almost sadly. "When I took this job, this is the last thing I expected to be up against."

"Brie is barely here," Mel said sympathetically.

"She'll understand, Mel. In fact, I'm going to have to talk to her about this."

"I never tell Jack...."

He gave a nod. "I'll ask her to be sensitive to that, but after what Brie's been through, I have to be up front about this. She's been lied to—things have been withheld from her. I can't keep something like this back from her. It's real important. We've barely begun...."

Mel held up a hand. "You know what you can and can't do—and you know we can't have these teenagers exposed."

He nodded. "I want to see her. Brie. When can I see her?" she asked, jostling David.

"I think as soon as ten minutes. Give me a head start?"

"Sure. At least."

Something wonderful happened to Mike's heart when his hand touched the door to his RV, just knowing she was there. Everything about that felt right. When he stepped inside, there she was, waiting. Brie had tidied up the place, put away their clothes and made up the bed. She was sitting at the small table with a tablet in front of her, writing, and looked up at him with those soft, glowing eyes.

He couldn't help himself—the first thing he did was go to her, lean down and kiss her. "What are you doing?" he asked, sitting opposite her.

"Writing my resignation to the prosecutor's office," she said. "And making a list. I'm going to start looking for an office. If I'm going to stay here, I'm going to work. And I'm going to stay here."

"An office?"

"Uh-huh. I don't know what I'm going to do, but I'm a lawyer. I can't work out of this space because I'll need my things. My computer, books, et cetera."

"I love hearing this. Are we sure we want to make Virgin River home?"

"I can do it, although I don't think I'm going to find an office in this little town. In fact, who knows where I'll find work? I might have to commute to one of the larger towns, or maybe I'll be taking whatever work there is in some of these small towns. But, Mike—do you want to leave Virgin River? Because I think you know—I'll go anywhere with you."

He reached for her hands and held them. "I love it here. The best part of my life has come to me here. I have a suggestion. Instead of looking for an office, think about looking for a house. One large enough for an office at home, or one with the space to build on. You could work out of our home."

"You think?"

"If we're going to go with nature, something tells me the need for more space will present itself before long. How do you feel about that?"

She smiled at him. "Like going forward with you."

"Am I getting ahead of you?" he asked her. "This is quick. Your brother, your father, your sisters—they're going to point out how fast we're moving. People are going to say we're crazy."

"I don't care," she said, shaking her head. "I haven't felt this good in well over a year. I'm due a little crazy happiness. When do you think we'll come down to earth?"

"Sooner than you think. I have some work I have to do. Police work. It's going to tie me up a little bit, but it's very important."

"Can you tell me about it?"

"I want to talk to you about it, but it's very sensitive. It could be upsetting."

"Okay. I'm good with sensitive. And I'll try to look upsetting in the face."

"Mel doesn't share things like this with anyone, even Jack. She hopes I might help investigate. I told her I was going to talk to you for a lot of reasons, but you'll have to be discreet with your brother. No question—he can be completely trusted, but this is an arrangement they have and I don't want to get in the way of that."

"Okay," she said.

"Mel has had some young patients she suspects have encountered a date raper. From what she describes, I believe she's right. I finally have some names—I'm going to do some interviews. See if I can get a fix on what's happened and who this could be. Then I'm going to get him. Or them."

Brie couldn't help it—a shudder of revulsion passed through her. God, she hated to think of anyone going through what she had. Mike gave her a moment to gather herself and finally she just shook her head, saddened to hear it. "How awful. Have you ever worked sexual assault? Are you up to speed on this?"

"I haven't worked a sexual assault unit, but I've worked with some of those detectives on cases that cross over, and have a little experience from that. And I've worked with a lot of kids, which gives me an advantage in this situation. I can get started without your help, but I'm sure I'll be asking for your advice. Can you deal with that?"

"I can try. I happen to know a lot about this—and not just

from personal experience. I've prepped a lot of rape victims for trial."

"I was hoping you'd be willing to help. I'm going to go talk to some people," Mike said. "Mel is dying to see you."

"She's at Doc's?"

"By now she might be right outside." He opened the door and saw her standing near the back door of the bar, bouncing David in her arms to keep him happy, giving them whatever time and space they needed. He gestured for her to come ahead. But Brie got up from the table and went to greet her. She opened her arms to Mel and the baby and they embraced as sisters would.

Mel slipped David onto the seat beside her at the small kitchen table while Brie got them each a soda. "How does it feel to be in my kitchen?" Brie asked Mel.

Mel smiled. "Took you long enough."

"I had to think it through...."

"You look beautiful," Mel said. "There is no doubt in your eyes."

"Do you think they talk? The men?"

"Not the way we do. Mike won't talk to Jack about you, I'm sure of that. Jack has been a real idiot about you and Mike."

"He's over that now," Brie said. "Someone brought us breakfast and left it outside, and I suspect it was Jack."

"Well, good. It's time he came around. I'd apologize for your brother's stubbornness, but you've known him longer than I have." She laughed. "Someone should have warned me he can be such an interfering pest. And bossy? Lord." She tilted her head. "One look at you makes it clear this is the right thing for you. For both of you. Mike is wearing some kind of halo."

"He should. He's an angel. I've never been treated with

such kindness and tenderness. Never. He spent months talking me through the dark days without a hint that he expected more from me. How many men do you know who are willing to invest themselves like that, when there might not be anything in it for them?"

"Mike's a good man," Mel said. "He wouldn't put a woman he cared about in a difficult position."

"I wasn't sure I'd even be able to respond to a man again, Mel. You can't imagine how nervous I was."

Mel simply waited quietly; if Brie wanted to be more specific she could. When a moment passed and Brie hadn't said any more, Mel said, "I'm just so grateful you finally worked it out, and that it brought you back to us."

Brie looked upward for a second, shaking her head, still in wonder. It was at times like this that she would miss her sisters most, but with Mel here she had the female connection she needed. That secret talk that women shared. "I had a lot to think about, to consider, but in the end, I'm here because of something that came up in Sacramento."

Mel lifted her brows. "Anything you can talk about?"

"I haven't had a chance to tell Jack yet—but Mike knows everything. The reason I came suddenly and without calling ahead is because Brad came to see me. Jerome Powell was found in Florida and the ADA is working on extradition to bring him back for trial."

Mel reached out and covered her hand. "God, Brie," she said in a breath. "How are you doing?"

"I'm going to testify against him. Of course. But I'm staying right here until that happens."

"Oh, baby. You know we'll all be there for you."

"It was bizarre—that I should get this news from Brad. He came to the house to tell me. But before he told me about

Powell, he asked for another chance, to see if we could re-kindle some of what we had. He's no longer with Christine."

"Whew," Mel said, sitting back in shock. "How do you feel about that?"

A slow smile spread on Brie's lips. "I showed him the door and then packed immediately. I'm done with that part of my life." Then the smile vanished as she said, "The other part, the trial, that's going to take a little longer. Be a little harder. Who am I kidding? A lot harder."

The very first occasion Mike had to present his business card officially came at Valley High School in the guidance coun-selor's office. Mrs. Bradford was a cautious and serious woman and, while cordial, she wasn't about to turn any of her students over to this man without being sure. He invited her to have him checked out with the sheriff's office if she questioned his authenticity. And he told her a little bit about how he came to be the new town constable, showing her the badge Hope had given him. He'd been to the high school before, talking to the principal and some of the teachers, but just on a get-to-know-you basis, never as part of an investigation. He ex-plained that, in his capacity, he wouldn't be making arrests of any kind, but that his interviews might help solve a problem.

He assured Mrs. Bradford that the students he wanted to speak with were in absolutely no trouble, but without even re-alizing it, might have information that could help him. "Think of it as something like a witness to an accident—someone might have information that can help resolve an issue, with-out even being aware of it."

Mrs. Bradford disappeared for about twenty minutes, and when she came back she was ready to have a few students called to her office to speak with Mike. He assumed she had called the sheriff.

Mike talked to a couple of girls who provided him with the names of teens they had seen at parties. Within an hour, Brenda Carpenter was delivered to the counselor's office and they were left alone together. He knew Brenda's parents, but in the months he'd been in Virgin River, he hadn't met her. He showed his badge again.

"What's this about?" she asked.

"You're not in any trouble," he assured her. "You're under no obligation to talk to me, but I hope you will. I want to ask you about a gathering of kids, a party you might have attended. Maybe recently, maybe quite a while ago."

"I don't go to parties," she said.

"Your name appeared on a list I have of kids who attended one or more parties I'm checking out. It could have been as long ago as last year. What I'm trying to learn about is a party in which there could have been drugs present."

"I don't do drugs."

"I'm not talking about pot. You might not have known if there were drugs present. Being used."

"Then how could I help you?"

"This is worth checking. And what you have to say, if anything, goes no further. I know your parents through Jack and, I promise you—I won't be discussing this with them or anyone else. I'm looking for information about a party at which people passed out or lost consciousness."

Her pupils shrank at once and her eyes narrowed. "What are you talking about?"

"Have you ever found yourself at a party where that happened? Where people—maybe they were drinking—passed out or lost consciousness? Because that information could help me."

Brenda just about leaped out of her chair. "Who told you about that? No one was ever supposed to tell about that."

He made sure his arms were open, that he appeared accessible to her, even if it was only on a subconscious level. "A student I interviewed claimed to have been at a party where this happened to her. I can't tell you who—it's confidential. I don't know whether you were present or not, which is why I'm asking."

"You're sure? It wasn't an adult who told you?"

"No," he said, shaking his head. "It was definitely not an adult. Have anything for me, Brenda? It's very important."

"Why? Why is it so important?"

"Because that sort of thing has happened, and I really have to make it stop before somebody gets... Well," he said, shaking his head solemnly. "Let's be honest for a second—the situation could be deadly. If I knew something, I wouldn't want that on my head."

"Deadly? How? From getting drunk and passing out?"

"If some kind of drug was used to cause a person to lose consciousness, yes."

She crossed her arms over her chest. "What do you want me to say?"

"Let's back up. Have you ever been to a party where that's happened?"

"I went to a party, once, a long time ago, where people drank too much. I don't think that's what you mean."

He shrugged. "That could be all it looked like, if something was slipped in a beer."

She took a breath. "Like I said, a long time ago."

"Do you remember who was there?"

"Why?"

"Because your name came up once, although there were several parties where that happened," he said. "Now, I'm just a simple guy, but I have an idea that maybe you went once and decided you don't like those parties too much. I'm not guessing why," he said, holding up his hands. "All I want to do is get some names from you—confidential—just so I can see if any of the same names turn up at these parties. Regularly."

A startled look came over her face, then there was a slow transformation—to anger. She was catching on. She knew now. She wasn't the only one. A guy or guys were going after the girls.

Mike turned a tablet with a pen on top toward her. "And anything specific would help, like whether a certain person was just there for a little while, a long while, was the host of the party, brought the beer, that sort of thing. That would be important. Thank you."

When Mike sat in his car forty minutes later looking through these lists, he knew Brenda was probably the patient who had become pregnant at a party with no idea how. Then something jumped out at him that spelled opportunity and relief at once. There was one name he recognized. It appeared on Sophie's list—that party had taken place about a month ago. A young man she remembered being there for a short time. The name popped up once more—at a kegger at the rest stop, again for a short time. But the name did not appear on Brenda's list, the party she had attended last spring, or on any others. Tom Booth. Tom would know the boys present at the party where Sophie passed out.

Mike could have gone back into the school and asked Mrs. Bradford to call Tom Booth to her office for an interview, but before he had much time to consider that the last bell rang, and he watched students pour out of the building and migrate to cars and buses in the parking lot. Paul had mentioned Tom was helping out at Jack's homesite after school, and he wondered if he might run into him there.

And he'd also run into Jack out at the job site. In thinking about it, he might be able to take care of two delicate situations at the same time. Brie had spent the night in his bed, in his arms—it had been a lot more intimate than a trip to the coast, or a dance at a festival. If Jack was going to have an issue with that, he'd rather they get beyond it without Brie being present. He was aware that she'd seen her brother that morning and had said the reunion was uneventful; Jack hadn't seemed to have had any bone to pick. However, that didn't cover the territory between two men who loved Brie—a protective brother and a lover.

Tom's little red truck wasn't there when Mike arrived at the building site, but the place was alive with activity, a lot of noise coming from inside the structure. Jack's truck was parked near the house.

Inside, Mike found a lot of men at work and Jack in the kitchen on his knees, working baseboards into place around newly installed cabinets. He watched him work for a moment and then said, "Looking real good out here, Jack."

Jack leaned back, sitting on his heels, and looked up at Mike. He pulled a rag out of his back pocket and mopped the sweat and sawdust off his face. Then he stood. Jack had a lot of expressions—there was the good buddy, the comrade, the steely-eyed killer, and there was one that he seemed to reserve for his role as commander and leader. It was not unlike the expression a father would bestow on the beau of a daughter— not quite deadly, not quite docile, but something in between. Purposely unreadable, giving away no emotion. "Thanks," he said simply, responding to the compliment.

"I thought if you had anything you wanted to say to me, I'd give you a chance to do that while Brie's occupied with other things."

"Yeah," Jack said. "Yeah, I have something to say. We've been over this, but just let me say this once more, so you know where I'm coming from. She's real special to me and

I've seen her hurt. Jesus, worse than hurt. You know what I'm talking about."

Mike gave a nod. "I know."

"This thing that's going on with you and my sister, I fought it. It really scared me, got under my skin...."

"I know," Mike said again. "I under—"

"Because I'm a fool," Jack said, cutting him off. He shook his head in frustration. "Christ almighty, Valenzuela—you've had my back how many times? You'd fight beside me in a heartbeat, put yourself in harm's way to protect me or any member of our squad. I don't know why I got my back up like I did. When a woman in your family gets hurt like that— you just want to put her in a padded box with a lock on it so no one can ever get to her and hurt her again, even if that's the worst thing you could do." He shook his head again and now his expression was readable. He was open. "I apologize, man. I thought of you as my brother before you even glanced at Brie. I know she's safe with you."

Mike found himself chuckling. "Man," he said. "Mel must have held you down and beat you over the head."

Now the expression got surly. "I'd just like to know why Mel always gets the fucking credit when I start to make sense. What makes you think I didn't just think it through and—"

"Never mind," Mike said, sticking out a hand. "I appreciate it." Jack took the hand and Mike's smile vanished. The look on his face became earnest. "Jack, I give you my word. I plan to do everything in my power to make your sister happy. I'll protect her with my life."

"You'd better," Jack said sternly. "Or so help me—"

Mike couldn't help but smile. "And we were doing so good there for a minute."

"Yeah, well..."

"You won't be disappointed in me," Mike said.

Jack was quiet a moment, then said, "Thanks. I knew that. It just took me a while. Guys like us…"

"Yeah." Mike laughed. "Guys like us. Who'd ever have thought?"

Jack rubbed a hand across the back of his sweaty neck and said, "Yeah, well, look out. You bite the dust like I did and all of a sudden you're breeding up a ball team."

"I'll be on the lookout for that," Mike said. "Show me the house, Jack. Looks like it's coming along real well."

"Yeah, we'll find Paul to give us a tour. I was going to make it good—he's going to make it a masterpiece."

After about thirty minutes of looking at every detail of Paul's work, Mike saw Tom Booth's truck pull up. Tom parked, got out and dug into his job of cleaning up and hauling trash. Mike timed his approach; he shot the breeze with Jack and Paul as the sun was sinking. Jack finally left to get a quick shower so he could help serve dinner at the bar, and Paul went back into the house to check on the crew as they were finishing up.

Mike made his way to Tom. "Hey," he said. "Could you give me a minute?"

"Sure," Tom said, dropping the debris at his feet and pulling off his gloves. "What's up?"

"I talked to you about some parties a while ago and—"

"Look, I told you, Mike—I dropped into a couple, just out of curiosity. What's going on here?"

"I'm looking for something," he said with a shrug. "Drugs."

"Drugs?" Tom asked. "I saw a couple of joints passed around. I cut out. You know my dad. I'd be in some military academy if I'd been caught around that stuff. Maybe a penitentiary. I'd be history. He's not a liberal kind of guy."

"Yeah," Mike said with a smile. "I figured that one out all

by myself. Actually, I was looking for something else. Something you don't see every day."

Tom's chin dropped and he looked down. "I didn't see anything," he said.

"Son. Look me in the eye and say that."

He lifted his gaze. "Seriously, I left when I saw a couple of joints come out. I got myself grounded for going somewhere they had beer. My dad, he's not the strictest dad on the books—I've had a beer with him. Innocent beer, no driving, no going out to a kegger in the woods, though. But..."

Mike waited. "But?" he finally asked.

"I was already on my way out, and I suspected something was going on." He shrugged. "Couple of kids breaking from the crowd, doing something a little sly, not gone long. You know?"

"What did you suspect?" Mike asked, his radar up.

"Have no idea. Ecstasy, maybe? Meth? I don't know. Something sneaky. Man, I wanted no deeper than a beer, seeing a joint from a long, safe distance. I'd be—"

"History," Mike finished for him. "Who threw the parties where you saw this?"

Tom lowered his gaze again, shaking his head. Then before Mike asked him to look him in the eye, he raised his eyes and said, "Look, I wouldn't mind getting the little shit in trouble—I'd love that. But really—I have absolutely no idea what might have been going on. If I knew something and thought someone might get hurt, I'd tell you everything, but I can't rat out a guy for drugs if he might've just been exchanging phone numbers. You know?"

Mike was quiet a long moment. Then he said, "I know. Let's go over who was at those parties again, okay?"

"I can do that," Tom said.

12

Of all the people in Virgin River Mel could have imagined having a positive mammogram, Lilly Andersen, who had borne and nursed seven children, was the last. Lilly, who was so dear to Mel. But there it was—the radiologist called and said the X-ray was significant. Lilly should see a specialist immediately.

It didn't sit well with Mel that in addition to this probable diagnosis, Lilly had lost a great deal of weight recently. She hoped and prayed the weight loss was from chasing one-year-old Chloe around.

Chloe. Only four people knew the truth—Mel, Doc, Lilly and Buck Andersen. Everyone thought Chloe had been an abandoned newborn whom Lilly had been fostering since

Chloe was three weeks old. But Chloe was her flesh and blood. Lilly's own child.

Now she had to tell this woman that she might have breast cancer.

"I'm sorry, Lilly. But at least we caught it, and if it's not good news, you can concentrate on the treatment. I've got you set up in Eureka for tomorrow."

"So soon?" she asked nervously.

"The sooner the better. Can Buck take you over there, or do you need me?"

Lilly, so typical, smiled that gentle, comforting smile of hers, touched Mel's hand and said, "Don't worry, Mel. I'll make Buck take a day off."

"Want me to talk to him? Because this is important."

"No, I can handle Buck. But they won't do anything like operate on me right away, will they?"

"No—but they'll do a biopsy. They might try to aspirate a lump or do more X-rays and blood work. If surgery is in order, I think they're going to get to it soon, however. The radiologist described the presence as significant. Have you felt a lump or lumps?"

"Not really—but I'm large and kind of lumpy anyway."

"Lilly, you're going to need help with Chloe. I really think you should tell your family the truth about Chloe. Your kids."

"We'll get by, Mel. I don't want you to worry."

"I'm not worried. Treatment now is good—the survival rate for breast cancer is great. But if you have to undergo treatment, you might not feel well. It seems like they deserve to know. And they're all wonderful, to the last one. They won't hold it against you."

She laughed and said, "If you don't hold it against me, I guess no one would!"

"You have to remember—if there's a reaction, it's only a

reaction. And temporary, until the facts settle. Don't be afraid of them, Lilly. They adore you."

"I'm lucky that way," she said.

But that was where Lilly's luck ended. Her breast cancer was advanced, aggressive and had spread to the lymph system and lungs. After a bilateral radical mastectomy, performed within a week of her visit with the surgeon, her new oncologist put her on a very strong regimen of radiation and chemotherapy. Chloe was living with her oldest sister, Amy, because Lilly was weak and ill.

Sadly it was common in police work to realize immediately who the bad guys were, yet not have the kind of probable cause or evidence required for a search warrant or arrest. Mike had deluded himself that it would be simpler in a town so small, where everyone seemed to know everything that was going on. But he faced the same problems in Virgin River as he had encountered in L.A.

After talking to Tommy and to twenty other teenagers, he had lists of names spread across several parties that had taken place from last May to recent months. There might have been even more, but Mike didn't know about them. Mike made one trip to Garberville to talk to nineteen-year-old Brendan Lancaster, who, along with Tommy's ex-friend Jordan Whitley, were the only two boys at every party. The few other names that turned up more than twice were probably shills—boys who were at the parties but didn't have a clue as to what was going on. Mike could tell in the interview—the shills responded with confusion that seemed authentic, yet Whitley's and Lancaster's alleged confusion was obviously contrived. Very few girls' names turned up more than once.

Where Mike got confused was the combination of drugs that caused people—girls, primarily—to pass out and possibly other drugs that hyped them up. It was a weird combination. Could there be roofies and either ecstasy or meth at the same party? Sounded like a smorgasbord—and a deadly one at that.

Mike was easily convinced that Tom Booth had no involvement with this group. He'd gone to one party at the rest stop out of curiosity, stayed less than an hour and had seen it wasn't going anywhere good. He'd decided to get out of there before it went south in a hurry. He'd been to a friend's house a couple of times before he met and started dating his girlfriend; beer was available but he'd never seen anyone passed out in any of those instances, probably because he'd never stayed long. He didn't know many people, but he'd given the names of the ones he did know, and the names added up, once again, to Whitley and Lancaster.

"I'll give you a clue," Mel told Mike. "Your boy has chlamydia. If there's more than one boy with chlamydia, they're passing it around."

"But I can't get to it," he told her.

"Then maybe you'll have to catch him."

"Maybe," Mike said, and a picture of him staking out a teen party waiting for these boys to drug and rape an unsuspecting young girl was enough to make him want to throw up. He thought he was probably going to have to get some help, which would mean going to the sheriff again, yet all he had was a list of names of teenagers who'd been drinking, maybe smoking a little pot, and had nothing else to say. Until he came across something more significant, he had nothing to report to anyone. He'd just have to keep talking to these kids, get Zach Hadley to sharpen his ears at the high school, maybe catch a break.

It was nearing Thanksgiving and Mike was caught up in this caper when Paul issued an invitation to a dinner at the general's house for Mike and Brie. It was Vanessa's idea to welcome Brie to the community—a generous thought that was typical of her. While the general—who had command of his kitchen—and the women were occupied, Paul and Mike stood out at the corral with a couple of beers in the light dusting of a late-afternoon snow. They had just been talking about the fact that Tommy was working hard out at Jack's homesite, really earning his money by keeping the site clean of construction trash, when he came riding up from one of the back trails with a girl on another horse.

"There's Romeo now," Paul said.

"New girlfriend?" Mike asked, squinting into the distance.

"The wonderful Brenda. He's been after her forever. I think the horses finally cinched it for him."

Oh, Jesus, Mike thought. This is going to freak her out. "Ah… Listen, there's a situation. I'll try to explain later, but do me a favor, okay? When they get up here, drag Tommy out of here. Tell him you need his help—firewood or something. I'll take care of his horse. I need a minute with the girl."

"Everything okay? Because she's a nice girl…."

"Yeah, she's a real nice girl. But I've had a little business with her—she's not in any kind of trouble, I promise. If I don't find a way to convince her I'd never talk to anyone about her, Tommy might lose his main squeeze over something as dumb as nerves. Cop nerves."

"You been flashing that badge around, partner?"

"At the high school, yeah."

"Oh, crap," Paul said. "You better make this right because Tommy's got his head screwed on straight after a little trouble with his dad, and it just might be due to the girl."

"Yeah," Mike said. "I can do this. Don't worry."

Sure enough, just as Mike expected, Brenda looked stricken when she spied Mike at the corral. She actually pulled back on the reins and slowed her mount. Mike tried sending her a signal, a narrowing of eyes and very slight shaking of his head, but she was a little lost. Scared. No way she wanted this new boyfriend to know what she'd gone through. No way she wanted to sit and tremble nervously through dinner with the cop.

"Tommy, buddy, help me out a sec, huh?" Paul said. "I need a hand getting in a load of wood. Mike will take care of your horse."

"You sure?" he asked, dismounting. "Maybe Mike should do wood while I help Brenda with the horses."

"Aw, his arm, you know—still iffy. Come on."

"You okay with the horse, Mike?"

"You bet," Mike said. "Your girl here can show me what to do."

"Ah, Mike—this is Brenda. Brenda, Mike Valenzuela, friend of the family."

"Nice to meet you," Mike said, extending his hand to the young girl. She accepted it limply, silently, surprise and worry still etched on her face.

Mike watched over his shoulder as Paul led Tommy away, an arm around him as they walked up the hill toward the house. Brenda dismounted and led the horse toward the stable.

"Brenda, don't panic. No one knows I've talked to you about anything. All right?"

"Sure," she said nervously.

"Easy does it," he said. "Tommy's a good catch. Don't cut and run because of me. I'm not saying anything to anyone. I've seen your folks at the bar ten times since we talked and haven't breathed a word. I told you, our conversation was in confidence."

"Yeah, but you've been all over that school. People are talking."

"Yup," he said. "And they're talking to me, too. Listen,

there's something you ought to know about your boyfriend here—I've been getting to know him and I think he's solid. If there's stuff you're worried about him finding out, it might be better coming from you—but that's just my opinion. I think he's a tough, fair kid. He's not going to get anything from me."

As she was leading her mount into the stable, she stopped. "You know more than you're saying. Don't you?"

"Yup," he said.

"You know who it was?" she asked without giving him any specifics. But he already knew the specifics. He could continue to play dumb with her or he could go out on a limb and hope it paid off.

"Yup."

"Will you tell me?"

"Nope."

"Why not?"

"I don't have a victim. Can't make an arrest or prosecute a crime without a victim. And just like I'm not telling anyone what you said—"

"Is there more than one person who could be that victim?" she asked.

He looked into her eyes steadily. "What do you think?"

"Oh, no." Tears gathered in her eyes—probably as the possibility of more girls going through what she'd been through flashed through her mind. "Oh, my God."

"Yeah, this isn't pretty, is it? Anytime you want to talk about this, work through it, you know how to reach me. I'm not asking you to do anything, but I want you to try to trust me a little. I'm going to give you some space, and I'm never saying anything about your personal life, or my relationship with you unless you give me the okay. Get that? Let's take care of the horses. And act like we just hit it off. Huh? Instant friends…"

"I don't know how to do that," she said, emotional.

"Sure you do. We're going to have a nice dinner, a visit with the Booth family. I'll introduce you to Brie—you're going to love her," he said with a smile. "I bet she was a lot like you when she was sixteen. Good grades, nice boyfriends, great family." His smile deepened. "You'll be fine. You gotta trust me a little, Brenda. I never sold anyone out."

"What if you never get a victim so you can make an arrest?"

"I'm gonna get him anyway," he said. "I'm trying to come up with ideas that don't involve you."

They got the saddles off and the tack out, then began brushing the horses. After about ten minutes she said, "Thanks. Mike."

"Hey, Brenda, I think we're on the same side. We don't want anyone else to get hurt."

It hadn't yet been two weeks that Brie had been in Virgin River, but to Mike it felt as if they'd been together forever. No matter what the evening held, whether supper at the grill and a quick walk across the yard to the RV, or dinner with the general and his family, when they were finally alone the door was barely closed before they were in each other's arms. They hadn't slept in a stitch of clothing since Brie's arrival and probably never would again. Mike thought about her all day and made long, slow, delicious love to her almost every night. Then there were the mornings…

"No one has this much sex," she whispered to him, breathless and satisfied.

"Even I never had this much sex," he admitted, just as breathless.

"It's a honeymoon, that's what it is," she told him.

"I've been on two honeymoons, and they were nothing like this."

"Well, I've been on one, and it was nothing by comparison." She giggled. "You're amazing, Mike," she told him.

He rose over her and looked deeply into her eyes. "You're a passionate woman, Brie. You have a powerful libido. It's a good thing you chose a Latino." He grinned. "We have a reputation for being able to handle hot women like you."

"You handle me, all right. Do you think this is going to wind down anytime soon?"

"If nature takes its course, it will. That's why I'm taking advantage of you right now. I know what's coming in the pregnant days."

"I just can't wait for the end of the day," she said. "I shudder on and off all day long, just thinking…"

"Aftershocks," he said, rolling onto his back. "I have 'em, too." He chuckled. "It's a miracle is what it is. I wasn't even sure I could do it."

"Huh?"

He rolled back onto his side and looked down at her. "I came out of my coma with a few things missing. Erections, for one thing."

"Seriously?" she asked, wide-eyed. "Because you're certainly having more than your share now."

"It took almost a year to come back, and then it was completely unpredictable. When I took you to bed that first time, I didn't know if it would work, how well it would work, if it would keep working.…"

"And yet you went for it?"

He shrugged. "I had responded to you before… I was hopeful."

"Mendocino," she said with a smile.

"You did know. I wondered."

"What if it hadn't worked that first night?"

He ran a hand over her naked shoulder and down over her

hip. "Helping you become comfortable with a loving touch was all I wanted. Pleasing you was the only important thing. I was prepared to make up for it. In many wonderful ways."

She closed her eyes. "You do have your ways," she whispered.

He laughed, deep in his throat, and took great pride in working a little of his magic. Nothing in his life to this moment compared to the happiness he felt when she responded to him, when she was swept away by the pleasure he could give her. And sweeter still was holding her afterward, whispering in the night, or talking softly in the early-morning light. Whether it was love talk, usually only stirring them up all over again, or just the conversation of partners planning their days, their lives. Then there were conversations about children, about a house on a hill, about life together that took them into old age. All of it filled him up inside, gave him the substance that had been missing from his life. He'd had women but this was the first time he'd had a true partner.

Brie propped herself up on her elbow, meeting his smiling eyes, her hair falling over her shoulders. "It's almost Thanksgiving," she said. "You're sure you want to stay here?"

He shrugged. "Mel and Jack can't leave—she has babies coming. Preacher and Paige are here—that's family. If you want to go to Sam's, I'll do that with you. But I don't want to go to L.A. yet."

"You aren't keeping me a secret from the Valenzuelas, are you?"

"God, no, I've told them all, every one of them. I even told them to look out—you're bilingual and tricky. But I'm not ready to share you. In my mother's Catholic household, it would be separate bedrooms because we're not married. Even though I'm thirty-seven and she knows we're living together—it's her Catholic home. We could stay in a hotel, but

I think we'll visit later. Just give me a little more time. I've never been this happy in my life and all day long I look forward to when we're finally alone together." He played with the hair that fell to her shoulder. "I'm greedy. This is the best my life has ever been."

"What about Christmas?" she asked him.

"What about it?"

"Will your family be upset it we go to Dad's for Christmas? Because my whole family plus Mel's sister, brother-in-law and the kids will be there—and I want to be with them."

"Then that's where we'll be. We can join the Valenzuelas another time. You have to remember, mija—my family is so large that my parents don't expect to have all the kids together with their own families every year. We'll do Christmas with them another year."

Thanksgiving fell on the last Thursday of the month and Preacher did the dinner in the bar. General Booth and his family were invited, but they drove down the coast to Bodega Bay to be with his sister and niece. There were several Virgin River folk who were included in Thanksgiving at the bar, people that Preacher and Jack had looked after for a long time, and it was a tradition to serve them the holiday meal in the bar. There was Doc and Hope McCrea, Connie and Ron of the corner store, Ricky's grandma Lydie, Joy and Bruce from just down the street. Now that Preacher and Jack were both married, they'd close the bar on Christmas, but Preacher liked doing his Thanksgiving feast, keeping the bar open in case anyone who was alone straggled in.

When Mel, Jack and Davie arrived for dinner, Mel called her two patients who were close to due dates to see how they were doing, and when the report was that everything was status quo, she asked for her one glass of wine for the trimester. "One of my girls is running a tish late, while the other one has a habit of going early," she said, raising her glass to Brie. "Any second now, we're having not one but two babies."

"You must be so excited."

"I still get a little wound up, waiting. I live for the babies."

"And you're still feeling okay?"

"I've been sick as a dog with this one. But I hang in. Jack promises he's not going to do this to me again. And I'm leaning toward a surgical procedure while he sleeps."

The turkey was one of Preacher's very best and the side dishes were perfect. The pies had been made by Paige, who had developed some amazing culinary skills since coming to Virgin River. Preacher had proven to be not only a fabulous chef, but a wonderful teacher. And she was a very apt student who had seemed to find her niche in the kitchen with him.

Mel and Brie helped with the cleanup and Jack helped with the trash and sweeping up while balancing David on one hip. Mike wiped down the bar and tables but, even so, Preacher was busy cleaning up for so long that he missed Christopher's story time after his bath. He did go upstairs, however, to kiss the little guy good-night, because he found he just didn't get a good night's sleep without doing that. Then he trudged downstairs to close up the bar and go to his quarters, where he would lie platonically beside the woman of his dreams, waiting for her invitation indicating that enough time had passed. Every day he wondered when he'd get permission to let it go. He really waited for ovulation day when he didn't have to hold anything back and which, by his calculations, was about a week away. And Paige was so regular, he had this figured almost to the minute.

When he walked into their bedroom he saw that Paige was sitting up in bed, pillows behind her, sheet drawn up over her naked breasts and a mysterious smile on her face. When he frowned and cocked his head, she pulled a pregnancy test stick out from under the sheets. "Ta-da," she said. "We did it, Dad."

Preacher almost fell down. His eyes actually welled up with tears. He put his hands up to his face to try to gain control, but he was overwhelmed. Three months of saving up, waiting for ovulation day, and he had begun to despair of them making a baby. But Mel was right! This is what it took! He could do this again, and again! But wait, he told himself. One baby at a time!

He went to the bed and fell to one knee beside it, grabbing on to that pregnancy stick. "Oh, God! Oh, baby! Are you?"

"Looks like it, yes."

"Oh, my God," he said, grabbing her, pulling her into his arms and holding her against his huge chest. "Oh, God!"

"Easy, John," she said, laughing.

He immediately let go of her. "Am I hurting you?"

"No." She laughed again. "Of course not. But, John, if this little stick is accurate, you're all done saving up."

"Paige," he said in all seriousness, "do you think so?"

"Yes, John, I think so. I'm late for the first time ever, and the test is positive."

"Oh, my Lord. Oh, my Lord. How do you feel? Are you okay?"

"Actually… I'm pretty horny."

"Not really," he said, stunned.

"Oh, really. This saving-up business—I guess you think you're the only one who missed it. Huh?"

"Well… You got a little pissy there for a while…."

"Well, John, you told everyone it was ovulation day! You're going to have to learn to be a little more discreet in the future."

"Anything you want, baby. Anything."

"Fine. Take off your clothes. Come in here with me. Do that thing you do…."

★ ★ ★

Mike drove out to Jack's homesite; it was the first week in December—damp and cold. Preacher had taken a call at the bar and asked Mike to go break the news. Preacher would work on shutting down the bar and closing up the kitchen.

Jack and Paul were both inside installing cabinets; Paul's crew had already quit for the day and were in the trailer getting together an evening meal. The sun was low in the sky and Tommy Booth was still picking up scraps and dragging them to the Dumpster. Mike got out of his SUV and waited for Tom to turn back his way.

Mike walked over to Tom. "I gotta get you home, buddy. It's bad news. It's Matt. There was an explosion. In Baghdad."

The expression on Tom's face was one of pure horror. He was frozen for a second and then he called out, "Paul!" It sounded as much like a scream as a shout. It was enough to bring Paul and Jack running to the porch of the house, and for some of the crew to appear in the doorway of the trailer.

Tom looked back at Mike. "Is he dead?" he asked in a terrified whisper.

Mike nodded and the tears instantly sprang to Tom's eyes. Mike grabbed his upper arm. "Leave the truck. I'll drive you. I'll get the truck for you later. You have to be safe—your sister has enough going on right now. She can't have anything happen to you."

Tom sucked it back bravely. "Yeah," he said in a breath. "I'm okay."

"You have to try to hold it together for her. We can meet up and fall apart later, bud."

"Yeah," he said. Then he ran for Mike's SUV.

Paul jumped out of the house rather than walking down the plank where the porch steps would eventually be constructed. He ran to Mike, Jack right on his heels, questions shining in their eyes. "The Marine Corps is at the house, Paul. It's Matt. Car bomb in Baghdad. He's dead."

"Jesus," Paul said in a breath. "Vanni!" burst from his lips. And he lit off for his truck before Mike had a chance to stop him.

"Jack, I sent Mel out to the house because of Vanni's pregnancy. You'll want to get over there. Brie will bring Davie in a little while."

Tom, Mike and Paul beat Jack to the house by mere seconds, but when he looked in the door what he found was a Marine Corps recruiter and a chaplain sitting uncomfortably in the great room while Walt stood beside his daughter. Tommy leaned on his dad and Paul knelt beside the ottoman on which Vanni sat, and held her in his arms. Before Jack could even enter the house, Mel drove up, parked and walked swiftly toward the house. Jack stopped her at the doorway. "Are you up to this?"

"I'm fine, Jack. I should see Vanni."

"Sure."

Then he watched as his wife, medical bag in hand, went to her patient. Mel put a hand on Vanni's shoulder and said, "I'm here, Vanni. I just want to be here," she said. What she didn't say was, to be sure you don't have any problems with your pregnancy on account of the news.

Shortly the house filled up even more. Preacher and Paige with Christopher, Brie with David. Preacher brought food that had been prepared for that night's dinner, plus a couple of bottles of good liquor.

Eventually the Marine contingent spoke with the general about arrangements and told Walt that a similar detachment had paid a visit to Matt's parents in Oregon once Vanni had been notified. They'd be available to help with the burial, when those decisions were made.

Paul took Vanni to her room, glancing over his shoulder to Mel, indicating she should follow. Once there, Vanni lay back on the bed and cried helplessly. Paul sat beside her, gently rubbing her back. Mel quickly checked her vitals, listened to the fetal heartbeat and gave her a light sedative that wouldn't bother the baby.

This was the first time Mel became aware of a truly special bond between Paul and Vanni even though she'd seen their reunion a couple of months before, even though she'd heard Matt ask his best friend to look after his wife. Right now, in the moment, Vanni was completely dependent on Paul. Not on her father or brother, but on Paul, who continued to keep at least a hand on her, if not his arms around her. "Paul, if you can, if it's all right with Vanni, lie down beside her and stay close for a while. The contact," she said. "Loving contact is good."

"Vanni?" he asked.

She turned in his arms, nodding and sobbing, and he climbed onto her bed with her, drawing her close as she cried.

"Call me if you need me. I'll be near," Mel said.

It was a long while before the sobbing finally subsided. Vanni's eyes were swollen and red, her breathing jagged. She turned to look at Paul and asked, "Did he know?"

"Know what, honey?"

"Did he know he was going to die? I heard him ask you to take care of us if anything happened. It was almost as if he knew...."

"He didn't know. When it gets hot, you think like that. That's all it was. You always wonder. Plus, he knew without asking I'd be here for you."

"What am I going to do?" She wept again.

"We'll get through it, Vanni. You have a lot of people around who love you."

"He'll never see his baby. His son."

"Sure he will. You think he won't be watching? I know the guy—he'll be watching."

They lay together on her bed and Paul held her. No one bothered them; no one checked to see if they were okay. Paul could hear the soft murmur of voices in the other room, but the only thing that mattered at the moment was Vanni and the baby. She faced him, her head on his arm, her belly pressed up against him, and he felt the baby move. Relief flooded him. It was bad enough that Vanni was going through this— he couldn't have anything happen to the baby. Matt's baby.

The room was dark. There was a soft glow from the hallway from lights in the great room and kitchen spilling over. Vanni's breathing became even and calmer—she slept, probably due to the sedative. He eased himself away reluctantly; he knew he wouldn't be able to justify putting himself back on her bed, at her side, his arms around her, so it was hard to leave her.

In the great room he found all his friends. Waiting.

"She's asleep," he said. "Mel, I could feel the baby moving, so I guess he's okay, right?"

"She's in her last trimester—the baby's pretty tough. Resilient. I'm confident she'll carry, though she'll have a lot of emotional pain."

"You want to call his parents?" Walt asked Paul.

"I can do that, yeah. Any idea what Vanni would want to do about the burial?"

"Yeah, but I don't know how it's going to sit," Walt said. "If anything happened in Iraq, they'd decided together that he's to come here. Not Virginia, where she's never going to live. Not Oregon, where their child isn't going to grow up. Do you think you can talk to his folks about that, or should I?"

"I can do it," Paul said. "When you say here…?"

"On my land," the general said. "I'm always going to be

here. This is going to be home base for Vanessa, at least. There's a kind of…the baby should have a link to his dad."

"And me," Tommy said. "And to me."

"Yeah, of course," Paul said. And he was beginning to long for the moment when he could be alone and grieve for his best friend. But it wasn't going to happen soon. He knew these people needed him to be strong.

A permit had to be obtained for burial on private property and a digging crew had to be hired from a cemetery in Fortuna. A site that could be seen from the house was chosen, up on a small rise under a big tree, a place from which a person could stand and see the many acres of General Booth's land. A contingent of Marines brought the body, a body it was not possible to view. It was never spoken of and no one really knew if it was a routine practice of the Corps to deliver an honor guard and twenty-one-gun salute to a ranch in the backwoods, or if a three-star general could whip that up with a phone call or two.

Folding chairs were placed around the gravesite; Vanni sat between her father and brother right in front, Paul sat beside Tom, and beside the general sat Matt's parents. In the gathering, besides Preacher, Paige, Jack, Mel, Mike and Brie were Joe, Zeke, Josh Phillips and Tom Stephens. They were there more for Paul than anyone, because when one of them needed to be shored up by his brothers, the Marines arrived.

The flag was removed from the casket, folded with precision and presented to Vanni, who pressed it lovingly to her breast. The rifles fired; the bugle wailed.

Mel held Jack's hand and pulled it to her belly. There was a stirring inside and she looked up at him with a small smile. He leaned down to hear her whisper, "Darling, you will never hear me complain about this baby again. Never. I thank God I have you…and your babies."

13

Despite everything, or perhaps because of everything, Christmas in Sacramento was filled with joy and laughter. Mel had many hands to help tend to David, allowing her to relax. Sam Sheridan's house throbbed with noise, food, love and celebration. Mike was pulled into the throng with enthusiasm, for the happiness that sparkled in Brie's eyes brought everyone's gratitude and relief.

Mel's sister, Joey, her husband, Bill, and their three kids joined the five Sheridan siblings, their spouses and, with David, nine little Sheridans, making it twenty-five in total, eleven of them camping out at Sam's house, using every bedroom, pull-out sofa, sleeping bag and beanbag.

The first night in town was a relatively quiet one, with Brie and Jack's sisters and spouses dropping in to say hello and welcome, heading back to their homes early, but on Christmas Eve it grew wild with everyone present at once. The street outside looked like a parking lot, dinner was big and messy and the dishes took forever to clean up, but the evening was young.

"We have a few traditions around here," Bob, the eldest of the brothers-in-law, said to Mike. "It starts on the patio."

"To the patio!" chimed in Ryan, the third in rank.

"This is where we come after dinner," Jack let him know. "First drinks, then the cigars come out and eventually the brandy—after which we generally have the women completely pissed off."

"Sounds like home," Mike said.

As the women held their usual gathering in the family room, the space heaters on the patio were lit by Sam.

"Do they do this at the Valenzuela house—segregate by sex?" Sam asked Mike.

"Yeah, but at my mother's home, the men take the garage, which holds a pool table and a refrigerator. In the refrigerator we have cerveza. It's kind of like a clubhouse."

"Hmm. I could get a pool table," Sam said thoughtfully.

Inside, the women were focused on pie, coffee and David, who was getting around very well and trying to pull himself up on furniture. He crawled around in his pajamas, ready to be put to bed once the noise level in the house subsided a bit. No one really seemed to notice when the doorbell rang. Donna, who was sitting nearest, answered. When she came back to the family room, she leaned down and whispered in Brie's ear. "Really?" Brie asked. "Hmm. Will you please get Mike for me?"

"Sure, kitten."

Brie went to the door and found Brad in the foyer with a small gift-wrapped box and a large, gaily ribboned basket of wine, meats and cheeses. "Hi, Brad," she said. "What are you doing here?"

"I thought maybe you'd had enough time to cool down now and think about things. I brought you something. This is for you, this is for the family."

He expects to be invited in, she thought. He still thinks we'll kiss and make up. He's crazy as a loon. "I'll take this," she said, reaching for the basket. She put it on the hall table behind her. "But you should take that back. I'll give the family your regards."

"Come on, Brie. Give me a chance."

She shook her head sadly. "Brad, you're much too late."

Mike came up behind her. She could sense his presence before she felt his hand on her shoulder. "Brad," Mike said with a nod.

Brie reached up and put her hand over Mike's. He slipped his other arm gently around her waist, holding her against him. Last Christmas came to mind, when Brad was with the other woman and her children and Brie was here, lonely and hurt in this huge crowd of family. And now, with Mike's warmth against her, his arm around her, she couldn't remember feeling more secure.

A strange look came over Brad's face and a huff of laughter escaped him. "No way," he said.

"You should go, Brad," she said.

"Come on," Brad said in disbelief. "You're not with this guy."

"Merry Christmas, Brad," Brie said. "Have a nice holiday."

Brad laughed. "God, I should've known. He was at the hospital. That's why…"

Brie turned to look up at Mike. She smiled at him. She'd be damned if she'd explain anything about their relationship to Brad.

Brad looked down uncomfortably. Then meeting Brie's eyes, he said, "You're sure?"

"Oh, yes," she said. "I've never been more sure of anything."

He took a deep breath and slowly turned, leaving Brie and Mike in the foyer alone. She leaned back against Mike and felt his breath on her neck. "God, I feel sorry for him," Mike said.

"You do?"

"I do. It must be torture for him, knowing what he's lost."

"You think he even realizes?" she asked him.

"Come on, Brie—he's a lot of things, but he's not stupid. He's figured it out by now. He gave up an incredible woman. The kind of strong, passionate woman who can commit to the forever thing, once her choice has been made. Not many chances like that come along for a man. Believe me—I know."

"He might not understand that," she said. "In the short time we've been a couple, you've touched me in places he doesn't even know exist."

"Hmm," he said, nuzzling her. "Not because there's anything special about me. Because you hold nothing back. Do you wonder what was in the box?"

"Not even curious. And there's a lot special about you. What do you want for Christmas, Mike?" she asked him.

"You." He turned her around and looked into her eyes. "Are you all right?"

"He doesn't have much effect on me anymore, Mike."

"No more questions about what went wrong?" he asked, running a smooth knuckle down her cheek.

She shook her head. "Six months ago I couldn't think of many reasons to go on living. I had no idea I'd find this kind of happiness with you."

"I didn't think I had a chance."

"You were so kind to me. So patient and loving, waiting for me to be ready. And so passionate—I couldn't resist you."

"My past concerns your brother."

She laughed. "His past concerned the whole family. He should worry about his own transgressions." She gave him a little kiss. "I'll worry about yours."

"You aren't afraid? Any fear that I don't know my heart?"

She shook her head. "When I'm with you, I don't worry about anything."

"Would you take a chance on me? Let me make promises that I swear by the Virgin I can keep?"

She laughed at him. "Do you really want to get the Virgin involved in this?"

"Before the babies come, mija," he said. "Because there will be babies."

"There is that talk about the water in Virgin River...."

He covered her lips in a steaming kiss, pulling her hard against him. "It's not about the water with us, mi amor," he said. "If we disappeared for a while, would we be missed?"

"Yes," she answered, laughing.

"When I woke up in the hospital, I thought to myself, why did I make it? When I was discharged and struggling for every step, unable to lift a glass from the cupboard, my constant thought was that I had misspent my life—carousing, living in the moment, acting carelessly. What every man wants, what my friends had found—that one woman they would give up everything for—had eluded me completely. And when you came along...angry over your divorce and determined never to give a man, especially a man like me, a chance, I knew I'd been cast into hell for sure, because I was feeling that for you." He gave her a kiss. "How did this happen? I know I don't deserve this."

"It started with a promise to break your heart," she said. "Somehow I got distracted."

"Will you marry me, Brie? I want you to be my wife. I want to be your husband, your partner for life. Can you trust me with that?"

"Sí, Miguel. I trust you with everything."

It was the first Christmas in many years that Paul Haggerty hadn't spent in Grants Pass with his parents and brothers and their families—because Vanessa needed him. She asked him if he would stay; she said it would make her Christmas a little easier. She didn't have to ask—he would move heaven and earth for her.

The person who needed Paul as much, perhaps even more, was Tommy. The boy was crushed by his loss. He loved his sister more than the average seventeen-year-old boy dared admit, but he'd begun to admire Matt in a heroic manner. He was enamored of his bravery and patriotism. He thought of him as a true brother.

It was typical of kids to take the opposite path of their parents, but even though Tom and his dad butted heads regularly, Walt had clearly raised a young soldier. Tom had been accepted into West Point already and was slated for at least a good long hitch in the Army, perhaps a career. This loss of Matt devastated him.

Paul tried to spend as much time as possible with Tom. He helped him take care of the horses and took him over to Jack's house to help out for a few hours here and there prior to Christmas. On Christmas morning a beautiful snow fell, dusting the pines and the trails, and they took a couple of the horses out for a ride.

"You think he was scared?" Tom asked Paul out of the blue.

But of course there was no confusion about whom he was

speaking. "Maybe not at that moment, since the explosion was a complete surprise. But in that situation, everyone is scared. You wish you could crawl into your helmet and wait for it to pass. But damn, it's exhilarating, Tom. The training, the physical challenge, putting it all to the test when it really matters. When everything's at stake. Not a pay raise, not an extra day of vacation—but your freedom. Your wife's freedom, your son's, your parents'. You think about that when you're really up against it—that there's purpose in what you're risking. Great purpose. That's what keeps pulling men like Matt back. Men like Jack. Jack did a twenty. If Matt had made it twenty, he'd have been as decorated as Jack."

"I don't know if I have the stuff," Tom said. "I want to do well, but..."

"It's not a good idea to go that route if you don't feel it. It's got power. The power of conviction. It's full of adrenaline. The rush. It's hard enough when you do feel it."

"How do you know?"

Paul shrugged. "I can't answer that, son. I wasn't sure till I was there. For us, me and Matt, it was Iraq the first time, and it was nothing compared to this. But once I got there, I knew I was supposed to be there. That's when we met Jack Sheridan, Preacher and Mike."

"But you got out."

"The reserves was enough for me, but that ended in Fallujah—where I took a bullet and donated a spleen. Okay by me—I wanted to serve, but I didn't want that career. I have the career I want. I love building houses. The most important thing for you to remember is you don't have to make this decision now. You have years before you have to do that."

"You think Vanni's going to be all right?" he asked.

"Not right away. She's going to have to grieve him. Eventually, though, she's going to get on with her life because she has that gift, that love of life. I've never known a woman as alive as Vanni. And she'll have a son to raise. She'll be okay. Just a matter of time."

"I hear her at night. Crying."

"Yeah," Paul said. "So do I."

They took the horses on a path along the narrow end of the river that cut through the general's property and Paul pulled back on the reins. "Tommy," he whispered. "Over there."

At the water's edge was the most magnificent buck Paul had ever seen. Drinking from the river, he had twelve points, six by six, a thick white throat, a long, handsome snout and black nose. God, he was beautiful. "There's an old guy. He's dodged the hunters for a few years."

"Look at him," Tom said. "I'd never be able to shoot him."

"His meat might be a little tough anyway," Paul said. "We're going to have to start bringing a camera with us."

They sat in silence and admired the stag. One of the horses whinnied and the deer's head came up. He sniffed the air and then turned and ran into the trees.

"You think it hurt him?" Tom asked. And again Paul knew it was Matt of whom they spoke.

Paul reached across the distance that separated them and put a firm hand on his shoulder. "Son, he didn't feel a thing. He might be wandering around heaven right now, wondering what the hell hit him. No pain. And I'm not just speculating—your dad got in touch with his platoon commander."

As they headed back to the house, Tom said, "Tell me about Jack. About these guys…"

"Jack," Paul said. "When Matt and I met him, he was already a marksman, a sniper, a decorated Marine, and we were kids. I served under him again when my reserve unit was called up— that's the group that still hangs tight. By the time Jack retired he held more medals than I could count. He saved a lot of lives—he served in five combat zones. He went in as a boy, but damn, he must have had some instinct about it because he was a huge success, a bona fide war hero. Then when he got out, he came to Virgin River and rebuilt that cabin into the bar and grill, married Mel when she got here and seemed like this pretty regular small-town guy.

"But he's no ordinary small-town guy—he's still a fighting Marine. There was an incident—a guy came out of the woods in the middle of the night, looking for drugs at Doc's. Mel was staying there. He broke in, put a knife to Mel's throat, threatened to kill her for the drugs. Doc heard something and called Jack, who was asleep at the bar across the street. He grabbed his handgun, a nine millimeter, and ran. He managed to get on a pair of jeans and that's all. Half-dressed, barefoot, a couple of big tattoos on those huge arms of his, and I don't know if you've ever seen that killer look he can get on his face— he must have looked like a wild man. He kicked in the door at Doc's and was face-to-face with this lunatic holding his woman, big serrated knife to her throat, and he had a little, bitty target." He held up his thumb and forefinger. "Right next to Mel's face. Now, you can see how he is with Mel—he worships her. No way he'd ever risk her life. But it took him about a second to make up his mind, to act. He took the guy out. Shot him in the head, killed him."

"No way."

"He did. He's the kind of guy who never hesitates. But he knows what he's doing—he knows what he can and can't do. Knows what he has to do. And then he does it—clearheaded."

"What a stud," Tom said.

Paul laughed.

"What about Mike? Valenzuela?"

"Mike? After our first hitch, he went to LAPD and stayed in the reserves, like I did. We were activated at the same time. We had some hard fighting in Iraq, but he got through that with a couple of medals. He held off insurgents at Fallujah, saving the whole squad. Joe and me were bleeding all over the place, and so were some others, but Mike kept them back till Jack and the rest of the platoon could effect a rescue. But then about a year ago back in L.A., as a police sergeant in a gang unit, he got taken out by a fourteen-year-old gangbanger in a playground. He took three bullets and it almost killed him. LAPD retired him and he came up here to recuperate—Mel helped him with his physical therapy. Now he's the town cop—bet he never saw that coming. And you already know about Brie, right?"

"What about her?"

"Well, it's no secret and you'll hear about it sooner or later. Brie was a Sacramento ADA, an assistant district attorney. She put away a lot of dangerous criminals, but then she prosecuted a serial rapist and lost the trial. The guy had brutally raped a bunch of women, and he walked. And then he raped and beat Brie."

"Come on—are you shitting me?" Tommy asked, appalled.

"No, that's what went on. Mike told me that they've found the guy and there will be a trial. Brie is determined she's going to testify against him and put him away so he can't do this to anyone else, ever."

"Jesus," Tommy said.

"Yeah," Paul said.

"Right here. These stories. This little dinky place full of big trees and pretty rivers and good-looking deer, and people are performing heroic acts and living out these huge dramas. Every day."

Paul laughed. "And I haven't even told you about Preacher. And Paige."

Christmas dinner at the Booth household was served at six—small and somber. Paul and the general cleaned up the kitchen and not long afterward Vanni just went to bed. Paul knew she wasn't sleeping well, as he could often hear her in the night. But she continued to go to bed earlier and earlier. Paul suspected she wanted to be alone, to grieve, to cry without impacting the rest of the household.

When it was down to just the men, Paul excused himself to run into town to pay a call on Paige and Preacher, and Tom took his little red truck in the same direction, to visit Brenda.

When Tom got to Brenda's house it was still all lit up, and it looked as if there were a lot of people inside. He knew he should've called, but he hadn't been thinking straight lately. When he rang the bell, she answered. "Hey," he said.

"Tommy! Hi! Wanna come in?"

"Um—I was wondering if you could come out. For a little while."

"Let me ask my mom," she said. "Here, step inside. Come on." She pulled his hand and he let himself be drawn into their house.

The moment Brenda's mom saw him, she stood up from her place at the table with Brenda's dad, brothers and sister, grandma and grandpa and a couple of other people. She went straight to him and put her arms around him. "How are you, Tommy?" she asked, giving him a motherly hug. "You getting by?"

"I'm doing all right," he said with a shrug. "Sorry. I should've called."

"It's okay, honey. How's Vanessa doing?"

He hoped he wouldn't get choked up. "Um. She's having a pretty hard time. I think it's going to be a while. You know?"

"Mom?" Brenda asked. "Okay if I go out with Tommy for a little while?"

"Sure, honey. Don't be too late. Tommy—keep an eye on the time," she said.

"Yeah, I will, Mrs. Carpenter." He held Brenda's coat for her. Then held her hand as he took her down the porch steps and out to his truck. Once they were in the truck, still sitting out in front of her house, still holding her hand, he said, "I'm sorry, Bren. I haven't called. I haven't given you any attention."

"I didn't really expect anything, Tommy. I understand— it's a really rough time. You feeling any better?"

"Right this minute, with you, I feel a lot better. Can we drive out to the woods? Maybe Jack's homesite? Brenda, I just have to hold someone." He smiled at her. "You're my first and only choice."

She squeezed his hand. "Sure."

He put the truck in gear and headed out of town. "You know—you're about the best thing that's happened to me since I got here. If I weren't going with you, this year would be—it would be total crap."

She laughed a little. "I feel the same way. My year didn't start out real good, either. It wasn't half as tough as yours, but it was still pretty crappy."

"You've been so great to me," he said.

"You've been pretty good to me, too."

"I mean it. A lot of girls are real complicated. Ever since we started talking, going out, you've been awesome. You don't worry about little shit, you don't get all moody, you're just so— Brenda, you're the best girl I've ever known."

"Thanks. You're pretty much the best guy I've ever known. There's only one thing wrong with you as far as I can tell."

"Yeah?" he said, smiling in spite of himself. "What's that?"

"You're going away next year."

"Yeah, there's that. Could be a long year. But I'll get leave— I'll be back here to visit. And you can always pick a school not so far from West Point when it's your turn. People do that, you know. Actually date for a long time. Go steady for a long time. Of course, that's all up to you—I don't expect anything."

"It would be all right to ask, though," she said.

"I wouldn't tie you down your senior year," he said.

"And maybe you don't want to be tied down your freshman year?" she asked.

"Whew," he said. "First of all, I don't think they let the little guys out much at West Point the first year. And second, if I knew you were my girl, I wouldn't even have to think about it. Being tied down to you—that would be worth my time, no kidding." He pulled off the road up to the top of the hill where the house was being built. He stopped the truck, leaving it running, and put on the dome light. "I have something for you." He opened the glove box and withdrew a small, wrapped box. "I bought this before… Before Matt… I had this big deal planned for giving it to you—a real nice night out, something special. For sure not sitting in my truck in the woods. Open it, go ahead."

"You didn't have to get me anything."

"Of course I didn't have to. Don't you think I wanted to?"

She tore into it and found a gold ID bracelet with her name on the topside and underneath, "With love, Tom." She read it aloud. "God, it's beautiful. It's just beautiful."

"You like it?"

"I love it! Here, put it on me."

Once the bracelet was latched, he put his hand against her soft hair. "I do, you know. I love you."

"Tom…"

"You don't have to say it back. I know I'm rushing you a little. Think it'll get me kissed, though?"

"At least," she said with a smile. She leaned toward him across the console, her hands on his shoulders while his found her waist, and the kiss was good. Hot and openmouthed. She made little noises while she kissed him, and he loved that. Kiss at an end, she said, "Thank you. It's the most beautiful thing I've ever been given."

All he wanted was to feel her warmth against him, and this wasn't getting it. Their make-out sessions had been a lot more comfortable than this—either at her house when no one was home, or out riding, on the soft ground under a tree, or in fresh clean hay in the stable. "I have an idea," he said, turning off the truck.

He went around to her side, opened her door and said, "Come with me. Let's hope Uncle Paul doesn't lock things up too tight."

"What are you thinking?" she asked, laughing, going with him.

He pulled her to the fifth wheel and, God bless Paul, the door swung open. He stepped up inside and pulled her up and right into his arms, covering her mouth with a passionate kiss. Then he pulled her down onto Paul's bed and held her there, tight. Close. "God, that's better. That is so much better."

"Tommy... You're not thinking we're going to, you know, do it...?"

"I hope we do it, Bren. But it's not going to be tonight. I'm not lying—I just have to feel you next to me. I've been feeling so damn empty. And alone. I just wanna hold you. So bad."

"But I bet you have a rubber in your pocket."

He laughed at her and buried his face in her neck. "I'm a seventeen-year-old guy. What do you think?"

"That's what I think."

"It's staying in my pocket, don't you worry. We seventeen-year-old guys, we don't even want to carry 'em. But it's the law."

"You're so funny...."

"Yeah, this is working," he said. "Snuggle up here, baby. You feel so good. Hmm."

"Tommy?" she said.

"Yeah?"

"I love you, too. I do."

"Aw," he said, pulling her closer. "That's so nice to hear."

"And if we fall asleep here, we're history."

"No kidding." He laughed. Then he slipped a hand against her breast, and she covered his hand with hers. "We're not gonna fall asleep, Brenda. We're gonna get all hot and bothered for a little while."

"Yeah," she said against his lips. "I know."

Preacher unlocked the door to the bar and let Paul in. They shook hands tight and hard, bringing them shoulder to shoulder. "Hey, man," Preacher said.

"Merry Christmas, my man. How was your day?"

"It was okay. Come on in. Paige told me to call her when you got here, then we'll have a drink. How's that?"

"Just what I need," Paul said, going to the bar.

Preacher called back to his quarters, then went behind the bar. "How's it going out there at the general's?"

"Real tough," he said. "Real, real tough."

"Yeah, I can't even imagine." He pulled down a couple of glasses. "Vanni?"

"She's hanging in there, but I can see the pain in every damn breath she takes. God, Preach—that girl is hurting all over. She's trying so hard to be brave, especially over these holidays, it just kills me to look at her. And she's growing by the minute."

"It's good, though, that she's got that baby in her. That little bit of him. There has to be some consolation in that." He tipped a bottle over two glasses. "And it's good you're there. I know she needs you there."

"I'm not sure it's a great idea. We spend an awful lot of time talking about Matt, and we'll have some fun things to remember, but it always ends up with her in tears."

"I don't know how you can get around that, man. She's gonna cry. At least she has a good friend to hold her up while she's doing it." Preacher touched his glass to Paul's. "If something happened to me and I left Paige with a baby in her, I hope to God one of my boys would be there for her."

"It's automatic, Preach," Paul said, taking a drink.

Paige came into the bar and walked straight into Paul's arms, giving him a big hug. "How are you holding up?" she asked.

"I'm doing okay, Paige. Thanks. How about you guys? How was your Christmas? I bet the little guy had a big day."

"Oh, you know he did. He now has everything but a car."

"And you?" he asked. "The man here spoil you like you deserve?"

"You have no idea," she said. "We've been sitting on a little news. We're having a baby."

"Well, damn!" Paul said. He looked at Preacher and grinned. "You finally came through on ovulation day, huh, buddy?"

He puffed up a little. "I did at that," he said, throwing his chest out.

"And John promises that in the future when we have personal business, like we're going to have sex all day and I'm going to stand on my head between rounds, he's not going to tell the town. Or the one-ninety-second."

"Aw, I think we took it pretty much in stride," Paul said, but he couldn't help grinning. "That's awful good news, Paige. I'm really happy for you."

"You know, it's not that easy," Preacher said. "Being married to someone like Paige and waiting for ovulation day. I think I did pretty good there. I should get a little more credit."

"I imagine it's pretty tough." Paul laughed. "You know, I needed that. Some great news, a good laugh. Congratulations to you both." He lifted his glass. "This last year has been awful tough. The past month has been pure shit. Let's toast a new year, with new stuff, good stuff. Here's to the new baby."

"I'll drink to that," Preacher said.

"And I'll just say hear, hear, and leave you boys to your business." Paige got up on her toes and pressed a kiss onto Paul's cheek. "We realize that you have some grief business going on, Paul. You kind of get lost in the shuffle with Vanni going through such a terrible time, but if you ever need to talk, escape, break down or blow off steam, we're here for you."

He gave an appreciative nod. "Thanks," he said.

Paul and Preacher talked a little while longer, then said good-night. It was in Paul's mind to go somewhere he could be alone and either hit something, cry or maybe scream, and he couldn't really think of anywhere other than the homesite. So he drove out there. But when he entered the clearing, he saw Tommy's truck. He killed his lights immediately. He assumed they were parking, Tom and Brenda. Then he saw that the truck was empty.

Oh, damn, he thought. Tommy was in a lot of pain. He was needy and vulnerable, seventeen and in either the trailer or the fifth wheel with his girl. Paul knew that Tommy hadn't seen much of Brenda in the past couple of weeks, given the events. And tonight of all nights, he was not only with her, he was way too alone with her. And there was a goddamn bed in that trailer.

Paul backed up, turned around and didn't put the lights on again until he was facing away from the trailer. He drove back to the general's house, let himself in and found Walt asleep in the chair, TV on and newspaper hanging off his lap. He roused when he heard Paul moving around. "Evening, sir," Paul said.

"Hmmmph," he grunted. "I must have nodded off. How was Christmas for Paige and Preacher?"

"Good," Paul said. "They have some big news. Paige is expecting."

"Ah, he did it," the general said with a chuckle. "He showed up for ovulation day."

Paul laughed. "He's in a lot of hot water for telling too many people about that."

"Yeah, I suppose. But it's so like him, don't you think? He's so damn transparent." He stood up and stretched. "I'm going to turn in."

"Mind if I sit up? The TV won't bother you?"

"Help yourself." The general extended his hand to Paul and Paul took it. "Thanks for staying on," he said. "I know it's damn hard on you, son. And I know you're here because Vanni asked you to be."

"I'll do whatever she needs me to do, sir. I gave Matt my word. And I'm awful fond of Vanni."

"You're a good man," he said, giving him a slap on the arm. And he went off down the hall, his step a little slower.

This has aged the hell out of him, Paul thought. He's buried a few hundred soldiers, but this one is taking its toll.

At ten Paul turned on CNN. At eleven he checked the news out of San Francisco. At twelve he was starting to think about driving out to the homesite, but at twelve-thirty the front door finally opened. Tommy was clearly surprised to find him up. "Hey," he said. "You're awake!"

"Yeah," Paul said, still undecided about exactly the best way to handle this. But it had to be handled while there was still the opportunity for a save, and neither the general nor Vanni was up to the job.

"Good. I need to talk to you about something, man. Let me get a soda. Want anything?"

"No, go ahead."

Tom came back to the great room with a soda, sat opposite Paul and scooted up to the edge of his seat. A little on the nervous side, Paul thought. "You want to take your coat off?" Paul asked.

"Oh. Yeah," he said, putting his soda down and shrugging out of his coat. "Listen, I have to tell you something. I kind of borrowed your trailer tonight—I hope that doesn't piss you off."

Paul raised his eyebrows, waiting.

"It was a situation. I would've asked your permission, but I swear I didn't plan it at all. It was real sudden. But hey, it worked out great."

"Want to attempt an explanation?"

"Sure. Yeah. I had a Christmas present for Brenda. I bought it before... Before everything happened. I had this big idea I was going to take her somewhere nice—like maybe over to the coast to dinner or something, but the shit hit the fan. So I took her out to the site to park where I could give her this beautiful bracelet I bought her." He smiled. "With your money, by the way."

"And what happened?" Paul asked coyly.

"Well, it worked pretty good. She loved it. It was good for many kisses, if you want to know. But that damn little truck, you know? So I got this idea—I spotted your fifth wheel and helped myself to it. Honest to God, Paul, I would've asked— but I didn't even think of that ahead of time."

"So. Were you having teenage sex in my trailer?" he asked.

"Oh, hell no!" Tommy said. "Jeez, man, I'm not having

sex with Brenda!" Then he smiled. "I am having some very nice making out with her, however."

"Listen, Tommy—maybe we should talk…."

"Aw, save it. I've had this talk a hundred times. I'm not having sex, much to my disappointment. I'd love to be having sex, don't get me wrong. But Brenda's a nice girl, and she doesn't move fast—which I happen to like, by the way. And besides, I'm still a virgin. You tell anybody that, I'll have to kill you."

Paul felt himself smile. "So, what did you do in my trailer?"

"Come on, Paul. Don't you think that's a little nosy on your part?"

"Under the circumstances…?"

"Man, I just wanted to feel something soft up against me, you know? This month has been so ugly. So horrible. Tonight was actually nice. We just kind of held each other, made out like rock stars and—" He got this look on his face, this dreamy faraway look. "She said she loved me."

"Whoa! Come on."

"I'm pretty sure it was the bracelet."

"Give yourself a little credit," Paul said.

"I'm giving myself credit for thinking of the bracelet. God, she is so hot."

"You can't use my fifth wheel to make out in," Paul said. "You're going to end up having sex. I can smell it. I'd feel like an accomplice or something."

"I hope you're right," he said with a laugh. "But I don't think you are. At least not anytime soon. Brenda's pretty worried about stuff like that. So…when did you actually lose it? You know."

"I was over seventeen," Paul said, smiling. "I think that's graphic enough. Do you have condoms, in case…"

"Oh, brother," he said. "Ask yourself. Did the general give the boy condoms? Holy shit, Paul—he watched me stretch 'em over bananas. I'm surprised he didn't make me model one. He's probably counting 'em every day when I go to school. I kind of want to throw a few away just to get his heart rate up. Yeah, I have condoms. And—I'm not willing to rely on condoms, how's that? I'm not having sex with anyone who doesn't also have her own birth control—and we haven't had that conversation, me and Brenda. You happy yet?"

"I'm getting there."

"I'm not going to take advantage of Brenda. I really care about her. Nothing that risky is going to happen between us until it's right for her. And when it's right for her, she's going to be safe and I'm going to make her safer. She's important to me, man. I'm not going to mess her up."

Damn, Paul thought. The boy's got serious game. "You can't use my fifth wheel to make out in," he said, but he grinned when he said it because jeez, the boy was so cute. It made him nostalgic. He remembered a certain prom date that he was sure, sure was going to be it for him. It wasn't. It came later, when he least expected it. Paul found himself almost hoping the kid could get lucky. "You understand, right?"

"Sure. But you're not pissed off about tonight?"

"Nah, I can live with it. You're sure nothing scary happened? Because if it did, even with a condom, we can still get ahead of it."

"Yeah, I know about that, too. The little morning-after pill. Believe me, the only thing I don't know about sex is how good it feels."

14

It came too soon—the trial against Jerome Powell for rape. In the third week of January Brie and Mike returned to Sacramento so that she could testify against him. They went ahead of time so that Brie could be prepped. When the trial date arrived, Jack was determined to be there, but Mel couldn't leave her women—Lilly had grown very ill and Vanni was in advanced pregnancy and in a state of grief. Paige and Preacher promised to back her up, as did John Stone, but still, it was very hard for Jack to leave her.

While jury selection and opening arguments were presented, Brie sat in the same room with her rapist. With her were her partner, her brother, her father, her sisters. She was definitely shored up—but the fact was she could have had the entire Marine Corps marching band sitting with her and she would still have felt shaken and vulnerable. She revisited the crime in her mind, over and over. They were all hoping that this ordeal could be dispensed with quickly.

There was a good case against Powell. Even though he'd worn a condom so as not to leave his DNA behind, the rape kit performed on Brie at the hospital had turned up hair, plus they'd found her gun in his possession. He claimed to have found it.

However, the defense had been able to suppress any testimony of earlier arrests or trials, which precluded Brie from explaining that her positive ID was based on the fact that she had prosecuted him. Since she had failed to convict him, she couldn't testify to that. The defense suggested she might falsely accuse him in a rage at having lost the case against him.

Brie didn't have to be in court as often as she was—she could have waited to be called to testify. But she wanted to get used to seeing him, to bolster herself before her testimony, and she wanted him to see her, to know how it was going to go down. The prosecutor was not going to accept a plea agreement under these circumstances, the crime being retribution against an officer of the court.

But seeing him every day didn't bolster her, or calm her. Now she knew exactly how her witnesses had felt. Brie barely slept, had trouble eating and felt as though she were vibrating under her skin. The illogical reaction—all emotional—was hard for her to accept. After all, he was in custody; he couldn't reach her. And right beside her were two powerfully strong men who would stop at nothing to keep her safe. Yet the very sight of him was making her sick.

Jerome Powell was six feet tall, tan from his stay in Florida, his blond hair thick and floppy, his jaw square. He had a big smile, one that certain women could be drawn to. He had very large hands, strong arms from working construction and was powerfully built. His eyes were dark, close together and sunken under hooded brows.

He glared at Brie. Sometimes he smiled at her, which made her stomach turn. Every time he turned his head to look at her, she felt Jack and Mike tense beside her. She looked up at their profiles, her lover and her brother, and watched the dangerous tics and tension in their expressions. These were completely fearless men—Jerome Powell should be as afraid of getting off as going to prison. But he sat calmly, unafraid, arrogant.

In the evening, conversation at Sam's was subdued and superficial. Mike, Jack and Sam took to the patio after dinner while one or two of Brie's sisters dropped by the house to spend time with her, being there for her. And at night, in bed, Mike would curl himself protectively around her, holding her closely, whispering to her that he loved her, that he was proud of her, that he could not imagine her courage.

"I could not get through this without you," she told him.

"I think you could, you're that strong. But I'm glad you don't have to. You'll never have to go through anything alone again."

When the day for Brie to testify finally arrived she went bravely and calmly to the stand to be sworn in. No testimony about her prosecution of him for previous crimes could be admitted by the prosecutor, so she was left to describe the details of her rape. As she took her seat and looked into the courtroom, she saw Brad in the back. Well, she thought, he was a part of it all, like it or not. Maybe they could all get their closure and get on with their lives.

"I had to work late and wasn't home until after midnight. I opened the garage door, but I parked in the drive because the garage was full of junk that I'd been meaning to clean out for months. My car door wasn't even closed when I was grabbed from behind, by the hair. He smashed my head into the top of the car. Then an arm came around my neck, choking me. I dropped my briefcase and was trying to get into my purse. I carried a gun. But the purse was flung away—I'm not sure if he did it or if I lost control of it in the struggle."

"Did you struggle, Ms. Sheridan?"

"I fought with everything I had, and he hit me, three or four times in the face. I blacked out for a moment. When I came to, I was on the ground and he was leaning over me. He was smiling. It was so evil, so terrifying, I froze. That's when he reached under my skirt and tore my hose and my underwear off. Well, not off. Down. He held a hand around my throat to keep me still while he undid his trousers with his other hand. I was choking."

She looked at her brother and Mike. Jack frowned and looked down, but Mike held her gaze. Steady. She knew that inside he was in terrible pain, hearing what she'd been through, but for her he kept a strong front, chin up, eyes level.

"Did he say anything?" the prosecutor asked.

"Objection. Your Honor?"

The judge put his hand over the microphone and leaned toward Brie. "Can you answer the question without introducing any prohibited information?"

"Of course," she said. She had to focus on the lawyers' faces. "He said, 'Look at me. I want you to see my face. I'm not leaving any evidence behind. I'm not going to kill you. I want you to live.'"

"And did that make you feel safe?" the prosecutor asked.

"He was putting on a condom as he said that. When it was on, he raped me, holding me down at the neck. I thought I was going to choke to death. I felt like I was being ripped apart. When he was done, he pulled his pants up and I watched— that condom went with him, inside his pants. Then he stood up and kicked me several times. I lost consciousness." She went on to describe the injuries she sustained as photos taken at the hospital were passed around the jury box. Her voice was steady, her words well chosen and clear, but tears ran down her cheeks and dripped onto hands folded in her lap. And inside, her stomach churned violently. It was almost enough to double her over.

"Did he say anything else?"

"Objection! Your Honor?"

"Sustained," he said.

"That's all I have for now," the prosecutor said.

The defense attorney got up and started asking her questions about the time of night, whether she was tired, did she wear glasses, was it dark or was the drive well lit, all aimed at throwing doubt on her ability to make an ID. The room began to sway before her eyes and she wavered a bit. The judge leaned over and asked her if she could continue. "You're looking a little pale," he pointed out.

"Let's just do it," she whispered back.

The defense took up an hour with questions about her schedule, her health, her mental stability, even her divorce. Finally he said, "Did you pick the suspect out of a lineup?"

"No. He fled."

"Did the police show you photos?"

"I did look at photos, yes."

"And that was how long ago?"

"Seven months ago," she said, and her face glistened in sweat.

"Do you see the man you identified in this room? This man you identified to police as your rapist?"

"Right there," she said, pointing. "Jerome Powell."

"And you're confident that a man you identified from a photo seven months ago is this man?"

Her head snapped up, her eyes wide, at attention. The prosecutor in her had kicked in.

"Yes or no, Ms. Sheridan."

She leaned forward. "No," she answered.

By the look on his face, the defense attorney immediately knew what he'd done.

"Your Honor, may we approach?" Brie's lawyer asked.

The lawyers went to the bench and a heated argument ensued, every bit of which Brie could hear. The prosecutor argued that he was entitled to explore that last answer while the defense argued that it would ultimately introduce testimony on evidence not allowed. At length the judge admonished the defense attorney that he had opened the door and the prosecution could proceed.

"Ms. Sheridan," the prosecutor asked, "how is it you're not confident that the man you identified from the photo is this man?"

"Because I looked at photos, but I didn't identify him from a photo."

"And how did you identify your rapist?"

"I gave the police his name. I knew him."

"And how did you know him?"

"I was an assistant district attorney when he raped me. I had just prosecuted him for the serial rape of six women— and I lost."

So much noise erupted in the room that the judge had to bang his gavel several times and threaten to clear the courtroom.

When the din had finally subsided, the prosecutor asked her, "Did he say anything else to you, Ms. Sheridan?"

"Yes. He said, 'I'm not going to kill you. I want you to try to come after me again, and watch me walk again.'"

The place went crazy with gasps and murmurings, the judge banging his gavel again and again. But it was at that moment

that Brie allowed herself to look again at Mike. Her lips curved
in a very small smile as she locked eyes with him. Even at that
distance she could feel the pride in his gaze. Love and pride
and commitment. He smiled at her and gave a small, almost
imperceptible nod. She'd done it. She'd got him. It was why
she'd come.

"That's all I have for Ms. Sheridan," the ADA said.

The defense tried to recover, asking Brie if there was any
chance she was out to get this guy, since she had failed to convict him before. Her voice clear and strong, even knowing that
possibility would be contained in the defense attorney's closing arguments, she said, "And leave another rapist out there?
My rapist? The police not even searching for him because they
thought they had the suspect? Not hardly."

"Perhaps you couldn't identify your rapist, Ms. Sheridan,
and saw your chance to go after the defendant."

"Objection," the prosecutor shouted. "Your Honor!"

The judge leveled his gaze on the defense. "Was there a
question in there or are you just testing me to see what it'll
take to find you in contempt?"

"Is that possible, Ms. Sheridan?"

"It is not," she said. "I saw him, I knew him, I identified him."

"You may step down, Ms. Sheridan."

She rose on shaky legs, grateful to be finished, to have finished strong. No way they could let him go now. No way a
single jury member could doubt. Now that the door was open
to Powell's motivation for raping her, they could look at his
past, at his previous arrests.

She stepped down and started toward Mike. Then she collapsed.

When Brie had delivered her final statement Mike saw her
face go pale, then white. As she left the stand and started to

walk toward him, he noticed that her eyes had become glassy and she wasn't walking in a straight line. He started to come to his feet just as she fainted. "Brie!" he yelled. The bailiff stopped him until the prosecutor identified him as her husband—though he was not.

Mike rushed to her. By the time he lifted her head, her eyes were opening. "I did it, darling."

"Can we get an ambulance here?" Mike yelled.

"On the way, sir," someone said.

"Lo siento mucho," she whispered. "I'm sorry you had to go through all this."

"Shh, it's okay, baby. You're done with it now. All of it."

"Te amo, Miguel. I love you."

"Te amo mucho," he said. "It's over, baby."

Every afternoon when it was almost David's nap time, Mel would drive out to the Andersen ranch. Doc went out there every morning and most evenings. They'd been doing this since the second week in January when Lilly's chemo and radiation had been suspended. There comes a time in every life when the curtain is coming down, and when that time is present and there's no way to turn back the clock, the best answer is dignity and peace.

When Mel arrived at the ranch, she greeted family members and put David down in Chloe's crib with his afternoon bottle where he would sleep for a couple of hours. Then she went to Lilly's bedroom, checked the morphine drip and kissed her on the forehead. "How's my girl today?" she asked.

"I think this is a good day to talk to the kids," she said weakly. "I don't want to miss my opportunity."

"Okay," Mel said.

"Will you help me?"

"Of course. Let's see who we can gather up."

Mel went to the living room and kitchen. Lilly's daughters were there, her sons out in the barn with their dad. "Your mom wants to talk to you about something important. Can you round up your dad and brothers?"

"I'll go," Sheila said.

Back in the bedroom, sitting down again beside Lilly and taking her hand, Mel said, "It's going to be okay, you know."

"I know. I owe you so much, Mel."

"Oh, it's the other way around. If I hadn't found Chloe on Doc's porch, I'd have made it all the way to Colorado Springs without ever knowing my husband, without having my children."

Only five of Lilly's seven kids were present, but that was enough for her to make a clean breast of it. Buck stayed in the kitchen with Chloe, bouncing her on his knee as he had with the six children before her. "This is going to shock you," Lilly said to her grown children. "I hope you can find it in your hearts to forgive me. I lied to you. I was a little bit crazy," she said, and then was sent into a coughing fit and had to rest for a little while, her children looking at each other in confusion.

"Whew," Lilly said when she recovered. "I have to get this over with. Chloe isn't adopted," she said weakly. "I gave birth to her, right here, in this bed. I covered my pregnancy with large and loose clothes and put her on Doc's doorstep. Mel?" she said, looking up at her.

"I'm going to see if I can help out with this," Mel said. "Your mom is so tired. Lilly was distraught at the thought of having another child to raise at the age of forty-eight, already being a grandmother seven times. She thought some nice young couple desperate for a baby would want to adopt her and that everyone would be better off—that Chloe would have young parents. But when no one came forward, Lilly took her back."

"I regretted it so much," Lilly said. "Your father thought it was crazy, but he was more afraid of what I might do if he didn't go along with the idea. I was really out of my mind. So I pretended to foster and adopt her—but she's your blood. I can't die without you knowing."

Lilly's oldest daughter, Amy, sat down beside her on the bed. She took her mother's hand, kissed it gently and smiled. "Well, that certainly explains why she looks like all the rest of the Andersens." She leaned over and kissed her mother's cheek. "You shouldn't worry so much. It's okay."

"I'm sorry I lied to you all."

"But you did the right thing when you brought her back home. We would have taken care of her for life anyway…."

"It's important that you know where she came from," Mel said. "Not just for medical reasons, but so she knows her legacy. Her biological family. We can't have our girl running around Northern California trying to figure out who her family is."

"If you have to tell her someday, please tell her that I loved her so much. And that I'm sorry," Lilly said. "Shew. I'm so tired. I hope this doesn't last much longer."

Mel stood and tinkered with the drip, giving her a little more morphine.

One by one Lilly's children leaned over the bed and kissed their mother.

"It's okay, Mom. Everything is okay and I love you."

"Thank you for another sister, Mom."

"We'll take care of everything—don't you ever worry."

"No one's mad at you, Mom. You're the best mother and grandmother in the world."

And finally, to her oldest boy, Lilly said, "Harry—you be sure to take care of Dad. He's really helpless."

"I got it, Mom. He'll be fine."

When it was just Mel and Lilly again, Lilly said, "There. I've been meaning to do that for a long time. Thanks."

"It wasn't me. You raised a wonderful family. They're the most loving people I know."

"It's much easier to go, knowing that. I'm leaving behind some good work. Really, a woman couldn't ask for more from a lifetime than a family like that. They make me so proud."

"A woman shouldn't go without knowing you've made them proud, too."

Four days later Lilly Andersen closed her eyes on the world for the last time and was lovingly laid to rest in the family plot between the orchard and the meadow with most of the town present to say goodbye. Mel wasn't able to have Jack at her side and was sorry about that, but there was a great deal of peace and relief in knowing her friend was no longer in any pain.

Jack went back to Virgin River the moment he felt he could leave Brie, though Brie and Mike stayed on in Sacramento. Brie wanted to hear how the trial ended and to hear the verdict. But Jack was aching to get back to his family, and although he'd talked to Mel several times a day, he hated that she'd had to bury a good friend without him. And he was very secure that he left Brie in good hands. Mike was more than just attentive—he was devoted.

As Jack drove into town he spotted Mel, all bundled up with David tucked inside her coat, just walking across the street to the bar. He pulled up to the bar and met her in front, folding them both into his arms. "God, I missed you. I'm going soft—I can't stand to sleep alone."

"I didn't," she said. "Someone was in my bed all night." She jostled the baby and David turned his wet, goopy mouth toward his dad for a kiss, which he got.

"Bllkk," Jack said. "When do you think he's going to stop leaking?"

"How was everyone when you left them?"

"Resting. Brie's doing pretty well. It'll take a while for her to get back on her feet—that trial was more traumatic for her than she expected."

"Everyone is waiting for news."

"Is Doc in the bar yet?"

"Yeah, why?"

"Maybe I can tell it just once. Here's something for you—guess who was there? At the trial?"

"Who?"

"Brad. Sitting in the back. When Brie got off the stand and fainted and Mike rushed to her, Brad just kind of hung his head and left the courtroom. He screwed himself pretty good. And he knows it." He slipped a hand down under his son's bum to place over Mel's belly. "How's this one doing?"

"Good. I seem to have passed the dark pukey days of the first trimester and am sailing through the comfort zone of the middle trimester, flying like a bullet toward my hugeness. We have to go get an ultrasound, see what you made me this time."

"I'm hoping for a girl," he said.

"Are you?"

"I have an idea you might cut me off at two."

"I'm not wild about throwing up or waddling, but I sure love carrying around a little piece of you. You're right—you make excellent babies."

"We all have our special talents," he said.

Brie and Mike were another two weeks in Sacramento, awaiting the end of the trial. As she waited, Brie was once again haunted by the violence done to her. Sometimes the

musty smell of that June night could come back to her; sometimes it was the smell of his sweat. His eyes would bore into
her in her sleep. The pressure of his hand around her throat
invaded her dreams and she would awake gasping, wondering
if this was the end. It caused her to be weak and sick.

Mike never left her side. When she couldn't keep food
down, his arms were around her as she lost it in the bathroom.
At night he held her protectively, securely, gently. When a
fright woke her with a gasp or near scream, he was right there
to softly bring her back to reality in the safety of his arms. If
he felt her shiver in a cold night sweat, he tenderly woke her
and talked to her until she felt all right again. In just a few
days Brie grew stronger, calmer and closer to closing the book
on that horrific experience.

For Mike, Brie's crisis gave him a stronger sense of purpose;
he had a problem in Virgin River that had to be resolved. He
hated the thought of any woman going through this kind of
trauma, and if there was a guy back in his small town who
was preying on innocent young girls, he was going to find
him and bring him to justice, if it took every breath he drew.
Ironically, after all these years of police work, he was revisit-
ing the emotions that had motivated him to get into law enforcement in the first place—a force that drove him to keep
the good people safe from the bad. To serve and protect.

When Brie and Mike returned to Virgin River they brought
with them a guilty verdict and matching wedding bands. They
were now ready to move ahead with their lives.

Jack was helping Paul put the finishing touches on the house
while Brie was helping Mel order furniture and accessories. In
addition, Mel was going to the Andersen ranch often, making sure the family there was doing all right. Most days she

left David with Brie when she had calls to make. She was also checking Vanessa every week as her time grew near.

With his sister ready to deliver any minute and Jack's house nearly finished, Tom had to hang close to home, so he was able to find the time to take his girl on after-school rides around the property, along the river, into the woods. The weather was cold but clear, the ground crispy underneath the horses' hooves. He loved riding with her, talking with her, kissing afterward.

"That whole business with Brie being raped—did you know about that? I mean before the trial and everything?" Brenda asked Tommy as they were taking the horses in.

"Yeah, Paul told me all about it. Not long after Matt died. It happened last year."

"Doesn't that make you feel strange about her now? Knowing that happened to her, that someone did all that to her?"

"Brenda, it's not like she did anything wrong. In fact, she risked everything to get that guy, make sure he was behind bars so he couldn't ever do anything like that again. You have any idea how brave she had to be to do that? Mike's so proud of her, he idolizes her. I think Brie might be one of the strongest women I've ever known. Brie and Mel and my sister, for sure."

Brenda dismounted when they got to the barn. "Wouldn't a guy feel funny about his girl getting raped? Like maybe not wanting to… You know… Seems like a guy wouldn't want to touch her after that."

"Like she was dirty? Come on," he said, laughing. "Don't think like that. When something bad happens to the girl you love, you just love her that much harder."

"Really?"

"Of course, really."

"She must've been pretty scared. About the trial and everything. I wonder if she ever thought about just not doing it—not testifying."

"I doubt it," he said. "It took a lot for her to go through with that, but she did it." Tom took the reins of Brenda's mount and led the horses inside. He got the saddles off, the bridles released. When she followed him into the tack room, he turned and pulled her into his arms. This was his favorite part. He kissed her. Damn, he loved the girl. "Wanna find a nice, soft bale of hay?" he asked her.

But she was crying. Little soft tears that made no noise.

"Brenda? What's up, baby? Huh?"

"I'm sorry," she said. "I have to tell you something you're gonna hate."

He wiped the tears off her cheeks. "What?" he asked gently.

"I'm not a virgin," she said with a sniff.

"Aw, Brenda." He laughed, closing his arms around her more tightly. "What are you worrying about? That's not as big a deal to me as you might think." He pulled away and looked into her eyes. "You're funny—here you're embarrassed because you're not a virgin and I'm embarrassed because I am."

"It wasn't someone I dated," she said.

"What are you talking about?"

"I'm pretty sure I was raped."

He frowned. "Pretty sure?" he asked.

But now that it was out and she couldn't turn back, Brenda crumbled against him, sobbing. Tom was no expert on girls, but he was smart enough to know he wasn't going to get the rest of the story until she calmed down a little. He sat down on the bench in the tack room and pulled her onto his lap, holding her while she cried. He murmured little words of comfort, stroked her back, held her close. It was quite a while before she could talk again.

"I lied to you, Tommy," she said, wiping at her face with

the back of her hand. "I did go to one of those rest-stop parties. One. With a couple of girlfriends and a date—a guy I went out with that one time. You take sleeping bags, you know? Because you'll have to sleep over, either in cars or on the ground, on account of drinking. Like camping, right? I got drunk real fast and passed out. When I woke up, I'd been sick all over the place and a couple of the guys said I'd really gotten wasted and was pretty hilarious—but I don't remember anything. Two months later I realized I was pregnant."

"Holy shit," he said.

"Yeah," she said, letting out a short, embarrassed laugh. "I was on my way to get an abortion when I had a miscarriage. Whoever it was gave me a raging infection. I hope he dies of it. There—it's out. Now you can break up with me."

"Why would I do that? I told you, I love you." He stroked her hair. "Who was it?"

"I don't know. I don't want to know. There were six guys at that party—I gave the names to Mike. He'd like me to tell the story to the sheriff—but what good's that going to do? I'm not like Brie, Tommy—I have no idea who it was. Plus, I'm not brave enough to do that. And I don't want the whole school to know I got pregnant. And really, I don't even want to know who it was because, God, what if there was more than one? Oh, God," she said, falling into helpless tears again.

"Okay, Brenda, honey. It's okay…"

"What can you think of me?"

"I told you—it's not your fault and I love you."

"I can't go any further with it. All I wanted since I realized what happened is that it go away. No way I'm going to blame anyone, testify against anyone."

"Maybe they could get the guy without putting you through all that."

"And what if I wasn't raped, really? What if I was just stupid drunk and let some guy—"

"No, you didn't," he said. "We've been together over five months. You're not like that. We've had a beer or two together—you're not like that. That isn't what happened."

"There might've been a drug," she said.

He pulled her close against him. It was hard, but he tried to focus on Brenda's feelings rather than building rage at what had been done to his girl, even before she was his girl. Of course he remembered the fight he'd been in with Whitley. It turned his stomach to think that little prick could've slipped his girl a drug and then used her. But he couldn't let himself think about that yet. He had to keep his arms around her, convince her he would never hold that against her. "Yeah," he said. "There might've been."

"Ever since that happened, I feel like trash. When you first started talking to me in school? When I told you I'd been sick? I hadn't been sick. I'd been knocked up while I was passed out."

"You are not trash," he whispered softly, not trusting his voice. "You're an angel. Pure as gold. You didn't do anything wrong."

"That's not how it feels. Tommy," she said miserably, "I dated before and I wouldn't give it up—I was saving it for someone really special. Someone like you—someone I really loved. And now I can't."

"No one else can ever take that away, Brenda. When… If… If it's us and we know it's time and it's right, it'll be special. I promise."

"How can it be? The first time should be so special. Now it won't even be the first time!"

He brushed her hair away from her eyes. "What can I do to show you that I love you just the same? Respect you? Huh?"

"I don't know...."

"I do. Come on, we're going to take care of these horses. Then we're going to find a nice soft bale of hay and I'm going to hold you. Hold you and kiss you until you believe me when I say I think you're the best thing that's ever happened to me. Everything is going to be fine."

"I was so scared to tell you."

"I know, Bren. It's okay now. I don't want you to ever worry about that again. Okay?"

An hour later, lying on the fresh hay in the stall, Tommy held his girl, kissed her, touched her gently in the places she'd begun to allow and told her how much he cared about her. He was careful not to try anything more or do anything less, and after a while she curved against him in their familiar way, trusting him. In case she wondered if she still turned him on, it took absolutely no effort on his part to demonstrate that he was just as easily aroused by her as ever before. Then when he took her home, he kissed her on the front porch and told her as far as he was concerned, she was perfect. Pure and perfect.

He might've been a little quiet at dinner, but around his house the past couple of months, that went completely unnoticed. A little later he told his dad he was going to run into town and would be back in an hour or so. Walt probably assumed he was going to see Brenda.

He parked his truck around behind the bar, just in case the Carpenters happened to be having an evening drink, something they did with their friends the Bristols from time to time. He walked back to Mike's RV and knocked on the door. Mike opened it. "Can I talk to you a minute?"

"Sure. Wanna come inside?"

"How about out here?" Tom said.

Mike grabbed his coat and stepped outside.

"Remember those parties you were asking about?" Tom asked, standing beside Mike but looking straight ahead.

"Yeah," Mike said.

"You think there might've been a drug that made people pass out?"

"Very possible," Mike said.

"Maybe things happened to people while they were passed out? Against their will?" he asked, still looking straight ahead.

"Could be."

Tom turned to look at Mike. "I bet I know who has some. I bet I can get him to sell me some."

"And how would you know this?" Mike asked.

Tom shrugged. "I'm just an investigative genius."

"You'd do this? A buy? There'd have to be police, you know."

"I know," Tom said. "In fact, I'll check and see if I can get some other stuff. If I'm going to do this, might as well get it done right. Might be meth or ecstasy or something. That interest you at all?" Tom asked.

"Pal, what interests me is getting anything that could hurt people off the street. If you think you can help me do that, I'd sure appreciate it."

"This what you've been looking for, asking all your questions?"

"Yup."

"Then let's do it," Tom said.

15

Vanessa had asked Paul if he could stay until the baby came and he said he could if she wanted him to. By his calculations, the house would be finished at about the same time Vanni gave birth. Jack and Mel would still have one or two things to do—carpet, appliances, paint—but the general contractor wouldn't be needed for that. And the house was shaping up very well—the hardwood floors sanded and varnished, master bath complete, plumbing and light fixtures in, walls textured for painting, porch painted and sealed. Furniture deliveries were scheduled. Mel was spending evenings packing dishes and things at the cabin.

And Vanni was getting huge.

She wasn't crying so much these days. It seemed as though a lot of her attention was focused on preparing to go into labor.

Oh, there were times she'd get a little weepy, which was certainly to be expected. But she was so strong—Paul just admired the hell out of her.

When he came home from the job site one day, she met him in the foyer. "Come with me," she said. "I have to talk to you about something."

"I should wash up first."

"No, just come." She took his hand and led him into the great room. She sat in one of the overstuffed leather chairs and directed Paul to another. This was the most animated Paul had seen her in a long time. Her cheeks were bright; her eyes sparkled. "Paul, the baby is coming very soon."

He smiled. "That's getting real obvious."

"You're my very best friend, Paul."

"Thanks, Vanni," he said, but he furrowed his eyebrows. Suspicious.

"I want you to be with me during the delivery."

"With you how?" he asked.

"I want you to be the one to encourage me, coach me, coax me. Hold my hand. Support me."

"Um… Isn't that Mel's job?"

"Mel is going to be very much a coach, but she's also going to be the midwife and she'll be busy with other things. Especially when the baby is coming out. I need you to do this."

"Vanni," he said, scooting forward on his chair, "I'm a guy."

"I know. Guys do this."

"I can't… Vanni, I shouldn't…. Vanessa, listen. I can't see you like that. It wouldn't be…appropriate."

"Well, actually, I thought about my brother or my dad and frankly, that really doesn't appeal to me. So," she said, lifting a video from the table beside her, "I got us a childbirth movie from Mel."

"Aw, no," he said, pleading.

She stood up and popped it into the VCR, then sat down again with the remote in her hand. "Jack delivered his own son," she said.

"I know, but in case you're interested, he wasn't thrilled about it at the time. And he refuses to do it again—he's adamant about that. And, Vanni, this isn't my son. This is my best friend's son."

"Of course I know that, Paul. But since it is your best friend's son, he'd be so grateful." She started the video. "Now, I want you to concentrate on what the partner is doing. Don't worry about the mother. Most of the time while I'm in labor you'll either be behind me, or helping me walk or squat to use gravity to help with the dilating, or reminding me to breathe properly. It's not like you're going to have your face in the field of birth."

"I'm starting to feel kind of weak," he said. "Why don't you ask Brie or Paige, if you need someone for that?"

"I could do that, but to tell you the truth, I'm much closer to you. And you're here—right here. You can do this. We'll watch the movie together and if you have any questions, just ask me."

He looked at the screen, his brows drawn together. He squinted. This was an unattractive woman, giving birth. Well, not just yet—she was working up to it. Her big belly was sticking out, which was not what made her plain. It was the stringy hair, monobrow, baggy socks on her feet and— "Vanni, she has very hairy legs."

"If that's what worries you I can still manage to shave my legs, even though I have to admit I've lost interest."

The hospital gown on the woman was draped over her belly and legs in such a way that when she started to rise into a sitting position, spreading her thighs and grabbing them to bear down, she was covered. Then the doctor or midwife or whoever was in charge flipped that gown out of the way and there, right in Paul's face, was the top of a baby's head emerging from the woman's body. "Aw, man," he whined, putting his head in his hands.

"I said watch the coach—don't worry about the woman," Vanni lectured.

"It's pretty damn hard to not look at that, Vanni," he said. "Concentrate."

So he looked up and saw that behind the woman, supporting her, was a man—presumably her husband—holding her shoulders and smiling and telling her to push. But Paul's gaze dropped, because how could he help it? And there, again, was the baby's head.

"This is cruel and unusual," he muttered.

"You go to war and shoot animals in the woods—surely you can do this," she said, getting very bossy as she did so. "Big animals—you shoot big animals. This is a lot nicer than that."

"Depends entirely on what you're used to," he grumbled. He watched as the man on the screen told the woman to pant, pant, pant and then push, push, push. Well, how hard was that? And the woman was sweating as if she had just run a marathon. She grabbed her own thighs again, pulled herself up, bore down with a grunt and a snarl as if bench-pressing 350, and holy shit! The head popped right out of her! "Aw, man," he whined again, ducking and swinging his head, bringing himself right to a standing position, turning his back on the TV. "Vanessa, where is your father?"

"I sent Dad and Tommy to the stable so we could watch this movie together."

"Vanessa, I cannot do this. It's not like I've been expecting to do this for a long time. Or if you were like some stranger, a woman suddenly having a baby in my taxicab or something—"

"Look, Paul," she said, pointing. He glanced back at the

screen over his shoulder and saw the whole baby come sliding out, all gross and mucky, right into the doctor's hands. And the cord, still attached, was threaded up inside the woman.

Paul sat down and put his head between his knees, because it would be so embarrassing to faint and have her revive him. "Vanessa," he said miserably, "you are making the biggest mistake of your life here."

Her hand was on his knee. "We can watch it several times until you get used to it. Desensitized, as it were."

"Please, God, no…"

"Well, if that's what it takes…"

He lifted his head in time to see the cord had been cut, and the baby was placed on the mother's stomach when this horrible-looking thing he knew to be a placenta came bubbling out. He thought, I'm gonna die. Right here, right now.

Vanessa made a terrible sound and he thought, see! She can't take it, either! But when he looked at her, he realized that wasn't the problem. With one hand on her big belly and a grimace on her face, she looked as if they were headed far too rapidly for real life.

"Oh-oh," he said.

"Yeah," she said. "Shew. It's okay—we have plenty of time. We can watch the movie again and again, if you need to."

"No," he said sternly. "I am never watching that movie again!"

"Then you're good to go?" she asked.

"I wouldn't say so, no."

"Okay," she said, clearly ignoring him. "I think you should go take a shower. Clean up. I've been in labor all day, but the contractions are getting serious now and I'm going to call Mel to touch base."

"Are you fucking kidding me?"

"We're gonna do it, Paul. I know you won't let me down."

"I bet I will," he said. "If I manage to stay upright through something like that, it'll be a miracle. I'm talking miracle!"

"I need you," she said. "If Matt can't be here with me, I need you to be here with me. Please?"

Oh, goddamn it, he thought. She's playing the Matt card. "Please?"

"Vanni, I'd do anything for you, honey. But this is a mistake. A mistake."

And she said, "Ohhhhh," while she held her belly. He stared at her with wide, horrified eyes while she tried to get through the contraction.

So that's what he'd seen on her face when he walked in the door. She was now having her baby and everything else was on the back burner. She was focused, like a mother wolf protecting her pup—not a grieving widow, but a mother. And she meant business. It amazed him how something like that kicked in. When the contraction passed she looked at him with clear but fierce aquamarine eyes and said, "Shower." Then she stood, holding her belly underneath, and went to the phone.

Paul went to his room, gathered clean clothes and headed down the hall to the shower. He made it quick, but clean. He shaved. Then he thought, I am shaving—why? To be smooth cheeked when I pass out? By the time he was coming out with his dirty clothes to take back to his room, he heard voices. Male voices down the hall and female voices in Vanni's room. And laughter—as if there was anything to laugh about!

He headed down the hall where there were men, where there would be someone sympathetic who could get him out of this. There he found Jack with David on his hip, Walt and Tommy. "Hey, there," Jack said. "How you doing?"

Paul got right up close to Jack. "Listen, Jack, you have no idea what she wants me to do," he said under his breath.

"Yeah, I do. She told everyone. Mel will be right out to get you as soon as Vanni's settled."

"You'd be better at this than me," he said.

"Yeah, I probably would." Jack grinned. "But I wasn't asked."

"I can't do this," he whispered.

Jack clamped a hand on his back. "Sure you can. You'll be fine. Count your lucky stars—at least you have a midwife in there with you." Jack smiled. "It'll be a good experience for you."

"I'm sure you're wrong about that."

"Paul!" Mel called. "We're ready for you."

"Aw, Jesus."

Jack leaned toward him. "Man-up, pal. Or they'll never let you hear the end of it."

Reluctantly Paul went down the hall. Mel, grinning very happily, met him outside Vanni's bedroom door. "How we doing?" she asked.

"Not so good, Mel. I'm pretty sure I'm not up to this. I'm very inexperienced."

"All right, Paul, don't worry. It's going to be a while before the baby comes, and right now all Vanni really needs is someone to rub her back, help her remember to breathe through the contractions, maybe give her a damp cloth for her forehead, or the back of the neck really helps sometimes. That's all."

"I can do that part."

"That's good. If you can't go the distance, that's okay. Just get us that far, okay?"

"I'll do what I can," he said. When he got into the room he was very relieved to see Vanni, clothed in a gown that didn't reveal anything, sitting up in the bed, cross-legged, smiling. So he smiled back. "How are you feeling?"

"Fine at the moment, thanks."

"Vanni, you should have told me this was what you wanted a long time ago. I'm totally unprepared to do this."

"Don't worry, Paul. You'll be fine."

"Probably not. I probably won't be—"

He stopped talking as he noticed he didn't have her attention anymore. She was looking off into the distance, running her hands in circles over her belly, breathing in with slow exhales. And after just a moment of that, her face contorted and the breathing came faster, harder. Then there was some groaning as the pain seized her. As the crescendo was reached, it began to subside, back to the slow exhales and circular hand movements, then eventually it went away and she looked back up at him and smiled.

Mel came back into the room carrying towels. "How's the back?"

She put a hand to her lower back and said, "Lots of pressure there, but it's okay."

"Here," Paul said. "Try to lean forward a little." He pressed his fingertips against the small of her back. "Does that help?"

"Oh, that's good. Very good." He moved his hands around the small of her back, then up to her shoulders, massaging them. "Oh, that's lovely," she murmured.

Mel stayed busy in the room, laying things out—instruments, blankets, gloves, basin. While Vanni went into and through another contraction, Mel simply organized her supplies, leaving Vanni's contraction to Paul. When Vanni couldn't lean forward during the contraction, when it pushed her back against the pillows, Paul just concentrated on massaging her shoulders and upper arms and neck. He found himself saying, "Relax and breathe, Vanni—in and out slowly. Good, good. How's that?"

"Uh," she said. "Uh, uh, uh! Ohhhhh."

"Mel?" he asked.

"Yes, Paul?"

"Can't you give her something?"

"No, Paul. She's doing great." Mel looked at her watch. "They're coming closer." When the contraction passed she said, "Let's get you up, Vanni. Stand up for me—get a little help from gravity. Paul, let's get her up."

Vanni swung her legs over the side and with Paul's assistance she stood up. When the next contraction came, she had to sit on the edge of the bed, which made it a little easier for Paul to rub her back. Mel slipped out of the room, pulling the door closed behind her. As the contraction passed, Paul urged her to stand again and they did that for a little while, up and down, up and down. And then, just as Mel entered the room again, Vanni let go with a great groan and her water broke, running in a huge gush to the floor. It splashed on Paul's shoes and soaked the carpet.

"Well, that's a good sign. Here, let me spread out a couple of towels and I'll check you, see how we're doing. By the way, a birthing party has begun out there."

"Really?" Vanni said. Then she groaned and bent over, panting.

"I'm sure it was completely unplanned, but when Jack leaked it that you were in labor, Preacher and Paige came out—Christopher is watching a video, but he's falling asleep on the couch. Mike and Brie are here, whipping up some snacks in the kitchen, keeping your dad and Tommy company. Jack's giving David his evening bottle, and…" She stopped talking as she helped Vanni back onto the bed. Vanni's knees came up, Mel pulled the gloves on and with one hand on her belly and the other disappearing between her legs, Mel said, "Well, now. Vanessa, you ought to do this for a living. You're making great progress. Stay like that if you can—on your next contraction, I want to see if I can spread you a little bit." She looked up over her belly. "Grab Paul's hand and breathe—it isn't going to feel good, but it might give us faster results."

Paul got down on one knee at the side of the bed and held her hand, looking into her eyes. "You doing okay?" he asked softly.

"I'm working very hard," she said, breathless.

"I know. God, Vanni—I wish there was more I could do."

"You're doing so much, Paul. Oh! Here we go! Ughhhh."

"Good girl," Mel said. "Very good. Very good." One gloved hand rested on her belly, the other disappeared again between her legs. "Pant," Mel said.

Vanni panted, but then inevitably she whimpered from the pain and Paul instinctively put his lips against her forehead and held on.

"Okay, Vanessa," Mel said, pulling out her hand. "You're almost ready to start pushing." She snapped off her gloves.

Paul noticed that when Mel withdrew her hand, there was blood on the glove. "Is that all right?" he asked. He gave a nod toward the glove.

"Perfectly normal," she said. "We'll be seeing a little more of that. You hanging in there?"

"Yeah," he said. And then he thought, I've been tricked pretty good. Like I could leave her now. "Fine," he said. "I'm going to get a damp cloth, Vanni. Be right back."

He went across the hall to the bathroom and first splashed cold water on his own face, then wet and squeezed out a facecloth and hurried back to her. It was a done deal—he was in now. He glanced at his watch and was amazed to see that three hours had passed since he'd come off the job site. He heard the sound of the TV droning down the hall and laughter from the kitchen. Soft, polite laughter.

When he got back he noticed that Vanni was showing the effects of hard labor—her skin was glistening with sweat, her hair was damp and limp, her face looked twisted with the pain. He knelt again; Mel had spread some towels on the damp carpet, but the knees of his trousers were already wet. He didn't care. He mopped her brow and held her hand through a few more contractions and then Mel gave the signal.

"Okay, Vanni—we're going to do it. If you feel the urge, push on the next one."

"Thank God," she said weakly.

"Paul, I want you to support her from behind, help raise her up a bit. Vanni, you know what to do."

Paul started to lift her and Vanessa said, "Not yet." Then in a moment she was lifted off the bed in a horrendous urge to bear down and, remarkably, he didn't have to be told it was time. He braced her from behind while she gave a huge grunt and strained, holding her breath, pushing for all she was worth. When she collapsed against the bed he asked, "Is he out?"

"Nah. It's going to take a while."

"But on that movie…?"

"That wasn't a first baby," Mel said. "He came out way too easily. First babies take time."

"How much time?"

"However much they want." Mel put her fetoscope in her ears, flipped Vanni's gown up over her belly and listened. She pulled the gown back down and said, "He's a strong one. He's going to keep you up nights."

Paul did his job—brow mopping, hand-holding, encouraging, supporting. It went on for almost an hour and he watched as Vanni got more and more tired and Mel stayed busy getting ready to catch that baby. While Paul supported Vanni he heard Mel say, "Hold it a little longer…right where you feel the pressure…. Okay, take a breath and push again…. Way to go!" Mel spread out the baby towel on the bed, brought her clamps, suction, scissors to the bed. Finally she said, "I think we're going to hit pay dirt on this next one, Vanni. Make it a good one."

"Make it a good one, baby," Paul heard himself say. "Ready, push. Push. Push. Push."

Mel handed Paul a blanket. "Spread this over Vanni's tummy, Paul. When the baby is delivered, that's where he's going. We're going to dry him off and then rewrap him in a clean, warm blanket. Okay?"

"Okay," he said, mesmerized.

Vanni reared up again, pushing. Paul did his job, just as he'd been instructed.

"All right!" Mel said. "We're almost there! I think the next push is going to do it, Vanni. Here we go now."

"Okay honey, here we go," Paul said. In spite of himself, he was leaning forward, watching, wanting to see this baby being born, wanting to be in on this all the way now. He heard the baby cry, heard Mel exclaim happily. He grabbed the blanket, did his job and out of the womb came this mucky, squalling infant. Oh, man, he looked unhappy. "Whoa," Paul said with a laugh. "He's pissed!"

Vanni laughed emotionally.

Paul stared in wonder at the new life, astonished by what she'd done. Astonished that he'd been there. Then he remembered—he was supposed to do things. Together, he and Mel dried the baby, and while he was helping with that, he couldn't help counting fingers and toes. He watched Mel clamp and cut, then he wrapped the baby in a new, dry blanket and carefully lifted him. Vanni was struggling to pull herself up a little bit, trying to get the pillows behind her back. Paul held the baby in one arm, assisted her with the other. Then he knelt beside the bed and watched as Vanni snuggled the baby close, gently kissed his head. And, Paul, not completely conscious, rested his lips against Vanni's shoulder.

She turned her head and looked into his eyes. Vanni reached up a hand to his face and wiped the tears from his cheeks. Tears he had absolutely no idea were there.

"We're in business," Mel said. "Good job. Good, good job."

Paul was exhausted. He lowered his head to Vanni's shoulder and just lay there for a moment, trying to imagine what she'd just been through. He felt her fingers in his hair. "Oh, Vanni," he whispered. He lifted his head. "What you did."

She started to smile, but then her face seemed to melt into a frown as the tears rose to her eyes and began to run down her cheeks. She looked up at Paul and whispered, "I wish he could see his son."

Paul brushed at the tears on her cheeks. "He sees him, baby. He's got the best seat in the house."

"Yeah," she said, the tears flowing. "Yeah, I guess."

Paul slipped his arm under her shoulders and held her to him while she softly cried, and he unconsciously dropped his own tears onto her hair.

"Let's get that baby on the breast, Vanessa. Redheads are such bleeders."

"Yeah," she said, tremulously. "Yeah, got it." She was pulling at her gown, but it seemed a little stuck and her hands were shaking. Paul gave the gown a tug and up it came, exposing one breast, but he wasn't noticing it as if it was a breast. It was as if it was just another part of delivering the baby. He helped her position the baby, who was screaming madly. And then suddenly he stopped and started rooting. And bang—he found it. "Ohhh," Vanni said. "That's it. Wow." Then she looked up at Paul and smiled. And the baby suckled, making precious little noises.

He hadn't noticed that Mel was gone until she returned with a basin of water and set it up on the changing table. She examined Vanni quickly, covered her up again and said,

"Okay, let me get this guy cleaned up for a viewing. How you doing, Vanni?"

"Okay," she said, wiping at her eyes. "I'm okay."

Paul kissed her forehead. "You're amazing, Vanessa."

"You, too," she whispered, and closed her eyes.

He stayed on his knees beside her bed while Mel took the baby, and for the entire time she washed him, Paul watched Vanni's face as she slowly drifted into exhausted sleep. He gently kissed the tears from her cheeks. A few minutes later Mel touched his shoulder. She was holding a bundled baby and said, "Here you go. Take him to his grandfather and uncle. I'll put this room and Mom right."

"You sure?"

"Absolutely," she said, handing him over. "You earned the right."

Walt and Tommy were most impressed with their new addition, as was the entire gathering. The camera came out and pictures were taken, the blanket pulled back to watch him kick his little legs, to exclaim on the size of his feet.

"Bet you could use a shot," Preacher said to Paul.

"Whew, partner, you'll never know," he said, scrubbing a hand along the back of his neck.

"What you got on your pants there, bud?"

Paul looked down. "I believe that's amniotic fluid. The carpet's going to have to be shampooed in there."

"No doubt." Preacher tipped a bottle over a few glasses. "I'm going to do that, you know. I'm going to be with Paige when the baby comes. I'm dying to do that."

"Well, I hope you're more prepared than I was. It really took me by surprise."

"But you don't regret it, do you?"

"Nah. It was awesome," he said.

"That's all I hear," Preacher said. "These guys, they don't want to do it, but then afterward they think it was their idea. Zeke, you know—he's done it four times. He says he'd do it four more, but I think his wife is going to shoot him before that can happen."

"Zeke is a paramedic," Paul said. "That might give him an edge."

"Yeah," Preacher said, sipping. "Also a sex maniac, I guess. A sex maniac who loves kids."

Jack joined them. "So—you made it."

"Jack, you are my hero. It was such a challenge to just be there, I don't know how you delivered David. Honest to God, I don't."

"I had directions," he said, lifting his glass. "I'm not doing it again, however. I'm going to keep a really close eye on her next time. I want to watch, that's all."

It was a celebration, albeit quiet and controlled so as not to get the baby wailing or wake Vanessa, who had earned a little rest. Christopher was out like a light on the couch, and David was asleep on Walt's bed with pillows stacked around him. Pretty soon Mel emerged and she was congratulated on a job well done. Everyone had their turn to hold the baby and then finally he was taken back to his room, his mother's room.

They all gathered in the dining room with their celebratory drinks, remnants of snacks still on the table. Paul stood in the doorway to the kitchen. Brie sat on Mike's lap, Paige leaned up against Preacher, his big arm around her shoulders. Jack stood behind Mel, massaging her shoulders. Walt had given Tom a beer, which he appeared to be handling like a pro.

"So when are the Valenzuelas stepping up to the plate?" Walt asked.

"We're working on it," Mike said with a grin. Then he kissed Brie's cheek. "Aren't we, baby?"

"Mike is working very hard." She laughed.

"Oh, you wanna look out for that," Preacher said. "Ask Mel. Crazy as it seems, having sex every day isn't a good way to get pregnant."

"John!" Paige scolded.

Before she could get her scold out, at least three people echoed, "Every day?"

"Well, Jesus, it's not against the law, is it?" Preacher asked, making everyone laugh the harder.

"Preacher, you are my hero, man," Tommy said. "I wanna be just like you when I grow up!"

Walt ruffled his hair. "My son is a damn liar. He wants to be just like you yesterday!"

"It's true," Tom said. "I'm not all that keen on babies, but the rest of it sounds pretty cool."

It wasn't long before people started to make noises about leaving, looking around for Paul. It seemed he had slipped away. Jack went down the hall and peeked into Vanessa's room, to find her sleeping peacefully.

Jack told the birthing party to sit tight while he looked to see if Paul had stepped outside for air. He put on his jacket and walked out around the house and down past the stable and corral. He didn't have to be psychic to figure this out. It had been a long and emotional day for Paul. He was standing up on that little hill not far from the house. The one from which you could see a whole lot of the general's land.

Paul glanced over his shoulder as he heard the frozen ground crunching beneath Jack's boots. Then he looked back at the gorgeous headstone. It read "Matt Rutledge, beloved husband, father, son, brother, friend." Jack put his hand on Paul's shoulder. "He'd be glad you were there, standing in for him."

"I was just telling him about it and I thought, shit, I don't even know how much of him is in there."

"None," Jack said. "He's moved on."

Paul hit his chest with a fist. "I still have him here."

"Of course. Everyone who loved him has him there. I think that's the point."

"I shouldn't have been the one tonight. It should've been him. She misses him so much."

"Look, we all have different paths, Paul. His led him there, yours led you here."

Paul sniffed and wiped at his face. "The house is about done," he said. "Vanni will be up and around in no time and I can't hang around here anymore. I have to get back. To Grants Pass."

"Yeah," Jack said. "But you'll be back pretty soon. You have strong ties here."

"I don't know about that...."

"Give her time, Paul. It's still a little raw, but that's going to change."

"What are you talking about?" he asked, looking at him in the dark.

"Oh, Jesus, I wondered. You don't remember. You got a little drunk and— No, you got a lot drunk and kind of let it slip about how you saw her first."

"No. I couldn't have."

"Take it easy. Just to me. You had the discretion to pass out before you told anyone else. So listen to me for once, okay? Because this is important. You already know this, but right now you think you're the only man who's ever been in this position. I married a widow. Remember? It wasn't easy. It wasn't quick—getting over that long, ugly hump of wondering where I fit in. It was goddamn humbling, if you want the truth. But, Paul, it was worth every sleepless night I invested. It's just that it takes whatever time it takes."

Paul thought a minute. He fixed his lips tight, as if he were struggling. "I have to get back to Grants Pass."

"But you come back here before long," Jack said. "Come back regular. I'm telling you, if you don't, you'll regret it."

"But I can't stay much longer, Jack. It's eating me up. I gotta get out of here. He was my best friend, and he's dead, and I helped his baby into the world, and—"

"And you want his woman. I know this is a rough patch, Paul, but if you're the kind of guy who cuts and runs, oh man, you're going to hate yourself." Paul hung his head. "Come on," Jack said. "People want to say good-night. They want to pat you on the back one more time."

"Can't you just leave me out here?"

"Nah," he said, turning Paul away from the grave with a hand behind his neck. "The general wants to tell you—Matt picked a name. They've made a few adjustments on account of his death—adjustments that were Vanessa's idea. Matt wanted to name him Paul. But they've settled on Matthew Paul. I think you should drink to it. And think to it."

16

Tom was quiet while he brushed down the horses with Brenda, but it didn't matter because she was talking a mile a minute. He'd invited her out to see the new baby, just a week old, and she was all jazzed about that. Then they took a quick ride and he listened to her go on and on about the cheerleading tryouts for her senior year that were coming up. He had already agreed to take her to the prom, though it was only February, and she had a million things to say about that. When the horses were put away, he grabbed her hand and led her into the tack room. He sat on the bench, pulled her onto his lap and kissed her deeply, lovingly. And he said, "I have to tell you something."

"What?"

"I love you. I know you believe that. And I want you like

mad, which you can't help but believe. But I'm going to do something—even though it might cost me everything. You and whatever I have with you."

"What? What are you talking about?"

"I talked to the police," he said.

She jumped right off his lap. "What?" she asked in disbelief, shaking her head to try to make it go away. "No."

He tried to pull her back onto his lap, but she skittered out of his reach, the look on her face one of sheer horror. So he stood up and faced her. "Not just Mike. Other police. A special detective unit, as it turns out. I'm going to help them get the guy who gave you the drug—because there was a guy and there was a drug."

"No," she said again, shaking her head. "You can't know that any more than I do."

"Yeah, we both know. It might even come back on you, but I'm not sure how. You might be asked what you know about it, and you'll say whatever you want. Maybe you won't say anything. But I had to, Brenda."

Tears immediately ran down her cheeks and she stepped back another step. "No, you didn't have to!"

"Yeah, I did, and I'll tell you why. Because I want to sleep at night. Because I don't want to try to imagine that sometime this summer or next year some poor slob like me is holding the girl he loves while she cries her heart out over being raped. I don't want to think of some poor girl—a good girl who's saving herself—waking up pregnant when she probably wouldn't have even scored a hangover! I'm not going to lie awake at night and wonder if there are a couple of kids like me and you, in love and playing it so carefully, so straight, getting ripped up by this asshole. I'm going to try to stop him even if you never speak to me again."

"But I told you, I don't know what happened! There's nothing I can do! And even if I could, I don't want to! God, Tommy, I don't want anyone to know!"

"I don't blame you. I didn't tell the police about you, but that's going to be irrelevant. Eventually they're going to want to hear from every kid who went to every one of those keggers and parties, to know what happened to them. And I'm sorry for that—you'll handle it however you want to. But I'm not letting this guy do it to anyone else's girl. I'm sorry you're mad, but I'm not sorry I did it."

"I hate you!"

"I had to."

"I hate you!"

"Yeah," he said, hanging his head. He lifted his head. "Well, I love you, and I'm sorry this upsets you. I hope someday, like in about a million years, you'll think back about this and even if you still hate me, maybe you'll have some respect for me doing the right thing."

She started to sob, shaking her head until her pretty, silky light brown hair fell over her face. "Why did you do this? Why? Now it's going to get out. I shouldn't have told you—I thought I could trust you! Now everyone will think I'm just a slut!" He reached for her and she pulled back. "Don't touch me! Don't you ever touch me!"

But he pulled her against him anyway and held her while she cried. And oh, man, she cried so hard he thought she was going to throw up. She started to gag, in fact, but he hung on until she exhausted herself. And he still hung on. "Why?" she kept saying to him. "Why? It wasn't for you to do—it was for me to do if I wanted to."

"Yeah? And if it happens to someone else because you didn't say anything? And if someone dies?" he asked, but he asked gently even as he held her. "I don't care that you aren't saying anything about it. That's your choice. You know what—you go ahead and hate me. You blame me if you want to, when we both know the real bad guy isn't me. Thing is, I have to live with myself."

She pulled out of his arms. "Well, I just hope you can."

He stared at her for a long moment. "I can," he said. "Come on, I'll take you home."

The next day after school Tom drove his little red truck over to Jordan Whitley's house. He ran up on the porch and knocked on the door. Jordan answered and Tom said, "Hey. Got my stuff?"

"Yeah, man," he said, laughing. "You're gonna love it." He reached into his pocket and pulled out a little baggie and an envelope. When Tom reached for it he said, "Hey, forget something?"

"Oh, yeah. How much did you say?"

"Just a hundy, man. You're gonna be so happy."

"What we have here?" Tom asked.

"Roofies, ecstasy, meth. Made to order."

"I changed my mind about the meth," he said, and Jordan took back the little baggie. "So, I get a discount right?"

"Sorry, pal. They don't exactly give refunds."

"Ah," Tom said. "You use this stuff a lot?" he asked. "The roofies?"

Jordan shrugged. "Coupla times. Just for kicks, you know."

"Yeah," he said, smiling. "Just for kicks." He handed him a wad of bills, accepted the drugs and stepped out of the way.

A detective came around from each side of the house, plainclothes, badges out and aimed at Jordan. One was a young woman in a ball cap with a ponytail strung through the back— she looked not much older than Tom. She could have passed for a college girl, young looking and petite. The other undercover cop was a great big guy in jeans and a jacket. Both had guns, cuffs and tasers on their belts. "Police!" the girl said.

"Jordan Whitley, you're under arrest. We have a search warrant. Turn around, hands up against the house."

The look on his face was priceless. It almost made Tom smile. Pure, horrified shock. "Hey!" he yelled. "Hey, what's up with this!" But before he could even finish his sentence this little bitty girl had him whirled around, his legs kicked apart and was patting him down while the big guy stood over him, daring him to move.

While they cuffed him, he looked over his shoulder at Tom. "You're gonna be so sorry, man."

"Yeah, probably," he said. "But I'll never regret it." Then he handed the envelope to the big detective and walked down the porch steps to his truck just as a patrol car pulled up and a uniformed officer got out. Down the street was a dark SUV with tinted windows, an unmarked police vehicle. Inside, watching the arrest, would be Detective Delaney and Mike. Tom went home to tell his family what he'd done.

Paul's fifth wheel was hooked up to the back of his truck, and his bags were packed and sitting out on the front walk of the general's house. Before going outside to leave, he put his arms around Vanessa and drew her against him, baby and all, and kissed her cheek. "Please come back very soon," she whispered. "I could never have gotten through this without you."

"I couldn't have gotten through it without you, too," he said. "You'll be okay now, Vanni. If you need me, you just call."

"I'm going to miss you more than you realize. You've been like one of the family," she said.

"I know," he said, and he thought, that's why I have to go now. Because I can't be like that to her anymore. Like a brother. It's killing me. "Thank you for making me feel so welcome, so much a part of everything."

"It was natural, Paul. It felt right, having you here. Now

that the house is done, I'm afraid you won't be around too much, and that's gonna be awful."

"Nah, I'll be around. I come down regularly to meet up with the boys, to hunt or fish or play poker. Even if there's no building to do here, there's always that."

"I'll be taking the baby up to Grants Pass to see Matt's folks. I'll call you, okay?"

"You'd better," he said. He kissed her forehead, then leaned down to kiss the baby's forehead. "I'll talk to you soon, I'm sure."

He went out front where the general and Tom waited, and Vanessa followed. He shook Walt's hand. "Thank you for everything, sir."

"Don't be ridiculous," he said. "We're in your debt."

Paul gave his hand to Tom, then pulled him in for a hug. "I'm damn proud of you, son," he said. "It was a hard thing, what you did. I hope it all works out okay." And as Paul said that, the general patted his son's back.

"Thanks," Tom said, but he looked down when he said it. Then, raising his head, he said, "I'm going to miss you, man."

"Yeah, me too, bud. Maybe I'll get down here for graduation or something."

"You know you're welcome anytime. Standing reservation," Walt said.

Paul nodded, picked up his duffel and suitcase, walked out to the road and threw them in the backseat of the extended-cab truck. He gave a wave and a toot of the horn as he drove off. He watched in the rearview mirror as Walt put an arm around Tom's shoulders and led him away. But Vanessa stayed, patting the little bundle she pressed to her shoulder, watching as he drove away.

Maybe someday, he thought. Maybe someday.

★ ★ ★

Jack put the last of the boxes from the cabin into the back of his truck and leaned into the cab to blow the horn. Mel came out of the cabin and just stood on the porch, turning in a circle. She brushed a little imaginary dust off the arm of one of the Adirondack chairs. He shook his head and smiled. She was having a really hard time leaving, even though the new house was big and beautiful.

"Mel, come on," he called.

"Coming," she said. But she stood there a while longer. She was getting a nice little tummy on her now. She wore jeans, boots and a yellow sweater pulled down over her belly, her golden hair falling in thick curls over her shoulders and down her back. She was such a little thing; she could look like a pregnant teenager, standing up there like that. But as Jack knew too well, this was no girl. His woman was all woman.

He went to her because she wasn't moving very fast. He took the porch steps in one long stride, lifted her chin and saw that she had tears in her eyes. "You going to cry again?"

"No," she insisted.

He chuckled. "We own the place now, Mel. You're not giving it up."

"I'm just remembering," she said. "Remember that night you brought me home and put me to bed after I'd had a couple of whiskeys on an empty stomach?"

"I remember."

"And you left fishing gear for me to find when I woke up in the morning?"

"Yes," he said, happy with the picture in his head of her wearing her brand-new waders and casting into the yard from the Adirondack chair. "I really thought I was going to get lucky that night."

"You got lucky in that cabin more times than I can count," she said. "David was born in that bed," she said.

"Talk about getting lucky." He laughed and pulled her into his arms. "Anytime you want to sneak out here and revisit the past, I'm your man."

"I'm remembering how it was when I first got here—there was a bird's nest in the oven." She looked up at him. "You rebuilt this whole cabin for me—trying to get me to stay."

"The second I saw you, I was doomed. I don't know what would have become of me if you hadn't stayed."

"You'd have fewer children, I think. Jack, I had so many happy days and nights in this little cabin. My whole life was changed here."

"And mine. Now come on, honey. We have a new house waiting."

"Do you think we'll be as happy in that new house as we've been here?"

He kissed her nose. "I guarantee it. Now, come on."

With a heavy sigh she walked down the porch steps with him and got into the truck. She watched out the window dreamily as they drove through town and up the drive that had become her drive, feeling moody and nostalgic as though she was moving to another state when it was really less than a twenty-minute drive. She sighed again as she got out of the truck and walked toward the new porch, the new house.

He grabbed her hand and pulled her back. Then, lifting her into his arms, he carried her into the house and stood just inside the doorway, holding her. It was fabulous—Paul had clearly outdone himself. The floors were shiny hardwood, the ceiling of the great room was vaulted and beamed, the new tan leather furniture that sat around the stone hearth was lush and inviting. He walked farther into the house, past a beautiful, huge modern kitchen, which he believed would be the center of many gatherings in the future. Silver appliances, black granite counters, dark polished oak cabinets and a long oak table that could seat ten or more.

"What are you doing?" she asked him.

He carried her into a spacious master bedroom with king-size bed and large, man-sized bureaus. "Taking a little tour." He pointed her toward the big new bed. "How do you like your new playpen?"

"Jack," she said, laughing and tightening her arms around his neck.

He kissed her, a long, deep and lusty kiss. "I think we have time to christen the new house before Brie and Mike bring David out."

"Oh, Jack, we have things to do around here."

"We certainly do," he said, laying her gently on the bed and leaning down to pull off her boots. "Yes, we do."

The sheriff's department's detectives were extremely co-operative in letting Mike listen in on some of the interviews they conducted with both Jordan Whitley, Brendan Lancaster and students who may or may not have been victimized by the suspects. He considered it very fortunate that only three Virgin River girls seemed to have fallen prey, because there were others around Valley High School who appeared to be suspiciously likely to have been drugged and raped. And, as Tom had suspected, there were more drugs involved—what was referred to as white dope. Two short weeks after these young men were apprehended a fount of information and piles of reports had been generated and confessions were falling like raindrops around the county ADA.

Brie's reputation as a prosecutor extended beyond the boundaries of the Sacramento Valley, and when she offered her services as a consultant to the local district attorney, they welcomed her help gratefully. The one thing she never thought she'd be able to do she did extremely well—she assisted in interviewing teenage girls who were likely rape victims. Her skills were impressive, but it was her compassion and finesse that probably assisted in prepping at least one girl for a possible trial. Carra Jean Winslow knew exactly what had happened to her, and who had raped her.

The most interesting thing to Mike—and so unsurprising as well—was that these boys, Whitley and Lancaster, were singularly unimpressive. They were neither clever nor savvy—they were simply idiots with access to dangerous drugs and the opportunity to use them. Lancaster had been present at a couple of raves held in a larger town down the coast where he had located and purchased GHB, sharing his wealth with Whitley. He also had a local marijuana dealer he worked with, and traded pot for meth and ecstasy. He had the stuff and was dealing. It boiled down to teens in search of a good time and the misfortune to have ended up being around these two losers.

It didn't take Lancaster long to flip and turn on his suppliers. This delighted Delaney, who'd been looking hard for white-dope dealers. He was also willing to flip on Whitley—he was pretty much the only witness to the rapes. Unfortunately for Whitley, the only person he could turn over was Lancaster—so it looked as if the rape charges might stick.

No names of teenagers were published in the local papers, but that didn't keep the word from spreading. In Virgin River, Mike found some of his neighbors wanted to express their gratitude for his work. He was given a case of good wine, half a butchered calf, a dozen jars of canned tomatoes that were put up last summer. He pulled a couple of bottles of wine from the case for Brie, but took the rest of the wine and produce to Preacher. Since he'd taken his job, Jack and Preacher hadn't allowed him to pay anything for his meals at the bar. That was the way things worked around here. All for one, one for all...

Mike leaned against his SUV, waiting outside the sheriff's department for someone, a young woman who had just completed her third round of questions with detectives. When Brenda Carpenter came out, a svelte young blue-jeaned girl with a book bag slung over her shoulder, he pushed off the car. "Hey," he said.

"Hey," she returned.

"I talked your dad into letting me give you a lift home. I thought maybe you and I could have a few minutes."

"What for?" she asked with a shrug. "There can't possibly be anything more you want to ask me. Not now."

He opened the passenger door for her. "Nah. No more questions. But I might want to tell you a couple of things."

She gave a heavy sigh, but needing that ride, she got in. Mike hurried to the driver's side, because once they were under way, she couldn't refuse to go with him. "Brenda, it was very brave, what you did," he said.

"I didn't have that much of a choice," she said.

"Well, but you did. You could have lied, you could have refused to talk to anyone, you could have feigned sick.... I can think of a hundred ways you could've been unhelpful—but you gutted it out. And knowing what that meant to you, I just wanted to thank you."

She looked at him. "Why thank me?" she asked.

"Well, it's my town—you're my family, my people. If I'm doing my job, I try to make sure you're safe. Believe me, I know from personal experience how hard it is to answer some of those questions."

"Yeah. Your wife," she said. "You must think I'm a pretty big sissy for holding out so long after what your wife was brave enough to do."

"Not at all, Brenda. Number one, my wife is thirty-one. Number two, she's not only a lawyer, but one with experience in prosecuting dangerous criminals. Three—she had some serious backup in me and Jack and many others. You're just a kid who was never sure what happened to you. You were up against a lot."

"Thanks. I guess."

"Really, kiddo. For me and Brie—we've been through some scary stuff and have kind of thick hides by now. Now all we want is a peaceful life in a peaceful town." He laughed. "Jesus, I hope that's not asking too much."

She was quiet for a long moment. "I'm sorry you went through all that. I know what it's like."

"Thank you, I know you do," he said. "Hopefully it's behind us now. We want a family, you know. You get to be my age, you don't want to miss too many chances at that."

"Were you proud of her? Your wife?"

"Oh, kid," he said in a breath. "She was amazing. She was so afraid, so sick inside, so vulnerable.... But one thing you learn as you get older—it's usually better to face the threat and the fear than try to dodge it. In the end the most important thing is that you have no regrets."

"Because it's never as bad as you fear?" she asked.

He laughed. "Did someone tell you that? Because sometimes it is as bad as you fear, or even worse. And sometimes you have to do it anyway, because the kind of life you're left with if you don't isn't really of the same value. Brie is a perfect example of that. She went after that guy for raping women, knowing that if she couldn't get him, he would be free to hurt more women and even free to go after her. But ignoring him would not only have the same effect, she would have to add to it that she never tried to do the right thing. Double pain.

Double regret. To try your hardest and then fail—no shame in that. To do nothing? It just ends up being harder to live with."

"The detective said he doesn't know what will happen to those guys… Doesn't even know if there will be a trial."

"They don't even know if they'll do time. I think almost all the drug charges were pled down for information that will help the police with bigger cases. I don't think they pled down any of the sexual assault, but if I were Whitley's lawyer, I'd talk him into a plea agreement rather than a trial. He goes to trial, he's so cooked."

"No time?" she asked.

"Don't worry, Brenda—he's over eighteen, barely. He's outta here—he won't be back in school with you. Since he made bail, he's been in another city with his father. He isn't going to be back here. He'd get tarred and feathered."

"What if…?" She stopped and thought a second. "What if I'd come forward sooner? Would I have saved anyone?"

"Don't know," he answered. "But, honey, when your number was called, you stood up, you told the truth and you helped get the job done. You should be very proud of yourself. I'm very proud of you. We all are."

The next afternoon at about four, Mike drove out to the general's house. He parked in front, but saw that there was someone down by the corral, forearms leaning on the top rail, one booted foot hoisted onto the bottom. That was who Mike was looking for and he walked down the small hill. "Tom," he said to the boy's back.

The boy turned, saw it was him and said, "How you doing?"

"Good. How about you?" Mike asked, joining him at the fence, aping his stance, one foot on the bottom rail, forearms on the top.

"Getting by," Tom said.

"You having any trouble at school?" Mike asked.

"Nah," he said. "There's a lot of talk, but I'm not answering any questions."

"What kind of talk?" Mike asked.

Tom shrugged. "Some people think they know that I got him caught, but no one's sure. Well, no one but Brenda."

"You did a good piece of work there, Tom. I know that was tough."

Tom gave a huff of unamused laughter. "Yeah, but then again, no. I felt like I had two choices—turn him over or just beat the living shit out of him."

"I would've felt exactly that way."

"Is it coming together? You guys get the little prick?"

"Yeah, he is totally gotten. He started spilling his guts almost immediately. For a while there he thought he could put it on Lancaster—but it turns out that Lancaster liked getting drunk and high, while it was Whitley's project to get the girls."

Tom winced. "Beautiful. I should've just killed him."

"It wouldn't have worn well on you. So, you're hanging in there?"

He shrugged. "I go to basic training with the Army right after graduation. Then the Point. I'll manage."

"There's lots of stuff going on between now and then. Prom and stuff..."

"Nah. I'm just doing time. I'll be gone before you know it."

"What about Brenda?" Mike asked.

"There's no girl, man. I sold her out. She's finished with me."

"You sure about that?"

"Oh, yeah," he said. "We don't talk. She won't even look at me."

"I saw her over at the sheriff's department—she wears that bracelet you gave her. The pretty one with her name on it."

"I know. I think she's punishing me with it. Gives me false hope."

"Maybe that wasn't quite it," Mike said. "Maybe she was just scared and mad, but not really finished."

"I wish," he said, leaning on the rail and looking down. "Nah, she said she hated me, and she's pretty much acting like it."

"You regret what you did?"

"No, can't get there," he said. "That guy had to be stopped. That stuff can't happen. It's wrong." He coughed. "I knew there was a price."

Mike clamped a hand on his back. "Tom, a man who will do what he has to do even though there's a price, that's a man I want at my back when there's trouble. You did the right thing."

"Sure," he said inconsolably. "Glad you got him," he added.

"I brought someone to see you," Mike said.

Tom straightened. "Yeah? Who?"

Mike inclined his head over his shoulder and Tom turned. Behind him about twenty feet stood Brenda, her hands clasped in front of her. Tom looked at Brenda, at Mike, at Brenda again.

"Oh, God," Tom said. "Brenda?"

He took a couple of steps toward her and she ran to him. Mike stepped back and watched with a melancholy smile on his face. Tom snatched her up into his arms, lifting her clear of the ground. She hugged his neck while he held her tight and he heard what sounded like laughter mixed up with tears. And then of course the sound was muffled because it was buried in kisses that were desperate and heartfelt.

"You can probably give her a ride home later," Mike said, though no one acknowledged that they'd heard. He shook his head in silent laughter and started back up the hill. As he was nearing the house, he looked up to see the general in one of his big picture windows. Walt slowly lifted a hand toward Mike and saluted him.

Mike returned the salute.

When Mike got back to town, it was already dinnertime. He was ready for a beer, but he went to the RV first to see if Brie was back from helping her brother and sister-in-law at the new house—a work in progress with wallpapering, unpacking, cleaning, settling. And he found she was there, wearing her bathrobe, patting dry her long hair with a towel. Every time his eyes even fell on her, he felt himself swell with pride that she would choose him.

It had been a long six weeks since the trial in Sacramento. The color was back in her cheeks, the sparkle in her eyes. Assisting the ADA in Humboldt County was gratifying for her; she was proud she could contribute. And she was enjoying the help she could give Mel and Jack, having a good time with her little nephew. It was so satisfying to know she felt secure and at peace once again. To have her in his life, to hold her and tell her he adored her, this was enough to make him feel as any king might feel.

"You're back," he said, going to her for a kiss.

"They're very close to being all settled now. I papered the new baby's bedroom, with no help from Davie, I might add."

"Are you hungry?"

"Ravenous. You?"

"It's been a long day," he admitted.

"And all that date-rape business? It's still falling into place for the ADA?"

"Better than I could have hoped, acting alone as I was. They're doing a fantastic job with it, and you were instrumental in that. These people can have it behind them soon."

"Which means we'll have it behind us," she said.

He threaded a hand under her long hair, gently massaging her neck. "There will be more cases for you, mija. Your skills are so valuable here. Thank you for that."

"We have other things to do, Miguel. For one thing, there's that baby. We need to get to work on that baby."

His grin was immediate and huge. "I thought I had been working on the baby," he said.

"You've been doing your best, I'm sure, if a little distracted by work. Now that all this stuff is handled, we can give it serious attention."

"How do you feel about takeout?"

"Excellent idea," she said, standing to loosen the belt around her robe.

A year and a half ago Mike Valenzuela lay in a coma in an L.A. hospital, his family wondering if he would live, and Brie Sheridan was trying to survive the reality of her husband abandoning her for another woman, and a few months later trying to recover from a violent crime. Neither had dared hope they would come out of these traumas with their health and sanity, much less a love that felt eternal. A love so fulfilling and endless that anything seemed possible. And yet for both of them, something had been born that exceeded their wildest fantasies.

"Do you have any idea how much I love you?" he asked her.

"That's the best part," she answered. "I do."

★ ★ ★ ★ ★

Escape to Virgin River and read the books that everyone is talking about!

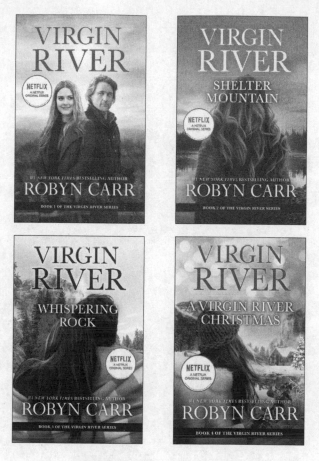

Connect with us at:

BookClubbish.com/Newsletter
Instagram.com/BookClubbish
Twitter.com/BookClubbish
Facebook.com/BookClubbish